MY BOSS'S SECRET

A SMALL TOWN ROMANTIC COMEDY

TARYN QUINN

This book is a work of fiction. The names, characters, places, and incidents are products of the writer's imagination or have been used fictitiously and are not to be construed as real. Any resemblance to persons, living or dead, actual events, locales or organizations is entirely coincidental.

My Boss's Secret
© 2021 Taryn Quinn
Rainbow Rage Publishing

Cover by Najla Qamber Designs
Photo by Sara Eirew Photography

All Rights Are Reserved.
No part of this book may be used or reproduced in any manner whatsoever without written permission, except in the case of brief quotations embodied in critical articles and reviews.

First print edition: November 2021
ISBN Print edition: 978-1-940346-70-0

ACKNOWLEDGMENTS

For some books, it takes a village. This book would not have been possible without our wonderful support team.

Thanks, Jenn, Kim, & Tori. You were life savers!

Sometimes we make up fictional places that end up having the same names as actual places. These are our fictional interpretations only. Please grant us leeway if our creative vision isn't true to reality.

Dealing with mental illness, in any form, comes with so many stigmas. We hope we did the subject justice.

CHAPTER ONE

April

Fiji

"You know what you need, Bunny?"

Ignoring my grandmother and her so-called helpful advice, I tugged at the bodice of my perfectly cute halter dress. At least it had been before we went on vacation. Now the flared sixties' style looked blah. Boring. I'd gone for sedate blue instead of island appropriate. But I didn't do tropical flowers. Or plunging necklines. Or anything too revealing—

"You need a good, hard bounce."

"I have a decent mattress," I said distantly, reaching behind myself to temporarily tighten the bust area.

I wasn't one to be showy, especially when it came to my overly large breasts, but I'd gone a size too big. With my runner's body, it wasn't logical to have breasts one pint of Ben and Jerry's away from tipping into Ds.

Still, baggy fabric didn't help hide anything, just made me look saggier than I was. Maybe I needed a new bra. I'd gotten the one I was wearing on sale forever ago.

"April Anne Finley, look at me." My petite grandmother stepped in front of me and leaned up to grab my shoulders. She was almost a foot shorter than me. "You're on vacation. Do you know what people do on vacation?"

I frowned down into her sparkling denim blue eyes. "Party like a rockstar?"

Something I had no clue how to do. I even had trouble partying like an office assistant, who one day might be a paralegal if I finally signed up for that program.

She laughed. "You could do that too, but I meant have a fling."

"Like sex?"

"Don't look so shocked," she chided, patting my cheek the same way she'd done when I was ten and baffled by some boy kicking my chair at school. "You don't have to sign on the dotted line to have some fun, baby girl. You desperately need more fun in your life."

"But I'm on vacation with you, aren't I?"

"Under duress, and don't tell me you wouldn't have been relieved if that codger boss of yours had pulled rank and said you couldn't go."

"Codger?" I had to snort. "Preston may be uptight sometimes, but he's 34. Far from a codger."

And I'd also been told by Colleen in computer support on the floor below us that he was hot, which I supposed I could see objectively. If I closed one eye and squinted and tried to forget he signed my checks with a flourish every week.

"In any case, you know you didn't really want to be forced to have fun on this trip."

"Well, no one mentioned anything about fun." My grandmother laughed and the sound made me grin despite myself.

Other than my two best friends in the universe, Ryan and Luna, no one made me smile more than my grandmother. When I'd been knee high to a grasshopper, as she used to call me, she'd been the only person capable of drawing me out of my crusty shell.

I'd learned far too early that people couldn't be trusted, and letting down your guard brought heartbreak. Until she'd brought pure sunshine into my life.

I'd been trying to repay her ever since.

"Okay, okay. Fine. I'm game for some fun. What do you have in mind?" I waggled a finger in her face. "No bouncing."

"Maybe not for you, but I have a date."

"A date?" I tried not to sound let down.

It wasn't as if I'd needed Grams to accompany me every minute. Our vacation was half over already, and we separated every afternoon after lunch to explore and to enjoy the hotel's amenities.

But if I had to have unplanned fun, surely she wasn't going to abandon me in my time of need?

Note to self: if Preston is a codger, so are you, toots.

"Yes. Surely you remember what those are like? If not, we have to remedy that."

"Never mind me. What about this date of yours?"

"He's tall, dark, and dreamy." With a wink, she skirted around the needlessly enormous bed in my room to retrieve her big white bag from the nightstand. She took out a compact and dusted her nose. "His name is Pedro." Her nose wrinkled as she dusted her chin. "Or was it Pablo?"

Only my grandmother. Or maybe Luna. Right now, Grams was exhibiting some post-heartbreak, decidedly Luna-ish free-flowing sexual energy.

And…*ick*. I mean, good for her, but for my mental picture reel? Definitely *ick*.

What did it say about me that my sixty-nine-year-old grandmother could get some on vacation when I hadn't even rated a second look from any of the many hot men we'd seen on the island?

Unleash the Kraken in your bra, and you won't have to wait long.

My inner voice was a brazen hussy. She was also horny as hell.

I wasn't keeping track, but it had been a long time since I'd been anything remotely close to naked with a man. Any day now, I expected dust to fly out of my hoo-ha. The esthetician who'd given me my Brazilian wax before vacation—*thanks, Luna, for inviting me to such torment*—had been the only one to see my lady garden since all my flowers had been replaced with dandelions.

"Is Pedro or Pablo a responsible man?"

Even before my grandmother coughed out a laugh, I winced. Yeah, it was not my place to be asking such questions. It would probably be more enjoyable for my grandmother if he wasn't.

"You're sure he's not a serial killer? On Asher Wainwright's podcast, he profiled a murderer who preyed on vulnerable seniors on vacation who—"

"Since you've been abstinent since the dawn of time and don't like 'unplanned fun', I will allow you to get away with lumping me in with vulnerable seniors. But just once." She jabbed a finger in the air in my direction. "Try it again and I'll salt your granny panties."

I giggled, and the sound was as foreign to me as it was to Grams from her startled expression.

"You need to laugh more, Bunny. It's such a lovely sound."

"I laugh."

"You do, but not enough." Her voice was gentle as she dumped her compact back in her bag and slung it over her shoulder. "Go have something exotic for dinner. And when you come back, I'll have a surprise here for you."

"You know I don't like surprises."

"Exactly why you need more of them." Hurrying over to me, she arched up to kiss both of my cheeks then headed for the door. "Don't take it all too seriously. Just remember: any guy you meet here, you'll never see again. So, feel free to be anyone you want."

"But I'm me."

"Sure. But you can try a new you on for size. Just for fun. No pressure." She grinned and shut the door behind her.

Her words echoed in the silence of my spacious room as I cast another disparaging look at my reflection in the mirror.

Regardless of this whole fun thing, I definitely needed to ditch this dress.

I went down to dinner at the hotel's dining room, one of our favorites spots to eat. I decided to try the lovo, a traditional Fijian meal typically for special occasions. Hot coals were placed in a pit in the ground to cook the meats and fish, which were bundled in banana leaves. The process took a few hours, so I enjoyed people watching and listening to the local guitar group.

Although some neurotic part of me worried about food safety, everything was delicious. And at the end, one of the men who'd helped to prepare my meal placed a plumeria in my tightly bound braid, and I found myself touching it over and over as I meandered back to my room.

He was a kindly older gentleman, but imagine if he wasn't? If he was my lover, and he'd put a flower in my hair...

Dammit, Grams, stop giving me ideas.

I wasn't used to thinking fancifully, and I didn't like it one bit.

Nor did I like stopping at the end of my bed to find a backless, short, siren-red dress waiting for me.

Backless. Siren red. A neckline that dipped way low in front.

Way, way low.

I held it against me in front of the mirror then stepped out of my halter dress to swap it for this one. Technically, this was a halter too, but it was much different.

I couldn't wear a bra. And when the silky, snug fabric wrapped over my curves and my nipples beaded, I didn't want to.

The vision in the mirror could *not* be me.

I undid my braid and shook out the wild waves over my shoulders. The dress swished against my thighs, and tiny crystals glittered along the sides of the neckline, drawing the eye down my body.

The woman in the mirror wasn't too curvy up top and too angular in other spots. Everything just seemed to fit together perfectly, as if this dress had been made with my body in mind. All I needed was shimmering shoes to complete the transition into Cinderella.

I spun around a few times to feel the airy material float around my thighs. Grinning, I hurriedly sent my Grams a note.

Thank you! It's so perfect. You knew just what I wanted, deep down. You always do.

Immediately, a text zinged back at me. It was just a bunch of laughing emojis. The next one, at least, was actual words.

Safety first! I figured rainbow was best. You know, so you can go with the mood.

That was my Grams, always speaking in complete sentences in messages. I was no better. But that wasn't my main concern right now.

What do you mean rainbow? It's red. Solid red.

She sent back more laughing emojis interspersed with a few devils.

Oh, is that the vibe for tonight? Hmm, I didn't think of one of those. I assume those are a personal choice in any case. Have fun, Bunny! Gotta go. Don't stay out too late.

Then a minute later…

Actually, yes, stay out very, very late. Like tomorrow.

Many hearts followed.

I glanced at my bed. A bright flash of color beneath my pillow caught my eye. I rushed over to pick up the item, which turned out to be a strip of condoms.

A very long, very colorful strip of prophylactics.

I dropped the strip as if it had singed my hand and pressed my palms to my burning cheeks. Oh my God, Grams had bought me condoms.

A *lot* of them.

A laugh spilled out of me, and I doubled over for a full minute until I got ahold of myself. Then I gazed down at my already beloved dress and smoothed my hands down my hips. Maybe she was just messing with me.

She had to be, right? Where else could this have come from?

I hadn't made any friends on the island. Not yet. Probably not ever, because I tended to stick to corners and shadows, always observing. Always wishing I could be brave and flirty like my two best friends until I reminded myself that hey, at least I was comfortable. Maybe I wasn't taking big chances, but I wasn't risking too much either.

My life was safe. Predictable. *Boring.*

Though it wasn't as if Ryan or Lu had found their forever guys yet either. Not that they were looking. I'd been the one everyone figured was born to settle down, and I almost had—until I'd made a mistake and lost everything. I hadn't even come close.

But that didn't explain where this dress had come from.

Maybe it had been delivered to the wrong room. My heart sank. God, would I have to give it back? That was the right thing to do. I was honorable. Always.

I sucked in a deep breath and forced myself to go to the room phone on the nightstand. I called down to the desk and asked the question I profoundly did not want to.

"Was something sent by mistake to my room?"

A pause. "Mistake? No, ma'am. The gentleman was very insistent."

"What gentleman?" I gripped my throat and stared at the door I'd closed and locked behind me as always. "What was his name?"

"He didn't give his name. But he said it was to be delivered to the lovely blond in 42. That is you, is it not?" He seemed to hesitate. "April Finley?"

"Yes, but there must be some mix-up. I don't know any man. There's no one." For an illogical reason, tears prickled behind my eyes.

He started to reply but a swift knock on the door startled me. Quickly, I thanked him and hung up.

I rushed to the door and then stopped with my hand on the knob.

What if I was being stalked by a serial killer with exceptionally excellent taste and a healthy bottom line?

What if I was the vulnerable one being preyed on now?

Another knock sounded. "I know you're in there. Open up."

I clutched my throat again. He'd been watching me. Following me. Buying me sexy dresses.

Maybe he wanted to debauch me. It wouldn't be hard. Missionary sex seemed like the ultimate indulgence right now.

Forget sampling my watermelon sugar.

The door had a peephole, so I used it. And gasped. Loudly.

Of course I had to meet a serial killer who was stunningly handsome. Even if his head was distorted by the optical glass in the peephole.

His rough chuckle went well with his bedroom voice. I hadn't known that was a thing until just now. "I saw you go in. Now I hear you. Do I pass inspection?"

I shut my eyes and dropped my forehead to the door. "Who are you, mystery dress man?"

"Names don't matter. I just want to see you in that dress." Somehow his voice dipped even lower. "Did you try it on yet?"

This conversation was bizarre. He was obviously a stalker and potentially dangerous to boot.

Did I say any of that? No, of course not. Instead, I asked something totally not relevant.

"How did you know my size?"

"So, it fit." The pleasure in his tone did something entirely not right to my dormant nerve endings. Specifically, the ones below my waist.

I cleared my throat. "It fit."

"You're about the same size as my baby sister, so I guessed. She's tall and lean like you. At least, most of you is."

My face heated again. He'd checked me out then. Even in my too-big halter dress. But he'd bought an extremely revealing dress for me, so he had to have paid attention to my…dimensions.

Dear God, what was I supposed to do now?

"Just let me in, okay? I promise I'm not dangerous."

He had a baby sister that he spoke of with fondness. Surely that indicated he wasn't psychopathic. "Isn't that what every dangerous man has said since the beginning of time?"

"I'm persistent, but I'm not a threat. I'm a man of the law, in fact."

My eyebrows reached for my hairline. "Complete with your dime store badge?"

"Not that kind." He laughed again. "I saw you two days ago. You were browsing in one of the shops, and you tried on this frumpy big hat."

I recalled it immediately. "It was not frumpy. I thought it was chic."

"Whatever. But you kept hemming and hawing, touching everything, buying nothing. So tactile. I wondered if all textures fascinated you, or just the ones you adorn your body with."

I was pretty sure that was sketchy sex talk. My nether regions offered a weak pulse of confirmation. "Watching people who are unaware is dubious behavior."

"If I'd approached you, you would have run. I saw you do it several times when men glanced your way."

"No one looked at me." I hated that my chin trembled. "No one ever does."

"Oh, beauty, you're so wrong."

Going on instinct, I opened the door. And nearly gasped again.

He was gorgeous. Tall and tanned with tousled golden-brown hair pushed back by his sunglasses and expressive eyes of indeterminate color. They might've even been green.

He was dressed casually in typical island wear—white linen pants, floral Hawaiian-style shirt opened just enough to show a smattering of dark chest hair, and sandals. The relaxed attire somehow showed off his broad shoulders and muscular chest even more.

"You're stunning." His voice was gravelly sex as he stepped forward to touch one of my loosened curls.

And I let him. I didn't move. Didn't say one damn thing.

I never took risks. But I was risking this, because I couldn't remember when I'd ever needed anything this much.

Then his gaze dropped to my hand and the long strip of brightly colored condoms I still clutched.

The corner of his sinful mouth tipped upward. "If you're game, so am I."

CHAPTER TWO

Bishop

I'd never behaved like this before.

Following a woman I'd noticed in a store. Wandering the island looking for her for the past couple of days. Knowing I was meant to find her.

Meant to *know* her.

Then I'd seen her at dinner tonight. I'd been on the opposite side of the restaurant, and she hadn't even looked my way. But that sunshine hair had caught my eye once again.

I'd gotten up half a dozen times, determined to introduce myself. Each time, I immediately sat down, transfixed by her slow sway to the guitar music. And her shy smile when the cook fastened a flower in her hair.

Gone now.

"These aren't mine." She was still flushing furiously as she gripped the condoms as if they were tiny latex pods of poison.

I touched her hair again, brushing it back behind the delicate shell of her ear. Her hoops were tiny. Barely visible. "Where's the plumeria?"

Even as I asked, I glimpsed the bright pink on the floor near the bed. I nudged her back gently. "May I?"

She swallowed visibly and nodded, hiding the condoms behind her back as if she could make them vanish. Her shyness was so damn adorable. And infuriating, because a woman this gorgeous shouldn't be afraid of anything.

She should be bold. Proud. A fucking peacock in bright red silk.

When she stepped aside, I walked into her modest room and retrieved the flower. I turned back to put it in her hair where she still stood uncertainly in the doorway, her back against the still-open door.

Must not close herself in with the big bad scholarly wolf.

"Wait."

I waited.

"You saw me two days ago."

I nodded. I would never forget how her long, fragile fingers had skimmed over every bit of fabric as if she'd never before touched anything so luxurious. The desire to give her the world had seized me by the balls. I didn't do shit like that. I dated casually when the need arose. But I didn't make commitments—not anymore. And I rarely went for repeats.

I definitely didn't fall into big hazel eyes and forget my own freaking name.

"Then what?"

"I waited for you," I said softly, feeling like the biggest chump who'd ever lived.

"You…waited?"

There, that little catch in her voice. Hesitation. Doubt. Everything I'd seen on her face as she deflected attention in the store. I didn't think she was even aware of the wall of ice she'd erected around herself.

Not much different than the one you've built, huh?

"I knew I'd see you again." To keep from reaching for her, I tucked my free hand in my pocket. "And tonight at dinner, I did. You never noticed me."

"How could that be possible?"

I didn't smile. My overlarge ego didn't appreciate that she hadn't, but it only made her more intriguing. It wasn't often that women overlooked me. That wasn't conceit, merely fact.

"I noticed you. I almost came up to you more than once, but I'll be honest." I ran the tip of my tongue along my lower lip. "I like watching you."

Her throat moved again and her big eyes flared wider. She was scared, yes, but she was interested. Maybe even curious.

Turned on.

Thank God. Arousal scorched my skin just from seeing her in that snug dress—one I'd chosen specifically for her—with her full breasts trying to escape the thin material.

"Is honesty rare for you?" Her voice was breathy, but I could tell fear wasn't all that was driving her. She was finding her bearings.

Soon enough, she'd join me in this dance. The one that had started between us before she'd even realized.

"With women I intend to get naked? No."

Bright flags of color appeared on her cheeks yet again. "You think highly of yourself."

"Yet you're the one toting around latex like you're leading the sexual revolution."

"That was an accident, dammit. My grandmother bought them for me."

I laughed. Stopped. Laughed again. "What?"

"Oh, shut up." In an unexpected fit of temper, she kicked the door closed. "So, now what? Am I supposed to get on all fours?"

Okay, I had not expected that. Or that her grandmother was her protection pusher.

With every passing minute, I liked this woman more. That was dangerous—for me, not her. And for the first time since I'd seen her, I wanted to run.

"What kind of prick do you think I am?"

"One who acts like it's hunting season and he's eyeing an easy lay." She crossed her arms. "Wrong, buster."

Buster. I nearly grinned. "Oh, you are far from easy. If I wanted easy, would I be here right now?"

"No, you'd probably be downstairs buying bikinis and Bahama Mamas for any beautiful woman who looked your way."

"So, you're acknowledging you're beautiful." Smugly, I matched her pose, careful not to crush the plumeria. "Finally."

"You're infuriating."

I stepped forward. "Yes. And this flower belongs in your hair."

Half expecting her to deck me—and half hard from almost wanting her to—I lifted my hand to slip the flower into her hair. But it was too wild and wouldn't stay.

How ironic.

I cheated and took off my sunglasses to put on her head then tucked the flower behind the earpiece. Except they were too big and fell off along with the flower.

"Now what, wise guy?"

Her impudence was doing the same thing to my dick as her temptation to do me harm. Masochistic? Perhaps.

"Do you have a hairpin?"

"Don't need one. It's all about technique." She plucked the flower from my fingers and did not tuck it in her hair. Oh, no, she tucked it into *mine*.

With a grin wide enough to make me laugh again like a besotted fool.

"Pink is your color." Her tone was admirably serious.

"With your fair skin, I'm sure it's yours too. All over." I trailed my fingertips down the inside of her arm, waiting for her to blush for me.

She didn't disappoint.

"Pity you'll never know."

"Would you prefer if I pretended I simply wanted to walk by the water with you? Is that the kind of game playing you like?"

"No. I don't like games. And I can take in the water just fine from my balcony."

I wasn't sure that was true. This didn't seem to be an oceanfront room. What would she think of my place right on the water?

I had to find out.

My gaze diverted to the brochure on the nightstand. It was open to a page featuring photos of oiled, firm bodies under the capable hands of a masseuse.

I could work with that.

"Besides, there are ways we can get to know each other physically other than sex."

She frowned, her lush lips tugging down so severely, it was nearly comical. I wanted to kiss the shallow indent in her chin.

Yeah, you're doing really well at this whole 'keep it about naked times' thing, dude.

"Why would I want to get to know you physically or any other way?"

She was direct. I liked that about her. Meant fewer chances she'd throw me a curve ball when I wasn't looking.

"Curiosity?" I rubbed at the frown lines between her brows.

I couldn't stop touching her and that didn't have a thing to do with sex. Or it wasn't only about that. I just liked having my hands on her. I definitely enjoyed her smart mouth.

I hadn't anticipated she'd be sharp-tongued. But of course she had to be, so that I'd be so impossibly fascinated, there was no way in hell I'd be able to walk away.

And not even due to the current situation in my boxers, although that was a valid consideration.

She folded her arms across her impressive chest and didn't respond. I tried not to look, but her body was as arresting as her face. So many long lines offset with irresistible curves. She was shorter than me, but not by much. Though her features were delicate, she didn't seem insubstantial. Unless I was mistaken, this was a woman who wouldn't break if things got a little interesting.

Once she got past the miles-deep wariness in her eyes, at least.

"You like massages?" I inclined my chin toward the brochure. "Have you considered getting one here?"

"I've never had one."

"No way."

Her chin lifted. "I don't like strangers touching me."

"I know a woman if that would make it easier."

She snorted. "I just bet you do."

"A masseuse," I continued evenly. "She does both regular massages and couples' massages. Not that I've ever had one of those, but I've seen the treatment rooms and know their protocol. They're extremely private, and they go as in-depth as you prefer."

Whatever level of depth I'd intimated, the depth she went to was a whole other level. "Are you serious? Now you want to pay someone to have sex with me while you watch? You are one kinky bastard."

I stuck my tongue firmly into my cheek. "So, you're saying you'd be into that?"

"Oh my God. Why am I even talking to you?" She flopped on the side of the bed and kicked off her sandals, revealing blue toenails covered with sand.

For Pete's sake, even her *feet* were sexy. And I did not have a foot fetish. Far from it.

If I made it off this island with my dick still intact, I was going to have sex with as many women as I could to get this fire she'd started inside me out of my blood.

"Intrigued?"

She stayed silent.

"Trying to guess if you're going to become infamous because you opened your door to a man who assured you he wasn't dangerous? By the way, according to Asher Wainwright's True Crime and other Macabre Tales, you should never—"

"You listen to Asher?"

"I do." I chanced sitting beside her on the bed. "You do too?"

I hadn't realized Asher's podcast had such far-reaching listenership, but his show was definitely was growing in popularity in this true crime-obsessed climate.

She nodded. "My besties and I have wine night and listen. We're a few weeks behind."

"Wine and gruesome murder sounds…delightful."

"You are entirely too sarcastic."

"And you are entirely too on to me." I traced a pattern on the back of the hand she'd rested on the bed between us. "I followed you back here that first day, after I saw you browsing. I know I shouldn't have. But I wanted some way to find you again." I swallowed hard and told the whole truth. "I was behind you when you went up to the desk and told them your room number and that you needed extra towels. So, that's how I knew where to send the dress."

When her mouth dropped open, I held up a hand. "I know it sounds awful. I wasn't stalking you. Not exactly. This is my resort too. Well, I'm at the other end, so I didn't have to come to the main building but—"

Her pale brows knitted together. "Other end?"

"Yes, I have one of the beachfront bures."

Her expression didn't clear. "What is that?"

"They're basically small isolated houses. From a distance, they kind of look like huts, but they have amazing amenities. The resort only has a half dozen of them and they offer the utmost privacy. I'm in the last one and my neighbors are all couples."

"Why is that?"

"They're mere feet from the water with plunge pools and outdoor showers and anytime access to private masseuses. The hot tub on the private deck is a perfect spot to watch the sunset with someone special." I shrugged. "People want romance."

"Hmm."

"You're a tough nut. I like that about you." The pattern I was drawing on her skin extended to her wrist. A delicate bracelet bisected by tiny shells rested there. Slipping my finger beneath it seemed intimate somehow, but she didn't pull back. "We could try a massage in my bure. I checked out the on-site facilities before I scheduled my own session, but we don't have to use the treatment rooms here."

"You must think I'm really stressed."

"Well, you do seem a little tense, but I don't blame you. We're strangers. You don't understand why I'd buy you a dress and follow you and generally act…weird."

"So, you're acknowledging this is odd behavior." That didn't stop her from turning over her hand and tentatively threading her fingers through mine.

Just the friction of our skin was electric. My head snapped up, our gazes locked, and I knew, just knew, she felt it too. My pulse kicked into overdrive and her breathing sped up enough for her glossy lips to part.

It took all my will not to lean forward and bite that pouty pink flesh.

"I understand what I've done would raise questions," I responded when I could finally speak.

"Just questions, hmm? Not for me to run away screaming?"

"I'd love to make you scream for an entirely different reason." I squeezed her fingers lightly. "Just give me a chance."

As the silence grew between us, I stared into her thickly-lashed hazel eyes. I'd beg her to run away with me in another minute.

To right where we were, so we never had to go back.

She smiled, so quickly I was sure I'd imagined it. "You do wonders for my ego. A man like you could have anyone."

"The only one I want is you. I have from the first."

She looked down at our joined hands. Her pale flesh against my much more golden skin somehow looked erotic. "I want to go dancing first."

"Anywhere. There's a club just—"

"You mentioned you have a deck. Is there room to dance there?"

"Yes." A slab of granite had wedged itself in my throat, and no matter how much I swallowed, nothing dislodged it. "And we would have the beach too."

"Okay. I need to text my grandmother where I'll be."

"Of course. I'm in 1401. You're close with her?" I coughed into my hand. "You must be if she buys your condoms."

"Smart ass." She shrugged. "I just ran out."

Don't be jealous of the nameless, faceless men she's having so much sex with. Even if you haven't seen her with anyone here. And no man shares this suite with her.

At least, there was nothing visible that seemed male. Regardless, I couldn't take the chance.

"Are you single?" It physically pained me, but I detangled our fingers while I waited for her answer. A shark chomping off my foot probably wouldn't have hurt much more.

Fine, at least a toe.

No need to be dramatic, even if I was practically ready to promise lifelong fealty to this woman. And I pledged to no one.

Not anymore.

Obviously, my dry spell had done more harm than I'd realized. It was past time to end it.

"What? Yes. Yes, of course. I haven't—I don't—" She took a deep breath that smoothed out the sudden jaggedness inside me. "I'm not that kind of person."

"Good. Me either."

"So, you're single too?"

"I am."

"Since last night?" Her lame attempt at a joke didn't make me smile.

"Since, oh, three years, eight months, and sixteen days ago. Give or take some hours and considering the time difference."

She tried to keep the shock off her face but failed miserably. "You can't have been alone that long."

"Yes, I can." My smile was a quick twist of my lips without the slightest bit of warmth. "I've had sex since then. Quite a lot of it, actually."

Her nose wrinkled. "Lovely."

I had to chuckle. "But not recently. It's been over a year since I've touched a woman. Equally as long since I've wanted to." I rubbed my thumb over her palm and watched her pupils flare from awareness. "And I've never wanted to touch anyone as much as I want to touch you."

"You're a charmer," she said after a moment, her voice nearly as raw as my own.

I laughed again. "Actually, those who know me in my real life would say I'm anything but. I'm a shark. A lion. An apex predator who eats the young of my prey for a bedtime snack."

"Sharp detour from charm into potential criminal past."

My laughter softened. She didn't seem afraid anymore, thankfully. "You're safe with me." I let my gaze roam slowly over her face. So many nuances lived inside her expression. I was as eager to peel back her layers as I was to have her naked and at my mercy. "As safe as you want to be."

"I don't."

It was my turn to be silent.

"I'm tired of being safe. My life is made up of routines and schedules and careful plans. No deviation, no rocking the boat. Right now, my grandmother is probably swinging from the chandelier with some young buck named Pedro Pablo and having the time of her life."

"That's a mouthful."

She pushed the fingers of her free hand though her long sunny waves. "She told me to get laid. Do you know how mortifying that is?" She pressed her face into her hand, her shoulders shaking.

Fuck me, was she weeping?

I did not deal well with crying women. Normally when I encountered them, I put them in the capable care of my assistant and told her to offer them fresh pastries.

Vienna wasn't here right now, and there wasn't a croissant in sight.

Then my mystery woman lifted her head and grinned. "You're off to a great start with the dress fit for Cinderella, but I want to have a hell of a story to tell—"

"No. Oh, no. Stop right there." I held up my free hand. "If you intend to tell your grandmother what we do in bed, I'm going to reconsider this whole arrangement."

She leaned toward me until our noses were a hairsbreadth apart. I could practically taste the fruity drink she'd had at dinner from the wisp of her breath on my lips. "Is that what we have? An arrangement?"

"Depends on what you want."

"No strings. Nothing to tie us down or hold us back for as long as we're here." The indent in her chin was going to kill me as that shy smile lifted her lips again. "And you're hereby instructed to give me an amazing story to tell my best friends."

"Best friends are far more doable than grandmothers."

"Especially mine. Both are hot as hell."

"Hotter than you?" If I moved a fraction closer, our lips would be pressed together. "Not possible."

She bit her lower lip, her white teeth piercing that full flesh. "It's time to dance, island stranger."

Before I could process it, she released my hand and moved away from the bed to grab her bag and head for the door.

I groaned and fell backward on the mattress.

"Coming?" she called sunnily, laughter rich in her tone.

I forced myself to my elbows just to take in the picture of her with her hand on her hip, flashing me a bewitching grin. Already she seemed so much more confident than she had just a few moments ago. If that was at all due to me, I was grateful.

Who knew it would feel so good to make someone happy rather than to delight in their misery? And God, wasn't I a pitiful sod if *that* was a revelation.

"You lead and I'll follow, Cinderella."

Her expression flickered and then we both glanced down at her bare feet. She'd forgotten to put her sandals back on.

When she bent to retrieve them, I rose and snagged her wrist. Her pulse beat strong and true against my thumb, racing just like my own.

If I could do only one thing for the rest of my life, touching her would be enough.

"Hello, I need my shoes."

"I have a better idea." I sidestepped her without releasing her wrist and picked up the bedside phone to call the concierge. The entire time, my gaze stayed riveted on hers.

When someone answered, I smiled. "Yes, I'm calling for 1401. I need a pair of high heels perfect for Cinderella delivered to me." When she tried to jerk away, I tightened my grip and twisted my head to see the tag on the footbed of her sandals. "Size ten."

Ten? I mouthed, cocking a brow.

She dropped the shoes and gave me the middle finger, making me grin. But she didn't try to yank away.

My mysterious stranger enjoyed being restrained. Duly noted.

"As you wish, sir."

The movie reference from the man on the phone made me smile. Too many hours babysitting Michaela back in the day had given me a broad education on the wild world of chick flicks. "Thank you."

As soon as I hung up, my Cinderella started to speak.

I laid a finger against her lips, silencing her. "Even apex predators appreciate heels on a stunning woman. Indulge me."

"Just as long as you remember to indulge *me*," she muttered.

"Oh, Cinderella, I've thought of nothing else all night."

CHAPTER THREE

April

I TEXTED my grandmother right before I crossed the threshold to my island stranger's pleasure palace.

While he was unlocking the door, I surreptitiously took his photo so Grams could send his picture to the FBI if my dismembered body parts washed ashore at a later date.

Was it selfish of me to hope he could deliver a few orgasms before my certain death? Probably. But I was overdue.

"Did I just hear a camera shutter? Hope you got my good side." He pushed open the door.

As heat scalded my cheeks, I moved behind him and aimed at his toned backside, nicely highlighted by his thin pants. "Yep." I clicked several times. "I did."

I managed to send the profile shot to my grandmother before he turned and grabbed me off my feet. My heart leaped into my throat while I struggled between a laugh and a scream. "Dammit, put me down."

"Whatcha doing, Cin?"

Cin. A nickname for a woman who wasn't me. But I liked it a lot.

"I told you I had to text my grandmother. Are you going to set me down now?"

"You needed to send a picture of my ass to your grandmother? Does she have a particular preference or what?"

I pinched his biceps—*whoa, someone worked out*—and he sent me a grin as he jockeyed me in his hold. But he most definitely was not setting me down as we crossed the threshold of his fancy little place.

He was carrying me inside like I was his bride, for God's sake. Like we'd gotten married on the beach, saying our vows while my hair blew in the breeze and his intent green eyes smoldered into mine…

"What are you thinking?"

I ducked my head. "Trust me, you don't want to know."

He reached up to grip my chin and made me meet his gaze. "You'd be wrong."

"Silly romantic fantasy. Threshold and all, you know."

His brow furrowed for a moment and then smoothed with a quirk of his lips. "I'm much better at wrecking them."

I frowned. "What do you mean?"

Abruptly, he put me down and I nearly tumbled into him. He steadied me with firm hands, and I reached up to adjust the flower I'd insisted on putting back in his hair when it fell. He'd laughed at me, but he hadn't argued. Just as he wasn't arguing with my foolish romantic notions now, even if he didn't know the exact parameters of them. I was sure he could come close enough.

"It's just this island. This place. This everything." I dropped my bag and waved a hand around us, slowly turning in a circle to take it all in.

The place was open to the sea, with the dark waves rolling just feet away from the glass doors. The deck he'd spoken of beckoned just beyond the glass, and the hot tub bubbled in the center of a ring of candles and flowers. On the other side of the hot tub, a short flight of steps led down to a plunge pool that looked like it dropped off into the ocean itself.

"Endless water." I passed the long, low, white couches and sunken chairs surrounding a rustic-looking coffee table where a million candles burned.

Flameless, I noted. No imminent fire risk.

Try not to be a buzzkill, okay? Women of the world don't worry about the place burning down.

A small desk off to the side held a laptop and a thick briefcase on the verge of busting apart. So, he worked on vacation. What did he do? Who was he?

I sucked at this whole 'no connections to real life' thing. But it was better. Less problematic.

Gauzy white curtains fluttered in the breeze, drawing me toward the deck and all that water. I didn't have my suit. I hadn't even thought to bring it.

"You don't need one." From behind me, his big hands landed on my shoulders.

Shit. Had I spoken aloud? I must've.

I glanced into the bedroom and noticed the bed took up almost the entire space. It was enormous. And in the center of all that pure white, cloud-like bedding sat the most perfect pair of heels I'd ever imagined, shimmering in the near dark as if they'd been inlaid with thousands of crystals.

I let out a soft noise and rushed toward them, picking them up to study them in the flickering light. This room was filled with candles too, set upon the nightstand and lined up in front of the large mirror on the dresser so the flames seemed magnified.

"These aren't crystals." Aghast, I glanced at him, where he lounged in the doorway like a lazy panther, waiting for his prey to land right between his massive paws. "These are real diamonds."

"So they are. This is your fantasy, right?" He moved toward me and tipped up my chin with his fingertip. "Put them on."

Obliging him didn't feel like a conscious thought.

I dropped the shoes to the floor and toed off my sandals. He'd made a joke about carrying me here, and I hadn't believed him then. Seeing these shoes, I did now.

I slipped them on and swallowed a gasp at how perfectly they cupped my feet. The heels were higher than my usual pumps, but they didn't hurt. I walked to the wide windows to stare out into the wind-whipped water, mesmerized by my reflection.

"Who are you?" I whispered.

"Who are you," he countered, brushing back my hair to kiss my bare shoulder. The touch of his lips on any part of me seemed illicit. Thrilling. Like I could be anyone when I was with him. Anyone in these clothes and in this magical place.

He reached around me and opened the glass doors so we could step out onto the wraparound deck. The burble of water hummed from a few feet away, but he didn't nudge me in that direction. Instead, he urged me toward the railing, his hands on my hips, his mouth against my hair.

I stared out into the night, marveling that this stretch of beach could be completely deserted although we weren't far from the other bures. Water crashed onto the white sand, flowing and receding, the sultry breeze tossing my hair back as I gave into the desire to lean against the solid wall of hard, hot man behind me.

Damn, he was hard and hot all over.

I jolted away from him as if I'd been scalded. He simply drew me right back, cupping my cheek as he turned me toward him and lifted my face to his.

Soft lips met mine, his gentle pressure and swamping warmth an invitation I couldn't deny. He didn't push me. Didn't thrust his tongue into my mouth and make demands that would send me running, no matter how brave I was trying to be.

He offered me the lightest hint of his tongue, sweeping against mine then slipping away so that I was left to pursue. To arch up against him and press my aching breasts into his chest as I wound my fingers into the dark golden hair that curled against his nape. A little wild and uncontrolled.

Just like us.

Tender licks of heat turned into hungry nips of teeth. I couldn't get enough of him. He delved into my mouth, and I tasted lime on his tongue, a surprisingly erotic flavor. The scents of ocean and salt and expensive cologne filled my senses while we devoured each other. I swayed on my ridiculously expensive shoes and he caught me again, dragging me up against his muscular body, my hard nipples shifting against my silky dress and making me moan.

He hoisted me higher, except this time, he caught my legs around his waist. And when he turned, I knew exactly where he was headed.

Since my arms were currently coiled around his neck and my mouth was attacking his, I had absolutely no problem with his destination.

I didn't hear him close the doors behind him. Maybe he didn't. Didn't matter. Ocean-tinged air flowed into the room as he tumbled me onto the huge bed and followed me down, caging me in with his long, muscular body. He pulled off my heels and tossed them aside, then he fisted a handful of my hair and held me in place against the pillow. His eyes were gleaming jewels in the candlelight as he lowered his head to lick my throat.

I bowed up, and he obeyed my wordless plea, pushing aside the panel of fabric that guarded first one breast, then the other. He sank back on his heels to stare at me, his fingers cupping and molding me while I strained and writhed and swallowed a moan at the cool breeze tightening my nipples to peaks.

It wasn't the wind. It was him. His hot gaze caressing me as the rough pads of his fingers touched me everywhere but where I needed him most.

And the bastard knew it.

He reached up to unhook the dress and tugged it down my body, his powerful gaze holding me hostage. I couldn't be embarrassed or afraid while he looked at me, keeping me in his thrall. His hand moved to my panties and I reached for him, incapable of not touching him a second longer.

And then he glanced down and started to laugh.

I shut my eyes. Damn, shit, fuck. Of all the times to wear those panties.

"What is this fluffy thing?" He flicked the nub on top of my mound. Not the nub I wished he'd flicked either.

"It's a cottontail. Like for a bunny? They were from my grandmother, because she calls me Bunny. A stupid gag gift. Somehow they ended up in my suitcase. I think Ryan stuck them in there to be a smart ass. But I'm a sparse packer and ran out of underwear—" Hearing the steady stream of babble coming out of my mouth, I covered my face with my hands. "Never mind."

"Who's Ryan?"

The cold whip of his voice made me forget all about my flaming cheeks. I dropped my hands and met his icy stare with a frown. "My best friend? She helped me pack—"

"Gotcha. I didn't realize Ryan was a woman." At once, his features eased and the light came back into his eyes.

And he went back to his task as if nothing had happened. But it had.

"Wait." I gripped his head in my hands when he lowered to where I'd so desperately wanted him to go two minutes ago.

Apparently, he wasn't in a talking mood.

He yanked down my panties and kissed me intimately, immediately applying a lot more pressure than he'd started with on my mouth.

I wasn't a sexual acolyte, but even I knew when someone was trying to distract me. And it was working.

"Jesus," I gasped, my hips tilting upward to get more of *that*. His tongue was everywhere. Against my clit, lapping in short, hard strokes. Sliding down to my entrance, snaking inside to tease me into clenching futilely around him before he was on the move again. Then his fingers replaced his tongue, two at first, then three, while he sucked hard on my clit.

It should've been too much too soon, but I'd been primed since the hotel room. The heat in my belly twisted tighter as his touch sped up, and he made his enjoyment of me clear. He didn't hold back anything. Not his groans or his obvious relish at his task.

"Goddamn, you taste good. You were making a mess of these panties, weren't you?" He lifted his head, and I caught the gleam of my wetness against his chin and the light scruff there.

Normally, I would've flushed, but I was too far gone. His fingers were still working me, in and out, in and out, swiveling just right to hit that swollen place deep inside.

"Watch me eat you."

I watched. I couldn't look away. His lips rubbed against my bare flesh and came up wet, making me arch and beg. He leaned up to capture one of my beaded nipples with his damp lips and sucked just right, intensifying the throb between my legs.

The one he'd created.

He growled against my nipple. "Clench me again."

I couldn't stop myself. The rumble of sound against my skin nearly made me come.

But then he drew his fingers out to lick them, one by one. "I want this honey all over me. All over my face and cock just like it's on my fingers."

I trembled and begged him wordlessly to go back to where he'd just been.

He slipped three fingers inside me, stretching me. "Tight as a virgin, baby. But you want my cock. Tell me you want it."

"I want it. God, I want it. Please." I was lost. So close. So wild. My hips bucked against the bed as his grin slashed into the near darkness, masculine and proud. His broad thumb swept over my clit, and I gripped the sheets and catapulted straight into the damn stars.

It went on and on. His mouth didn't stop. His fingers were tireless. I just kept coming. I couldn't stop shaking. All I could do was twist the bedding in my hands and try to hold on while he ravaged me.

By the time he finally undressed and slipped inside me, I was nearly incoherent. I wrapped my arms and legs around him and tried to open for him, to make room, but even after all that, it wasn't quite enough.

"You're a fucking fist. Came half a dozen times and still." He bit my earlobe with a grunt of frustration. "I want in." His teeth razored down my throat. "Let me in, Cinderella."

I slipped my hand down between us and went for my clit, rubbing hard while I hooked my leg around his hip and swiveled.

"Fuck, yes." He slid in the rest of the way, filling me unbearably full.

I didn't have a lot to compare him to, and a very long stretch of abstinence might be making me fanciful, but holy shit.

"I'm not going to be able to walk tomorrow," I gasped.

"Good. Because you're not leaving this bed." He hauled back and sank in again, even deeper this time, his groan echoing in my head.

I dug my nails into his back, savoring his low noise of pleasure. I leaned up to lick his damp throat, rocking my hips against his. "So, fuck me already."

"As you wish."

He pulled back and thrust in again, his strokes choppy and rough. His corded arms braced beside me on the pillows as he worked himself in and out of me. He wasn't careful now. His jaw locked tight and his golden skin glistened in the candlelight as he grabbed my hand and brought it between my legs once more, guiding me to touch myself as I had before. His mouth found mine in the darkness as our bodies strained and ground together, and I raked my nails up his back with my free hand to grip his bunched shoulder.

Our fingers tangled together over my pulsing clit. I didn't think I could come again. There had to be a breaking point. But he made me a liar when he pulled out and slid home one last time, the base of his cock slamming against our soaked fingers and setting me off again.

He buried his face in my hair as his hips jerked against mine. Still spinning myself, I managed to reach down to grip his taut ass, still flexing as he pumped inside me. I used my nails and he groaned helplessly, jerking again as if just that flash of pain extended his orgasm.

"Fuck me."

I couldn't help laughing at his dazed exhalation. "Think I just did."

He lifted his head, his hair adorably mussed and his expression already verging toward sleepy. "You sure did."

I brushed his hair back from his forehead. "You held up your end well."

"Appreciate the vote of confidence."

"I aim to be of service."

"You certainly were. Thank you for the best experience of my life." He kissed me, so sweetly that my heart ached.

I kissed him back. I didn't have words for that one.

After a minute or two, he eased back and looked down between us. He was still inside me, and he didn't seem to be in a hurry to go. "Like times a thousand plus fifty."

"Is that all?" I teased, wiggling to remind him he was a really big dude and my ribs were about to shatter.

"No. More. Shit, condom." He reached down to hold onto it as he withdrew and climbed off the bed to take care of things.

I looked up at the ceiling and giggled. And kept right on giggling as I heard the water turn on and off in the next room before he rejoined me on the bed.

"What's so funny?" He rolled next to me, washcloth in hand and a satisfied smile on his far too handsome face.

How did a woman walk away from a face like that? Or those hands, or those eyes, or those smiles that seemed to land somewhere inside me, lighting me up all over?

But I didn't voice any of that. Instead, I pointed at the ceiling. "There's a skylight."

He followed my gaze upward. "Indeed there is."

"I thought I came hard enough to fly through the roof."

His laughter burst through the room before he dropped his head to my breast. "That'd be a feat, wouldn't it?"

I threaded my fingers through his hair and grinned up at the twinkle of stars against the darkness. "Close enough."

CHAPTER FOUR

Bishop

"Do you think it's weird we've had sex in multiple positions, but we don't know each other's name?"

I stroked a hand down her still damp hair, currently spread over my chest as she nibbled at a chocolate-covered strawberry. We were on our second platter this afternoon. The first had been part of breakfast.

My girl had a healthy appetite in more ways than one.

"If you want, I'll tell you my name." I tried to sound casual. This wasn't any big thing, even if it felt that way more with every passing moment. "I'll tell you anything you want to know."

My heartbeat kicked up as she leaned up to offer me a bite of berry, smearing chocolate over my lips with a giggle as I nipped her fingers and chewed. Her laughter was already my favorite sound in the entire world.

Right after the sound of her moans. That breathless hitching cry would always rank first. I was a lucky SOB that I'd heard her make that noise pretty damn often already.

She fed both of us for a few minutes, trading off. One for her, one for me. Until the platter was empty and she flashed me a pout. "All gone."

Before I could offer to order another ten dozen strawberries if it would make her happy, she pushed the platter aside and shifted onto her belly, baring her beautiful tits at me, all pink and swollen from my scruff, lips, and teeth. She might not want strings, but she would wear my marks for as long as they lasted.

Not long enough. They're as temporary as you are, pal.

She folded her arms on my chest and rested her chin on them. "What's your favorite color?"

I tried to school my features to keep my disappointment from showing. It wasn't any big deal. We'd made an arrangement, and I was a man of my word. Besides, I was the king of one-night-stands.

Even if this had already gone so far beyond that, both in duration and intensity.

I tapped her nose. "I offer my name, and you ask for my favorite color?"

"A name is given to you, not chosen for yourself. But you pick your favorite color. So, that's more personal."

"Hmm. Black."

She wrinkled her nose. "Why black?"

"Because it's every color all in one."

"Indecisive and fickle. Got it."

"I'm not the least bit indecisive. I went for you the first time I saw you." I rolled her under me, thereby knocking the empty berry platter off the bed.

"Whoops." Her sunlit hair spilled every which way as she laughed up at me, her hazel eyes sparkling in the afternoon sunshine. "We made a mess."

"Not the first time." I notched my already interested cock between her thighs, still slick from the shower we'd had not long ago.

That was our second since last night, thanks to our nighttime—and daytime—entertainment. I'd lost track of how many times I'd come. The same went for her.

All I knew was my cock was sore but happy. Just like the rest of me, except for the knocking on my brain every time she reminded me how temporary this all was.

"What's yours?" I tugged on a lock of her hair, wrapping it around my finger like a corkscrew. It was thick and shiny, and she always moaned when I gripped it while she licked her way down my body. She hadn't sucked me off yet, but the day was young.

The hourglass wasn't ticking down audibly second by second, like a metronome. That was all in my head.

"Wow, seriously?" She sounded awed. "I figured this topic would be a nice refresher, and yet you're still knocking at heaven's door."

I glanced down between us, smothering a laugh as I shifted away from the wet pearly gates. "Damn right it's heaven. But I need my latex wings before I fly in."

"You're ridiculous. And cute. But ridiculous." She cupped my cheeks and kissed me hard, rolling on top of me to straddle me in the center of the bed. She stretched her arms over her head on a yawn, and sweet mercy, my tongue practically lolled out of my mouth.

At first, she'd been shy about being naked with so much glass surrounding us. I hadn't moved to close the curtains either. Who wanted to block the view to paradise? Then she'd realized how private this part of the beach really was, and she'd relaxed. I hoped that maybe my influence was rubbing off on her too.

Just like her giggles and easy affection when she wasn't thinking too hard were having the same effect on me.

"These fucking tits." I grasped one in my palm, rolling the stiff nipple between my fingers. "I'd like to go to sleep between them. Wake up there. Live in the valley between your mountains of glory."

"Mountains? Oh my God. You're a dork." She dipped down to kiss me, her thick ropes of hair sheltering us briefly from the unrelenting sun streaming in through the French doors.

"Your dork," I said between kisses.

"Mine," she agreed all too readily.

We'd created this fantasy world and for now, we could live here and pretend it would never end.

At least for a little while longer.

"Green," she said a few minutes later when we ran out of oxygen and needed to gasp for air.

"Green?"

"Yeah." She traced the edge of her pale pink nail under my eye. "This exact green. It's like emerald shot with lighter streaks of peridot."

My ears went hot. "My eyes are not striped, thank you."

"No, not striped. Not exactly. The color's like…layered. So when your expression shifts, different facets—"

I grabbed her and she squealed out a laugh when I shifted her under me again. "Kindly." Kiss. "Shut." Kiss. "Up."

"They're still manly," she assured me when I allowed her to speak again. "Beautiful eyes are an asset, not a curse." She pressed her face into my biceps as I glowered. "I don't hate you because you're beautiful."

"You're a menace."

"Your menace," she shot back.

A glowing ember settled in the empty pit in my chest where my heart had once resided. "Mine is right." I caught her lower lip between my teeth before I set about proving it.

Again.

And again.

As obsessed as I was with having her gorgeous body wrapped around me at all times, I did have to check in with work. Vacations—even doctor mandated ones—didn't care about my abundant client cases.

We'd used up the condoms I had and a couple from her strip, courtesy of grandma. I was quite fond of that woman, even if the providing your granddaughter with protection thing struck me as extremely strange.

Even my dad wouldn't have done that for me, though he had offered me a five-thousand dollar bottle of vintage wine "to enjoy together" when I'd brought Rina home with me from college. By then, I'd been way past losing my virginity, but I'd also been under the drinking age. But boys will be boys, and rich dads liked to spoil their favorite sons.

I hadn't been the favorite even then. But I'd been further up the totem pole than I was now, that was for sure.

"My hands are a mess."

Her voice broke through my busy inner dialogue. I glanced over at her as she studied her nails and wrinkled her nose.

"They're beautiful," I said distantly, flipping through emails on my phone.

Nothing that pressing. Lots of client emails forwarded from Eli, one of the junior associates in my firm, because of course I had to handle every-damn-thing, vacation or not.

The problem with being extremely hands-on with your clients? They expected that white glove treatment 24/7, 365 days a year. Especially since I didn't *take* vacations.

I wouldn't have taken this one either if my doctor hadn't basically ordered me to. She hadn't listened to any of my excuses either.

And I had many of them.

"Says the man who helped wreck my nails."

"So, let's book a manicurist along with the masseuse."

I looked up to find her staring at me from where she was curled up in the chair. Her hair was wrapped on top of her head in a towel and she wore only a loosely belted plush hotel robe. Her cute feet were bare.

We'd debated going out and exploring, but we'd contented ourselves with other, more personal sights. Besides, I'd rather gaze at her than at stalls of sunglasses and bags any day.

"They'd have to come here because I don't have any other clothes with me. If I wear the Cinderella dress back to my room, my grandmother will think I'm a hussy. We have adjoining suites."

"You mean she'd be thrilled you were a hussy, since you haven't gotten any since the dawn of time."

She tossed a rolled-up newspaper at my head, nailing me with it, and I rubbed my forehead and grinned. Damn good aim.

"Just because you can get some anytime you step outside, you don't have to judge."

"Not judging. I told you it'd been awhile for me too."

"A year. *Pfft.* I have underwear older than that."

"Do they all have bunny tails?"

"You're asking for it."

I tossed aside my phone without looking where it ended up. "I am. Are you going to give it to me?"

"Do you still want it to be operational after you're gone? Because I'm pretty sure we're in the red zone now." She pressed her legs together with a wince. "I mean, absolutely no complaints but—"

I didn't hear anything after the "you're gone" part. It was just a haze of white noise in my ears.

I rose to move to the room phone. "We both can use that massage. And they have estheticians on staff so you can get a fresh manicure."

"Wait."

I paused with my hand on the phone. If I clenched it harder than necessary, she couldn't tell. "Yeah?"

"You mean that sexy couples' massage, right?"

"Yes, if you're okay with it."

She bit her lip.

"I've seen you from every possible angle. What's the problem?"

"Not all angles," she said stubbornly, sliding her hands under her arms as if she was chilled.

Which was patently impossible. The room was temperature moderated to be absolutely perfect, with a warm breeze floating off the ocean.

"Any that are left, I'll see by the time we're through." I put extra emphasis on the final word to see if it affected her the way it did me.

She never even blinked.

"Not just you. He'll see me."

"The masseuse I'm contacting is female." I tightened my jaw. "Her partner works here as well. Then you can choose which one you feel more comfortable with."

She immediately brightened. "Sounds good. Thanks."

I rolled my shoulders and turned to make the call.

After I finished, I found her on the deck. She was leaning on the railing, the shoulder of her robe dipping off alluringly. I kissed her bare skin, and she smiled up at me, but the lines of tension were back around her eyes.

Was she worried about the whole massage deal or were second thoughts slipping in? As seductive as this whole scenario was, I was already chomping at the bit to know more about how her fascinating mind worked.

Fuck it all, why wasn't the physical enough now? It always had been before.

I hadn't been lying last night when I'd said it was the best experience of my life. I was just a greedy bastard. I wanted more than her sighs and her kisses and her smiles. I wanted the time to learn all about her.

Dial it back or she'll run. You know that.

I lowered my chin to the top of her head and took a long breath of her rich vanilla scent mixed with the sea. "You're going to burn out here." I tugged the robe back into place. "Delicate fair skin."

"How do you do it?" she asked softly.

"What?"

"Just roll with everything as it comes. Not that I know you that well. I'm trying not to think about how little I know about you." A hitching laugh left her as she shielded her eyes and turned back to me. "I need my damn sunglasses."

"I can have your things sent over here. Or I can order some clothes and some sunglasses for you to be delivered."

"And what, I'll just never go back to my room? Never talk to my grandmother? I've already swiped away all her messages. I know she wants deets, but they can wait."

"Deets?" I swallowed. *"Deets?"*

She grinned and turned her face into my chest. I wasn't wearing anything but my boxers, but I had a good base tan going already.

Mediterranean skin, my paler than snow mom always said. She was the light one and my father was the dark. Balance in all things.

I'd given up long ago finding that for myself.

"Not that detailed. She just wants to make sure I'm having fun. I haven't in so long." She peeked up at me, her hair falling forward around her pretty face. "Why me?"

"I could ask you the same question."

"It felt right."

Truer words. So right, I couldn't imagine walking away. "Right for a couple days," I said lightly, wanting her to argue with me. To deny it.

She kissed the spot where my heart pounded so hard that I wondered how she didn't see it through my skin. "The best kind of right. No worries about what comes after. It can stay this wonderful, perfect thing."

I filled my hands with her hair and relished the sensation of her in my arms. Curling against me with more trust than I would've ever expected.

"How did you end up here?" I stroked her hair. "Just needed a getaway with your grandmother?"

She sighed, her breath puffing against my chest. "We're on her honeymoon."

"Come again?"

"Yeah. My sixty-nine-year-old Grams can get remarried years later—well, she intended to, anyway—and I haven't even managed it once. Not that I'm ready for marriage," she added hastily. "Besides, my cat doesn't like men."

"So much information." I pressed my finger against her nose until she gave in and smiled. "Marriage isn't all it's cracked up to be."

"How do you know? Were you married?"

The hint of suspicion in her voice would've made me laugh if I hadn't wanted to avoid this line of conversation altogether. "Just saying. Obviously, it wasn't that great for your grandmother or else she'd be with her guy instead of you. Or wait, are you saying you came with them on their honeymoon? Which is a bit…odd."

"Too odd for you?" Only her fluttering lashes clued me into her bullshitting me.

"Nothing about you is too odd for me. We should go meet them.

Go on a double date. And hey, we have some condoms left, maybe they need some? We could share."

"I can't with you." She looped her arms around my neck. "No, they broke up and Grams decided she wasn't wasting a perfectly good trip."

"What happened?"

"I think they realized they were settling down too fast."

"At almost seventy? Assuming he's her age too."

She jerked a shoulder. "You don't know my Grams."

"No." But I wanted to, I realized. She sounded like a character.

And I never would, because we'd put this…whatever the hell it was in a box, and we were both determined not to drag it back into our real life.

Or I *had* been determined before last night.

"She knew I was overdue for a change of scenery since I haven't been on vacation in forever," she continued, interrupting my thoughts, "and my boss almost lost his mind because I dared to give him only a week's notice. He's kind of a hard ass. But Pres—" She broke off as chimes sounded in the next room.

"Do you need to get that?"

She shook her head. "No. That's just Grams texting. I'll reply later. She's probably just saying you're hot. Which you are. But I don't want to talk about it."

"Thanks. I think." I rubbed her ass through the robe. "You didn't show her my ass, right?"

Her eyes widened. "Oh, you mean that sneaky naked shot I took? I thought you missed that." She laughed when I poked her in the side. "No. That's just for me." She sighed. "I just want to be with you. Nothing else intruding. Is that too selfish?"

"And you wondered why I want your clothes sent here, or better yet, I want to buy you a whole new trip wardrobe?" I nibbled her earlobe. "You looked so fucking sexy in that red dress and those Cinderella shoes. I didn't get to see your moves yet."

"Oh, you've seen a lot of them. I wouldn't mind dancing with you though. We could skip the massage—"

"Do you trust me?"

She swallowed audibly. "Would I be here if I didn't?"

"Then trust me that you'll enjoy this. It's a different sort of experience for me too. We'll figure it out together."

"If you've never had a couples' massage, how can I trust you that I will enjoy it?"

Her pragmatism made me fall silent. "Hmm. Good point. Okay, don't trust me. Maybe it'll suck. We can wing it together. The tables will be in the same room. And if Orlo doesn't touch you the way you prefer, then we can swap."

"Orlo?"

"Yes."

"I don't actually know what I prefer." She bit her lip. "Can I keep my robe on?"

"How about your cute bunny panties? As long I'm the only one who can pull your fluffy little tail…" I trailed off and laughed as she leaned up on her tiptoes to stop me from talking.

"Shut up, sexy island stranger," she breathed between kisses.

"Shutting up, my sexy Cinderella."

CHAPTER FIVE

April

What was I doing on my wild, freewheeling, sexually-liberating vacation?

Perching on the side of the claw-footed tub made for two and whispering into the phone to Luna, since Ryan was not home. I'd called twice and gotten voicemail both times.

What happened to being there for your bestie? She should be home from work by now. Which yes, she was actually working at my job for me this week, so technically, she'd done plenty for me already, but I needed more right now. These were desperate times. And I couldn't ask my grandmother because she'd be like "hell, yeah, give it a go, shake those tatas!"

My tatas had already been shaken plenty. For strangers was something entirely different.

Um, hello, the guy outside in his boxers talking to the masseuses while you freak out is a stranger too, Einstein.

"How's vacation? Are you getting a tan? Though that probably would take longer than a week, huh?"

I snorted. "You know all I do is burn. Where's Ryan? I called her twice, and she's not home."

"Oh. Hmm. Well…"

"Lu?"

"It's a story," she hedged.

"Is she okay?"

"She's very fine. Like the kind of fine we all aspire to. Her energy is a little chaotic at the moment, but I have faith that she will balance the scales. If not, I'll kick his ass."

I set my teeth. When both of your besties were witches, and you were so not, you had to get used to lots of woo-woo talk. I had to admit some of it was even fascinating. But not right now when I had to act a whole heck of a lot more confident than I actually was.

"Whose ass? What are you talking about?"

"Ohhh. So she didn't tell you anything at all? Ohhh."

Normally, I would have felt a prickle of irritation that they'd discussed something I did not know about yet. I understood logically that they'd been close before I became the third spoke of our trio, and that meant they'd probably always share secrets I wasn't privy to. But it still stung sometimes. For once, I wanted to be someone's first choice.

For it to be real and to last.

"Whatever it is, I'll find out in a few days."

"You sure will," Lu said ominously. "So, tell me all about your tropical vacay. Please tell me you got some hottie beach ass. Minus the sand fleas."

I didn't even laugh. "When you get a massage, do you get naked?"

"What?"

I repeated the question.

"Sure, if the energy feels right. My practitioner is also a Reiki—"

"Lu, regular non-witch speak. It's kind of an emergency."

"Reiki is hardly solely the practice of witches. It's a form of spiritual…" She trailed off at my heavy sigh. "Okay, okay. Yes, I usually strip down and Sven places a towel over my butt. Why? Are you getting one? Don't you hate being touched by strangers?"

"Yeah, but I kind of fucked one, so…" Shocked at myself, I clapped a hand over my mouth. I rarely even swore, but when a man said he wanted to taste your honey enough, I supposed you lost your inhibitions. Maybe it was heat stroke.

Or sand fleas.

The music in Lu's apartment immediately quieted. "You kind of fucked a stranger? How do you kind of fuck someone? Please tell me you didn't just blow him without a gift with purchase."

"No. God, no. I didn't even blow him yet. But he blew me. Is that a thing? I mean, oral sex. Anyway, he wants to do this couples' massage. I want to try it, but if the woman is super gorgeous like…" *Don't go there.* "Well, if she's super gorgeous, I'm going to feel totally inadequate."

"Did you feel totally inadequate when you had sex with your stranger?"

"No," I whispered. "He acts like I'm the most beautiful woman on the planet. He must be blind."

"April Anne Finley, you stop it right now. If he's with you, he sees all the amazing qualities we do every day with you. You're smart and funny and sweet, and you have those dreamy hazel eyes."

"I'm pretty sure he's in love with my breasts."

"Well, duh. I'm half in love with them myself, and I'm straighter than a ruler. Except that one time in college, but that was due to the margaritas, I'm almost sure."

It made me laugh when I'd been certain I couldn't. "Thanks, Lu. So I should do this?"

"You absolutely should do this. Walk in that room with those knockers loud and proud. Any woman would love to have your body and your brain and your buns of steel."

"If you say so." I took a deep breath and stood. "Wish me luck."

"Luck. And I want to know everything when you get back."

"Absolutely. Wine night with Ry, who obviously has a story of her own."

"Oh, she does. And you definitely will not believe it."

"Huh. What about you?"

"What about me?" she asked with a trace too much innocence in her voice.

"Do you have a story too?"

"Maaaaaybe."

Her long trill made me grin as I said a quick goodbye. Letting the robe drop to the floor, I threw back my shoulders and marched to the door, hauling it open.

And looked into the wide eyes of two petite female masseuses whose heads barely reached my cleavage.

Behind them, my mystery man sat on the arm of the couch, gaping at my naked body. His wolfish expression was far different than the startled ones of the masseuses.

"Talk later," he said into the phone before tossing it over his shoulder.

Distantly, I heard a crack before he strode past the portable massage tables and gripped my shoulders, dragging me up onto my toes. His mouth landed on mine, a hot caress of pure desire, and I kissed him back, linking my arms around his neck as he lifted me up and carted me into the bathroom and slammed the door.

"We need to—they're waiting—they can hear—"

"Who cares? Open your legs."

I opened everything to him. I didn't have locks strong enough to hold fast against him and his feverish kisses and devouring gaze as his hands roamed and teased and possessed.

Who was I kidding? I'd been lost to him from the moment he'd knocked on my door.

When we stumbled out fifteen minutes later, the two women were busy straightening towels on the portable tables.

"Orlo was busy," he said against my hair, sending me a glance of pure male satisfaction when my knees buckled with the first step. He drew me hard against his side and kissed my temple. "Sylvie, Lai, we apologize for the delay." His voice was as rich and smooth as fresh cream. "We're ready now."

The massages weren't anything like I'd expected, but then again, after being carried off beforehand by a sexy stranger with lust in his eyes just for me, two businesslike women with strong hands taking turns rubbing out the kinks in my sore muscles didn't really rank.

It was hard to even think about anything but him as we stared at each other across a distance of a few feet while strangers touched us. While strangers touched me.

Pure hedonistic decadence.

The only tension was the hum of heat between the two of us. It didn't seem to matter how many times we had each other. It never abated. Never lessened. Electricity practically crackled in the air when he turned over so Lai could massage his chest. He didn't even look her way. His head remained tilted toward me so that as her hands capably stroked his skin, it was *me* he was imagining, his pupils wide with desire.

I wetted my lips and he did the same, and I couldn't stop from clenching around air, wishing he was inside me. Even the scant distance between us was too much.

"Tensing," Sylvie said in her lilting voice. "Just relax."

Hard to relax when I was still hornier than a tree frog, but I tried.

They massaged me from my scalp right down to the soles of my feet and many parts in between, although nothing the least bit salacious. Afterward, I bundled into my robe for a mani and pedi, during which I asked for assistance with my color selections.

Instead of laughing at me, he looked at the chart and helped me pick. He even bossily insisted on a deep pink hue for my toes.

I humored him since my body was buzzing in a way it hadn't since —ever. Absolutely never had I experienced so much pleasure.

Or chafing, but that was a separate consideration.

I wasn't used to this level of pampering. Usually, I did my own nails, although occasionally I'd spring for gel nails when I needed a pickup. I'd had a pedicure exactly once before for a wedding. While I didn't always love being fussed over—my female gene was missing on that score—my companion's soft sounds of appreciation made me enjoy the process far more.

Had anyone ever looked at me the way he did? And I didn't even know his name. I couldn't even find him again after this if I wanted to.

Admit it. If you knew who he was, he would take over your life. You'd do whatever it took to keep this going. Flights across the country to wherever he lived, probably someplace tony like Beverly Hills. You hate to fly, remember?

Most of all, he wouldn't allow me to live my safe, comfortable life and stick to the predictable routines that I preferred. Everything would change. *I'd* have to, whether I wanted to or not.

My temporary brave persona would have to become permanent. And I might like playacting right now, but I couldn't keep this going. A large part of my personality involved nights lounging in fuzzy pajama pants and a ripped sweatshirt with a pint of rocky road with added cherries and my sewing projects, usually of the cat-related variety. Sure, I was branching out a bit there with my in-progress Christmas prezzies for my besties, but we weren't talking big changes.

Lu always said there was a secret ninety year old inside of me, and she wasn't wrong. More often than not, I felt more like Grams' elder than the other way around.

Besides, Kit-Kat hated men. And Kit-Kat was my family. I wouldn't subject her to something she hated just because he knew how to lick me until my head popped off and rolled on the ground.

I was not a jetsetter. I was not independently wealthy. I was just a small-town girl living a fantasy—and fantasies ended. They were *meant* to. Real life would just reveal all the holes and cracks and destroy the chemistry we'd found here.

Being practical was what I did best.

My mystery man gave the masseuse duo a hefty tip, waving off my offers to chip in. Not that I had his kind of money. I couldn't even sneeze at his sort of spending.

His latest delivery after the women left demonstrated that in spades.

"What is all this?" I rifled through the dresses and tops and skirts paired with lacy underthings—all sized appropriately of course, since the guy never missed a trick or a cup size, apparently—and heels to match. That wasn't all. He'd also included super high-end diamond-encrusted sunglasses, a pair of flats, and a pair of Dolce & Gabbana slippers soft enough to make me whimper when I slipped my feet inside. "You are either a demon of temptation or a god of women's fondest unspoken desires."

"I wanted you to be comfortable." He shrugged as if this haul hadn't cost at least half of my yearly take-home pay. "You mentioned dancing and you can't wear yesterday's outfit."

"You were just afraid I'd put my halter dress back on. Admit it."

"Since it's back at your hotel, impossible. Besides, you shouldn't hide behind folds of material that disguise everything you are."

I gave into the need to try on the La Perla bra and panty set and tried not to gawk at my own shockingly curvy reflection in the mirror.

"Or," he said silkily from behind me, "we could just stay here and I'll pull those off of you with my teeth."

Playfully, I crossed my arms over my chest. "You're not harming the LaPerla, buddy. What kind of sick man are you?"

He lowered his mouth to my hair, his gaze never leaving mine in the mirror. "One who's becoming obsessed with you."

My heart beat in rapid time with my traitorous clit. It always got me in trouble with this man. Then again, what didn't?

"Island romances," I said with all the lightness I could muster. "They aren't real life."

"Says who?" He reached around me to unclasp the bra I'd just fastened. My breasts spilled free, my pink nipples almost lewdly hard. "We make the rules."

"Right now, it feels like *you're* making the rules."

"Tell me you don't like it. Not having to think. Not having to decide." He trailed an open-mouthed kiss down my neck and I could do nothing but watch him in the glass and *feel*. "Your only job is to enjoy."

I knew I should stop this. Fun and games were one thing, but this was all moving far too fast. Sure, we were just having a fling, but the deeper I got, the harder it would be to forget him. To be alone again, knowing that I'd probably always stay that way.

Lightning had already struck once. How could I get this lucky again?

Just take a chance. Ask his name. Where he lives. Maybe he doesn't have a mansion on the west coast. He could live in like...Cincinnati. That isn't that far away.

"I do like it. But this all—this isn't the real me. I'm not like this at home."

"Neither am I. I don't have a woman like you taking all my attention." He filled his hands with my breasts and twisted my nipples between his fingers. "I love how you look at me. As if I'm the gatekeeper to a whole new world."

I couldn't help smiling even as lust pooled low in my belly. "You are. You have no idea how long it had been since I'd had a non-self-administered orgasm."

It was not the right thing to say.

Not even close.

"I like knowing I'm the only one lucky enough to have you. I'm greedy. So fucking greedy for you." His teeth razored down my throat, making me shiver. "But I want to see it."

"See what?"

"You know what. Slip your hand in your panties. Let me watch you come for me."

In my head, I screamed. I couldn't do this in front of a man. It was too personal. But the side of me that wanted to be the sort of woman who *could* lowered my hand to my panties. They were cut high on the thigh, a rich vanilla with a lacy sheer panel. Romantic and sexy.

"The color reminded me of your scent."

"Which?" Was that really me who sounded so flirtatious as I ran my fingertips just under my waistband?

His chuckle skated along the back of my neck like a kiss. "Your perfume and *you*. You smell delicious. Like a treat I could eat forever and never get my fill."

"Yet here I am, doing your work for you." The sensation of my fingertips against my bare mound made everything seem more sensitive. I couldn't stop my inward gasp.

"Tell me how it feels."

"Weird."

"There's my dirty talker. Want me to help?"

"No. I can do it." I took a deep breath. "I mean, you can help all you want after, but I can do this."

He rested his chin on my shoulder, his gorgeous green gaze a steady flame as he watched me in the mirror. "I can't wait to watch."

I turned my head and kissed his cheek and the scruff growing thicker as the day slipped into evening. He shifted to look at me straight on and it was easier to touch myself when I was lost in his kaleidoscope eyes. I felt powerful now. With him supporting me, I could do anything.

Be anything.

It didn't make sense. We barely knew each other. But my fingers moved downward of their own accord, my clit swelling in anticipation. Moisture slicked my skin and sensations swamped me, impossible to differentiate. Excitement. Need. Embarrassment.

And under them all, the desire to please him—and myself.

Face burning, I teased myself as I would at home. Sliding up and down, reveling in the thrill building in my core. I darted over my clit, circling there for a moment before slipping down to where I quivered. Dipping inside with just the tip of my finger, then inching in more as he gripped my hips.

The steel brand of his cock against my behind was wordless encouragement to move faster, harder, to join another finger with the first. I was panting now and it was getting harder to maintain eye contact with him. I wanted to close him out. To lose myself in the need building inside me. I felt too exposed, too overwhelmed. My skin was so hot and tight and my clit was hammering as I fucked myself, so much harder than I would have if I was alone.

But his narrowed eyes and parted lips and quickened breaths were turning me on every bit as much as my own hand. *More*. He was my drug, and I was already addicted.

"You're so close." He spoke against my lips. "Let me taste."

I started to pull my hand free, but the brutal lock of his fingers around my wrist stilled me as he moved around me to kneel at my feet. "Don't stop."

Breathing fast, I nodded.

He peeled aside my panties and bent to lick between my rapidly moving fingers, making me moan and drop my head back before I had to look again. I had to watch. I couldn't miss a moment. My gaze shifted to the mirror and I gripped the back of his neck with my free hand, my fingers weaving into the golden brown curls at his nape. Holding him there while he sipped at me as delicately as he would the finest champagne while I worked myself into a frenzy.

Then his tongue swept over my aching clit and I detonated, bending forward over him, trapped and forced to accept his pleasure from the forceful clamp of his arm around my thighs. I stared into his eyes as I came, shocked and shattered both, absorbing his groans mixed with the noises I made as if now *I* was the stranger.

I'd never met this wanton woman in the glass before. I wanted to get to know her better.

I was still quaking when he rose up my body and cupped my cheeks to kiss me with my flavor flowing like wine between us. I fumbled for his boxers but he lifted my wrist to his mouth and kissed it, his eyes intent on mine.

"I owe you a night of dancing. I want to see you moving in the moonlight."

I tried to find my voice as I dropped my gaze to the sizable erection tenting his boxers. "And I want you in my mouth." I leaned up to nip his insolent lower lip and summoned the last of my courage. I'd never given a blowjob. I'd always been too awkward. But with him, I ached to try. "I want to taste you too."

His groan sent a bolt of liquid fire through my already overwrought system. "You're making it hard to be honorable."

"Harder than you already are?" Teasingly, I tugged at his waistband, looking closer at the dagger tattoo high on his left thigh. I'd seen it before and the stark black ink had fascinated me, but he'd always diverted me before I could examine it thoroughly.

This time, he wasn't quick enough.

It was a dagger all right, sharp and lethal. And the circle I'd thought was just part of the design was actually a ring.

A band.

He realized too late my attention had snagged on something other than his cock. He framed my face in his hands, his confident smile already in place as if he wasn't stiff enough to hold up the damn ceiling. "Believe me, you constantly bring me to new heights. First, I want to feed you."

"Is that a ring?" My words caught in my throat. "Like a wedding ring?"

Smoothly, he drew my hands away and settled his waistband back into place. "Divorce is my business, honey. I told you I'm a shark. And it's made me a very wealthy man." He kissed my forehead. "What's your poison? Surf or turf?"

What I really want is the truth.

Somehow I managed not to say it. We'd agreed not to get too personal. Maybe divorce *was* his business, and if so, that brought his profession dangerously close to mine, even if he operated on the other side of the world.

Not that I knew he did. It was just a guess. Maybe some kind of twisted wishful thinking so there was no way this could continue.

Perhaps there were other reasons why it couldn't.

His job didn't explain his tattoo. There was more there than professional pride in his cutthroat style.

I'd stake my far too expensive panties on it.

CHAPTER SIX

Bishop

THERE WERE certain truisms about women. Some of them I'd become aware of after becoming a divorce attorney, others had been gleaned through painful experience.

A woman might say she was fine with a casual arrangement. She might be adamant about not sharing about her own life. But if you hold back something she deems pertinent, she will think of nothing else until she strings up your balls and you cough up the truth.

Or I suspected that was her plan, anyway.

I wined her—within reason, because I wanted her faculties to be fully intact. I was, for all intents and purposes, a stranger, and despite all we'd already done, I didn't want her to be unaware in any way.

I dined her—feeding her shrimp and some kind of fancy potatoes and asparagus at the little round table on my deck beside the ocean.

I danced with her—to Elvis and to the sounds of the Fijian guitar band playing down the beach. She swayed in my embrace and she laughed and kissed me, her body long and lush in my arms. Anticipation simmered in her eyes as the moon climbed in the dark, rolling sky and shone its spotlight on the endless waves crashing onto the sand.

All the while, I knew she was thinking about my tattoo. Wanting to probe without risking me turning her questions back on herself. I had plenty of my own.

Who are you?

Where do you live?

Why don't you want more when it's obvious we are so good together?

It was damn lowering to realize I'd do just about anything to keep this going. Me, the guy who'd practically vowed to become a monk after Rina.

That had lasted a few months and then I'd gone the other way. If a pretty woman smiled at me, I went home with her. Left the next morning and didn't call her again.

Along the way, I'd dated a couple women longer than that, but they were rare. In time, I'd stopped thinking about the opposite sex altogether.

I'd dived headfirst into work and focused on making bank. In my profession, it was easy to do if you were tenacious and knew how to attract the right clients. I developed a reputation for having no fear in the courtroom. I didn't stop until the men and women I fought for cleaned the damn clock of their usually cheating spouses, whether that spouse had a doublewide and a ten-year-old Chevy or a mansion worth seven-point-five mil. I didn't discriminate.

What I hadn't realized until, oh, about yesterday, was that my skill at my chosen profession had made me into a goddamned hard bastard. I'd known I wasn't the freaking toasted marshmallow I'd been in my college days, that I'd honed my softer emotions so they worked for me instead of against me. I had a strong sense of empathy and I understood when to use it to convince a judge to see my point of view. I also knew when to tuck it away so I could go in for the kill.

What I hadn't fully grasped was that I'd forgotten what it felt like to want someone. Not just sexually. To crave their laughter and their expressions and the sound of their voice filling all the hollow spaces.

That I'd spent just over a day with her didn't seem to matter. Island time was something different altogether.

And I didn't know how to lose. Not anymore—and not when it was this important.

After dancing, we indulged in a long soak in the hot tub. I reached down to grab her ankle in the bubbling water and brought it up to my shoulder where I could kiss her petal-soft skin. I moved higher, well aware she was already curling her toes as she sipped her champagne and watched me through eyes sleepy with satiation of several different kinds.

No one ever accused me of playing fair.

"I have a bird named Santiago. He's a parrot. He has a filthy mind."

She stared at me for a second then let out a surprised laugh. "Okay."

"Earlier when you came out naked for your massage, I was on the phone with my pet sitter. She was telling me he's developed an interest in the poodle down the hall."

"At least he's open-minded."

"He is. And probably would blister her ears with God knows what if she got within his shouting space."

"Your bird shouts?"

"Sometimes. He's feisty. One time, he heard me swearing a blue streak after I got off the phone with a client who called me after hours, and it all went downhill after that." I turned over her foot and nibbled the side of her big toe, wrinkly and pink from the water. "Tell me about your pets."

Her eyes twinkled. "Pet, singular. Just my cat, Kit-Kat."

"For the candy?"

"Yes. Also, it's to disarm people into thinking she's sweet. I adopted her from the shelter, and they told me she had a few quirks." She shook her head.

"Like what?"

"She drinks out of every water glass. You turn your back, and she's into them. I basically only use tumblers with tops now for myself and my guests."

I sank my thumbs into her delicate foot arch. "That doesn't sound so bad."

"She *really* can't stand men. She tried to bite the mailman."

I had to laugh at that one. "Well, that must cut down on your social life."

"Are you fishing?"

"Does it help I have a large rod?"

She splashed me with her foot. "I don't date much."

"Why is that?" I asked instead of saying what I wanted to.

It probably makes me a jerk, but I'm glad.

See, I could keep things casual. I was practically a pro.

"I have a busy life." She shrugged and finished off her champagne before setting it on the edge of the tub. "About the only man in my world right now is my boss. Speaking of, I need to get him a souvenir."

"They have a gift shop. Get him a stuffed flamingo. He'll love it."

Her laughter pitched higher. "You don't know my boss. Trust me, he would have no use for a stuffed anything."

"So, you should definitely get him one then. Tomorrow, we'll explore the island. Do some shopping. Whatever you want to do."

"An alpha male voluntarily offering to go shopping? What is wrong with this picture?"

"I'm assuming you've never been to Fiji before. You should get the full experience." I moved through the frothy water to join her on the other side. "I don't want you to look back and have regrets."

She cuddled into me, tipping back her head. Her skin was rosy pink from the steam and the champagne. And possibly from me too. "I couldn't regret anything from this trip." She trailed her fingers through my chest hair and headed downward, her fingers skimming my happy trail before giving my cock a long stroke. "Not one minute."

I tucked her damp hair behind her ear. "Me either." I kissed the cluster of freckles beside her lips. "I want to make more memories with you."

So I can't ever forget.

"Like hot tub sex?" She wiggled on top of me, rising up until her gorgeous tits were level with my mouth.

Focused on the ruby-red tips so close to my face, I spoke without thinking. "I've had it before, but it wasn't like this." I drew one of them between my lips, only realizing from her expression what I'd said.

Dick. I was honest to a fault and sometimes that was *not* a positive trait.

Normally, I would've shrugged off my mistake, but I was all too aware that we were operating with limited time. Comments like that weren't going to convince her to tell me who she was.

I could've found out her details through dubious means. Like using my powers of persuasion on the hotel staff, or if that didn't work, I could flash my credentials and my money to get my way.

But I couldn't do that to her. Manipulating her that way would undermine everything we'd shared. If she wouldn't tell me herself, I'd have to accept that.

Somehow.

"We could go snorkeling," I said abruptly.

"What?" Her laughter eased the knot in my chest. "You snorkel?"

"No, but I've always wanted to. My doctor suggested—" I broke off, glancing away.

I didn't want her to pity me. The fact that I was overworked and stressed the fuck out was my own fault.

She feathered her fingers over my jaw and turned my face back toward hers. "Your doctor?"

"Yeah. He thought it'd be good if I took a vacation." My lips twisted. "His particular way to relax is snorkeling. Something about being one with the sea creatures." I gripped a hank of her wet long hair. "But I've found other ways to relax with you."

"You have. But you're so not relaxed now." She fisted my cock, giving it a hard squeeze that sent heat searing down my spine. "I wonder what we could do to fix that?"

I grabbed her and tipped her back in the water, splashing it everywhere. She squealed and clung to my neck, winding around me so tightly that her heartbeat raced against mine as delight danced in her eyes.

It was so easy to laugh with her. The logjam in my chest didn't feel so tight anymore when she was in my arms.

"How am I supposed to give this up?" My mouth covered hers before she could reply.

I didn't want to hear her answer.

CHAPTER SEVEN

April

For the first time in my life, I fell asleep in a man's arms.

I was a notoriously restless sleeper. I'd tried all manner of things. Melatonin, vitamins, excessive exercise. Some of the time, wearing myself out from physical projects at home did the trick.

Then I'd discovered the joys of endless orgasms. I was usually a one and done girl, if even that. My previous partners had been scattershot at best at making sure I was satisfied.

No one compared to *him*. He took the pursuit of my climaxes like claiming new territory in a foreign land. He knew I wasn't like him with a little black book a mile wide, and he seemed determined to ruin me for all other men.

And now he'd done something even more unforgivable—he'd worn me out so thoroughly that I'd fallen asleep coiled around him just like I did with my boyfriend pillow at home.

Worse, because I'd never awakened aroused and practically humping said pillow.

Luckily, he'd seemed just fine with me eagerly rubbing against him in the middle of the night. He hadn't even sounded sleepy.

"That's it. Use me how you need. Take exactly what you want, Cinderella."

That name in his low, sexy timbre did crazy things to me, and I hadn't even had to do much before I was coming against his cock. That illicit hard, bare flesh pressed to my clit aroused me unbearably.

We'd gone to sleep nude, and that was new too. All of this was so unexpected and overwhelming and wonderful.

He hadn't tried to get some relief for himself. He'd just turned me so he was spooning me from behind and buried his face in my hair, banding his arm securely around my waist as if he was afraid I'd evaporate before morning.

I slept better than I ever had before. Or probably ever would again.

The next morning, I sent my grandmother a text without reading hers first. I knew she wouldn't be up yet—she wasn't an early riser like me—but I didn't want her to worry.

She probably already was, due to my sudden pressing need for multiple Os.

Horny cow.

But I didn't want to go back to the real world just yet, so a message would have to do for now.

My fantasy was slipping away, no matter how hard I clung to it. And to him.

Hi, sorry I haven't been in touch. Everything is fine. Better than fine. It's nothing serious. Just fun. I hope you had a good time with PedroPablo. Love you.

I'd barely sent the text before she replied.

Bunny! Thank God. I was about to contact the authorities to report you'd been lured into sex trafficking.

I'd been lured into sex, that was for certain.

I smothered my laugh against my arm to not wake up the man finally sleeping behind me. He hadn't seemed restless last night, but every time I woke to go to the bathroom, I had the sense he was awake.

Maybe we were more alike than I'd realized. I'd have to try harder to wear him out today.

I was running out of time, and I wanted him to have at least one good night's rest while we were together. Especially now that I knew he had a doctor, and it sounded like for more than occasional physicals.

A surge of protectiveness rose up inside me. Maybe we shouldn't be having so much sex?

God, there was a statement I'd never thought I would make, even in my own head.

No trafficking, Grams.

Just sex though?

I sent back a winking smile.

I don't wonder with that pretty face. He's the kind of guy a woman can't walk away from.

He's also the kind of guy it's dangerous to keep.

If I even could.

Sure, he was interested now when it was all frantic and romantic with hot tubs and moonlight and crashing waves on the beach. What would happen when we resumed our normal lives? Sex would become routine and sporadic. And some other mystery woman would catch his obviously wandering eye…

Better to walk away with an unforgettable memory that reality couldn't shatter. I knew that better than anyone.

Is he stepping out on someone?

I didn't answer, because I knew what was coming next. I wanted to shut off my phone before it could, but I knew.

Something that starts that way can never end well. You know that.

Oh, I knew. Hot, shameful tears burned my eyes so I typed quickly while I tried to blink them away.

How are things with Pedro Pablo?

Who? Oh, him. He stood me up at dinner.

Uh-oh. So, my grandmother had been alone for a day and a half? I sent back a hasty response.

God, no. What a jerk. I'm sorry.

Don't be sorry. I met someone else. Roger asked me to island jump with him.

Who the heck was that? My grandmother had a more active social life than anyone I knew.

Well, she did now. While I was growing up, she hadn't dated. She'd put all her time and effort into raising me after my grandfather died. My parents had made flaking out an art form. Eventually, the two-hour visits to her cute little bungalow had stretched to four then six. Then they had become overnights.

Then one day when I was nine, my parents simply hadn't returned at all.

I'd never forget waiting for them all night, staring out the window. Sure, they were just out having fun, but they'd be back. They always came back.

Except they hadn't, and my grandmother had put her life on hold to care for an overly curious, hyperactive kid with separation anxiety.

I'd do anything for my Grams, including being there to support her if she wanted to have the time of her life. She'd earned every minute.

Even if it scared the hell out of me that she might get hurt.
I took a deep breath and quickly replied.

What is island jumping?

He wants us to explore and for me to extend my stay. With you already occupied, I decided to move my ticket out a week. I can do the same for you if you want? Will Codger flip his tie?

Hope flared inside me and was ruthlessly squelched. First of all, there was no way in hell Preston would be open to me staying away for another week, no matter how big a souvenir I brought him.

Briefly, I debated sending him a box full of his favorite Colombian caramel coconut coffee to sweeten the deal, but even that wouldn't be enough.

Then there was my bestie. Surely Ryan wouldn't want to work longer for him. She might've already quit.

Though it was strange she hadn't texted to vent. Maybe that was the story Luna had referred to?

Nah. Ry and Preston went together like fried chicken and pickles. They probably hadn't spoken to each other after the first day.

I frowned and responded to my grandmother.

Do fried chicken & pickles go together? They seem like they wouldn't. But I don't like pickles so I've never tried to eat them w/chicken.

Are you hungover, Bunny?

I had to swallow a laugh. I was more than a little sex-drunk but definitely not hungover. I'd had a couple of glasses of champagne the night before, but I'd eaten plenty and it had been over a matter of hours. And he'd made sure I alternated with water so I didn't get dehydrated.

I sneaked a peek over my shoulder. He really was the sweetest—

Where the heck had he gone?

Earlier, I'd awakened and taken a quickie shower—focused on actual cleansing since our *other* showers had been more about creative uses for the spray—before I returned to bed. The bedding had been bundled up on his side enough that I'd assumed he was under there. Sort of strange for a dude to cover up so much, but he kept the place a literal icebox.

At least that was the excuse I gave myself for my constant headlight situation.

But nope, at some point, he'd just…vanished.

I rolled out of bed and put on my robe, then I shoved my feet into the positively decadent slippers he'd bought me and wandered out onto the deck. I probably should talk to him about the whole spoiling situation. Despite the gorgeous red dress he'd gotten me, I wasn't with him for his money, even if he obviously had plenty to spare.

Fantasy aside, *he* was the reason I would never forget these days together. The trappings were nice, but they didn't matter without him. He made me laugh and crave him and enjoy every moment. I'd found out more about myself on this trip than I'd ever managed to on my own.

And I didn't know his name. Didn't know exactly what he did for a living or where he lived or what his astrological sign was.

Jeez, this channeling Lu and Ry thing was definitely working if I wanted to figure out his astrological chart. Compatibility mattered.

Then again, we knew we were compatible, at least in bed. And that was exactly why we weren't going to push our luck with anything more than a fling.

Why risk ruining perfection? Even if that excuse was seeming more like a cop-out every time I repeated it to myself.

Another text came through.

Bunny? Are you off using all the red condoms?

I giggled despite myself. Red had been my favorite color since I was a little girl, although I had definitely developed an appreciation for green. Wonder why.

No. I'm not hungover or…busy. I'm actually looking for my guy. He seems to have disappeared.

Even as I typed those words, I didn't tense up. The April I'd been before Fiji would've been scared of that very thing. Kit-Kat and I both had uncharitable thoughts toward guys, though I tried to shove down mine. They couldn't help being fickle. Besides, I was hardly a supermodel so I couldn't be shocked if—

And I was officially not thinking that way anymore.

But *he* wasn't the sort to disappear without a warning. I didn't know how I knew that, but I did. Maybe it was because he seemed to notice my feelings about the smallest things. He paid attention. But he also didn't seem like a man to invest time or money if he hadn't already taken time to calculate the value.

Oh, look at who's big shit now? Of course he wouldn't run out on you and your French manicured toes and waxed hoo-ha.

He hadn't assisted with the waxed hoo-ha, though he'd offered to pay for that too if I wanted a touch-up. Since I wasn't doing *that* again one millisecond before I had to, I'd declined.

I'm sure he'll be back soon. Have to say he looks familiar. I must be imagining things. He's so handsome. He reminds me of one of those demon hunting boys on TV. Or is it vampires I'm thinking of?

She sent a string of vampire emojis while I grinned and shook my head.

But ice skated between my shoulder blades. My grandmother never forgot a face. She didn't have an eidetic memory, but I swore she had the next best thing. Hers was far better than my own.

Could my mystery man be someone famous?

I squinted into the bright sunshine and moved to the deck railing to look up and down the white sand beach. Nearby, a couple from a neighboring bure was playing volleyball over a net they'd set up in the sand. The woman noticed me outside and waved, calling out a hello. Her husband did the same.

People were so nice here. Welcoming. Or maybe I was the different one. Could my happiness be palpable enough to draw people toward me instead of away? When I was home, I normally had no trouble keeping my distance. No one seemed to notice me much in any case.

You're not home right now. And you're different now to boot.

I called back my own hello, then threw back my shoulders and marched inside to grab my sunglasses. Also courtesy of my hot as hell lover, who was entirely too generous.

I slipped them on and decided to swap my robe for the long swingy pink sundress Mr. Richie Rich had selected for me. Yet again, it had a high-end designer label, and yet again, it fit perfectly. The summery material swished around my calves just the way I liked and spun out around me as I tested it with a twirl.

He had an uncanny way of knowing what I would look good in. Better even than I did. I should probably be affronted about that too, maybe even insist I liked my own clothes just fine, but my clothes were often bought because of their modesty or their sale price. I never really chose pieces I loved.

I loved this sundress. And when I looked at myself in the mirror on the back of the closet door, I loved my smile.

Most of all, I loved this feeling inside me. Excitement. Pleasure. *Hope.*

I walked back outside, closing my eyes as the breeze off the water lifted my hair and it settled again around my shoulders. Every part of me seemed brutally aware and responsive. It was as if I'd been sleepwalking all this time, and now I was finally awake.

Sexually and otherwise.

When I couldn't stall anymore, I replied to my grandmother.

I don't know who my guy looks like other than himself. He's just so amazingly himself.

She wasted no time responding.

And if those aren't the words of love…

CHAPTER EIGHT

April

Yeah, I so wasn't addressing that pink elephant in the room right now, thanks.

No one fell in love that fast. Not anyone regular, anyway. It wasn't as if I was some oversexed Hollywood starlet who fell in love as easily as she blinked. I was ordinary April Finley, legal assistant. Lover of ornery cats, bargain D-I-Ys, complicated sewing projects, and gourmet hot chocolate.

Still, thank God she couldn't see me flushing right now. I had to be beet red—and not because of my light sunburn. I really needed to get the sunscreen from my suitcase. Vacation was almost over, but I didn't want to go home looking like a lobster.

Already almost over. How could it be possible?

I made myself answer before I turned into a crisp. I'd have to go inside to wait for him or else check out the nearby shops for sunscreen. I was probably the palest person on this island, which also hammered at my self-confidence. I'd gotten used to the milky hue of my skin years ago, but it was hard not to compare myself to all the curvy, golden bodies running about so freely in bikinis. Not a pale ass in sight. Next time, I'd spring for some self-tanner.

What next time? How are you going to afford Fiji again on a legal assistant's salary?

Even if I saved—hell, even if I finally signed up for that course to become a paralegal—it would be awhile until I could make it back here. And I wouldn't be staying in a bure with all the amenities, that was for sure. More like the cheapest possible room.

I gazed out at the tranquil turquoise water frothing onto the white sand and sighed as I set my chin on my palm. But the view was free.

I frowned down at the shell bracelet on my wrist. It was pretty, but I really needed more mementos from this trip. Maybe an armful of bangles like one of the masseuses had sported yesterday. Their clang was so light and cheerful. I'd just go shopping while I waited rather than fretting like some sailor's wife pacing along her widow's walk.

Now there was an image.

And I officially needed to stop chatting and start exploring—on my own, if need be.

I sent back another text.

Like. Serious like. He's incredible. But no one falls in love in a few days.

Oh, my sweet summer child. You can fall in love in a moment if you allow yourself.

I replayed her words over and over as I shopped. I strolled through the different open-air markets, savoring the experience of browsing. Every piece of jewelry I picked up, I imagined my mystery man's reaction. Every kitschy thing I found, I pictured him laughing with me.

You're sunk, chick.

In the back of my mind, I was also searching for a small souvenir for my boss, but I especially wanted to find something for my guy. I wanted him to have a tangible reminder of this trip too. I didn't want to go too romantic. Just enough so that with a glance, it would bring these intense days and nights rushing back.

Not that I could ever forget them.

In a funky shop run by a pair of loud, boisterous women who were clearly sisters or cousins or best friends, I bartered for a pair of bookends stained and carved into the shape of whistling doves, one of the birds I was told was found in Fiji. The green bodies and yellow heads were so cheerful and cute, not that my boss especially appreciated either of those things. He also wasn't one for much color, preferring navy or black suits most of the time. I wasn't a colorful sort either when it came to most of my attire, and what had that gotten me?

I smiled down at my pretty pink sundress with the hand-stitched showy flowers in a deeper pink along the hem. I was tired of neutrals and blues. It was time to enjoy the full range of colors.

Maybe that was true for Preston too.

"You got a good deal, *totoka*."

Since I didn't speak Fijian, I didn't know what the owner's last word meant, and I was too bashful to ask. I just smiled and thanked the women profusely before I continued on my way.

My next purchase was for my lover. I didn't know his taste or what kind of office he had, or even what he did. But the glass globe paperweight done in swirling greens and blues immediately made me think of his eyes. They were so vivid and unique.

And you're so screwed.

Not only that, when I was holding the world in my hand, it made what I was doing—what *we* were doing—seem not so futile. Sure, we wouldn't be together after Fiji. But the world wasn't really that big, right?

Okay, that was a lie, but knowing he was out there couldn't make me feel any more lonely than I had before. Especially if somehow we found a way to skip that whole messy ending thing.

I was absolutely awful at them.

At the next shop, I perused the swimsuits in between darting glances over my shoulder. I'd never enjoyed flaunting myself, since I was always too aware of my flaws. I was too angular in some places, too round in others. But this body was mine. I'd lived in it for twenty-six years, and I was tired of hiding.

"Can I get this one?" I called too loudly to an assistant, fingering my first ever bikini. Crocheted bikini, no less.

And hot pink. Virulent pink.

Most likely, I'd end up wearing my striped tankini far more than I ever did this pink number. But it didn't matter. I'd always have the memories of when I walked on the wild side.

And lounged. And laid.

Much laying.

After I did the walk of shame to the reception desk and got a new room key, I took my purchases back to the room and tried on my new bikini before I found the note in my guy's slashing handwriting waiting for me.

Hoped I'd find you naked in the hot tub, but maybe we can reenact that later. I just have a quick errand and then I'll be back. In the meantime, try not to open that item next to the couch.

Already grinning, I craned my neck and saw a huge package wrapped in brown paper leaning against the back of the sofa. It was the size of a giant picture frame. Or…mirror.

We already had enjoyed some of the mirrors in this place. If that was another freestanding one, we probably could have an orgy in front of it.

No, no orgies needed to be added to my repertoire. I was enjoying *him* plenty and didn't want anyone else.

Might never want anyone else.

I crept closer to the item. I wouldn't peek. I really would not. But if I ran my hands around the outer dimensions just to see if I could get an idea what it might be…

In front of the sofa, there was another folded note on the floor. I snatched it up.

Maybe I should say it more strongly. This is a surprise. I want to see your reaction when you open it. No peeking.

Dammit, it was like he could see me. Or else he knew curiosity killed April.

I sighed and glanced around. *Could* he see me? I almost wouldn't put it past Mr. Moneybags Controller-of-All-Things.

Why did I find that hot? What was wrong with me?

Probably too much stimulation after a long sexual drought. It couldn't be good for the psyche.

Fine, I wasn't going to look. I was just going to wait patiently for him to finish his errand, even if I had to wonder what he was up to now. In the meantime, I'd just try on my cute new bikini and hope all my island indulgences hadn't made me go up a size.

At least some of them were calorie-free.

I was bent over examining my ass hang between my legs when my grandmother texted me. Flushed, out of breath, more than mildly embarrassed, I grabbed my phone to read what she'd said.

I'm leaving soon, dear. You're sure you'll be fine on your own with your gentleman?

Already? We didn't get to talk much.

You're busy. I get it. And your man sure is fine. *winky face* Mine too.

I sat on the sofa, clutching the note from my fine man in one hand and my phone in the other. This whole trip was supposed to be about my grandmother, not about following my lustful loins wherever they led me. She hadn't been as depressed or brokenhearted over her failed engagement as I'd expected—actually, she hadn't been those things for even a minute that I'd seen—but I couldn't imagine her just going off to island jump with a man I hadn't even met.

Not that she'd met mine either.

Ugh, God, what were we doing? I had to see her in person. Texting didn't accurately convey emotions. Maybe she was burying her pain in sly emojis and island beverages and naughty activities with a younger man. At least I thought he was younger. What if he was some kind of huckster, just waiting to secrete her somewhere I could never find her again? Sure, my guy hadn't turned into a spree murderer—yet—but what were the odds we could both just have freewheeling fun with colorful condoms and couples' massages and pink butt floss, aka bikinis, without negative consequences?

Probably not very good.

Quickly, I sent her a message.

Are you in your room?

Yes, I'm packing. Why?

I stood up and grabbed the bag with the coverup I'd picked up in another shop. I dragged it on over my bikini and hurried over to look at my reflection. Butt floss hidden.

Yay me.

I bent to search for the flip flops I'd worn to shop. I'd kicked them off in a hurry after returning since I'd had a few too many fruity concoctions while on my spree—it was five o'clock somewhere—and my bladder had protested.

Yanking up the tangled sheets, I looked under the bed. Where the heck were they? Only I could lose shoes that quickly. It wasn't as if I had a powerful kick.

Sparkles out of the corner of my eye made me sigh and grab the heels he'd given me. Not the best choice but I'd take them off on the sand and just wear them to walk through the hotel. Besides, it wasn't as if I could wear my new fancy slippers. But I'd shove them into my bag for when I got a blister from the sexy-as-sin, not-meant-for-sand heels.

After sliding my feet into the heels with a little happy sigh—that would unfortunately be gone after I walked in them for a few minutes—I grabbed my phone and answered Grams.

Wait for me.

I didn't wait for her to text me back, just silenced my phone and threw it in the beach bag I'd been using as a purse. It was hot as blazes out, or else I'd just been running around too much, so I grabbed a bottled water and dumped it in my bag with the few purchases I hadn't yet unpacked.

My stomach growled so I plucked a croissant off a tray left from last night's decadence and ate it while I passed the neighboring bures. Everyone was so friendly, and I found myself calling out greetings and laughing although I rarely chatted with the neighbors at home.

I was always so serious there and didn't take time for things like that. Much like my equally serious boss who was probably still stunned I'd dared to take an impromptu vacation after eighteen months.

Truthfully, so was I.

It didn't take me too long to arrive at my hotel but the journey there wasn't nearly as much fun as leaving with my guy had been. Of course, there was no one to carry me over this threshold. No one to grin at me with challenge and interest in his mesmerizing eyes. The rest of him wasn't any slouch either, but he conveyed a wealth of information in just one glance.

I crammed the last bit of flaky pastry in my mouth and forced myself to focus on my grandmother.

You'll see him again soon, so no more mooning, Finley.

Turned out I didn't know exactly *how* soon.

I entered my room and was just about to fling open the connecting door to my grandmother's suite when her light laughter filled the space. Followed by the deep commanding tone I would know anywhere.

My clit pulsed out a weak hello while my brain whirled.

I didn't want them talking. Not because I was ashamed of him, far from it. He was sweet and gorgeous and witty and had manners for days. He made me laugh and made me come and made me wish I hadn't set up stupid rules that I didn't know how to break, because breaking rules was not my thing.

God, I'd even made a rule so I could *break* them.

But aside from possibly revealing things to him I didn't want him to know, my grandmother wouldn't make it easy on me to let him go. Maybe that was for the best, but even so, that was my choice. The whole making decisions for me thing had been exciting and freeing when it hadn't been about important issues.

This was different. We'd decided on how this would go, and now he was doing an end run around me and trying to take the decision out of my hands.

Not that I was terribly surprised. He didn't strike me as someone who abided by what he was told very often.

My grandmother's voice rose, but her tone held laughter not rancor. "I must say, I'm rather surprised Bunny would make such an arrangement with you. But if she did, she has her reasons, and you won't get any more out of me."

I pressed my ear to the door to catch more of their conversation, my heartbeat a hollow echo in my head. I needed to stop this. I also needed to hear what they'd say.

I was on a speeding bus headed to hell, and my armor was a string bikini and sex heels.

"Oh, I don't want to break our agreement. I just wanted to surprise her by picking up her bags, and I was hoping to meet the woman who means so much to her. And I can tell the feeling is mutual."

Despite myself, I smiled. He was an astute guy. Probably why his tongue had such unerring accuracy.

Or else he'd slept with the equivalent of twenty cheerleading squads, but I preferred to focus on his powers of observation.

My grandmother laughed. "You're a slick one, aren't you? Think you can wind your way around an old bird without her being any the wiser. My Bunny will see right through any games. That's not the way to win her."

I winced and covered my face with my hands. Probably shouldn't mention what it had taken to "win" me—and most of the time, talking had *not* been involved.

"I don't see any old birds around here, but I'll take any advice you'd spare."

"For one, she won't appreciate any high-handed maneuvers. Oh, it might work once or twice. A girl does enjoy being spoiled—and surprised—now and then. But keep it up and you'll find yourself with something other than your hat in your hand and a possible restraining order."

His laughter was deep and rich..

Grams had a very good point. Getting presents was awesome. Making decisions without my input and replacing my wardrobe as if I was a doll to play dress up with was not.

Minus the red dress and the Cinderella heels and the plush slippers my arches were crying out for even now.

"You're right. I got hung up on giving her the whole fairytale experience. Making her happy is addictive." His smile resonated in his words, and I found myself smiling back, then touched my own lips as if his were against mine even now. "I'll just leave her things where they are. We can come back and get them, or she can get them herself."

"The boy can learn." My grandmother laughed.

He laughed with her, and they said a few things too low for me to discern. Then my grandmother gasped loudly enough I teetered on my heels and nearly overbalanced from my full beach bag.

"I see it now."

"See what?" His question was easy, relaxed.

"I knew I recognized you. I thought it was from that show with the vampire brothers. One of them is sleeper sexy, not as overtly sex on wheels as the older brother."

I closed my eyes. *Please God, don't let her explain how she ranks the appeal of the Salvatore brothers.*

But she didn't go into that. Instead, she went in a direction that was far worse.

"When Bunny sent me your photo, something clicked in my mind.

I figured it's the bone structure. You could fill in on that show, you know."

"Sorry." His tone was thick with humor. "I haven't seen it."

"Well, broaden your mind. Anyway, that wasn't it. I've seen you on TV, but not on a rerun. You do those commercials, don't you? You're the bye guy."

I frowned. What did that mean?

He cleared his throat. "I didn't come up with that unfortunate nickname, but I was convinced by a PR firm that it was hooky enough to catch attention. I stopped doing those commercials more than a year ago, by the way. We only ran them in the tri-state area with a brief expansion into the south. After that, I was so inundated with business, I no longer needed to advertise."

"I can only imagine. Handsome, slick divorce attorney like yourself, you must've had to beat the horny wanna-be divorcees off with sticks."

Divorce attorney. Like my boss, my boss's brother, and their father, who planned to retire soon. Shaw, Shaw, and Shaw, LLC was my place of employment.

I clutched my stomach. Well, his tattoo certainly made sense now.

His chuckle was smooth, saying without words that she was right on the money.

Lovely.

I knew all too well how women swarmed around my boss, and he gave them no encouragement whatsoever. He also didn't serve clients outside of New York unless they were a personal referral.

My guy had who knows how many likely attractive and soon-to-be single women flitting around him at any given time. Like I could compete with that? I could halfheartedly pretend to fun and exciting for a few days, but my true staid, steady personality lurked underneath. I wasn't the kind of woman who could keep a man like him intrigued for long.

Good thing this was all just very temporary. I'd been smart.

"I don't mix business and pleasure."

"Never?" My grandmother pressed.

"Rarely," he hedged. "If I do indulge, I make it clear I'm not interested in anything that lasts longer than a weekend reservation. I learned my lesson well in that arena."

A ripple of pain went through my belly though I firmed my shoulders. *Me too.*

Just more confirmation we'd made the right choice by keeping the pressure off. And if my grandmother slipped and said my real name instead of bunny, so what? We both knew the score.

"If that's the case, why are you here warming me up to plead your case? Your temporary arrangement with my granddaughter must suit you right down to the ground."

"It does. It did." He let out a baffled laugh as I closed my eyes and tried to ignore the traitorous flutters in my chest. "I don't understand it myself, but I'm not ready to let her go. I can't."

Oh, God. The backs of my eyes heated. I fought every urge to open the door and tell him I felt the same. But how could I do that? Never mind my eavesdropping. There was no way we could last, and then I'd ruin the best memory of my life by reaching for more than I was meant to have.

It would end. It *always* ended with me. Every real relationship of any sort in my life had ended before I was ready, other than with my best friends and Grams.

Even my parents had split on me, for God's sake.

My grandmother's voice gentled. "Sounds like that's a conversation you need to have with her."

"She doesn't want to go there. The first woman—shit." He blew out a breath. "Wait a second, where are you located? If you saw those commercials, you have to live in one of the markets we serve."

I grabbed the doorknob. He served those markets because he lived in one of them himself, obviously, and if she told him where we were from, he would follow suit and everything would fall apart.

But she didn't answer his question. "Preston Shaw," she said instead.

My boss? What the heck?

"I saw a picture of you two together in the paper," she said slowly. "Oh, dear."

My throat closed and I gripped it to keep from throwing up. *Oh, dear* indeed.

"Yes. He's my best friend. Where are you—"

The beach bag slipped off my arm. The sound reverberated in the base of my skull like a gong.

I didn't wait to hear more. I just grabbed the beach bag I'd dropped and my still-packed carry-on and escaped.

Running was the only option I had left.

CHAPTER NINE

Bishop

I STARED at my mystery woman's grandmother as a *thunk* came from the connecting suite. Her concerned denim blue gaze flew to mine before she quickly jogged to the door between the rooms and flung it open, with me right behind her.

The room looked undisturbed, just as it had when I'd came here to get "Bunny's" belongings.

I still didn't know her name. She hadn't even given me that much. I'd thought her grandmother might, but she'd called her Bunny and I didn't feel right asking.

None of this felt right anymore.

The concierge had opened the room for me, since he'd handily seen us leave together the other day. He shouldn't have, of course. I could be anyone. Possibly even one of those serial killers on the podcast she enjoyed.

I did too. What did that say about the pair of us?

That you fit together. You knew it from the first glance.

Her grandmother hurried through the room and stopped beside the small dresser, lifting her fingers to her lips. "Her carry-on isn't here."

I strode past her to the door to the hallway and pulled it open, already certain she was long gone. We were only moments behind her, but that was enough.

She could be headed back to my bure. That was the logical assumption. She'd overheard us, maybe had gotten annoyed that we'd discussed her in her absence, or that I'd pulled a Bishop move and tried to orchestrate her life by getting her things without asking first.

A bad habit with me. It hadn't started with her. No, that particular compunction had started over three years ago, when I'd decided the best way to ensure I always got the outcome I wanted was to control as much as possible in my orbit.

No spontaneity. Nothing unplanned. And no decision made that I didn't have my hand in.

It worked in business and it had worked in pleasure—until her. Until her grandmother had reminded me that a forced decision wasn't a decision at all.

I could lock her away in my bure and never let her leave. Keep her there with fancy clothes and inventive sex and sweet nothings whispered over delicious dark chocolate and fruit.

But eventually, the haze would clear. And the fantasy would end.

I was beginning to think that it had already.

My first instinct was to go after her. To talk it out. Maybe even admit that I wasn't able to settle for less with her. It had been so long since I'd found a real connection with anyone. She had to feel the same, right? No way in hell could this…*thing* be one-sided.

But I didn't move. Why had she run? If she'd heard us talking and she was pissed, she had a voice. She could use it. Why not barge in and tell us how she felt?

Why just turn around and leave?

You know why. She doesn't want more. Sure, she likes the sex. Likes your face and your money and your attention. You're a good vacation fling. Period.

Her grandmother was speaking to me. Her voice buzzed in my ears like a horde of flies, circling my head.

Had *she* even looked at the picture? I'd asked her not to peek, but

I'd also asked her for more without saying the words. She'd declined one, why not the other?

I took a deep breath and walked up the hall in the direction I'd assumed she'd gone. Why, I had no clue. I didn't say goodbye to her grandmother, didn't even attempt to search for my manners.

What difference did it make now?

I couldn't say precisely why she'd chosen to run, but I knew deep down in my gut she had. Already I felt empty in a way I hadn't since I'd arrived on the island.

I hadn't known the hollowness in the center of my chest was loneliness. Even misery. I hadn't known because those weren't feelings I allowed myself anymore.

Now I was steeped in them. Drowning.

I rounded the end of the hallway, walking as if it was all I still knew how to do, my feet soundless on the carpet. One foot in front of the other. How I lived my life. I'd just keep walking until my soles were numb and I didn't remember anymore.

Easier that way.

Then I made the mistake of looking down the hall. My gaze landed on a glittery shoe, tilted over on its side.

I rushed forward and grabbed it from the floor, my ears throbbing with my frenetic pulse. The heel was broken. Snapped almost off.

So much for these being high-end.

She'd loved these shoes. And she'd left it behind, broken and discarded.

I wasn't making myself into a metaphor. I just was not. Besides, if I was broken, that had happened before she'd come into my life.

What was one more slice off what remained?

I started to rip the heel the rest of the way off, but I stopped. I couldn't do it. Nor could I reply when her grandmother came up behind me and laid a hand on my back. Her gaze dropped to the shoe I held. Our eyes locked, and the pity in her expression said without words what I already knew.

Better to leave than to be left. When would I ever get that fucking message?

Not today.

Her grandmother had seen my commercials. Somehow she knew Preston—well, if her startled look and her "oh, dear" had held any weight. I could solve part of this right now and ask for her granddaughter's real name and address. Force her to talk to me if she had indeed chosen flight rather than fight.

But asking was another kind of weakness, and pride was all I had left.

Actually, it was questionable at the moment if I had even that. Because I opened my mouth, the question lodged in my throat, the words begging to get out.

Tell me who she is. Give me that, at least.

Before I could, she shocked the hell out of me by grabbing my face and pulling it down to hers. She whispered in my ear, "just wait," before she hurried up the hall in the direction she'd come from.

What the hell did that mean?

I pushed a hand through my hair, my gaze fixated on that damn shoe. I wanted to throw it against the wall. Obliterate it under my heel. I didn't want a visible reminder if I couldn't have her. I wanted them all to disappear as quickly as she had.

Instead, I gripped it that much tighter and went back to my bure to fucking wait.

By nightfall, she hadn't come. I hadn't expected her to.

I fell asleep eventually. My dreams were wild, chaotic. I couldn't process them. Lots of storms breaking over the ocean, sharp bolts of lightning crashing into the tumultuous sea. After one of those dreams had me rearing up in bed, panting and disoriented, I opened my eyes to see the very same storm rolling in outside the open glass doors to the ocean.

Naked, sheened with sweat, I walked to them and pulled them closed on a gust of wind. And I strode to the wet bar and splashed some dark liquid into a short glass, swallowing it quickly so that the burn in my throat spread into my chest and down through the rest of me.

The next time, I skipped the glass and just drank from the bottle.

It was late the following day when I finally pulled myself out of my alcohol and exhaustion fueled stupor. I fought off the hangover with Advil, water, and a punishing run on the beach in the now blazing sun. It felt as if my calves were burning—and my skin matched equally once I was finished—but I was spent enough to not care anymore.

Almost.

The time rolled by, and I didn't watch the clock. I slept, I drank, I kicked the stupid painting every time I passed it.

I wondered if I could set up a bonfire on the beach. It would make some damn good kindling. What did I care if they kicked me out of this place? It was almost time to leave, and I was never coming back.

She was never coming back.

I still could not let it go. Not if there was any chance she could still be here, and I could still find the way to reach her. Convincing people to see things my way was what I did. I was a freaking expert at it. Or so I'd once believed.

Like a pathetic sap, I went to all of the places I'd seen her alone. Futile expedition, that was. I'd just arrived at her hotel again when I remembered I was supposed to meet Preston at Lonegan's to talk over some work shit, something I did not care one iota about. I was also nowhere near home.

Biting off an oath, I called my best friend.

"Hey, what's up?" he asked. "You on your way?"

Not exactly.

I shoved my sunglasses up on my head. Damn blinding sun was pissing me off as much as everything else was right about now. How had I ever believed this was paradise?

Far as I was concerned, paradise was now a dark room with an endless supply of bourbon.

"I'm still in Fiji. Shit went sideways. Needless to say, I'm not going to be at the bar tonight. Sorry."

I hadn't been able to leave. An idiotic part of me hoped that she hadn't left the island, and she was just hiding in plain sight somewhere, hoping I'd find her again like I had the first time.

The idea made my breath quicken as I crossed the lobby, my gaze darting from person to person as if the possibility really existed she could be here. It wasn't too late.

I hadn't lost my last chance.

"Fiji?" Preston's voice spiked. "You didn't tell me you were there. And you said you met a woman?"

"Oh, I met a woman, all right." The words tasted as bitter as the leftover alcohol coating my throat.

"What happened? I thought you were in love and all that."

I snorted. Love. Right. What the hell was that, anyway?

"All that is correct. Until she ghosted me."

Static filled the line, and for a second, I thought we'd lost the connection. I didn't want to talk to anyone right now—at least anyone who wasn't *her,* as lowering as that was to admit. "If I can't find her, I'm catching a flight tonight."

"You're still looking? And um, just for curiosity's sake, her name isn't April, is it?"

"No," I growled.

As if I even knew her name. I hadn't wanted to shock uptight, moralistic Preston by admitting we'd never even given each other our names, so it had just been easier to fib.

Also, that whole falling in love concept when someone didn't even want you to know who they were was a little hard to explain. Much easier to lie.

"Thank God." More static filled the line.

"If what she told me was even her name." Since I knew Bunny *wasn't* her real name, the bridge to the truth I was perched on was shaky. But I wasn't ready to come entirely clean yet. At least not until I was in person with my best friend. "We only did first ones. Now I'm questioning everything."

"Okay, what did she look—"

A voice came across the hotel intercom, warning of more

inclement weather due in soon. Naturally. Why not? I'd have to see how bad it was supposed to get and come up with a plan to get home.

So much for my pointless search. It was obviously for the best. Wasting any more time on someone who didn't even have the courtesy to say goodbye—even if it was just to tell me to fuck myself via a Dear John letter—was below even me.

"Sorry, man, I have to go. We'll reschedule that meeting in a few days. Whatever you need."

"Sure, don't worry about it. I'm sorry about this."

I shut my eyes. "Me, too, Shaw."

Time to close the chapter on my Cinderella for good.

CHAPTER TEN

April

AND THAT WAS how I ended up on a flight back from Fiji to the US wearing a pair of Dolce and Gabbana fuzzy slippers, an eye-searing bikini, and a flowing printed coverup with one spiked Cinderella heel in my beach bag.

I also had my carry-on full of electronic equipment, my toiletries, and a few souvenirs for my friends I'd hastily crammed in the other day, along with some extra pairs of underwear, socks, and a spare nightshirt.

Oh, and my teensy-tiny vibrator.

Hey, if I wasn't going to have a romance with an actual *man* on vacation, I'd intended to be able to at least have it with *myself*.

What I did not have? Any of my actual clothes other than my new bikini and coverup. Any of the clothes my still unnamed mystery man —also known as the bye guy, oh yeah, there was relationship material —had bought me. My huge wrapped present that I'd never even gotten a look at because he'd asked me not to peek and I'd obliged him, not knowing I'd run away like a coward and never see it at all.

God, I was a fool.

I should've stayed. So what if my boss was his best friend? That wouldn't be awkward if we stopped seeing each other.

Definitely not.

I moaned and rolled onto my side in my airplane seat, belatedly catching an aghast expression from my seatmate.

"I'm not sick," I said hurriedly. "Just having romantic trouble, I swear."

The older gentleman fussily moved closer to the window and watched me out of the corner of his eye.

Fabulous.

It was a miracle I'd even managed to switch my flight to this one in the first place. And I didn't even know where I was going once I got to the airport.

My home was available, of course, but I couldn't go home alone right now. I'd texted my grandmother to let her know I was okay, that I'd just needed to head home immediately, and oh, could she maybe grab the rest of my belongings from my suite and not ask any questions?

Please.

Then I'd wished her a great time island-hopping with Roger and told her to keep me updated and sent a prayer to the travel gods that she wasn't canoodling with a mass murderer before I turned off my phone.

I couldn't bear a conversation now. I didn't have an explanation for my behavior. I was just a throbbing ball of stress, guilt, confusion, and woe.

And my sunburn freaking hurt. I was the only one who could get burned in like fifteen minutes.

Many, many hours and two connecting flights later, I got an Uber from the Syracuse airport back to Kensington Square. It was late, and I was jet-lagged and didn't know which way was up, so I stumbled into my apartment and checked on Kit-Kat, who promptly turned her back on me and started to wash. My neighbor had come by twice a day every day to feed her and give her fresh water and clean the litterbox, but you would've thought I'd thrown her to the werewolves from the green death glare she sent my way.

That didn't stop her from waiting outside the bathroom door

while I took a quick cool shower to get rid of the travel grime. After, I pulled on my rattiest pair of flannel PJs. They had clouds on them and were nearly threadbare from wear. I crawled into my bed and nearly wept when my cat curled up beside me on the pillow. She was still watching me judgmentally, but she gave in and rested her head against mine.

I'd never needed the show of solidarity more.

I fell into a deep, dreamless sleep. When I woke, it was Saturday afternoon New York time, and I had to pee with the fire of a thousand suns.

Kit-Kat watched me take care of business from her station on the sink. I knew what she wanted, and it wasn't to be close to me.

"Gimme a second, cat, okay? I'm hungry too."

She finally gave me that second once I'd filled her dish with her wet food twice. A delicate face wash later, she swished off to sleep in her favorite patch of sun under the window.

And I curled up on the couch and stared at my silent, turned off phone.

I shouldn't have left. With each hour, I knew that with more certainty. It had been a cowardly act, more fitting of the me I'd been after Jeremy had dumped me. I'd grown some since then. My self-esteem was still questionable, but I thought I'd made some progress.

Apparently, I could let a devilishly attractive stranger finger me in front of a mirror while I helped, but I didn't know how to have an adult conversation about wants and needs.

I'd been so sure nothing could work between us for a million reasons. Distance had definitely been one of them. What were the odds he could live near Kensington Square? Not good. And I hated to fly. I'd loaded up on Dramamine before my flight home from Fiji, and I'd still white-knuckled it most of the time.

I still didn't know where he lived, but he probably wasn't based all that far from here, considering that whole commercial thing. And Preston.

His best friend. God. Would that ever stop flooring me? I didn't think so.

They were so different, at least on the surface. Both driven men, at least from what I could tell. Wealthy, powerful, well-educated. Miles above my associate degree and commensurate pay scale. Someday I might go for that paralegal certificate, but that was still firmly in the *maybe* realm. I hadn't reached for that brass ring. Even the silver.

My mystery man was a bright, shiny gold, and I didn't want to eventually be his tarnish.

My shoulders shook and I bowed my head to get myself together. I couldn't sit here alone and second-guess myself forever. I needed someone to help me out of this self-created spiral.

I needed my best friends.

I tried Ryan's home phone and got voicemail. Didn't that just figure? I hung up without leaving a message and debated calling her cell, since she rarely turned it off. But right now, Ryan was one degree away from my boss, even if I'd been the idiot who put her there.

At the time, it had seemed so reasonable. I was only going away for a week.

How could the span of a week—even less—change so much? Me especially. Even my apartment didn't feel like mine. It was as if I'd been dropped down into the place of a stranger.

I belonged on a white sandy beach with a man with changeable eyes the color of the sea before a storm.

Swallowing hard, I called Luna's cell. The call went to her voicemail too.

Not shocking. It was the weekend and my friends had active social lives. They didn't spend their free time watching D-I-Y YouTube crafting videos to create seasonal displays with popsicle sticks, hot glue, floral stems, and colorful gourds. Or studying new sewing patterns.

I sniffled as I studied the arrangement I'd made a few weeks ago for my coffee table. Whatever. It was cute. Besides, it wasn't as if I had a trust fund or a divorce attorney's largesse. Or both in the case of my boss. I had to make do with what I had.

He was a decent boss. I wouldn't have worked for him for a year and a half otherwise. But I wanted him to stay firmly in the realm of my superior. That was one of the reasons I'd asked Ryan to fill in for me at work. There was no way in hell she'd ever spend one second more with Preston than she had to.

Lines not blurred. Mission accomplished.

I curled up on the sofa and clutched a throw pillow to my chest. I was still sleepy. A nap might help my mood, although I hadn't done much since I'd woken up.

Or maybe I should go for a walk. I popped back up again. I had that harness thingy in the closet for Kit-Kat. I'd never actually put it on her, but she might want to enjoy the late summer day too. She liked to watch the sparrows and the squirrels out the window from the lofty height of her kitty condo, right? This would be even better. We'd both get some sunshine and some exercise and fresh air.

Half an hour later, my hands were covered with Band-Aids, Kit-Kat was sulking under the bed, and my desire to enjoy the great outdoors had been extinguished.

So, I'd just slather aloe on my sunburned skin with the fingers not bandaged while I listened to Barbra Streisand's "The Way We Were" and wallowed.

Luna texted me a while later when I was spooning up boxed macaroni and cheese and watching old "Friends" reruns.

Bish, u home? What's with u calling & leaving no voicemail?

I dumped a handful of crushed goldfish crackers into my mac and cheese.

Are u not answering me now? That's ok. I'll just come over.

Hastily, I grabbed my phone with cheesy crumb-laden fingers. The mess made me grumble, but I did not want company. At all.

I'm busy. Sorry I bothered you. Chat soon.

My phone buzzed. I sighed, answering on the second ring. "Hi, Lu."

"What happened with the couples' massage? Did they slip accidentally on purpose into the no-no places?"

I laughed loudly enough to spew crackers. My own fault for eating before I picked up the phone to Luna. It was always dangerous to talk to her with a full mouth—including texts. She was apt to say just about anything.

"No. It was fine."

"Just fine?"

"Well, I mean, it wasn't, like, sexual."

"Not sexual?"

"Stop repeating me. It was hot seeing my guy naked while he was getting a massage, yeah, but the women weren't hot. Which was good since I wouldn't have wanted some Pamela Anderson *Baywatch* babe oiling him up."

"Girl, you need to update your pop culture references. Welcome to 2021. Next time, say someone like Dua Lipa or Megan Fox."

"Dua who?"

She sighed. "I was hoping you'd get off. Loosen up a little."

"I'm loosened. I'm so loosened that I practically passed out more than once from extreme loosening." And with that, I promptly burst into tears.

"Uh-oh. Not good. Not good! Goldilocks, you're gonna have to scram." The sounds of a ruckus came over the line, filled with plenty of giggles interspersed with a much deeper voice that indicated Goldilocks probably had a penis. At least I assumed.

What a week this had been for all of us. Unless Luna's "friend" had been around longer than that. You could never be sure with her. She acted as if she was an open book, but she definitely had some pages glued together not for public consumption at the back.

"You don't have to send him away." I tried to swallow my tears when she returned to the line. "I don't want to be a cockblock. I'm totally fine. I have HBO Max and food and my cat, who is around here somewhere even if I can't hold her right now because of earlier."

"Earlier?"

"Ever tried to walk a cat?"

"Goddess, no."

"Good. Don't." I couldn't help shuddering.

"Okay, obviously that's a conversation for later. You said you have food. You went shopping?"

"Not since I've been back, no." I sniffled. "I emptied my refrigerator before the trip because of spoilage concerns, but I have another blue box."

"If that's code for some kind of drugs, I don't know it. And spoilage concerns sounds so very April."

I cried harder.

"All right, hang tight. I'm coming and I'll grab a pizza on the way. Once I'm there, we'll grab an Instacart order and spend the night watching trash movies in our living room blanket fort. Sound good?"

"Yes. Thanks, Lu. Can you grab Ry on the way too?"

"Ry's…unavailable right now. She's fine," she added hurriedly. "She's on a spiritual quest."

"Huh?"

"She fell onto some dick and it got her all mixed up."

I knew the feeling. But God, it was so good—until it all went bad.

I frowned. "Wait, what dick?"

Luna rushed ahead. "On top of that, Rainbow is in town. Or she was. They're off in the RV exploring together."

I rubbed my forehead. "I have a feeling somehow I won't like this story."

Lu's sigh was long-suffering. "Yoda, you are correct. I'll be there soon, babe."

Grabbing a throw off the back of the sofa, I gave in to the desire for sloth and set my half-empty bowl on the floor—I never did that, since I was a member of the "no dirty dish shall touch my sink club"—and rolled myself into a burrito. It was a warm day, but I was still chilly due to the AC and my cracked heart.

The last one I was just assuming was to blame for my broken

temperature gauge. It definitely had increased my appetite. I wasn't one to eat tons of junk food, but I had a feeling I would be tonight.

So much for fitting in that bikini. Oh, well. It wasn't as if I'd be cavorting on any other beaches soon.

Lu showed up with her double cheese and pepperoni pizza in hand an hour later. She took one look at me, set the pizza on the kitchen counter, and drew me into a huge hug.

"You're burned." She drew back and tapped my nose before dragging her enormous bag off her shoulder. "I brought supplies, so don't worry, I'll fix you right up."

"Stuff from Luna Falls?"

"Of course. You know I get my goods from the best witches." She winked, her blond space-buns bouncing.

She looked adorably chic as always in pink denim overalls, a bright yellow T-shirt, and colorful high-top Keds.

And a bright red hickey just under her ear.

"So, who's Goldilocks?"

"Hmm?" She was still rooting through her big bag, tossing items on the counter with impunity. Balms, candles, tarot decks. Essential oil sprays, a random stick of incense, a velvet pouch I knew contained crystals.

And strawberry-flavored lube.

Rather than commenting on that particular item, I picked up a tin of lavender salve and lifted the lid to sniff. I swiped my finger through the mixture and leaned over to rub it under her ear, making her jump.

"Hickey," I said by way of explanation.

She flushed from her throat to her hairline. So not like Luna. She didn't embarrass easily, unlike me.

"Oh, that. Thanks." She snatched the salve and did the honors herself. "I hope you got some of those too, by the way."

I didn't reply. I actually had some on my breasts, not an area I intended to reveal anytime soon.

"If you did, this stuff works wonders."

"Do you have any that makes them stay forever?" I asked miserably, sliding a hip onto a stool at my counter.

Luna stopped rubbing her skin and frowned, capping her tin. "That good? Or that bad?"

"It was good. Amazing. I didn't want to ever get out of bed."

"Sounds promising. So why the hell are you back here, looking like someone stole your cat?" Luna glanced around. "Where is she, anyway?"

"Still hiding. She'll be happy to see Aunt Luna."

"I'll go find her for snuggles in a few." She clambered up onto a stool with far more difficulty than I had since she was half a foot shorter. "Okay, grab the plates and some wine. Time to spill."

"Technically, I just ate dinner."

"Are you satisfied?"

What a weighty question.

Since no, I definitely was not, I got the plates. The bottomless hole inside me felt like it would never be filled. Jamming it full of gooey, cheesy pizza was as good a start as any.

"Where's Grams?" she asked as we dug into the still-hot slices.

"I abandoned her."

Luna choked and grabbed for her goblet of wine. She waved me off when I started to come around the island, then set down her drink and took a bracing breath. "Metaphorically?"

"No, literally. I ran off to have sex with a stranger, didn't come back, texted her sporadically, then planned to see her off before she went island-jumping with a serial killer, but instead, I ran off again, except this time I didn't stop until I was home."

Luna blinked her large baby blue eyes at me. "You must be tired."

"Huh?"

"That's a really long way to run."

I let out a laugh, shocked I still could. "A plane or two was involved."

"Start at the beginning."

I told her all of it up to the point right before my big escape. From the dress to him appearing at my hotel room to carrying me over the threshold of his bure and the Cinderella shoes and all that came afterward. Leaving out a few dozen, um, intimate details.

"Damn, girl, even in an overview, that sounds like a lot of sex."

I bit my lip. "It does, doesn't it?" I shut my eyes. "Did I mention that he made me come back-to-back more than once?"

"Back to back? Sounds like you didn't stop. I would hate you right now if my own plum hadn't been thoroughly plundered earlier today."

"Yeah, tell me about Hickey Man."

"That's a lovely nickname. Goes so well with Goldilocks and Teach, my other choices. But nice try, Finley." She finished off her slice and piled three more onto her plate while my eyes widened. "We're still talking about you."

I sighed. "Lu, he lives here."

Luna threw down her napkin. *"Here?* Like here here, in Kensington Square?"

"I don't know exactly." I jerked a shoulder. "Maybe in New York State, maybe Jersey, but God, I overheard him talking with Grams and found out he's a damn divorce attorney who does commercials as the Bye Guy, *and* he's besties with Preston."

"Preston?!" Her screech threatened to break the sound barrier. "Oh my God, you're going to be double dating with him and—" She stopped and shoved half a slice of pizza in her mouth. "Sorry, starving," she said, chewing loudly.

I narrowed my eyes. "You never eat this much."

"Told you I'm hungry," she said between overly large bites, making me think she didn't want to have to answer questions. I knew the feeling. "Okay, backtrack. Bye guy? Commercials? You missed a step or five."

I pushed aside my plate and braced my elbows on the counter to drag my hands through my normally quite boring hair. I'd slept on it wet and hadn't bothered brushing it today, so it was not my usual look. "I don't even know, except I freaked out at the idea this guy who was supposed to be a stranger and just a fling could be my damn neighbor, and I didn't even know it. Preston being his best friend jammed all my circuits and I couldn't think. How can I sleep with a guy who is close to my boss?"

"Uh, quite easily. Not like you're sleeping with *your* boss, Apes. I mean, people do that too," she added hastily. "Whether a temporary boss or otherwise…" She coughed into her hand. "Anyway, don't make molehills into volcanoes."

I straightened and crossed my arms over my chest. "You're being weird."

"Am I?" Her expression was pure angelic innocence as she peeled off a pepperoni slice and popped it into her mouth.

"You are and you know it. Is Hickey Man your boss? Even your temporary boss?"

She giggled, bending over at the waist. "He works in a Catholic school, teaching little kids. How could he be my boss? Unless, hmm, I was his teaching assistant." She sat back up and tapped her chin. "Do they have those in elementary schools? No matter, would be hot to roleplay. You can only do that doctor and nurse thing so many times."

"I was gone a week," I said under my breath. "Only a week. It feels like I've been gone a lifetime. Has anything else monumental gone on while I was away?"

Lu hummed under her breath. "So, how about those Yankees?"

I tipped back my head to stare at the ceiling. "I feel like I'm missing something big, but gotta say, I can't handle anything else right now. Between having the most amazing couple days of my life and fleeing from my sexy stranger and my grandmother, who may even now be international news since I never got to meet her new lover, I can't deal."

"I kinda gathered that. We'll just table anything else for a bit and watch some movies and rub sweet smelling balms on each other. You know, the sort of sleepover that would make our dudes sure we're secretly lesbians. Or at least hope we are." She leaned forward and clasped her hands near her mouth. "Just one rather specific question."

"Okay."

"What kind of thrusting power are we talking here?"

"Turbo jet," I said immediately. "My eyes rolled back until I saw Jesus."

She nodded serenely. "Just as I suspected."

CHAPTER ELEVEN

April

I WOULDN'T SAY I crept off the elevator at Shaw, Shaw, and Shaw, LLC on Monday morning approximately twenty-two minutes before my scheduled work time, but—okay, yes, I would.

And I did.

I freaking hugged the damn elevator wall and peered around the corner, looking both ways before I stepped out. Then peered again in both directions.

Twice.

A little much? Yes. Probably. No, definitely. Even if Preston's best friend had decided to visit him in the office—which he certainly never had before, or I would have met him—I didn't have to fear his presence like I would the bogeyman.

I hoped.

To be fair, I didn't know how *he* reacted when he was angry. My gut feeling was that he would be explosive. It only stood to reason, since he was that way at…other times.

Hello, inner prude. I missed you last week. You really didn't have to return though. It's not you, it's me.

Maybe he wasn't angry. Maybe he'd shrugged off my absence.

Fling, right? Stuff happened.

Even if he had spent a small fortune on me, including that large wrapped object I hadn't gotten to see and really wished I had.

No one had ever bought me such expensive gifts. Especially not a man.

One who probably either hated my very memory or moved on without a backward glance. There didn't seem to be any in-between in my head.

"April? You're back." Dexter Shaw, Preston's younger brother, emerged from the hallway that led to the conference room and hive of offices. "Baby, you told me you'd text, and what did you send me? Absolutely nothing. Not even a digital postcard or some eye candy of you in your bikini." He waggled his brows.

The steel stick up my spine—and possibly up my posterior too—softened enough for me to smile. Only Dex could get me to relax so fast. He wasn't hard on the eyes either, but the sexual chemistry between us ranked about minus one hundred. He was like a slightly older, pain-in-the-ass brother, not a potential screw buddy.

Not to mention, he was indirectly my boss. I could never contemplate contaminating the sanctity of my calm workplace with sexual relations with my employer.

My job was my oasis in the center of a chaotic world. Before getting the job with Preston, I'd worked at the law firm of a sweet elderly couple. They were in the first slate of interviews I'd had after completing my Associate's degree, and I'd stayed with them for almost five years until Mr. Seville passed on. His wife lost the will to practice law after his death, and it had been hard for me to search for another position because they were all I'd ever known.

A go-getter, I was not.

Ry and Lu had pushed me to spread my wings and to lose the guilt that I was abandoning Mrs. Seville, even though she'd made the choice not to continue working. We stayed in touch even now, and she'd helped me find the position with Preston. Her glowing recommendation had been what had set me apart when it came to nailing this job.

It had helped that Preston and I had similar work ethics. We both put work above all else, including meals most days—Preston even more so than me. His clients came before everything.

I frowned. My boss was always here before me. Here before Dex. Here before the cardinal that always greeted me with a song as I hurried in each day.

Yet his glass-walled office was dark.

Dex hadn't let my silence deter him from talking. Nothing ever did. I cut him off mid-sentence and blurted, "Where's Preston?"

He reached up and stroked his clean-shaven jaw. "Did you hear a word I said?"

"No," I admitted, moving to my desk outside Preston's office and placing my purse in the bottom drawer as I always did. "Sorry, I've got a lot on my mind."

Dex eased a hip on the edge of my desk and flicked open the button on his suit jacket. Beneath it, he wore a Marvel Universe graphic T-shirt. Only Dex. Must not have any court appearances today. "You literally just got back from vacation. How can your mind be cluttered with anything but sun, sand, and se—fun?" He grinned at my arched brow. "Almost forgot who I was talking to for a minute."

"I do have…things like that."

"Good to know. It's healthy."

I made a noncommittal noise in my throat. "Trust you to think so, since you're the healthiest guy in this building then."

He laughed. "Oh, I have a feeling my brother might be threatening my record there. Way to go on that score, by the way. If you had to go on vacation on short notice, you certainly thought ahead on how to soften the blow."

I reached for my locket. I'd left it home on purpose while I traveled to Fiji, not wanting to bring my security blanket with me on my wild vacation. "You mean giving Ryan the heads up on bribing him with coffee?"

His laughter turned sly. "Oh, she bribed him with something, and it didn't come in a cup. Well, two cups, maybe."

When my frown grew, he sobered. "You really did not hear a word I said."

"No." I dropped into my chair with a thud, certain I would not like what was coming one bit. "Tell me. Please. Don't draw it out."

"It's not as bad as that face you're making. Actually, some think it's pretty damn awesome, me included. My brother's never been this happy. But you're not happy at all." He gripped my chin and tilted it upward. "You have a sunburn too. Fair Irish beauty."

"Yeah, I didn't have sunscreen—"

At that moment, several things happened at once. The elevator stopped and the doors slid open as slowly as they would in a box office smash. Unnaturally slowly. So slowly that I had an instant to take in every nuance of my boss in just his shirtsleeves with his arms around a woman who'd pressed herself against him as if she feared being blown away in an unexpected windstorm—and had decided to anchor herself to him with her lips.

That woman was my best friend Ryan, amazingly gorgeous hussy that she was.

Apparently having just realized they'd arrived on their floor—of their office building, not Adult World's private cinema level—they detangled their lips long enough to step off and notice they had an audience.

Me, staring at them as if my worst nightmare had just embodied a physical shape, and Dex, who was still cupping my jaw while he gave his brother a thumbs-up for scoring the winning touchdown in the sex championship.

I was fairly certain that had happened a time or seventeen in the week I'd been gone.

Just a week.

My bestie was looking at me apologetically and mouthing words that could've been "I'm sorry" but read to me like "I stabbed you in the back, oopsie!"

If that wasn't enough, I noted through my shock that my heretofore nearly chaste boss was looking between his brother and I as if he'd caught *us* screwing on the floor under my desk.

Part of me wished I was there right now, but that part of me was *not* my lady trampoline.

"Guess I didn't need to fill you in with the deets, anyway, huh, April? I didn't have a clue we'd have a porno reenactment right in the reception area. But then again, Dad said he practically caught them in the buff in the records room, so who's surprised? Not I. Cleanup in aisle three, if you know what I mean." Dex finally turned his grin my way and belatedly seemed to realize a bomb had gone off in the center of my world. And my best friend was directly responsible.

Not entirely responsible. It took two. But before a week ago, my boss had been as repressed as I am.

As I *was*. Oh, God, vacations were the actual devil.

"Hey, you all right?" Dex's voice dropped as he reached up to clasp my shoulder in what I assumed was a gesture of support. Or solidarity in the face of so much sex. I didn't know, but Preston certainly grasped an intent behind the gesture I did not.

"You are not doing this shit with my assistant. I don't care what you've obviously done in the past. Nor does what's going on with me give you any right to bring your wickedness out into the open."

I gasped. "What are you insinuating, you—you office fornicator?"

Ryan's lips twitched, but she wisely crossed her arms and remained silent.

Preston, however, was too fixated on his sibling to care about my protests.

"And if you think my good mood precludes you from having to hide your illicit activities, I haven't had *that* much sex, Dexter Benedict Shaw."

Dexter didn't have a chance to respond before Ryan resoundingly punched Preston in the arm. "Watch it, pal, because you can have even less."

Instantly, my previously sexless employer reached out to stroke Ryan's long dark hair in a way that was only appropriate in an office setting on *Boss Me, Daddy* on Pay-Per-View. Did Pay-Per-View even still exist? I didn't know. "A metaphor, Miss Moon. Just a metaphor."

"Miss Moon? Is that some roleplay thing you guys do?" Dex circled his finger before tucking his tongue in his cheek and glancing at me over his shoulder. "Maybe the next time I flip up your skirt, I'll call you Miss Finley."

"Dexter," Preston barked, finally removing the hand that I was practically certain had immediately detoured to my best friend's ass. And she was not complaining one bit. "My office."

"You're not the boss of me." But Dex's singsong response didn't stop him from easing off my desk. He strolled toward Preston's office before he gave me a cheeky wink. "We'll chat more about this later. Thanks for wearing a dress, though. You know how much I love seeing your—"

"Dexter." Preston's jaw ticked as he strode toward his door. "Now."

Dex just grinned at me and followed his brother into his office, The door slammed hard enough to rattle the pretty vase I usually filled with fresh flowers.

It was empty now. Like my cold, barren heart.

Ryan examined her manicure. "So, wanna take bets which one blows his stack first? I'm going to say it'll be Dexter. Because he's actually had plenty of sex, thank you very much."

My bestie's deep, husky voice was usually one of my favorites on this planet. Right now, she might as well have been Freddy Krueger using all ten knives to carve his name into the chalkboard in my skull. "Dex's had plenty of sex?"

"Well, I can't verify for certain there, but probably. I meant PMS."

"PMS?"

She laughed as if this was all fun and games, and hey, too bad that my entire life was now dangling off a cliff. "Oh, sorry, forgot you never heard me call him that. Preston. You know, for Preston Michael—"

"Shaw. Yeah, I get it. How funny. Har-de-har-har." I jerked to my feet and pointed at my face. "See me laughing? Don't I look like I'm having a grand time?"

"No, you do not." She frowned. "What's up, Ape?"

"You took advantage of a situation I invited you into, then you defiled the records room that I spend half my time in?" I shook my head. "I mean, seriously, Ry? Could you be any more filthy?"

Ryan looked momentarily taken aback, but it didn't take her long to recover. No, my best friend happened to not only be drop-dead beautiful, she was also whip-smart along with being the hussiest hussy who had ever hussied. "I have to assume you're exaggerating. If you spend so much time in there, maybe get off your phone and, I don't know, organize it properly, maybe? Those files are a wreck."

My head snapped back as if I'd been physically struck. "How dare you."

"Oh, I dare. I dare so hard." Ryan marched forward and slapped her hands on my desk, knocking back my blotter. Which had a big tea stain—no coffee for clean living Moon—on one corner of the green felt.

I did not even want to know how or why she'd spilled her drink. Nope. Did not.

If that wasn't enough, there was a hunk of shimmering rock beside my notes cube, one more sign she'd just moved in and taken over my spot as if she owned it.

Temporary assistant, my burned buns.

I grabbed the blue crystal and thrust it up between us, getting right in her face. "And this. *This.* You couldn't just pretend to be a normal, semi-competent assistant for one freaking *week* to help out your best friend?"

A flash of pure pain crossed through Ryan's blue gaze. "You don't sound very much like my best friend right now."

Immediately, I wished I could snatch the words back. All my words. I didn't want to hurt her. She was my family. Deep down, I knew I was being ridiculous. She hadn't planned for any of this to happen any more than I'd planned on—

"Oh, God." I sank into my chair and buried my face in my hands. "I'm so sorry, Ry."

She didn't yell at me or refuse my apology, two things she had every right to do. But that wasn't my intuitive, understanding bestie's way. Instead, she came around the desk to crouch beside my chair before she drew me into a quick, hard hug.

"It's going to be okay, I promise." Her voice was gentle against my hair as I closed my eyes tightly, hoping I could keep the tears from spilling.

It didn't work.

"I'm acting like a complete jerk. You didn't ask for this to happen."

"Uh, absolutely not." She snorted, still not letting me go. "The last thing I ever planned on was falling for a damn *lawyer*. Are you kidding me? He probably starches his shorts."

I laughed halfheartedly through my tears before easing back to wipe at my cheeks. "You said falling."

"Hmm?"

"Falling, Ry. Not falling into bed."

She let out a long, slow breath, rocking back on her heels. "Yeah. I love him. Don't ask me how."

Before Fiji, my inner pragmatist would've laughed and waved her off. Love that happened that quickly wasn't real. It was shiny like fool's gold, but not something that could last.

Despite my bitchy tirade just minutes before, a genuine smile broke through my woe. "Oh, Ry. Does he love you too?"

Normally, my tough, fearless bestie would've blown off the question or made a joke. Not this time. "Yeah." She rose and rotated the ring on her thumb, a smile playing around her lips. "He said he does."

"Then I'm happy for you. Truly." I bit my lip as her head lifted, her eyes narrowing on mine. "I'm really sorry I acted like such a horrible person. Not even like a friend. More like an enemy. I don't deserve such—"

"Hey, can it. You said some shit. You were shocked and scared and caught off-guard. And dealing with some stuff of your own, hey?"

When I pressed my lips together to keep from spewing all the confusion and pain inside me, she ducked her head until our eyes were level. "C'mon, Ape, share. I just admitted I'm in love with a freaking divorce lawyer, for goddess's sake. How can it be any worse?"

I'm in love with his best friend. Also a divorce lawyer. Quite a pair we are, huh?

But I didn't say that. Whatever had happened on vacation couldn't be love. Not that quickly. Infatuation, lust, sure. Love was built over time from getting to know a person.

I didn't even know his name. I absolutely could not possibly love him.

Not yet.

A bang sounded from Preston's office.

Ryan rolled her eyes. "One who thinks he knows everything too. The awful part is he's not always wrong."

"Tell me how it happened. You and Preston."

She waggled her finger. "No get out of jail free cards to avoid telling your tale, missy."

"How do you know I have one?"

"I know you, crumb cake." She glanced at the closed door and the low hum of voices coming from the other side. At least they didn't sound murderous, unexpected bangs aside. "Gotta say I never expected…*that* from you."

"What that?"

She inclined her chin toward the door. "You've worked here long enough to know Dex isn't exactly the faithful sort. *I* know that and I only worked here for like half a minute."

A laugh rolled out of me and just kept on coming. I banded my arms around my waist and tipped forward in my chair. "He hit on you."

She placed a consoling hand on my back. "Kind of, but I think it was more to make PMS mad."

"That nickname is the best. How come I never thought of it?"

"Since half the time you call him Mr. Shaw—probably even in your own head—I have to assume PMS is too disrespectful for you."

"Well, I called him an office fornicator, so I guess the gloves are off."

We laughed together for a minute before Ryan tapped her lips. "Was it just a fling? He's hot as hell."

"Don't let Preston hear that."

"He's not my particular catnip, trust me. But I have eyes and an extremely functional libido." Delicately, she cleared her throat. "Is he good in the sack?"

I was already flushing, and I wasn't even sleeping with the dude. *That* dude, anyway. I had slept with someone, and good didn't even touch him or his masterful member.

Call it a dick, dammit. You are not retreating into prudishness just because you're not on island time anymore.

"Dick." I raised my voice. "Dick!"

Surprising no one, my boss opened his door at that very moment and stopped on the threshold, obviously hearing my battle cry. He cleared his throat as Dex chuckled behind him. "Miss Finley, my office, please."

"Oh, stuff it, PMS. She has a first name. And apparently, she also really likes dick, to which I say hooray. Dick for everyone!"

"Hear, hear," Dex said heartily. "Let me know if I can help either of you with your celebration."

Ignoring him, my bestie dragged me to my feet as my face, neck, and entire upper torso area burst into flames. "C'mon, Ape. Have your meeting so we can go to lunch with Lu and talk trash about these clowns."

"Excuse me, lunch?" My boss consulted his heavy gold watch. "It's not even ten o'clock."

"So? You wore me out this morning, and you didn't feed me, so I'm hungry." Ryan gave him a look that dared him to challenged her.

He wisely remained silent, merely stepping aside as Dexter moved past him and headed down the hall to his own office, whistling a jaunty tune.

Me? I needed a cold shower and a dark room, in that order.

Definitely not dick. I needed a dick diet. I'd developed an unhealthy fixation.

"If you want to go to lunch, that's fine." Preston only sounded moderately stiff, a minor feat for my typically tighter than a drum boss. "But I need to speak Miss—" He cleared his throat. "April first."

"Miss April? I suppose that's an improvement over Miss Finley, but seriously, pal, loosen your tie."

His aristocratic brow lifted. "Yet I call you Miss Moon and you don't have a problem with such."

"Yeah, well, I'm a kinky bish, what can I tell you?" She marched over to him and grabbed his aforementioned tie to haul him in for yet another porno-worthy kiss.

I should've looked away, but this whole thing was fascinating to me. If someone like Preston could loosen up enough to fall this quickly, maybe it wasn't so improbable or impossible.

Then again, who wouldn't fall in instant love with Ryan? She was amazing. Especially since she didn't seem to hate me, when she had every right to.

Ugh, I was never going to forget my meltdown this morning. My chaotic emotions were no excuse.

As Ryan and Preston quietly laughed together, I smiled. She was right. Everything was going to be just fine. Nothing had to change at work. I'd just overreacted.

As usual.

I kept telling myself that until Ryan said she'd be back to get me in an hour, and Preston gestured for me to come into his office.

Life as I knew it ended again at that moment. It had already ended once a few minutes ago, but I'd had a momentary reprieve.

I should've known it was too good to last.

"Please sit," he said as I lingered awkwardly in the doorway, smoothing down the sides of my navy pencil skirt.

I wanted to comply, but I had to clear the air first. My need to get things between us back on even footing was practically making me twitch.

"Mr. Shaw—"

"Preston, please." He raked a hand through his hair. "I'm not sure why we didn't dispense with the formalities a long time ago."

"We did sometimes. Just sometimes formalities are easier. Boundaries are easier." I reached for my locket. The metal seemed to warm under my fingers, steadying me. "I want to apologize for calling you an office fornicator. That was uncalled for."

"When did you call me that?"

"When you were ranting at your brother for also being an office fornicator." Now would be the time to say that Dexter wasn't—or if he was, he wasn't with me.

My boss lowered into his chair and rested his forearms on the edge of his desk. Along the way, he'd rolled up his sleeves. He'd also lost his jacket at some point. Very unusual for the always business-appropriate elder Shaw brother. Well, besides their father, anyway.

Ryan had probably mauled him in the elevator. She lived a charmed, sexually free life.

Damn her.

"Okay." He shook his head as if he didn't quite know where he was. I understood the feeling.

Neither of us spoke. This meeting was off to a scintillating start.

"You wanted something, sir?" I asked after he made no attempt to move things along.

"April, would you please sit?"

I sat.

"I know we've always kept things on a certain level in the office for both of our comfort levels. I want you to know that you're the best employee I've ever had."

"More than Ryan?" I had no idea what devil had perched on my shoulder to make me ask such a question, but I didn't try to dismiss it and change the subject.

This inexplicable office romance fascinated me. And now I was hungry for my extremely early lunch and gossip and Preston was the only conduit in sight.

He reached up to loosen his tie a fraction. "Miss Moon has many gifts, but clerical work isn't among them. Other than her facility in the records room."

Don't snicker. Just do not.

"Oh, I heard all about her facility there."

"My brother was out of line. I apologize if he embarrassed you."

"Pretty sure I wasn't the embarrassed one," I said under my breath as my boss started stroking his tie up and down, up and down. A nervous tic if I'd ever seen one.

He'd never had one before. Side effect of too much sex? I hoped I didn't develop something similar. Although my sex spate had ended with…not a bang. More like a cowardly whimper.

"Or if he's embarrassed you in other ways. Or made you feel at all uncomfortable." Preston didn't comment on my statement. Just as well. "Despite…recent events, this isn't that kind of law firm. We respect professional boundaries."

Now would be the right time to say that Dexter had not deflowered my previously plucked petals in the records room or anywhere else. Yet I didn't, because somehow I preferred my boss and Ryan assuming I'd slept with Dexter rather than the man I'd actually slept with, who was just as close to home to Preston.

Not because my mystery man wasn't worthy of shouting about to the rooftops. This was just simple misdirection.

Here, look at this shiny thing, so you don't find out about the shiniest phallus.

I didn't know how long I could keep the ruse going, but some part of me found it titillating. And hey, if Dex didn't care who thought we were humping like oversexed jackrabbits, why should I? It wasn't as if Preston had any room to talk.

"I appreciate that, sir, thank you. Your concern isn't necessary. I assure you, Dexter has always treated me with utmost…gentleness."

Which wasn't a lie. I mean, he didn't exactly act *gentle* with me. Most of the time, he behaved more like a gnat-like sibling, but he also had never tried to grope me in the conference room.

Wonder if my bestie had enjoyed that table too? I supposed I'd find out later.

Assuming this agonizing meeting ever ended.

"I just want you to feel comfortable speaking frankly with me. Any of the changes in the office we'll discuss today won't alter the fact that I'm always here to listen if—"

"Changes?" I edged forward on my seat, although my knees had turned to jelly. "What changes? Are you getting rid of me?"

Of course he was. His girlfriend could do my job. Maybe she wasn't a wizard at clerical work according to him, but she was still his lover. Plus, she apparently had some heretofore unknown skill at filing.

Unless that was just an inside joke between them about her suck-and-blow abilities.

Figured it had to be my sexual sore spot since I'd never given one. Not that I was about to hone my talents in that area to keep my job.

I rubbed the throbbing in my temple. Dear God, I was losing my mind and needed an Excedrin. Some sleep would help too, since I'd gotten, oh, none last night, and I was still vaguely jet-lagged.

Now that I was about to be joyfully jobless, I'd have plenty of time to nap. And day drink. And remember when I'd thought my place of employment was more important than anything, including multiple orgasms.

Dummy.

"No, absolutely not." To his credit, Preston's jaw locked as if I'd said something abhorrent. "I just told you you're the best assistant I've ever had. Anyone would be thrilled to have you working for them."

"Thank you, but then what changes are you talking about?"

He gave me a tight smile. "Actually, I'm getting rid of me. I'm hoping to bring someone in to take my place in the firm."

CHAPTER TWELVE

PRESTON

Needless to say, April didn't react well to the impending transition.

April was typically a rational woman not prone to fits of emotion, one of the reasons I'd hated the very idea of her taking a vacation. What would I do for a week without her sensible pragmatism and the way she wielded a calendar?

Unshockingly, I'd hated every second—until I'd fallen head over heels with a witch. I'd blame April for that, but it was the best thing that ever happened to me.

I owed her immeasurably. And I'd repaid her by sending her into a state of seeming catatonia that had now lasted for nearly five days.

April had done her job as capably as always, despite her early, extra-long lunch with Ryan and Luna on Monday. She'd come back to work that day wearing a smile—and with red-rimmed eyes—but I hadn't seen her smile again in the ensuing days. She answered by rote, arrived on time, left on time, and engaged in absolutely nothing more friendly with me than the usual pleasantries. At this point, her reception was so chilly I almost wished she'd called me an office fornicator again.

Even the bookends she'd presented me as a souvenir from her trip hadn't chipped the ice between us, despite my profuse praise of their "high polished sheen" and ability to hold books completely straight. She'd given me a thin smile and retreated to the safety of her desk.

The days of her reminding me to eat lunch when I forgot were firmly in the past. Now she'd probably just let me starve to death in my office of glass and call in a clean-up crew to dispose of my skeleton.

I understood she hated change or a disruption in her daily routine. We were very similar that way. The best way I could allay her fears that her job would remain stable even after I'd taken my exit was to introduce her to the new person who'd be helming the firm in my stead once my father and I helped with the transition.

First, I had to convince Bishop to take the position. I wasn't above light extortion and possibly begging. I'd start with buying him a round of drinks and a hearty meal before the begging began.

When I finally got him on the phone on Thursday, we made plans for a late dinner at Lonegan's on Friday night.

I glanced around the packed bar, filled with people talking, laughing, and whooping it up over the football game on the TVs stationed in every corner. Not the best choice on my part for an important conversation, but my buddy loved it here, and they had good food.

Things were off to an inauspicious start. Bishop was nowhere in sight.

While I waited for him, I played a stupid game on my phone called Plant-Eating Zombies while simultaneously eating my way through a plate of fried vegetables.

Hey, I'd missed lunch. *Thanks, April.*

I'd almost asked my jackass younger brother to attend, as he was supposed to be the other managing partner once I finally moved on. But I was still pissed at him for acting as if potentially sleeping with my assistant was no big deal. I wasn't sure he had. I wasn't certain he hadn't. He wouldn't clarify, and as usual, he seemed to enjoy making my life difficult.

Some might say I had a lot of nerve coming down on him for the same thing I'd done with Ryan. The problem wasn't that they'd hooked up—well, not entirely. I just wanted to make sure he knew he couldn't just roll on from her to the next woman, his standard MO.

Good time Charlie—err, Dexter—wasn't going to treat April with disrespect if I could help it. Along with the fact she was my stalwart assistant, she was my girlfriend's best friend. One of them, anyway. There were boundaries.

So, Dex had been left out of this meeting until I figured what his deal with April actually was. It was impossible to tell, since the man lived to fuck with me. It was basically his favorite thing. He'd even tried to make me jealous by asking out Ryan before I had.

He'd actually ended up pushing me toward her. I supposed that meant I owed him one.

Good luck there.

I glanced at my watch again. Bishop wasn't a clock-puncher, but he wasn't usually a half hour late without texting. He might've had a late client meeting. I hoped it was that and not something worse. He'd been holed up for days since he'd gotten back from Fiji, and I had a feeling we might not even get to the subject of him joining the firm in my stead tonight.

There were other pressing matters. Like if he was going to even show at all.

When I grew tired of virtually munching on plants, I switched over to texting my girlfriend, who basically told me to buzz off because she and La-la-Luna were about to record an episode of their Tarot Tramps podcast. To soften the blow, she promised to be waiting for me in my bed after I was done with Bishop.

Since I hadn't even *started* with the dude, I hoped she didn't doze off. Or else I'd be forced to wake her up with my tongue.

Oh, the hardships I endured.

A cheer went up near the doorway, so I assumed another touchdown. I turned in my seat to check out the score and frowned as my gaze zeroed in on Bishop holding court in the doorway, bending down to listen to something the cute, perky blond waitress was whispering in his ear. He was grinning and gesturing with the bottled Bud he held, clearly making sure he split his attention between the waitress and the two women equally interested in chatting with him. My best friend used to be known for enjoying the ladies—though not in the same numbers as my brother, thank God—but he'd been all about work for a bit now.

Guess he'd decided to keep his streak going after Fiji. And despite his lazy smile as he sipped and chatted, I knew the guy well enough to see the neon warning sign flashing over his head even from across the room.

He was cruising for trouble. At the speed he was traveling, he was definitely going to find it.

I grabbed my phone and sent him a text, since he didn't seem terribly concerned about my current location.

I know I'm not wearing a miniskirt, but let's go, Stone.

He yanked out his phone and lifted his head, his gaze narrowing on mine. He sent me an apologetic smile and then must've taken his leave, because an actual round of "boos" rang out.

Even Dex couldn't have gotten that reaction. Probably.

Bishop meandered his way through his crowd of admirers before finally undoing the button on his jacket and dropping down opposite me in the booth. "Hey, man, sorry for the delay."

I cocked a brow. "It's hard being so popular."

He set down his beer and sent me a grin. "Don't hate me because I'm beautiful." As soon as the words were out, he scrubbed his hands over his face. "Have you been here long?"

"The better part of an hour, but who's keeping track?" I leaned forward, putting a hand on the menu he immediately put in front of his face. "Have you slept?"

"Today?"

"Today. All week."

He jerked a shoulder and went back to the menu. "I'll sleep when I'm dead."

Quips aside, my best friend looked like shit. Deep furrows dented his forehead and the grooves around his eyes were deep enough to swim in. Neither detracted from his easy charm and the good looks that led opponents to write him off as a pretty boy who couldn't close a case.

How wrong they were.

And if he'd sometimes relied on that very thing when he didn't want someone to study him too closely, who could blame him? We all had ways to cope. But I knew him far too well, and I wasn't buying one ounce of the bullshit he was selling.

"So, did you put in an order for us?" He popped out a pair of glasses from his inside jacket pocket to peruse the menu, a sure sign he hadn't been sleeping. He was supposed to wear them for reading and usually didn't, unless his candle was just about burned out.

"Since when do I order for us? Am I your girl?"

He peered at me over the top of the laminated plastic. "No, because I heard you've been stepping out on me. You sure are pretty, though." He reached over to pinch my cheek just as the waitress he'd been flirting with in the doorway sashayed up to the table.

"Emmy," he said with that same casual grin. "Are we in your section?"

The lowered lashes smile she gave him said eloquently she wished he was in *her* very private section, and I wasn't invited.

Fine by me. I was needed elsewhere.

"I switched with Sue. She had a hot date. Friday and all." Emmy clutched her pad to her chest and eyed him up and down. "Speaking of hot dates, how come you're in here and not making some lucky lady's night?"

"Because I'm making Preston's night instead." The grin he aimed at me made me smile despite myself. I knew he was in his worst kind of deflect-and-pretend-everything-is-awesome mode, but Emmy didn't know him well enough to care.

She might not have cared even if she *did* know, which was why my buddy usually settled for sleepovers instead of searching for someone with substance. He'd given up on a woman like that existing for him.

Or he had before his trip, anyway, which I suspected was at the root of everything.

Fiji. That still niggled at me. What were the odds that both he and my assistant could have gone to the same place during the same week? I mean, the place was not tiny, a fact I'd verified after talking to him last week. Not tiny like Kensington Square, in any case, and to my knowledge, they had never met while they were home.

But them being there simultaneously almost seemed like…kismet or something.

My moonbeam Ryan was responsible for thoughts like this. As she was also responsible for Bishop taking advantage of my silence—sue me for considering if she'd found her way into my bed yet—to order a large pizza heavy on peppers and onions, which he knew were my least favorite toppings.

I didn't say that, however. I just sat back in the booth and crossed my arms while Emmy lamented Bishop's long, tough, *stressful* week and threw out about sixteen hints that she was free this weekend as she twirled her long ponytails.

"What?" he asked innocently once she'd wandered off, hips swaying.

"You know exactly how she wants to help you to relieve your stress. Just put us all out of our misery."

"Aww, Shaw, don't tell me your well in that arena has already dried up? Wasn't it just last week you were lost in a sex fugue state?"

"Keep your voice down, asshat. I'd be in one right now if I wasn't sitting here with you while you demonstrate your lack of game."

His eyebrow climbed. "Guy has sex for the first time in a millennia, and suddenly, he's an expert."

"Nah. Definitely not an expert. But we're way into advanced innings now."

"How advanced?"

I shrugged and tucked away my phone. "I love her and want her to move in with me. That advanced enough for you?"

He gripped his beer bottle, eyeing me steadily. "That's advanced, all right. You've known her like, what, a week?"

"In person, two now. We emailed and texted a bit for a week

before that." Quite contentiously for the most part, but he didn't need the details right now.

"Doesn't that seem soon to you?"

"No. It seems like perfect timing. She came into my world, and everything changed."

His smile seemed entirely forced. "You sound like a cheesy love song, dude."

"Yeah, well, I'm happy."

"Then I'm happy for you. I am," he insisted at my questioning look. "I just don't want you to be fucked over by someone looking for a payday from a rich, lonely guy."

I snorted. "Save your concern for another man then. Ryan couldn't want my money any less than she does now. In fact—"

"Ryan?"

I laughed. "Yeah, confused me too at first. I expected her to be a guy, but she's definitely not. Anyway, she's like the least materialistic person ever. She acts like I'm pampering her if I get takeout Denny's. Where the hell are you going?" I demanded as he jerked to his feet.

"I need to walk." The muscle in his jaw was jumping so hard that I could detect it even in the low light of the bar.

"Okay, okay, let's walk. Let me tell Emmy to box up the pizza. We'll get it to go."

Bishop didn't answer me, but he stood in the same place while I went up to the bar. I paid our check and explained we'd been unexpectedly called away. Emmy's face fell so far, I almost felt sorry for her—until she returned my credit card with her phone number on the slip. And it was not for me.

I'd give it to him later, once I knew what was going on. I wasn't sure a meaningless bounce was what he needed. Maybe a monastery was a better solution.

Grabbing the pizza box, I motioned to Bishop across the bar and he followed me outside. It had started to rain, and the streets gleamed wetly under the streetlights as we walked silently to my new Jeep.

He stopped dead and stared. "What the hell's this?"

"Got a new vehicle."

"A truck? You?" Shaking his head, he pocketed his glasses. "You planning ahead for the 2.5 kids, Shaw? Jesus."

I wasn't aiming for kids, exactly, but yeah, I was planning ahead. "The Lexus never suited me."

"Since when? Since your hot little assistant filled in while—Jesus. Jesus." He leaned against the side of my Jeep and raked his hand through his hair.

"Have you become religious? If so, my girlfriend the witch will probably try to counsel you onto another path."

He didn't move. I wasn't sure he was even still breathing. "The witch?"

"More like a kitchen witch, but yeah."

"What the fuck is that?"

"Look it up. I'm not your *Witches for Dummies* guidebook."

"I'm not the dummy here."

"Jury's out on that."

"A *witch*, Shaw? Like with a broom and cauldron and cackling?"

"Do some research. Your mind needs opening."

"Right." He snorted. *"My* mind's the flawed one."

I leaned back against the Jeep beside him and resigned myself to getting soaked. He didn't seem concerned with petty considerations like damp clothes. "Don't knock it until you try it."

"How many women could be named Ryan?"

Since he'd asked the question under his breath, I wasn't sure if I was supposed to weigh in.

Then he glared at me, slicking his already dripping hair back from his face. "Well?"

"Are you looking for statistics or anecdotal research?"

"Do you have statistics?"

"Hmm. No."

"This is why I don't hang out with you more. You're exasperating."

"You don't hang out with me more because whenever you ask, I'm working." I flicked water off the pizza box. I should put it inside the Jeep, but I didn't want to set him off again since I wasn't quite sure what had done it the last time.

This was why I avoided socialization. It was almost as full of pitfalls as dating.

"Yeah." He frowned. "Good point. Why aren't you working?"

The evening's agenda hadn't panned out thus far, so it was time to admit defeat. "Remember how I said I quit my job? Recall that?"

"What?" He practically roared the word.

"I told you on the phone when you were in Fiji."

He rubbed his forehead, swiping away water. "Yeah. Shit. I've been so wrapped up in my own stuff. No excuse." Turning toward me, he clamped his arms around me in a bear hug. "About fucking time. We need to celebrate."

I hugged him back then retreated. "Yeah, hold off on that. Can we discuss this out of the rain?"

"Yeah." He shook back his damp hair, scattering even more rain on me. At this point, what was some more?

But he didn't move.

"Stone, if you've got something to say—"

"You mentioned someone named April on the phone."

A tiny noose descended around my throat from unseen hands above me. Did this count as some kind of kismet, as well? Had I pissed off some goddess in a previous life? I'd been allotted enough fortune to meet and fall in love with my moonbeam, but that was it.

Now I was paying the piper. If Bishop and April had hooked up in Fiji, and she'd run from him...well, I was the closest thing to the woman herself and therefore, suitable to kill.

Then again, so was Ryan.

I drew myself up to my full height. If my feet squished, so be it. "You'll have to get through me to get to her."

"Oh, is that so?" He stepped closer.

I moved forward until I was nearly standing on his shoes. Rain pelted us with the ferocity of the glare in Bishop's eyes. "That's so. I love her, and I'm prepared to withstand your wrath."

"You love her," he said slowly.

"Yes."

"Since when did you come up with so much love for so many

people? The last time I saw you, you were lamenting the fact that a woman from the Chinese takeout place had dared to ask you out."

"I wasn't lamenting. But when a guy says no after the third time you've tucked your number into a fortune cookie…"

"Preston, shut up and tell me why the hell you're in love with April."

"April?" I sputtered out a laugh as I shook back my wet hair like a dog. Not flattering, but the comparison was apt. "What? Sorry, pal, talking to the wrong Shaw brother there. Though love isn't the word I'd use for Dex's feelings for her. If he even has any. The fucker won't be straight about what happened between them."

"Dexter touched April? When?" Bishop grabbed my shoulders. "Start talking before I go over to your brother's place and talk to him myself. And I can assure you, I'll get the answers I'm looking for."

All at once, I realized the joke was over. And it was on me.

Usually, I processed information rapidly. It was actually one of my best skills under normal circumstances. But I'd been off all night, probably due in no small part to my mind and other vital appendages being focused on Ryan's naked body.

Add in the fact that Bishop seemed incapable of saying his direct thoughts along with my being out of practice at handling his doublespeak, and it seemed as if the chances of my buddy taking over my position in the firm grew slimmer with every passing moment.

Maybe he shouldn't. My best friend was clearly on the ropes. He was exhausted and running on empty. I'd chalked up most of it to emotional chaos. But there could be more. He hadn't taken a vacation in forever and pushed himself way too hard.

If working at my father's firm was slowly killing me, why did I want to saddle my best friend with working there? Divorce law was a perfectly acceptable specialty, but I wanted to focus on the other specialties of family law—the ones that dealt with keeping families together, not tearing them apart.

As for Bishop, I wasn't sure what he wanted. He might not be happy where he was now—and that was more a gut feeling than anything firm—but my role in my father's firm was far from an improvement. If Bishop didn't want to take over for me, I couldn't blame him.

I squinted at him in the slanting rain. "We need to figure this out."

He didn't respond.

"Let's backtrack," I added before he hauled off and hit me. He wasn't prone to such actions, but love made fools of us all.

Not to mention missing dinner.

"Then start talking some sense, because right now, you aren't making any."

I switched hands on the pizza box and used my sleeve to wipe off my cheek. "You told me on the phone her name wasn't April."

His jaw locked. "I didn't know it was April."

"You're saying it *was* April? You went on vacation to sleep with my assistant?" I gave him a good hard shove, belatedly realizing our increasingly loud argument had gotten the attention of more than a couple of passing customers. "She's gotten damn popular lately."

"There you go again, asshole. What are you intimating is going on with her and Dexter? If he's been fucking her too—"

"*Too?* Here I was thinking you might want my position in the firm, and you're balling my assistant."

CHAPTER THIRTEEN

Bishop

I STARED at my best friend with the increasingly angry rain slashing between us and echoing on the cardboard box Preston was now brandishing like a shield. One thought was looping over and over in my head.

Her name is April.

She wasn't just my mystery woman anymore. My Cinderella. The woman who'd filleted my heart and tossed it into the sea before taking off without a backward glance.

And I could make fun of my best friend for falling in love with a witch? I'd become more fanciful than any twisted fairytale.

As for the rest of what he said, what the hell?

"I have my own firm," I said as if we'd just met and he was ten steps behind.

"Yeah, you do, but you're not happy there." He lifted his voice above the rain. My clothes were sticking uncomfortably to my skin and still, all I could think of was April. "You keep dumping more and more work on Eli."

"No, I don't. He likes the work. He's taking on more by his own choice. As is Cord."

"Even so, where you are now, you're just a cog in a wheel. One of the biggest cogs, but if you came to work at Shaw, you'd be the top dog." He blew out a breath and said something I couldn't comprehend. He seemed at war with himself. "Shit, why am I arguing for this? I'm not his shill."

"The top dog with Dexter, you mean?" I could barely keep from spitting the name, although before the last hour, I'd liked the dude.

I wasn't as close to him as I was to Preston, but we'd always gotten along just fine. Truth be told, on the surface, I had a hell of a lot more in common with Dex than Preston.

Christ, did April have a type? Did she like players, despite all her assertions to the contrary? And when exactly had they hooked up? Had I primed the pump, so to speak, for her to come back and get naked with Preston's brother?

I growled and turned to brace my fists against the hood of Preston's Jeep. Damn good thing Dex wasn't here right now because I wasn't at all sure I wouldn't kick his ass.

And for what? Maybe sleeping with a woman I'd slept with too? One who had told me she hadn't been with anyone for a long time? But she'd run out on me without a word, so could I trust anything she said, period?

Even if it had seemed as if I could. I'd looked into her gaze and knew how she felt deep down. Words got in our way sometimes, but her expressive hazel eyes told the truth.

Or so I'd thought.

"Look, let's get inside. Whether we talk here or my house, I don't care. Our damn pizza is probably waterlogged."

Considering the cardboard box seemed to be sinking onto itself and was totally drenched, that was a good guess.

"Yeah." I exhaled. "All right, a few minutes in the bar." I motioned for him to head inside.

At least the rain had cooled our tempers. God knows we were both soaked through to the bone.

Emmy took one look at us and offered to remake our pizza on the house. She even brought another basket of fried vegetables to the surprisingly isolated table she found for us in the back of the bar.

As soon as we sat down again and mopped our faces with the napkins, Preston leaned forward. "Start at the beginning."

I didn't bother trying to divert him. More than anything, I needed to talk to my best friend. "Yeah, well, before I start there, you need to know I wasn't entirely honest on the phone."

He merely cocked a brow.

"I didn't know her name. We decided on no strings and she stuck to that. I called her Cinderella. Scandalized?"

"What, people having sex without benefit of a wedding ring? Well, I'll be." He placed a hand over his heart and rolled his eyes. "I'll have you know that Ryan and I desecrated the bench in my yard."

"I'm thoroughly stunned."

He shrugged. "I'm opening my mind. Continue."

"The pineapple slices were actually chocolate-covered strawberries, because they had to substitute fruits after I got off the phone with you. I was just planning to eat them off her when we talked. But we did enjoy the strawberries."

"I'm so glad."

"And I never got around to asking her to come back with me. I was getting there though." I unwrapped my silverware and poked listlessly at a fried cauliflower before dragging it onto my plate.

"So, you lied about a lot."

"Not lied, exactly. I just painted a picture of what I wished was reality. If I'd thought she would come back with me, I would've asked."

"So, you hang back and hope for the best? That's your style now?"

He had a valid point. What the hell was I doing? I wasn't the sort of guy not to make my thoughts known. Or to just stand back and let things happen to me.

"We knew each other for under two days. I made it seem like it was longer. I figured you'd tell me I was fucking crazy, which wouldn't have been out of left field. It was. It *is*. But it felt right. She made me laugh. I haven't done that in so long." I speared my cauliflower and popped it in my mouth, burning my tongue.

Fit my life lately.

"Here you go, gentlemen." Emmy nudged aside our basket of

vegetables with the piping hot pizza. "Hope you enjoy. And here's a fresh stack of napkins." She slid them on the table and offered me a wink. "Let me know if you need any assistance."

"Thanks so much. You're a lifesaver." I flashed her a weak smile and ate a fried zucchini, ignoring the accompanying sting from my burn.

We ate in companionable silence for a few minutes.

"I'm done with women."

Preston snorted as he pried off peppers and dumped them on my plate. Apparently, he was giving the onions a go. "Sure you are. Just like my brother. The two of you are supreme horndogs." Before I could speak, he held up a hand. "I'll admit, I forgot some of the finer points of the joys of sex. You can say I've seen the light."

"Don't rub it in." I ate Preston's discarded peppers. "It was so good. I mean, so, so good. Like good enough you don't even care she won't give you her name if she'll just keep sleeping with you."

"Huh."

"Fine, that's a lie."

"Another one? You're stacking them up."

"She's has me all twisted up, man. I didn't want to let her go, but I couldn't figure out how to make her stay."

"Here's a novel idea. Try telling her what you want."

"I was going to, then she split. Broken Cinderella heel and all." Recapping that final afternoon was no picnic, but I had to get it out.

All of it.

"I never intended to take that vacation, but my doctor said it was an imperative. Once that ocean air and sunshine soaked into me, I realized I'd needed it. I hadn't even taken a weekend off in forever. I hadn't been with a woman. I hadn't even spent time with friends."

"Your doctor?"

"Yeah. I've been having some issues." I ate a slice of pizza then went back for more fried cauliflower, since Preston didn't seem to be touching it.

"Like what?"

"Stress-related. I had a full work-up. I'm fine. Just dealing with some quickened breaths and rapid heartbeats. Panic attacks is what they're called." I hoped like hell my cheeks weren't red. Admitting the word panic was part of my life on any level wasn't easy. "But at first, I thought I was having a heart attack."

"Jesus, Bishop, what the hell? Why is this the first I'm hearing about this?" Preston reached across the table to grab my forearm. "Are you okay? Level with me."

"I'm fine, seriously." His concern made me smile. Best friends or not, we didn't spend the amount of time together we once had, mostly due to work conflicts.

"Can I help? If there's anything I can do, just give me a damn hint. You're family."

Emotion clogged in my throat and I laughed to make it dissipate. "Same, brother. Better than my own, except Mickey."

"Mickey is pretty awesome." Sitting back, Preston crossed his hands over his stomach as he studied me. "Did you even get a tan? I can't tell in this low light."

"Yeah, a little. We spent a lot of time in the room."

"I'm still having trouble reconciling this with April. *My* April. Metaphorically speaking," he added as I lifted a brow. "Don't get me wrong, she's a fine assistant. Very capable and intelligent. But she's not exactly wild."

"Who's to say who we are? Don't we get to decide that?"

"You leaped to her defense so readily." He flashed me a quick grin. "I'm glad to see it. For her and for you. I was beginning to think you couldn't get any deeper than a puddle with a woman any more. Fucking Rina." He didn't even bother de-peppering his next piece of pizza before he started to eat.

Either they were growing on him or he was more consumed by my story than I'd realized.

"We'd only just begun to get to know each other. But it felt good, being with her. I wanted to learn more about her. To see if we were compatible in more ways than just—"

"Being naked?"

I pulled another slice of pizza onto my plate. "Something like that."

"So, you went to Fiji and fell in—"

"Fell in interest," I said, cutting him off.

"Right. Fell in *interest.* Anyway, and then you came back here and went back to the same job that was slowly draining the life out of you."

"So melodramatic." At his hard stare, I released a long breath. "Yeah. Okay. Fine. It takes a lot out of me. But that's my own fault."

"You go harder than two lawyers, so yeah, that is your own fault. But you can walk away, you know. You're not chained to your damn desk."

"Walk away from being a lawyer? Or just walk into the spot you no longer want?"

My buddy gazed at me for a long moment before dumping his half piece of pizza with a splatter of cheese and grease. "That's fair. But I never really wanted it. I just never had the balls to admit what I did want. Or to even take the time to explore my options." He finished his slice and went back for another, then dropped a few peppers on my plate almost sympathetically. "Have you ever considered yours?"

"I'm good at being a lawyer."

"No arguments. You're the absolute best."

"That doesn't mean I can't check out other avenues." I ate a few bites, chewing and swallowing. "Tell me about the kinds of cases you have on your plate right now."

A short while later, the large pizza was mostly gone, and I'd decided I was going to spend Monday at Shaw, Shaw, and Shaw getting the lay of the land. Whether that meant I'd be leaving my firm remained to be seen.

"This isn't a guarantee of anything."

"I get that. I appreciate you taking the time to give it a shot. And if it doesn't feel right, just say no. I'm not sugarcoating my father's firm. This may just be you climbing out of one cesspool into another. I don't want that for me—or you."

I nodded as we paid the bill, ignoring Emmy's generous offer to pick up the tab for us. We also tipped her heavily. "I appreciate you entrusting your family's legacy to me. If it works out," I added.

"Yeah." He cocked his head, jockeying the box of leftovers I'd foisted onto him. I wouldn't have eaten what was left. "My father's a dick. So that is part of that whole legacy."

"Familial dickdom is often passed down. Not too surprising."

"Yeah." He exhaled roughly. "You're not trying it out because of April, are you?" He didn't let me answer before he continued. "If you are, I don't begrudge you that. I would've followed Ryan to the ends of the damn earth to make a go of things with her. As it was, I almost did." He chuckled. "Freaking Rainbow."

I didn't know what that meant, and I was too spent to ask. "April is a factor. I want to see her again. But now that I know she's here in Kensington Square, I wouldn't need your job to talk to her."

"Truth."

I pushed my fingers through my drenched hair. "I just can't believe we were that close all along. What are the odds?"

"Kismet," my best friend said sagely. "The universe is always at work."

"I'm kind of scared of this woman of yours."

"You should be. But just remember—my woman is best friends with *your* woman, so talk is cheap, dude."

I laughed and dipped back my head to stare up at the cloudy sky. The rain had momentarily slowed. Pity. It matched my mood.

What the hell was I supposed to do now?

"It'll all work out. Trust me. And I'll see you Monday morning."

"You will." I held out a hand to him, and he pulled me in for a quick, hard hug. "Thanks. For everything."

He drew back, still examining my face far too closely. "Thank *you*. Sure you don't want to, I don't know, shoot some pool? It's been a while since I've trounced your ass."

"You wish, Shaw. Go home to your woman." As thunder crackled in the air, I made myself laugh. Maybe the storm wasn't over yet. "See, there's your sign. We'll talk later."

He frowned at me, and I tried not to laugh at the image he made with his wet hair sticking out at all angles from his head. I also wouldn't be jealous thinking about him going home to cozy up with his witchy chick while I went home to Santiago, who still hadn't forgiven me for daring to leave him in the care of the pet sitter. He still wanted to get out to see the poodle down the hall, but too bad, bird. If I wasn't getting any romance, neither was he.

Especially the cross-species kind.

"You could come with me."

"I'm not a threesome kind of guy, but thanks for the offer." I grinned and backed up toward my black Nissan SUV. "Have a good night."

"We'll see, since now I have onion breath, you bastard."

I laughed and climbed behind the wheel. The laughter lasted until Preston's taillights disappeared out of the lot. He was clearly in a hurry to get home.

Who could blame him?

I was curious about the woman who'd snagged his attention, even if I'd made fun of her…occupation? Was witchery a job or a vocation? In any case, regret curdled in my belly. He seemed happy. Happier than I'd ever seen him, aside from our petty argument and difficult conversation. What kind of best friend was I to tarnish something that seemed so good for him?

A crappy one.

A crappy, jealous, selfish one.

But I'd make it up to him. I'd cook dinner and have them over some night soon. That way I could also properly vet the new chick without being distracted. That was what a friend was supposed to do. I could be happy for him and still look out for the guy. It was my damn job.

As for the other job on the table, I wasn't going there tonight. I couldn't deny that the idea of being entirely my own boss—other than working with Dexter, who was currently at the top of my shit list until I determined otherwise—intrigued me, but there were too many other considerations.

I'd worked my way up in the Pierson law group until my name was nearly as synonymous with the firm as the founding partners. Walking away from that history required an offer worthy of—

"Bullshit," I muttered.

That was money-minded Bishop talking. This was about so much more.

Loyalty. Fidelity. Family.

Three things with a price tag way more than money.

With a flick of my wrist, the truck came to life and the windshield wipers swished futilely at the deluge. The next time we went to Lonegan's, it would be under much different circumstances. I intended to make sure of it.

And somehow, though I'd demolished part of a pizza and some fried vegetables, I was still hungry.

I needed something more. Something that involved Mickey time.

It didn't take me long to reach the university section of Syracuse, the city just outside Kensington Square. I drove down tree-lined streets lined with stately mansions, their warm lights burning to keep out the dark. College students clutched warm cups of coffee as they talked and laughed, seemingly unconcerned about the rejuvenated storm. They huddled under hoodies and umbrellas as they kissed and did God knows what else.

Squinting, I made sure none of those cozied-up students happened to be the one I was looking for. Luckily for both of our sakes, she wasn't.

I shot into the last open parking space at the curb in front of a frat house at the end of the block. It was obviously a party night, judging from the noise level and the amount of students spilling down the towering flight of steps from the wide open front door. While I watched, some enterprising young man did a headstand on a porch railing and tumbled into the hedges with a beer-fueled shriek.

Had I ever been that young and stupid? Definitely on the second. The first felt very far away right now.

I grabbed my phone and texted my sister.

Tell me you're home.

She replied quickly.

And if I'm not?

If you're not, come meet me at the diner.

Aw, damn, I'm studying. Now u put the idea of whipped cream on a stack of hot waffles in my head.

Now she'd put it in mine too. I'd be doing a couple extra sessions at the gym this week.

Works for me. I'm parked outside of PZP. I'll drive us.

Now u're talking. Give me 5.

She only needed four. That was my always speedy baby sister.
"Hey, jerk." Michaela shook off the rain as she slid inside my truck and gave me a quick once-over. "You're soaked."
"You too."
"Nice night out there. Finally decided to show proof of life, huh?"
"Yeah, well, I like to do that now and then so you don't find another brother you like better." The words were out of my mouth before I realized what I was saying.
I did my damnedest not to remember I had a brother most days. I wasn't sure if Mickey did too. We didn't talk about Key.
"Not gonna happen," she said lightly before rolling down the passenger window to lean out and yell something indecipherable at someone passing on the sidewalk. She slid back inside with a giggle that made the weight strapped to my shoulders fall away, just for that one moment. "Sorry." She snapped on her belt. "Had to say bye to my man."
"Your man? Since when?"
"Since last week. Would you rather I have a woman?"
I thought about it as I signaled away from the curb and merged into traffic. "Depends. Both sexes have their strengths and weaknesses."

"True. But I'm strictly dickly." She punched my upper arm. "What about you?"

"I'm definitely not strictly dickly, and you shouldn't be either. The semester just started. You need to be focused on your last year of classes, not…dick."

"You're worse than Dad. He doesn't ask me about boys."

"No, as long as you don't come home pregnant, I guarantee he doesn't give a solitary shit."

"There's truth in that statement. What about you?" she asked again.

"I guarantee I won't be coming home pregnant."

"Ugh, you are not even funny. I mean, you were on vacation, right? You bought the killer dress for your princess."

"My princess?"

"She sounded like one the way you described her. I expected you to text me you'd run off to elope or something and then nada."

"If we wanted to elope, Fiji theoretically is the place some would run to. So we would've been perfectly located for such."

"Bishop."

I headed downtown to the all-night diner, well aware I was pissing off my sister. My mood had already lifted just from the easy, familiar rhythm of our conversation. "Hmm?"

"What happened with her?"

"Nothing princess-worthy, sorry to inform you."

"She didn't like the dress?"

"Oh, she loved the dress."

"And the Cinderella shoes? I found the perfect ones."

Michaela had definitely been my secret wardrobe weapon, that was for sure. "You did. She kept staring at them. Until one broke when she was running away from me." I let out a dry laugh. "Actually, I'll take it back. There were some fairytale aspects, minus the pumpkin chariot. Unfortunately, I didn't have one of those on standby."

"Aw, Bish. You should've stopped me."

"From asking questions? Nah. It is what it is. And you helped me, so you deserve to know what happened."

"A total bust happened is what it sounds like." She flopped back in her seat. "She wore your cute clothes and split? That's cold."

"Not exactly what happened." I signaled into the parking lot behind the diner, veering into one of the few free spaces. Date night and apparently, the diner was the happening place to be.

No wonder women got so excited about Cinderella shoes if diner meals were among the options being presented to them.

"Then?"

I unsnapped my seatbelt. "Let's stuff ourselves, and you can tell me about your man."

"Not if you're not telling me about your princess. Although she's sounding more like an ice queen at the moment."

I didn't respond. She'd put waffles in my head, and that was preferable to thinking about April. The name fit her. Like the first blush of spring before full bloom.

Yeah, I needed to stop the sappy comparisons before I started talking in haiku or something equally flowery. Or worse yet, found my own kitchen witch. I needed to look that up.

When we were tucked into a booth in back with our waffles smothered in mounds of whipped cream and maple syrup, plus a plate of crispy bacon to share—make that three extra gym sessions this week—I told her the sanitized version of what had happened in Fiji.

She didn't say a word until I was finished, when she leaned forward and exclaimed, "You didn't chase after her? You just let her dick you over?" At a level just loud enough for the nearest three tables to cease all conversation to stare at me.

Hey, I'd be curious to see who the dickless wonder was too.

"Thanks, Mickey," I muttered, squirting an unnecessarily large amount of maple syrup on the remnants of her waffles.

She just kept eating. Sugar was her drug. And it better have been her only drug, or I'd do my best dad impression and totally blow up her spot.

Whatever that meant.

"Sorry, but it's gotta be said."

"And you said it so most of Syracuse could hear. Appreciate it." I set down my fork and leaned back in the booth. "Turns out, I know where she is."

"What? You do? Where is she? Did she ghost you and just hide on the island until you left?"

"No, I'm pretty sure she left that day and came home." I took a deep breath. Saying the words would make it true, and then I'd have to do something about what I'd learned. "She lives in Kensington Square." At least I assumed she did, since she worked for Preston. Or close enough.

Michaela's brown eyes widened comically. "No."

"Yes."

"Nooooo."

Now I was smiling. I couldn't help myself. "Yessss."

"What are the odds your shipwrecker would live in the same town? Oh my God." She pressed her fingers to her lips. "How completely *meant*."

CHAPTER FOURTEEN

Bishop

I RUBBED the furrow between my brows. Was the entire world made up of foolish romantics now, or was it just the people who were important to me?

"Not you too." Weariness lined my voice. "And at no point were we on a ship."

She waved that off as insignificant. "It is. You can't argue it. You live here forever and never meet, then you go to a far-off land to screw like—"

"Hey, hey. Keep it clean or I'm not telling you any more perverted bedtime stories."

Her grin over the rim of her soda held much mischief. "I can tell some to myself."

I covered my ears. "Not listening, la-la-la."

Her expression turned serious as she shoved aside our nearly empty plates and leaned forward to snatch my hands, pulling them down from my head. "What're you gonna do? For real."

"The question of the hour." I gripped her hands. "She ran from me, Mick. I searched all over the damn island. I get that she was probably pretty pissed that I'd talked to her grandmother without asking her first—"

"As she had every right to be," my sister interjected. "Don't do that 'I know better than you' shit. Chicks don't like it. Humans, period, don't like it. Sisters absolutely hate it."

My lips twitched around a smile. "Duly noted. But she didn't even say goodbye."

"How could she? Like there was any way in hell you would've let her just walk."

"What do you mean, I wouldn't let her walk? How could I stop her?"

"You could and you would. Your words are enough. You're very commanding when you want to be, Mr. Million Dollar Divorce Lawyer. And spoiler alert—you always want to be."

I frowned down at our linked hands. I still hadn't let her go. This conversation wasn't exactly making it easier for me to move back, either.

"I wouldn't *force* her to stay to talk to me. What kind of man do you think I am?"

"A strong, proud one who lashes out when he's been hurt. Dude, you've been hurt a lot. And you're jaded and ready to draw blood at the first chance someone is pissing in your Cheerios."

I locked my jaw and glanced away, studying the rain-slickened windows at the front of the diner where the neon pink Open sign blinked on and off. My sister knew better than anyone what had gone down almost four years ago. It had probably been a mistake to dump all of that on my barely eighteen-year-old sister, but after what Key had done, I'd had literally no one to turn to except her and Preston, my best man.

Even my parents hadn't been on my side. My dad had aligned himself with Key, as always, and my mother had claimed she was neutral like Switzerland. Total bullshit. Our relationship had never been the same since.

"And now you're not going to talk to me, because I hurt your wittle manly feels."

Not laughing at her was impossible, so I didn't try. "I'm definitely still talking to you. You're right."

"I am?"

"Yeah." I squeezed her fingers, grateful she was letting me hold on just a moment more. "I treat every negotiation like a case. I can't do that in a personal relationship. Especially with a woman. It's just been so long."

"Did you forget your steps?"

"Yeah. I think I did. She's not an opponent I can strong-arm. I tried hanging back and playing cool, and she left."

"You playing cool is anyone else making demands."

I narrowed my eyes. "But if I don't take control, if I don't show that I'm capable of—"

"Ripping her throat out if she so much looks at another man?" Mickey's voice gentled. "She's not Rina, Bish. At least she better not be anything like her, or I'll kick your ass myself."

"No. April's nothing like her. Even after not spending all that long with her, I know that."

The waitress returned to collect our dishes, but first, she gave me a lengthy glance before diverting her gaze to our linked hands.

"Bit young for you, isn't she?"

"Oh." I laughed uncomfortably. "She's my sister."

That didn't make her glacial gaze warm. If anything, her voice turned frostier. "Real nice, buddy." She swept away our plates with a "harrumph" that made Mickey dissolve into giggles.

I wasn't much better.

My sister shook her head. "Man, some people have really dirty minds."

"That's the truth. But real life is usually worse than most people even guess." My shudder wasn't entirely fake. The things I saw on a weekly basis were often horrifying.

And going to Preston's family's firm likely wouldn't change that. If it was much better than what I routinely dealt with, why would he be checking out?

He wouldn't. It wasn't just about family dynamics either. Issac Shaw wasn't a prince. He definitely didn't play by the rules. Truly, I was surprised Pres had lasted there as long as he had.

Was it any coincidence he'd made the decision to leave as soon as he'd found someone else to worry about other than work? Probably not. We all just wanted someone to come home to at night.

And I needed to stop having thoughts like that. I had someone to come home to, and his name was Santiago. He wasn't great at spooning, but he gave out his own snippy version of kisses.

My sister retreated across the table to check her phone, a grin creeping across her face.

"You like him."

She blinked. "He who?"

"Your man." I did air quotes.

"Yeah, he's a good dude. Seems to be, anyway. Early yet. What about your girl?"

"Not again."

"Did we solve your dilemma?"

"No. You don't even know the half of it." I pulled out my credit card and handed it to our disgusted waitress when she returned. She bustled away as if she couldn't stand to be near heathens like us.

She'd pegged one of us correctly as a heathen, but not for the reason she suspected.

Fame-hungry divorce attorney, at your service—if you've got the green.

But there were other opportunities on the horizon.

Preston's footloose, fancy free brother was a managing partner at Shaw times Three, LLC, and he couldn't be trusted to run the firm alone. With Daddy Warbucks—also known as the elder Shaw—retiring, the idea of Dexter piloting the plane was, frankly, a disaster waiting to happen. Just because the fit wasn't good for Preston didn't mean it would be bad for me.

But was I ready to walk from a very successful career with the Pierson law group just to help out my best friend?

And significantly reduce your stress levels and maybe get closer to achieving that fabled work/life balance you've never figured out? And oh, hey, get to work with April? Remember her?

Mickey flicked her finger against my glass to get my attention. "Um, hello, big brother, sitting right here. Stop thinking so hard smoke comes out of your ears and start talking. What else is going on?" She rolled her eyes. "As if there isn't enough already."

Quickly, I told her about Preston's little surprise this evening. Rather than seeming shocked, her eyes widened and she squirmed on her seat. "Yes, yes, yes! Dr. Vader will be so happy. When do you start?"

I frowned. "That's it? Just yay, you're doing it?"

"Preston's your best friend. Like in the whole world."

"Yeah." No arguments there. "But did you miss the part where I'll be taking his place? We won't be working together."

"Maybe not full-time, but you could. Don't you guys like consult on cases or whatever? You know he'll keep his hand in, especially in the beginning."

"More like especially with Dexter."

"Yeah." She winced. "Pres thinks he's a total slack-ass, right?"

I shrugged. "Let's just say he has more to occupy his time than work."

"Babes, babes, and more babes?"

"Not my concern." Unless he didn't do his share of the work or, more importantly, was dipping his wick in April's pot.

Look at me, already thinking as if I might actually take this job. I hadn't even considered all the pros and cons.

Hell, I wouldn't even *know* all the pros and cons until my meeting with Preston on Monday.

"Not unless you're smart enough to realize when a plum opportunity just falls into your lap. You said April's his assistant. You need to work less. To not swim with the sharkiest of deadly sharks. You've already proven you can dominate them all. Now you can prove you can be a decent boss and maybe help some Moms and Pops find their way to their happily-ever-afters." She nibbled on her thumbnail. "And hey, maybe find your own."

"I'm a divorce attorney, not a marriage therapist."

"You don't offer counseling as part of your package? Maybe you should. Don't you think some people make a mistake?"

I rubbed the sudden piercing pain in my forehead. "Some people's mistake is ever getting married in the first place, Mick." I lowered my voice. "And call me crazy, but I'm pretty sure I'm the last person who should ever offer marriage counseling to anyone. Forget professionally. I shouldn't even mention the words."

"So, that's just your badge of honor now? You're 'Bad at Love' like Halsey, so that gives you an excuse for acting like a dick for all eternity?"

"Hey."

She held up her hands. "Just saying."

"You do realize that a divorce attorney makes an income from people, I don't know, actually getting *divorced?*"

She let out a heavy sigh. "Yeah, like you're scrounging through the couch for change. You're already a bazillionaire. Think about the greater good."

"Don't let Dad hear you talking like this. He'll disown you for sure."

"Lucky me, I have no need for cheddar because my big brother freaking adores me and would give me all his worldly goods." She batted her lashes and held her hands under her chin as if she was praying.

I signed off on the check when Disturbed Waitress reappeared. Once she'd left again, I laughed and shook my head. My sister was still in praying stance. "God help me, but I do."

"As you should. When you were on your own, who was by your side?"

"You," I pointed out.

She waved that off. "Yeah, but I'm not hiring anyone. Yet," she added with an air of significance I would explore later.

"Fine. Preston."

"He let you sponge off him for months."

"I wouldn't say I sponged—"

"I would. He made certain you ate and slept, and I'm sure he talked shit about bitches and hoes—"

"Michaela," I warned.

"Hi, Rina is both, so don't even go there with me."

"She's also your sister-in-law," I said tiredly.

"Right. Like I have anything to do with the two of them."

I should've argued with her that she should. They were her family, and unlike my parents, she shouldn't have to choose between us.

What's the difference, jackass?

I didn't know, exactly, but there just was one.

"You owe Preston, even if he'd say otherwise. But he's trusting you with his family biz. That's gotta be huge for him. And it seems like you're just writing it off as not an option, as if you're happy. As if you've been happy for years."

I shut my eyes. "Taking a job for a chick is a catastrophe waiting to happen."

"Yeah, maybe, if that's why you'd be taking it. She's just…frosting. Decadent chocolate ganache, but the cake is your best friend and the chance to, I don't know, conquer a different frontier or some shit. You'd be taking care of your health. And maybe you could even get to know April outside the bedroom." She slapped her palms to her cheeks. "I know, *gasp*."

"I never exactly said—"

"If a guy falls in love with a chick in a night or two, they didn't have marathon Scrabble sessions. I'm a college student, not a cave dweller."

"I'm not in love with her."

"Right. Just like I wouldn't have Harry Styles' babies if he decided he found sociology nerds hot." Even as I laughed, she stared imploringly into my eyes. "Just think about it. Seriously, why would you say no?"

That question replayed over and over in my head after I dropped off Mick. The rain had finally stopped, and instead of heading home to tend to my doubtlessly aggrieved bird, I drove in circles until the chaos in my mind smoothed out into a semblance of certainty.

I stiffened my shoulders and hit my best friend's number on the in-dash screen.

He took so long to answer that I finally remembered he was probably playing marathon Scrabble this very minute. I even hoped he'd gotten a high score 7-letter word. Now he needed to recover enough to pick up the frigging phone.

As if he'd heard me, he came on the line.

"Bishop?" He sounded perturbed, not as if he was in a state of orgasmic euphoria.

That made two of us.

"Yeah. Did I interrupt something?" Somehow I managed not to snicker like a twelve-year-old boy, but it was a close thing.

"Look, man, you okay? I didn't like how we left things before."

I growled. "Are you gunning for sainthood?"

"Huh?"

"You're supposed to be PO'd at me because I interrupted your sex bliss."

"Oh. That. Am I? Maybe I would be if we hadn't already had it twice. Hey, stop hitting me, dammit."

I had to laugh at the obvious sounds of a struggle. I liked Ryan already. "Good. Then you can listen to me for a minute."

"Sixty seconds. Clock's running, Stone."

I tapped my fingers on the wheel. "After it all went down with Rina and Key, I took advantage of your generosity."

"You absolutely did not."

"I did. I lived on your couch for half a year and took my sweet ass time getting my shit together. You have thrown me my allotment of ropes already for one lifetime, and now here you are again."

"Wrong. You're doing just fine without me."

"Without you, I wouldn't have gotten back up." I shut my eyes. "You and Mick," I corrected. "You're my family, and you stood with me when no one else did. I never thanked you properly for that. And now you're offering me a chance to guard your family's legacy, and I was almost too much of a thoughtless dick to see the gift you were entrusting me with."

Heavy silence descended on the line. "You've been drinking," he said finally.

I had to grin. "No."

"Something harder?"

"Definitely not."

"Hit your head on a curb?"

"Not lately."

Preston hesitated. "I hate to have to ask this, but you'll have to forgive me."

"Shoot."

"You're not planning some kind of revenge on April, are you? Because I'd stand with you against the devil, Stone, you know that. But I can't be part of something that could hurt her. She's dealt with enough, and beyond that, she doesn't deserve anything but your best treatment. No matter what mistakes she's made."

I only heard part of what he said. "Dealt with what? What has she dealt with?"

"I only know bits and pieces. She's not one to mix business and pleasure."

"What do you know?"

"I'm sorry. You'll have to ask her."

"Goddamn you and your ethics, Shaw." Hell if I didn't admire him for sticking to them. There were far too many times in my life I'd thought I was entitled—even righteous—to abandon mine. "Thank you for thinking of her first." I let out a raw laugh. "Even risking my wrath."

"You don't scare me." He coughed. "But that one time we were opposing counsel, I really did have strep throat and couldn't come to court."

I hadn't laughed so hard in a long time.

Correction. It wasn't that long in actual days, even if it felt that way. Not since Fiji.

"Just promise me you're not doing this for any reasons other than you're saying. You're a dangerous animal when you've been hurt. I know she hurt you, though maybe she had a good reason."

"Pretty sure Rina thought wanting to ride my brother's dick was a good reason too." I pinched the ache in the bridge of my nose.

"Christ."

I sucked in a deep breath. Michaela had been my compass since she'd been old enough to string sentences together, and once again, she was pointing due north.

Even when I didn't believe in anything, I believed in my baby sister. She thought I should do this. So, I was giving it a fucking go.

All I could lose was everything.

"I promise, Pres. You can trust me."

"By God, I do. Don't make me regret this, Stone."

Staring out into the darkness, I punched the gas as I neared my place. "Let's hope neither of us have any regrets. This isn't a guarantee. Just a trial period. I have my own clients to think about, and you know how thorny it is to extricate yourself. I have to see if this is the right move for me to make."

If I even knew which way was up anymore. But I had to try.

"Goes without saying. No strings."

My lips twisted. "Funny you should say that."

CHAPTER FIFTEEN

Ryan

"Are you sure this is a good idea?" Lu's voice was worthy of a stage whisper.

"Yes. I took her to lunch, but I know she didn't tell me everything. Now she's ignoring my texts."

"Well, she was just on vacation. She's probably got a mountain of laundry."

Lu and her endless optimism. I gave her a sideways look. "April? C'mon. Besides, we usually text or chat the whole time we do laundry. Unless…distracted."

Okay, so both of us were decidedly distracted these days. And I was definitely falling down on my best friend duties. I was never a woman who ignored her friends for some dick, and I wouldn't be now.

Even if it was exceptional dick.

"Do you think kidnapping is the way to go?"

I flipped my braid over my shoulder.

"Hey." Luna swatted my arm. "I'm behind you."

"Sorry." I peered around the old oak tree on the corner. She lived in a two family house just down the street, and we probably looked suspicious as fuck. The big tree was sort of shading us. "Look, we need to get her drunk and get the real details. PMS is driving me crazy about this thing. April isn't acting herself."

"She told me all about Bishop. Not that she knew his name at the time. I mean, I thought I was bad with the Goldilocks thing."

I arched a brow at her. "We all have stuff going on with our guys. All of us need a girl's night—or day as it were."

Lu blushed and looked away. "Three Musketeers action is definitely on tap."

"Good. Now help me kidnap our best friend."

A woman walking her dog came up on us. "Did you say kidnap?"

I straightened. "Not really. I mean yes, we did." I blew out a breath. "She's our best friend. It's for boyfriend explanation purposes." He wasn't really a boyfriend, but I was going to get the cops called on us if I didn't get this chick to see the light.

"Oh." She toyed with the ends of her hair. "I wish my girlfriends cared enough to do that."

Lu peered around me. "You need new friends. Was the guy a jerk?"

"Definitely. But maybe if they were honest with me instead of patting me on the head, I would have booted him faster." The big white dog she was walking leaned on her and looked up at her adoringly. "At least I got the dog in the divorce."

I crouched in front of the dog. She had sweet little cow print markings on her nose and an autumnal collar. "You got the best deal didn't you?" The dog's tail wagged and she gave me a nose bump before returning to her mistress.

I stood. "So, yeah we're going to make sure she doesn't make a mistake."

"Go get her." She tugged the dog's leash lightly. "Let's go, Olive."

Luna leaned against me with a sigh. "I can't with the cuteness." She bumped my arm. "Her aura was blue, but after you talked to her it was a nice glowy yellow. PMS must be making you mushy."

"Shut up."

"So, are we doing this for Apes or for you?"

I crossed my arms. "Is it bad to say both?"

"No. Makes you honest."

My arms dropped immediately. "More PMS rub-off."

Lu snorted.

"Hussy."

She nodded. "Accurate. And your aura is a lovely pinky-purple these days. My bestie is in lurve."

"Shut up. We're just…doing whatever it is we're doing. Don't make it weird."

"Mmm-hmm."

"Can we just go?"

Things were still so new between PMS and me. I didn't want to pick it apart. I just wanted to keep enjoying it, and that was the end of that story, thanks.

I grabbed Luna's hand and dragged her down the sidewalk to April's house. I had my backup key to get into her place. Sometimes I needed to feed Kit-Kat when April went to visit her grams.

Luna bumped up behind me as I screeched to a halt. April was on her porch, locking her door. Perfect, we didn't even need to convince her to put shoes on.

She spotted us. She went from blank to surprise to suspicious in a few heartbeats. "What are you doing here?"

I linked my arm through Luna's to drag her along. Suddenly she seemed less than excited about this outing. "We're here to kidnap you."

"What? Why?" She blew a stray curl from her messy bun out of her face. "Can't we just have lunch like normal people?"

"Your two best friends are witches honey. There is no normal."

I had long legs and hurriedly climbed the stairs to snag her keys out of her hands.

"Nope. We're having a girl's night."

"I can't. Kit-Kat still hasn't forgiven me for my trip."

"Kit-Kat will be fine. I already cleared it with your neighbor to look in on her."

"Why? I don't need a girl's night."

"The fact that you're fighting this so hard says you do."

"It's been a long—"

"A long week of sitting at your desk doing busy work so you don't have to speak to anyone?"

She frowned at me. "How would you—Preston." Annoyance stiffened her shoulders.

"Our pillow talk involves the office quite a bit."

April's eyes widened. "God, why?"

"Because he's worried about you."

April twisted her fingers. "But during…post coitus? I'm not comfortable with that."

"Post coit-what? Are you watching *Bridget Jones* again?"

April flushed.

I lifted a shoulder. "We talk when we talk. Most of the time we're naked. I can't help that."

"Stop." She held up a hand. "He's my boss. Or will be for a little bit longer."

"PMS is worried about that. He doesn't want to leave you in the lurch, but that place is killing him."

"Maybe it's killing me too." She hooked her thumb into the strap of her purse as if she didn't know what to do with her hands. "I'm quitting. I think."

"What? You can't do that." Luna took a step forward.

"Can we not do this on the porch?" April whispered furiously.

I took the keys from her and unlocked the door. "Evidently we're doing this at your place."

"My house isn't made for a bunch of people."

"Oh, and mine is?" I used her keys and opened the door, dragging them both with me. "Lu, use Insta and get us some food and wine."

"On it."

April's place was feminine farmhouse chic meets thrift store rehab. The soft blue kitchen table was new. A rather lovely floral centerpiece in complimentary yellows and peaches anchored bamboo placemats set up for four people.

I hadn't been in her apartment in awhile. We tended to use Luna's rooftop or our favorite diner when we met up. To be truthful, those were becoming rarer. All of us had a lot going on, but keeping friendships strong was the cornerstone to a full life.

Men were great—more than great. Sometimes not so great, too. They were confounding on a number of levels. I was learning that in spades, but I was pretty sure April was hip deep in the muck of relationship sabotage.

Was it a relationship if you didn't know his name?

Hmm.

April sighed and went to her closet to hang up her purse. Because of course she wouldn't dump her bag on a chair like the rest of us when in a snit. Nope, she methodically hung up her bag and light jacket.

"Would you like something to drink?"

"I want you to not be perfect April for a moment."

Her back went straight as a broom handle.

I went to her, dragging her in for a tight hug.

April's arms were limp at her sides. "What's going on? Is someone dying?"

She wasn't exactly the most demonstrative woman. She always seemed to be holding herself back just a little. As if she was afraid to share too much, give too much, or maybe that it would be taken away.

"Yeah, your love life if you don't start telling us about what really happened in Fiji."

She patted my arms awkwardly. "I told you. I don't think I need to go into blow-by-blow details."

"I'm always down for TMI," Luna said and rushed us, then wrapped her arms around both of us.

As usual, her hugs were literally like warm sunshine. Enough that April relaxed and hugged me back then leaned her head on Lu's shoulder.

"I appreciate the solidarity moment, but there's nothing to tell."

Lu snorted. "Sure. You got rocked into a different zip code a dozen times over. There's plenty to tell." She drew away and unearthed her phone from her rainbow boho bag. "I found a new place that will do one of those charcuterie boards. Pairs with wine and everything. They deliver."

"Excellent." I drew April into her living room and pushed her onto the couch. "We're gonna talk smack about dudes, eat too much, and maybe get a little drunk."

April nibbled on her lower lip. "Maybe we need ice cream too."

"Can do," Luna said with a delighted laugh. "I mean, as long as gelato is cool. This place is a little boujee."

"Salted caramel," me and April said together.

"With chocolate sauce." April slipped her shoes off then curled into the corner of her couch.

I put my hands on my hips. "Were you going somewhere?"

"Does it matter?"

"Kill the prim voice, babe. You've been avoiding me since our lunch."

She picked at the corner of her blush painted nail. "I wasn't. I just don't know how to process all of this. I'm not brave like you two. I don't…do that kind of thing."

"What? Get fucked until you're hoarse from screaming?"

April flushed. "Yeah, that."

I tipped my head. "So, me and Lu are loose women?"

"What? No. I just said you were brave." She sat up so tall I was expecting her spine to rattle.

"You know it's a special thing to find someone like that, right? It's rare."

She went back to picking at her nail until she finally curled it into a fist to stop herself. "I know it's rare. But it's not real. It wasn't real. It was the vacation, the bure, the—"

"Bur-what?"

"Bure. I don't know, that's what he said it was called. It was right on the water and I could hear the waves when I slept." Her cheeks pinked up even more if that were possible. "The little bit that I actually slept anyway."

Lu sat beside her with a sigh. "The water is my favorite. I listen to the ocean or the rain on an app—well, I used to." It was her flush.

"I'm usually passing out with a certain teacher beside me these days."

April laced her fingers together, the knuckles white with pressure. "Doesn't it seem weird that all of us found someone around the same time?"

I sat cross legged in front of her on the floor. "Bit of a chain reaction, it seems. You left PMS in my care and then went and hooked up with his best friend."

April closed her eyes. "I can't even have a vacation fling correctly. My boss's friend? I don't even know his name."

I opened my mouth.

April held up a hand. "No. Don't tell me. I don't want to know."

"Which is very un-April of you." Luna bumped her.

She melted into the couch, scrunching down as she pulled a pillow over her face. "I think it was better that way. Keeping all that reality at bay made it easier to let go."

"Very intuitive of you." I reached for the pillow and flung it onto the love seat behind me then patted her leg. "It's okay to take what you need, Apes. Even if he was just a moment. If you really want it to be only that."

She crossed her arms. "What else would it be?"

Luna played with one of her rings. "Well, maybe it's meant that he was PMS's friend. You know, that way you could find him again? That it didn't have to just be a one-time thing."

She fidgeted in her seat. "No. Definitely not. He's a big deal lawyer. I like to stay home and make crafty things or refinish an old dresser from a tag sale. We have nothing in common."

"Oh, and a witch web comic artist and a lawyer in the middle of an identity crisis totally should work." I snorted.

"Or a witch and a Catholic school teacher?" Lu interjected.

"Yeah, but you guys thrive on chaos. It's comfortable for you. I'm not like you."

I flopped onto my back. "Excuses, April."

"What Ry means is you don't have to be afraid of feeling something for your crazy vacation fling. Maybe it's even good for you."

"Yeah, at that moment in time. I agree. I really liked wild April then. But it's not the *real* April."

I stared at her ceiling. I knew April had a lot of baggage. Less than stellar parents dumping a little girl on her grandmother was bound to leave its scars. Not to mention more than a few shitty romances.

There was a knock at the door. Lu popped up off the couch and ran for the door. April quickly followed. There was a flurry of activity as April stowed the gelato, then they set up the table with the big box of meats, cheeses, and fruit. Lu and April were in their element with making things pretty.

I hauled my butt off the floor, a plan forming in the back of my mind. Maybe April just needed a little more confidence. Even if she never met up with PMS's bestie again—hell, I hadn't met him either.

But it seemed that April would need to deal with her wild fling in the real world. Even if it was a periphery type thing.

Maybe if we boosted her up a little, she could deal with the office changes a little better.

I had a feeling Bishop would be around a lot more, the way he and Preston were talking. PMS was keeping things close to the vest, but I knew he wanted to close things up at triple Shaw. Once he'd gotten over the hump of knowing it wasn't what he needed anymore, the man was antsy to get things settled.

Whether that meant the whole firm would be dissolved or he got new lawyers in to take over remained to be seen. I wasn't sure how much to say to her. The boundaries of a relationship were new to me. April was my best friend, but I also had to be mindful of things told to me in confidence.

And it's not like PMS had even said it was confidential, but I was an intuitive witch, dammit. And I didn't need to be a witch to know you didn't blab your boyfriend's shit to everyone. Especially when things were still so in flux.

I crossed to them, the lure of food far too great. "Man, look at that spread."

"I know. This place is super cool." Lu popped a grape in her mouth. "I'm definitely keeping them in mind for our tarot nights."

April nibbled on a piece of cheese. "Tarot nights?"

"Yeah. We have a few tarot curious people over at Luna's apartment building." I filled a plate then sat down.

"Oh." She fixed a stack of crackers in her April way, then picked up a plate and took a few pieces of cheese and pepperoni. "Are there a lot of people involved?"

I shrugged. "Three or four people. One of them is an older woman. She's a trip. We should introduce her to your grams. They'd probably hit it off."

Lu pointed at me with a wedge of cheese. "Oh, yes. Bess is amazing. And becoming quite the card reader." She threw a quick smile at April. "Maybe you should let her practice on you."

"Me?" April's eyes went huge. "No. You know I don't do that."

"It would be fun. Oh, maybe she can read for Elizabeth instead. She'd get such a charge out of it."

"My grandmother?"

"Definitely," I interjected.

Luna popped the cheese in her mouth and chewed quickly. "Text your gram to come to our next class night. I know she'd love it."

"I don't know." April bit the corner of her lip. "Not to mention, I don't know when she'll be back. She's still traveling with her new guy."

"I guess everyone was getting lucky on that trip, hey?" Luna poured wine in plastic cups that had come with the spread.

"I appreciate that you guys were worried about me." April reached for a bundle of green grapes. "It kinda feels like trip hangover. I can't seem to get back into the groove of things at the office. And now with Mr—Preston's news. I just don't know if I want to stay there."

"Even with the transition of lawyers, closing up shop won't be instantaneous. PMS has a lot of cases to finish up."

April snapped a few grapes off the stems. "I know."

"It's not like you to quit unless you have something else. Or do you?" Luna got up to go to the fridge. She came back with a jar of cherries and plopped a few into her wine.

Huh. That was new. Luna liked just about every veggie or fruit but not usually in her wine.

April sighed. "No."

I closed my hand over hers. "That doesn't seem like you."

She flipped her hand under mine to hold onto me. "I know. But it just feels…different there."

"You're just reacting to the vibe in the office." I didn't want to get into what she probably was doing. Between her own need to turtle and all the exasperating emotions going off in the office, she was literally reacting to the energy in the room.

She was probably far more intuitive than she would ever own up to.

"Maybe," April said with a shrug.

I scooped up some brie and peach jam. "So, I have an idea."

April looked wary and Lu bounced.

"I love when she gets ideas."

I snickered. "I think we need a trip to see Georgia."

"Oh." Lu rattled the cherries in her cup then slugged them back like a shot. "I'm good for a trip into Luna Falls," she mumbled as she chewed.

"Luna Falls?" April's eyebrows shot up. "Is that your…"

I grinned at her. "Where our witchy folk live?"

She swallowed. "It sounds terrible when you say it like that. But there's a lot of rumors about that town."

"Cursed," I whispered.

"No. That's silly."

Luna Falls was magical, but it wasn't cursed. People just didn't understand why there was such a strong energy there. Most people couldn't find it unless they were meant to.

Because there were a whole lot of protection spells around the small village's borders. It was a fascinating place and for witches it was always a safe place.

And Georgia was just what April needed, whether she knew it or not.

CHAPTER SIXTEEN

April

WHAT WAS I DOING?

There was always a piece of Ryan and Luna that I never could quite reach. Maybe I never wanted to. I liked logic and order and their…faith? I wasn't sure that was the right word for it, but it was as good as any. I didn't understand their draw toward divination, herbs, and crystals.

Crystals were one thing. It was mineral and stone—pieces of the earth compressed to make something beautiful. They only had as much power as you gave to them.

At least that was the way Ryan always explained things.

But traveling to Moonstone & Obsidian's storefront was a whole different thing. I couldn't even say I knew how I got there. The winding roads between Kensington Square and Luna Falls were like driving in Boston without any street signs.

Streets didn't make sense and turns chopped off into dead ends or one way signs, rerouting the Jeep so many times I lost count.

Even the crisp fall day had turned foggy the closer we got to the town limits. Not that there were signs—at all. But suddenly, the wisps of silky fog dissipated as quickly as they formed and the sun was bright and bold as it had been when we left my house.

We pulled in the small parking lot beside the whitewashed building with a jet black tin roof and matching shutters. The door was an earthy red with dents and nicks in the wood, as if it had been pushed open by a thousand hands in one thousand years.

I blinked.

Since when had I ever been so fanciful?

We parked and Ryan hustled me across the gravel lot and through the door. A chime announced our arrival. Luna slipped around me and rushed to the crush of bookshelves that made up the vestibule. They weren't regular shelves.

It was as if each shelf was bolted into another haphazardly in different sizes, thicknesses of woods, and add-ons. Crooked skinny shelves held small satchels and palm sized notebooks, then the next shelf would be taller to hold oversized books. Some were ancient—as in should probably be behind glass, old—and others were as modern as a best seller's list, and everything in between.

Again, it seemed fanciful to think that way, but this place was otherworldly in a way I couldn't describe. Even the air felt different.

The deeper we got into the vestibule, the more the books aged. An earthy green cabinet with pristine glass filled one corner. A lock that would probably fit in a Tolkien movie seemed to keep them apart from the rest of us.

Dark leather tomes without names on the spines were tucked in shadows. On the other side of the space, a bean bag chair was stuffed into a corner with a pile of books piled on a tiny end table that seemed barely strong enough for a teacup.

The whole space was alien and yet invited you in and said it would be okay to sit there and read a book without purchasing it. I trailed my fingertips along the spines. Some leather, some fraying paper. Something urged me to pull one free and sink in to see what it was about.

Fiction seemed intertwined with books about botany and metaphysics. A startling amount were about caring for plants, followed by crystals, and finally more esoteric things I didn't understand.

Ryan urged me forward. The room opened up and light filled the room. The air was suddenly heavy with herbs and dried flowers. It enveloped more than annoyed, which was incredible since I got headaches from strong scents so easily.

Another unique shelving unit framed a perfect circle archway from floor to ceiling drawing us further into the store. Instead of books, this was a forest of clippings in various stages of propagation. Roots floated in crystal clear water. Some small as a thimble, some large as a fishbowl.

More shelves, more plants, and an incredible array of bottles greeted us as we stepped through the...why I wanted to say portal, I have no idea. Maybe it was just the feel of the store, and the lore of the town. I don't know, but it felt like everything was new and strange to me.

Suddenly a woman with jet black hair came out from behind the counter. "Ryan Moon, I didn't see you were coming today."

See?

Ryan rushed forward and clasped hands with the woman for a moment before Luna skipped into the room and launched herself at the woman.

The proprietress—or maybe she was just an employee, but something told me she was more important than that—laughed and enveloped Luna in a warm hug.

"What a delightful surprise." She drew back from Luna and then skimmed her gaze down her middle before smiling even wider. "Your energy is much different."

"Is it?" Luna toyed with one of the stacked necklaces she often wore. "I wouldn't know anything about that."

"Wouldn't you though?" She gently patted one of Luna's wildly curling space buns.

Ryan waved me forward. "Georgia Rose, meet my best friend April. Apes, this is Georgia. She owns this store."

Georgia cocked her head. Her dark eyes were assessing and completely void of another color. Usually with brown eyes there were facets of other colors, but not here. Just deep, dark, espresso brown. "Hmm."

I pressed my lips together and swallowed hard. "Maybe I should go. I'm not meant to be in here."

Georgia gently encircled my wrist and drew me deeper into the workshop. I didn't know exactly what it was, but there were bottles and small drawers lining the walls. "No, you wouldn't have been allowed in if that were the case."

"I don't…believe in that kind of thing."

"Doesn't matter what you believe in, April. I believe enough to ward my spaces. When you came in here you felt nothing but interest and welcoming warmth did you not?"

"I…well, yes."

"Then you were meant to be here."

I blew out a slow breath. *Be open minded. Be open minded. It won't hurt you.*

She linked her arm with mine. "Nothing in here will hurt you. And obviously your friends knew you were ready to come here."

Ready? What, like to convert?

Georgia laughed. "I mean be open minded."

I blinked. "I didn't—"

"I can read your emotions, not your mind. Now, what seems to be the problem?"

"I don't…there isn't…"

"Confidence. Okay. I can work with that." She drew me over to a large scarred table. Candles in a rainbow of colors were tucked in boxes without tops, bottles in just as many colors were crammed in little nooks. Everything was clean and tidy. There was just a lot of… well, everything.

"I didn't come here to take anything. Or buy—or whatever."

"I know."

I looked over my shoulder for Ryan and Luna but they were gone. "I'm sure you have other…" There was no one in the shop.

"Other customers? No. As you can see, this was a moment meant for you. Just you and me."

I sighed. "I don't know what that means."

She lifted a hand to my cheek. "You've been hurt so many times. Not just men either." Her hand was cool and warm at the same time.

My eyes stung, and I made a valiant effort not to let tears spill over. Such a simple statement, but there was no doubt in her eyes. How could she know?

"A lot of people have pain in their past."

"Not everyone holds their pain like a trapped bird. The minute you let it free, you'll feel so much lighter."

"I—" I didn't know who I'd be without it. Would I be the April in Fiji? Brave and fearless in the arms of my mystery guy. Not content to sit on the sidelines.

Not so achingly lonely.

The tear escaped before I could blink it away.

"Tell you what. We'll just start small. A little confidence boost never hurt anyone, right?"

"No. I don't imagine so."

Her eyes drifted down to my locket and I automatically fingered it, hiding it in my fist.

"I think we'll start with your talisman."

"It's my grandmother's locket."

"Lockets hold much power. Paper and history wrapped in gold with skin on skin contact of generations."

My heart fluttered. Her words were soft and full of knowledge at the same time. I'd never met anyone like her. "Just me and my grandmother."

"Ah. Your mother never wore it?"

I shook my head. "A little gold locket wasn't her kind of jewelry." My jaws snapped shut. I'd never really told anyone that. But it was true. My mother had been looking for a better life since she was old enough to understand her own power.

At least that's what my grandmother told me.

"Many things hop a generation. Hair color, twins, powers." She arched her brow with a sly grin. "May I?" she held her hand out.

I held onto the locket tighter.

"I promise I won't hurt it. Just enhance it."

I snuck a peek around the room and still no Ryan or Lu. Something told me to give it to her. I didn't understand it, but Georgia Rose had a way about her. I wasn't entirely sure it was about her being a…witch? I didn't even know.

I reached around and unhooked the locket and held the chain and locket in my hand for a moment longer before I handed it to her.

"Thank you for trusting me with it." She flipped it and read the back. "Elizabeth."

"My grandmother's name."

She opened the hinge and smiled at the photo. "Your grandfather?"

I nodded. "She said he was the love of her life."

"As with most things, we outlive the men…" she gave me another secret smile, "or women who mean so much to us. Elizabeth has a strong love for you. But you feel like she's moving on."

Did I?

Even on our trip it felt like she was leaving me behind.

Georgia touched my hand. "She's not. She's letting you free."

"I don't want to be free."

"Yes you do." She took the locket over to the table. "You've been restless for months. Maybe even years. You can only ignore it for so long, April. I think your grandmother understands that."

Before I could reply to that far-too-deep statement, she pulled a white candle and a yellow one out of a box. A few bottles, a leaf of some kind, and a book of matches.

"We're going to just dip our toe in the water with you. As with any magic, it only works if you believe it. I can work up the most powerful spell in the world, but if you don't believe—it's pretty useless."

"Then am I wasting your time?"

"Not at all." She gestured me to sit next to her at the table. "Take that notebook. Write down something you want to change about yourself."

I picked up the pen. "I will be brave."

"I am brave," she corrected.

I looked at the paper. I nibbled on the inside of my cheek, then wrote down the words and added another.

She glanced over. "See, you're getting it."

I tapped the pad with my pen. "I am brave and capable."

"Now we're going to make a sigil."

"That sounds like a lot."

"It's easy. Cross out the vowels and duplicate consonants until you get down to a few letters."

I made neat slashes through the letters, then looked up when she slid a paper in front of me. "What's that?"

"How we'll make the sigil."

She took me through the paces of creating an odd looking line drawing.

"Now add a few of your own flourishes."

"Won't that ruin it?"

"Definitely not. It's your sigil. Whatever makes you happy is correct."

I made a few little diamonds and a little flourish on the longest line in the drawing. "Okay. I think that's good."

"Perfect." She took the locket and laid it in a gold tray. She sprinkled a few things on it and rubbed an oil inside and out. "This won't hurt the metal." She lifted it to me. "What do you smell?"

"Rosemary?"

"To remember who came before you." She opened the locket and sprinkled a little salt in it and held the skinny white candle up to me. "Take the matches and light the candle and think about fresh starts. About calming your mind."

I picked up the matches and blew out a slow, calming breath. I lit the candle. She moved it over to the locket and dripped a little bit of the wax over the bits she'd added to the other side. I expected her to blow it out, but she tapped it out with her fingers.

"Wow."

"Well if I blew it out, I'd blow away your intentions."

"Oh. I suppose that makes sense."

"Much of the practice is common sense wrapped in intention."

We repeated the same thing with a yellow candle, which was for mental blocks and clarity with a side of confidence. Then she helped me draw the sigil on the leaf—which was a bay leaf. Then again we went with fire.

I listened as she explained about the element of fire and how it activated things. As well as burning the sigil to do the same.

Luna and Ryan chose that time to come back to find me.

"Thanks for deserting me."

Ryan grinned. "I knew you were in good hands. And that you'd do better without us hovering." She tucked her chin on my shoulder. "And lookie lookie, you sure are."

I tipped my head against hers. "Have you ever used a sigil?"

"Many times."

"Georgia is a pretty amazing teacher."

"That she is."

Georgia mumbled a few things under her breath that I couldn't catch. Then she handed me back my locket. It was still warm to the touch.

"Will the wax hurt it?"

"No. Not at all. Eventually it'll fall away and then you don't need it anymore."

I quickly put it back on and was surprised when it was still warm against my skin. Not like it burned or anything, but if I believed in energy I'd almost wonder if that's what it was.

"Your friend is welcome here anytime."

Ryan and Luna took turns hugging her and surprisingly, I allowed myself to be drawn in for a hug as well. Georgia smelled of deep, earthy things. It matched her layers of dark clothes and long dark hair. The sun caught it and reddish tones fired in the dark. As she stepped back, the same happened with her eyes.

Was it just a trick of the light?

"You're welcome at Moonstone & Obsidian anytime. Even if Ryan and Luna aren't with you."

"I'd never find it again. I got lost just thinking about all the turns."

"You'll find your way here if you need it again."

With that she nodded to a few people who'd come into the store. It was as she said, when I needed her undivided attention, it happened. Suddenly the store was filling with people. Some obviously into the craft and others I'd never have guessed. A woman in a linen suit, another in hiking clothes, and still another in a poppy colored dress that seemed far too dressed up for a weekend afternoon.

It said so much about my own biases as well as the rest of the world.

I was quiet as we left. I couldn't stop fingering the locket, nor wondering if such a thing as spells were real. Already I felt a little lighter for the first time in days.

Maybe just believing really was all it took to start moving forward again.

CHAPTER SEVENTEEN

April

"You are the master of your destiny. Only you can find the key that will get you to the next level."

I scowled at the voice of the motivational speaker intoning from my car's speakers. "I'm going back to Asher's podcast," I told him. "I'd rather hear about The Liver Licker than this nonsense."

Not that The Liver Licker was exactly cheerful morning fare, but it was more interesting than this.

I was going to try a different podcast tomorrow. Ry and Lu had suggested a tarot reader they liked who did energy forecasts. I still wasn't sure about any of that stuff, but it had to be better than mastering my destiny through the power of positive thinking.

Frankly, my skills in that arena sucked.

I turned off my car and flipped down my visor to check my makeup. I was early as always, and this was just an ordinary Monday. I hoped.

I really wanted my life to just take a pause so I could catch my breath.

In the meantime, I wouldn't do anything rash—like quitting. I hadn't ever really wanted to. I loved this job. I even loved my boss's idiosyncrasies. Imagining him naked did nothing for me, but Ry had that area covered, and I was so happy for her. For *them*.

If Preston needed a new area of law to practice, good for him. He was chasing his dreams.

As for who would be taking his place, I was letting go and letting spirit handle it. I didn't know who or what exactly *spirit* was, but that was the advice Lu had texted me this morning as I was blow-drying my hair. So I was running with it.

Spirit, do your damn thang. Gently, please.

I grabbed my bag, made sure my bagged lunch was inside, dusted off a few gray cat hairs, and stepped out into the street. A car drove past far too close to me, making me hurriedly shut the door and press against the side. Whew. Spirit was doing a good job so far.

I rounded the hood, ducking between my little sedan and the hulking black SUV parked against the curb in front of it, and stepped over the large puddle in the gutter. Luckily, I had long legs and—

And I missed the motherfucking curb and landed on my ass on the grate. I let out a howl of pure agony as the ache sung up my bones and cold, muddy water drenched my peasant skirt right up to my new undies.

I glared at the cloudy September sky as I shook my fist. "Not a good showing, spirit!"

Not so distantly, a door closed. I ignored it as I grabbed my pretty canvas bag out of the puddle. I gave an unhappy cluck of my tongue as I futilely rubbed at the muddy streak along the blue bottom. Ah, hell, the whole thing was ruined.

I closed my eyes and prayed for deliverance. Better yet, maybe I'd wake up in my bed at home and realize it was all just a bad dream.

"April?"

That voice. Silky and rich like chocolate cream pie with a bourbon finish that warmed the belly...and other things.

Dear God, it couldn't be. This was just part of my dream.

And okay, now it was getting really intense, because the chocolate cream pie voice was gripping me under my armpits and plucked me out of the gutter as if I wasn't long and gangly and sputtering my carefully blown hair out of my mouth. But that gave me a precious second to grasp that I was being lifted upward and settled into his arms as if I belonged there.

As if I'd never left.

God, why did I leave?

"April."

I'd dreamed of hearing him say my name, but definitely not in this situation. He jockeyed me carefully in his embrace, looping his arm under my knees as he lowered his head to peer into my eyes. "Are you hurt?"

A perfectly reasonable question from a man who'd just seen a woman land on her ass in a muddy, leaf-strewn puddle on a hard grate. And a perfectly reasonable answer would've been…

No, I'm fine. Please put me down now.

Also, I didn't mean to run away from you in Fiji. Well, I did, but you shouldn't have sought out my grandmother.

But was it that bad, really? No. In retrospect, who even cares?

Sorry, I may be concussed from hitting the pavement and from getting lost in your greener-than-green-with-a-hint-of-blue eyes.

Wait, can you get a concussion from falling on your ass? You know, reverberations and such? I haven't been eating much for the last week, but I still have plenty of padding. So, I'm gonna say no.

"April?" He frowned at me, not seeming the least bit uncomfortable holding me as if I had broken a leg. Which I had not.

A heart, however, seemed much more likely. And it was my own, from my own doing.

I shouldn't have ever left him.

"Okay, you're not replying to me, so either that isn't your name or you're really injured. Hold up your hand. How many fingers do you have?"

I started to comply, since he could probably command me to step into traffic in that sex voice of his and I'd go. Then I shook my head, laughing at my own foolishness.

And then I did something else entirely.

I kissed him.

I used the hand he'd asked me to hold up to tilt his head toward mine as I curled against him without a single consideration that maybe he couldn't support my weight. His arms were like iron around me, keeping me aloft without breaking a sweat.

God, he smelled like some fancy cologne mixed with the ocean. If I could've done anything but mold my lips to his as if he alone contained the only source of oxygen in the world, I would've broken free to bury my face in his neck and just *absorb* him.

Just soak him in like the water outside our place in Fiji until every sensation inside me belonged to him.

"April." His groan into my mouth kindled every bit of sorrow inside me for him and set it burning. "God, April, I missed you."

"Yes. So much. God. Don't stop kissing me." I wrapped my arm around his neck and drove my fingers into his hair, shifting to get even closer, to meld into his body if it were possible, until a bolt of pain screamed through my hip and I yelped.

"April, baby—"

"Just keep going," I panted as he immediately drew away, grabbing his face and pulling his lips back down to mine.

"No, stop, wait." Breathing hard, he extricated his mouth from mine again and looked me over as best as he could without setting me down. "What hurts? Talk to me."

"Dammit, where I hurt most has nothing to do with that grate."

His lips quirked for half a second before his concern overtook the humor in his expression. "I'm going to set you down and then we're going to the urgent care center—"

"It's nothing that bad."

"You cried out. You're hurting."

"Yeah, but it's bumps and bruises. Nothing that some Advil and seven orgasms won't cure." His expression clued me into the fact that I was acting like wild April again, with horny, sex kitten April as an extra cherry on top. Maybe my locket really did have magic now. "I mean, I can give them to myself."

"We'll discuss that later. In the meantime, urgent care."

He set me down and just like that, my happy anticipatory sparkles fizzled into dormancy.

"I don't want to go to urgent care, and you using your big deal lawyer voice on me isn't going to change my mind." I wobbled and looked down to see my damn heel was broken.

Again.

"What the hell? Are heels not made to quality standards anymore? Or else it's your presence, snapping women's shoes instead of panties?"

Instead of answering me, he drew something out of his suit coat pocket and held out his hand to me, slowly unfurling his fingers.

The broken heel from my blingy Cinderella shoe sat in the center of his palm.

My eyes filled, and I didn't know why. "My ass hurts," I said with a sniffle, rubbing the part in question and hoping like hell he'd let it go.

Like I'd hoped he'd let me go even as I'd wished every part of me that he didn't. That he wouldn't. That for the first time ever, someone would pick me no matter what.

And keep on picking me even when I was an asshole and ran away from the best thing I'd ever found.

"I can't call you Cinderella anymore, now that I know your name." His voice was so soft, but I still heard every word even over the early morning sounds of horns honking, and traffic, and the low hum of voices from passing office workers, hurrying to their offices. "April. Spring blooming and the sun rising like your hair." His Adam's apple bobbed. "The heel snapped the rest of the way in my suitcase. But I kept it with me, just in case. A talisman, if you will."

Another talisman. What were the odds? Spirit was shrieking at me now.

Then again, so was my cold and soaked foot from the water flowing through the opening in my broken shoe. *Ugh.*

I bent to pry off my damaged shoe and winced as I stepped outside the puddle onto bare pavement. "Here's another one then." I pulled off the heel the rest of the way and put it into his hand. "Now you've got two. Rate I'm going, I'll have more for you by the end of the—oh, shit."

He tucked away the heels in his magic pocket, his brow rising.

"I'm late now. I'm never late."

"Pretty sure your boss will understand. In fact, he'll probably insist you go home and get cleaned up and have some breakfast before you worry about work."

I narrowed my eyes as he plucked my dripping bag from the ground. "Oh, he will, will he? And you know this because you're his best buddy. Which, by the way, is entirely weird and creepy and—"

"And that knowledge kept you from kissing me, right?" He tucked his hands in his pockets. "If you pick where we're going to eat, I'll try not to make things weird or creepy."

"Too late." My pulse kicked into high gear. With effort, I fought to keep my voice steady. "Besides, I can't just go to breakfast on your say so."

"I guarantee you won't be penalized. Here, put the rest of your shoe in here." He held open my bag until I obliged him. "Might as well take off the other shoe too. Better not to walk around unbalanced. You can change at home."

"But I'm already late—"

Without warning, he swept me back up in his arms and started heading around the big black truck parked in front of my small sedan. "You can't walk around barefoot," he said in a patient, practical voice that really would've annoyed me if his damn pheromone-infused cologne wasn't making me lightheaded.

He unlocked his truck—of course I'd fallen conveniently located to where he'd parked—and somehow opened the door and maneuvered me onto the passenger seat. If I whimpered when he set me down, it wasn't because my backend hurt like a bitch. I was just…tired of standing.

That was a good excuse.

He placed my bag beside my feet. The guy didn't miss a trick. "Let's skip going out for breakfast. I have a better idea."

"Strawberries and chocolate with my stomach as a plate?"

"Hmm, that has possibilities." He leaned forward and gripped my chin, lightly laying his lips on mine. "Did I mention I missed you?"

He started to pull back, and I grabbed his silky tie to halt him in his tracks. "Wait. You're being awfully calm about all of this. Still bossy as all hell, but calm."

"What was I supposed to do? Pitch a tantrum? Demand to know why you didn't pledge lifetime loyalty to me after roughly thirty-six hours of orgasms?"

"Shh."

He grinned at me. "Here I thought you'd argue the hours of orgasms, not tell me to be quiet."

"That's next. But hello, I work on this block. I can't be overheard discussing—"

He ducked his head to kiss me again, except this time he didn't stop at a light, brushing tease. He delved into my mouth as if he had endless amounts of time to spend exploring me, and he just happened to be beginning with my lips.

"How about that," he murmured, easing back once we were breathing heavy. "Can you be seen kissing a big deal lawyer before you've even been to work?" His thumb caressed my lower lip. "You have no idea how much I want to do that to the rest of you right now."

His irises were blazing and when he shifted back, the steely hardness beneath his belt brushed my thigh. "I think I have an idea," I said shakily.

"So, to answer your question…"

I fingered my locket. Breathing was optional, right? So was thinking. What wasn't optional? Not squirming against his fancy leather seats in my damp panties. "I had a question?"

"More like a statement. That you're surprised I'm calm." He took a deep breath. "I'm not calm. Every fucking nerve inside me feels like it's jumping. But I'm not going to mess this up again like I did last time."

"You—what?"

"I messed up. If I hadn't, you wouldn't have thought you had no choice but to leave." He didn't give me a chance to reply before he backed out of the open door and closed it softly behind him.

What? He didn't blame me? Better yet, he didn't hate me for just leaving instead of having a conversation like an adult?

As soon as he climbed behind the wheel, I turned toward him. "I still don't know your name."

He stared straight ahead. "You didn't look me up?"

"How?" I toed off my other shoe and stuck it in my bag. Mud streaked over my feet. Awesome. "As Preston's best friend?"

"Much as I hate to admit it, you can find me as the Bye Guy online. Advertising never dies." He pulled out his phone, pressed a few buttons, scrolled a couple of times, then showed me the screen as a slick commercial played, complete with jaunty jingle. And there he was, doing his best impression of an upscale car salesman, standing behind an official-looking desk as he told the camera to contact him to get every damn penny you're owed—and maybe more than that too.

The camera panned over a sleek office building I was fairly certain was near here and a bronzed sign for the Pierson law group. Beneath that, the name Bishop Stone, Attorney at Law was in all caps. A couple other names were beneath his.

Once the commercial ended, he flicked a button and the screen went dark.

"Wow."

"Yeah. Wow." He leaned back against the headrest and turned his head to look at me. "Disgusted?"

"Terribly. Even if I don't have a heel to stand on, considering I work for a divorce lawyer."

"That you do."

"I love my job."

"Then you're lucky." He tossed his phone in the cup holder and turned on his truck.

"Bishop." I tested out how it sounded on my tongue as I placed my hand on his forearm. Silently, he gazed at me. "People need divorce attorneys. Just like they need all kinds of other lawyers. Like defense attorneys for all sorts of crimes. People mess up every day."

"They do."

"You're helping them to—"

His laugh held a bite. "I'm helping to line my pockets."

"Why shouldn't you? You take a percentage of what you help them to get. You earn that percentage. If they didn't agree, they wouldn't accept your terms."

"I realize that."

"Then?"

"Winning is addictive."

"You're very good at your job." I didn't have to see any corroborating evidence to know that, and not simply because I saw the kind of cash he was flashing around in Fiji.

He was a commanding, powerful man on a personal level. I could only imagine facing him from the opposite side of a courtroom.

I shivered as I sneaked a look at him out of the corner of my eye. God, the image of him prowling around a courtroom shouldn't be hot, but after seeing him in his expensive, finely cut suit, it so was.

Not to mention seeing him in absolutely nothing at all.

Bishop merely tapped his fingers on the wheel. He didn't have to answer. I knew it already. I also knew that he wasn't entirely happy about that fact right now. Was he having a crisis of faith regarding his work as Preston seemed to be? Best friends and all. Water seeking its own level, yada, yada.

"Preston is a good guy."

His smile was brief. "The very best."

"You're close, right?"

"Yeah." The smile appeared again. "Since college. We don't always have a ton of time to see each other, but we don't have to spend time together to pick right up where we left off." He glanced at me. "Is that how you are with his girlfriend?"

"Absolutely. And Luna. They're a little closer to each other than they are to me, but they let me pal around with them—" At his frown, I paused. "What?"

"Don't sell yourself short. Ever," He reached out to cup my cheek.

I couldn't stop myself from leaning into his palm and letting out a little sigh. If that was a sign of weakness, I'd accept it. Anything to keep his hands on me.

"That's what I was saying to you."

"Hmm?"

"Preston wouldn't have an asshole for a best friend. He just would not. So, don't act as if your success is somehow tainted because of your field."

He reached over to cup my other cheek too and drew me toward him to kiss my forehead. "I went mad without you." His voice scraped over my skin.

I couldn't stop myself from trembling. "You weren't the only one." I squeezed his fingers. "I'm so sorry. It was a cowardly thing to do. I wanted to take it back right away and I couldn't. I just…couldn't."

Searching my eyes, he swallowed several times before speaking. "Did you ever think maybe you ran because you knew we'd find each other again? That we had to?"

"That doesn't make sense." But I clung to his hands just the same.

"None of this makes sense yet it happened." He released my face and retreated to his side of the truck before putting on his belt. Then he reached for my hand as if he couldn't bear to even be that far from me.

"I live at 16 Holly Way. It's a two-family house."

With a quick nod, he signaled out of the space and merged into traffic, his hold on me steady and reassuring.

We didn't talk on the way there. It wasn't far and he didn't need my directions. Kensington Square wasn't exactly a big, bustling metropolis.

He pulled into the driveway I indicated and parked in my slip in front of the multi-car garage. I was suddenly nervous.

Actually, nervous made me sound calm compared to the manic fluttering in my belly.

"Um, you may want to steer clear of my cat."

His thumb rubbed over the back of my hand. "Okay."

"She'll probably try to engage you. Just…don't."

"Engage me how?"

"She swats at legs. Or springs out of hiding places. If you can not react, that would be better. I mean, for you. She won't be intimidated by you, regardless. But don't yell at her. That just makes her more rage-y." I darted a glance at him.

His brow was hiked halfway to his hairline.

"This is a normal-sized cat? Not like one of those hybrids?"

"Hybrid with what?"

"Bengals? Don't ask me. The wild cats they cross with regular pets."

"No clue. Kit-Kat is just a normal tortie cat."

"Who springs out of the shadows and goes for hapless men's throats." He undid his seatbelt and leaned over to move my hair away from my neck, nuzzling me.

"I was just warning you. Do that again."

"I will if you take off this damn seatbelt." He did the honors for me and tilted my face toward his, his mouth about to capture mine.

"Preston," I gasped.

He dropped his forehead against mine. "Really?"

Not laughing was impossible. "I never called to say I'd be late."

"Allow me." He pressed a button on his in-dash screen and Preston's name and number came up on the screen. "April is detained," he said in lieu of a hello. "If you need anything, contact me. Otherwise, I'll be in touch."

He clicked off before Preston could so much as grunt.

"See?" He turned off his SUV and shifted back toward me. "Problem solved."

"You're incorrigible. This isn't exactly painting me in the best light."

"Why? I can guarantee his thoughts are centered strictly on your best friend at this point, not you. He's probably already trying to get

Ryan to substitute for you for the day so they can play kinky office games."

"Like what?"

"I can think of a couple, if you're really that curious." He undid his tie in record time and rubbed the silken material against my cheek. "I wanted to start on my knees, but if you'd rather we start on yours…"

Danger! Veering out of known skill set. Abort!

Flashing him a strained smile, I jerked open the passenger door. "Um, I have to pee." I jumped out of his truck and only realized after I slammed the door shut that I hadn't grabbed my bag.

Before I could rectify that, Bishop climbed out and met me on my side, bag in hand. "I've got it," he said, motioning me ahead of him up the steps.

I deliberately tried not to see things through his eyes. The porch was homey and quaint with big vintage-style pots of fall flowers in cheerful golds and oranges, but I couldn't miss the little flakes of peeling paint. On the cheerful sunflowers welcome mat, I turned back. "I need my keys."

He offered the bag and I dug them out, fitting the right one into the lock and then again at the first door after we went inside.

"First floor?"

"Yeah."

"Not the best for a single woman living alone—" He stopped and smiled tightly. "Forgot the attack cat."

"Right." I gave him a pointed look before we stepped inside my apartment. Now that I knew he was a high-powered attorney, I understood how ingrained his take charge personality was. That didn't mean I intended to let his bossiness have free rein.

Surely spirit couldn't want me to be *that* open-minded.

We stepped into my small, tidy apartment, and I took a quick assessment to make sure a band of rowdy gnomes hadn't broken in when I wasn't looking to create havoc. Nope, everything was in its place. The coffee table was cleared of the newspaper and the remotes were in their usual pile. My current sewing project was in its bag beside the couch, nicely tipped against the side. The half-done fall bouquet of flowers I'd be hanging on my front door was on the shelf of the side table, tucked away.

He set down my dirty bag just inside the door before taking a long moment to wander around the living area. "Do you actually live here?"

"My mansion's being renovated." Knowing he probably did live in a mansion—or the next thing to it—made it harder to joke, but I was determined to not make things awkward.

Well, any more awkward than they were already. The man knew more about my cup size than he did my actual *life*.

He walked to my small fireplace and ran his fingers over the tops of the pictures frames gathered there, quirking his eyebrow at me. "No dust? I need the name of your housekeeper."

"Her name is April, and you couldn't possibly afford her."

His gaze drifted down me in a languorous way that made my nipples bead against my thin top. I was nearly sure he saw it too, since he licked his lips in a wholly wolfish way that had me pressing my thighs together. "Maybe we could work out a trade."

"Oh, yeah?" There was no helping the catch in my voice. Between his charged glances and the way he positively dominated my small living room, I felt like a live wire in danger of sparking. "Like what?"

"Like I'll spread you out on that sofa and see how fast you can wrap your long legs around my neck."

Back to breathing being optional. Good deal. "And for my part?"

He studied the picture he was holding of my grandmother and I at my high school graduation for a long moment before setting it down and moving to the next framed photo, this one of Ryan, Luna, and I the first night they'd recorded their podcast. We were all flushed and drunk with our arms around each other's shoulders. Not that I'd done anything but show up to the afterparty that evening, but I'd had to drink with them in solidarity.

"For your part, you'll scream my name every time you come. And you'll be coming a lot." Before I even had time to process that, he tilted the frame toward me. "You're sexy as hell when you're drunk."

I winced. "That obvious?"

"Well, the bottle you're clutching behind the little blond's back is kind of telling." His grin took me by surprise, all the more devastating in its unexpectedness. "She's not Ryan, is she?"

"No. That's Luna. Ryan's the dark-haired knockout. Preston totally scored with her."

"Funny. I would've said the guy who got to go home with you was the one who scored."

I brushed my hair behind my ear, inwardly groaning at the wet leaf stuck in it. "That night, I went home alone."

"Pity. When was this?"

"Not long before I started working at Mr. Shaw's—" I cut myself off and cleared my throat. "We like the formalities. It's been a process trying to see him as an actual man who's sleeping with my best friend."

"If it helps, I don't think sleeping happens much." He tapped the glass. "You're wearing your necklace here. The one you have on now." He swerved to look at me, as if he was comparing me to the picture. "You didn't have it on in Fiji."

"No. I left it home. Do you pay so much attention to your court cases too? You must be one hell of a human lie detector if so."

"I pay attention to what I care about. You weighed less here."

"Gee, thanks."

"You're beautiful both ways. All ways. But your curves are gorgeous. I love the way you eat as if you don't care who is watching."

"That was just with you." I hadn't realized the truth of it until I said it. "Maybe that's why I've barely eaten for the last week."

It was meant to be a joke, but not only that. I wanted him to know —to understand—that I hadn't only hurt him by leaving. I'd also hurt myself.

Today was the first time I could truly breathe again since I'd flown off that island and away from him. And I didn't know what the hell to do about it.

Maybe just take it minute by minute. Let go and let spirit take over, remember?

He set down the frame and moved toward me in a few long strides. "Take a shower, get cleaned up. Then we'll eat."

"If I'm Cinderella, you're bossy."

Disputing it would've been pointless and we both knew it. His calling Preston stunt was a prime example, even if he had made things easier for me. Still, calling in late was for me to do, not Bishop.

But he was trying. *Ish.*

"I'll be bossy," he murmured, "if you'll be mine."

CHAPTER EIGHTEEN

Bishop

I WAITED for her to freak out.

Great job at going slow and keeping the pressure off, moron.

She stared at me for a long moment before she shook her head and escaped down the hall with a vague, "make yourself comfortable."

Easier said than done when I could hear the water turn on in the bathroom and understood full well how close I was to her naked, wet, likely soapy body.

Down, boy.

I pressed a hand against my eager cock, which didn't exactly have it lowering to half-mast. The situation was dire enough I briefly considered investigating if she had a half bath elsewhere in the apartment. Pre-gaming might be wise unless I wanted to embarrass myself.

But if I needed to come in my damn pants like a teenager to make her understand what she did to me, so be it. I'd just embrace my torment.

I glanced around her ridiculously tidy living room. It was this put together without her even realizing she'd be having someone over. Talk about a neat freak. She was probably quick in the shower too, but I'd have at least a few moments to myself.

Ones where I would not even *think* about touching my dick.

Now what?

My inner attorney wanted to investigate her place while I had a couple minutes alone. Nothing too invasive. Just a little preliminary scoping things out. But the part of me that was working my ass off at not fucking this up kept me rooted to the thin blue carpet.

This place was full of blue. Blue walls. Blue rug. Gauzy blue curtains. The place was quaint and cozy, if a bit reminiscent of a hut for a Smurf, right down to the low ceilings.

Well, at least until I wandered into the next room, which I assumed originally had been meant to be a dining room. April had made it into more of a combined library-slash-crafting space with lots of wide white shelves and low white benches with lots of pillows and pale wood tables everywhere. Most of them contained various projects in progress, mostly of the home decor variety with a fall or holiday theme. Sprigs of fall flowers with bows in various stages of completion, oddly shaped vessels and vases standing at the ready for those blooms. Creatively decorated tags meant for names or prices were mixed in with small painted plaques with cheerful sayings.

Home is where the heart is.

Love fills this home.

Family is spelled love.

And then a surprising inclusion: *The cook says it's takeout night.*

Its slim canister held a pair of wooden slatted forks and a rolled laminated paper that I imagined was supposed to indicate a restaurant menu.

Clever.

The bookshelves held more of the same—some finished projects, some shelved for a later date—interspersed with big craft how-to books and magazines. A few romance novels were tucked in here and there, most of them dog-eared and probably well-loved.

I picked one off the shelf and flicked through a few pages. So, she had a romantic soul. I wanted to indulge it.

Indulge all her appetites, including the ones that had led her to put a cat bookmark on page 191 on a scene with a blindfold and a feather.

Hmm, I could work with that. Maybe not a feather, unless I came across any enterprising pigeons on the windowsill. But I could improvise.

I put back the book and looked around, savoring being in a space that felt so light and airy and like *April*. She was all around me, and I never wanted to leave. Even her luxuriant vanilla scent seemed to waft from the see-through curtains. The morning's clouds had burned off, leaving only a blue cloudless sky and abundant sunshine, filling the room.

Metaphor? Maybe.

I fucking hoped so.

A basket overflowing with ribbons and lengths of brightly-colored fabrics sat on the rug next to a corner table with an honest-to-God vintage-looking sewing machine. One of those old fabric tomato things sat next to it, covered in tons of pins. Beside it sat a pair of scissors with a cap that was shaped like a middle finger.

I grinned. My girl's backbone showed up in unexpected places. I wanted more of it. More of her.

The chair in front of the machine was built well enough not to list under my weight as I sat down. Idly, I picked up the basket of fabrics, tossing it aside with a…manful squeal when it yowled and exploded with projectiles of fur and fabric in all directions.

I clutched my chest and caught my breath as I tried to process what had just happened. Only fully comprehending when I noticed the pissed-off pair of green eyes peering at me from under one of the tables.

Guess I'd disrupted Kit-Kat's catnap.

I got down on my knees and braced myself on my forearms as I inched forward. "Hey there, pretty girl." In fact, I did not know if she was pretty, but her eyes certainly were. They were even more beautiful in their absolute disgust.

We'd gotten off on the right foot, all right.

"Hi there, Kit-Kat. I've heard a lot about you. I don't suppose you've heard about me? Probably not, since your mom didn't even know my name until today. So glad we finally have that out of the way."

The cat seemed unconcerned.

"Listen, I'm sorry I interrupted your nap. That was rude of me. But I didn't see you buried in there. It looks like a nice place to sleep, though. I haven't been sleeping much, so if I could get some rest in a basket that comfortable, I'd probably check out too. And the sun was shining on you too, wasn't it? Cats love sunshine. Humans too, but not your mom because she's too fair and she burns too easily."

More staring.

"I wanted to talk to you privately, so this is a good time as any. I don't know how long you've lived with your mom, but you have the insider information I don't. What does she like? I don't mean the usual female stuff like flowers and candy, although I wouldn't mind that intel too." I propped my chin on my palm. "But maybe her favorite food? Favorite movie? I happen to know her favorite color, but that might've been pillow talk. Maybe she really loves lemon yellow or something."

"It used to be blue, but I've developed an appreciation for green."

At April's soft reply, I jerked into a sitting position and glanced up to find her lingering just outside the doorway with her long blond hair wet and loose around her shoulders. A ridiculously soft and fluffy gray sweater dipped off one shoulder, revealing a dark gray bra strap, and a pair of tight jeans that rode just below her belly button and exposed a teasing gap of skin. Her jeans hugged her and left nothing to the imagination.

But I was imagining just the same.

My gaze traveled down the long curves of her legs, finally landing on her bare feet and baby pink toenails. Toes that were currently curling into the rug.

I wanted to elicit that reaction from her for a whole different reason.

Soon.

Very soon.

My throat had gone dry. I couldn't speak. Probably a good thing or else I would've let out another of those manful squeals as Kit-Kat skulked out from the table and pranced toward me with her tail held high before she climbed up on my lap, gave me a flat stare, and curled up on my folded legs as if she'd decided I was better than a basket of fabric.

I could guarantee no part of me was softer than that material. Especially since Kit-Kat was using…certain engaged parts of my anatomy as a body pillow.

At least she hadn't tried to bite me. Any part of me. But the day was young.

April's laughter filtered through the embarrassed buzz in my head. I frowned and looked up at her, mesmerized all over again by the picture she made in the doorway, cheeks flushed, eyes sparkling, with her hand cupped over her mouth.

I was so fucking in love with her, I couldn't see straight.

"Looks like I've already been replaced." She frowned at my lap. "Is she laying against your—"

"Mmm-hmm."

"And that's not a trick of the light?"

"If it is, it's a shaft straight from heaven."

A giggle burst out of her. The best sound ever.

"So, about that whole hating men thing—"

She lifted her hands. "Literally every one she's met in my presence. Leave it to you. You didn't even have to bribe her with soft chicken."

"Seems like she prefers hard cock at the moment."

"You're terrible."

"*I'm* terrible? You're wearing a sweater I want nothing more than to dive underneath to see what kind of bra you have on, and I'm stuck over here with a cat on my lap."

She wetted her lips. "You want pussy, right?"

I was so twisted up it took me a minute. When I got it, I growled—especially as she teasingly unbuttoned her sweater as she strolled toward me. With each inch of skin revealed, I swallowed.

She didn't stop.

The bottom of her bra was some studded contraption that cupped her breasts with peekaboo lace and an intricate fabric cage. The shoulders of her sweater fell lower, and she tilted her head, playing the role of seductress to the hilt.

"In case you're wondering, these aren't my usual work clothes. I wore these for you. And for me." She let out a breathy sigh. "I wanted to see that look in your eyes as you peeled them off of me." She toyed with the panel of lace that guarded one shell pink nipple. "But I think I want to peel them off myself."

"You're so damn gorgeous," I gritted out.

"You make me feel as if I am." She stroked the waistband of her jeans. "Am I supposed to pretend I don't want this? Maybe string you along, make you wait, see if you're genuine about wanting more than getting inside me." The sound of her zipper opening sent a shiver down my spine.

"I do want more. A fucking lot more."

She pursed her lips and eased her fingertip into the vee she'd made. Her gaze locked on mine, never leaving as she nudged aside the scrap of gray guarding her pussy. Her finger slid inside and just as quickly back out before she took a shaky breath and held out her hand to me.

I caught it in both of mine, dragging them into my mouth and sucking her taste inside me greedily.

Kit-Kat made a plaintive sound and streaked off my lap, darting out of the room with her furry tail twitching.

I lurched to my feet and pulled April into my arms, feasting on her lips and transferring the hint of sweet flavor she'd taunted me with. She barely had a chance to kiss me back before I was on the move down her body, yanking at the lace. I tugged first one tip then the other between my teeth. Alternating my kisses between them, not tempering the pressure, giving her an edge of pain that made her cry out. I jerked her zipper as far down as I could get it so I could wedge my hand inside.

She was positively dripping.

"Oh, fuck, baby, let me take care of you." I dropped to my knees before she could argue, yanking her jeans down over her ass and pressing my face to her mound. "This. This is what I couldn't get out of my head." I didn't want to tear her tiny scrap of nothing, but I felt big and clumsy and desperate as the fabric rent between my fists. And then I was on her, my mouth wild against her soaked flesh, lashing between her swollen lips as she speared her fingers through my hair and hauled me deeper into her inferno.

I wanted to burn. To lose myself inside her. My fingers sliding into the molten clasp of her made us both groan. With my free hand, I jerked down the zipper of my trousers, fisting my weighty cock with a hiss of relief.

"Yes. God, yes," she whispered, and I thought she meant what I was doing with my fingers. But when I glanced up, she was watching me brutally work my cock, enough that a stream of arousal trickled from the tip. "That's so hot."

"You're hot. You." I moved my hand upward to cage her proud little clit between my fingers, licking it hungrily while my other hand pressed my luck. Knowing she was eating me up with her eyes had me going faster, harder, trying to show off for her even as I was crazed to taste her coming undone.

"I want you to come."

"Want me to come?" I repeated, almost unable to hear my own voice over the loud hum in my ears.

She nodded frantically.

"Then come in my mouth. Don't make me beg." I grabbed her leg and hiked it over my shoulder, nearly overbalancing her when the jeans bunched around her other ankle made her stumble. But she righted herself by gripping a handful of my hair, and that was all it took to have my cock spurting all over my goddamn pants as if this was the first time a woman had touched me.

For all intents and purposes, it might as well have been.

She cried out, following me, rocking into my lips and my questing fingers and the appreciative groans I couldn't hold back. Feeling her quake under my mouth made my orgasm linger even longer, and I could do nothing more than tongue her through the final pulses.

Then I saw the big purpling bruise wrapping around the side of her hip.

"Fuck, are you okay?" Forgetting the mess I'd made, I jerked to my feet to turn her around so I could check out her ass and the backs of her legs, yanking her jeans away as she released a breathless laugh.

"Only you. Can you dry clean a floor?" Her own question made her dissolve all over again.

I glanced down and shut my eyes. "So, guess neither one of us is going to work today."

"I have a dryer. And a shower. And a steamer, although I'm not sure how it does with certain potent fluids…"

Rising, I shed the rest of my clothes and quickly tried to clean up the mess. Then I captured her mouth with mine and swallowed her laughter until neither of us were feeling amused anymore.

She ran her fingernails lightly over my chest down to my stomach before diverting lower to where my dick was already rousing to participate. She scraped her thumb nail gently up the underside and I hissed out a breath. "Now where were we…?"

"I don't want to hurt you. You fell, you have to be sore, you—"

"I really, really want your cock."

As if I'd ever say no to that.

"Ask and you shall receive." I glanced around, bitterly disappointed a King-sized bed hadn't materialized since the last time I'd looked.

Luckily, my woman was far more able to think on her feet than I was and rooted through the remaining fabric pieces in the basket to find a large one to drape on the hastily cleaned floor. Bonus points, it had some kind of fleecy liner that added at least a millimeter of padding.

But love was pain, right?

She nuzzled my jaw and pointed toward the carpet. "I'll get on top."

"Oh, hell, yes, you will." I couldn't lay down fast enough.

I'd probably have to buy her new carpet depending on the quality of her rug cleaner. Ah, fuck it, it had been worth it. So, so worth it. I'd redo her whole damn apartment if necessary.

She crouched over me, leaning forward so her locket necklace dangled free over the lace that still partially hid her full breasts from my view. I fumbled behind her, shoving off her sweater and going to work on the intricate hooks and loops that had me swearing. She laughed and fumbled with me, angling forward so that the moment the hooks gave way, one of her tits dangled right into my mouth.

I bit down on her flushed nipple, forgetting to check myself, and the sound she made was pure unadulterated pleasure. I sucked on it even harder, reaching up to fist a handful of her wet silky hair. Her eyes widened, going unfocused as she tilted her hips to rub her pussy against my bare cock. We panted and writhed together, arching against each other without thought. I couldn't stop myself from thrusting into her. On a wild cry, she enveloped my length, sinking down until I couldn't go any deeper.

Until we were locked together. Hot, wet, indescribably *right*.

Some alarm bell clanged in the back of my brain. Since I was currently drawing her breast between my lips and surging into her hard enough to possibly snap her vertebrae, I didn't much care. Did not even give one flying fuck if that alarm bell meant the police were about to mow down the door and arrest me for being stupid and horny and in love with this woman I was only beginning to know.

Apparently, she wasn't any more concerned, because she braced her hands on either side of me on the carpet, her hips bucking against mine with such intensity that I knew she'd hurt later.

Outside *and* in.

I reached down to grab a handful of her ass, careful to avoid her more bruised side, squeezing her so rhythmically that with every flex of my hand, she jerked up and down my dick. Such dirty sounds. Delicious. The smell of sex was thick and ripe in the humid air, and I had to pull my mouth off her breast to arch higher to suck on her throat. Leaving marks wherever I could.

"Better invest in turtlenecks," I managed to get out against her skin a second before she rolled her pussy down my length with such wet suction that I had no choice but to drive up to the hilt inside her again.

I was going to come. There wasn't time to warn her, and if I'd been capable of dragging free of the sweet heat of her body, I wouldn't have.

Couldn't.

She let out a keening cry and then I was falling with her, except it was more like soaring as I jerked upward and spilled myself inside her. Endlessly. I couldn't stop the wild heaves of my hips as I drained into her and she held on, gasping as the sensations rocketed from my body into hers. She coiled her arms around my neck, kissing me with a lifetime's worth of passion as I anchored her in my embrace.

Never letting go. No matter what.

"Mine." I knew I said it. Knew I groaned it again and again while that fierce urge to claim my mate reared up inside me.

Of *course* she was mine. How could she be anything but?

She framed my face in her trembling hands, kissing me so gently while sweat dripped into my eyes. "This is crazy. You know this is crazy." But when she eased back, tears starred her lashes. "But God, it feels like you're mine too."

I reached up to grab her hand and pulled it to my chest. "I am. I swear it. I—" I swallowed as spots encroached at the edges of my vision and my skin went from flushed to clammy in an instant.

God, not now. Not here.

I shut my eyes as tightly as I could, breathing through my nose as I'd been taught to do. Inhale for a count of four. Hold for a count of eight. Exhale for a count of—

"Fuck, sweetheart, get up. Please. I'm sorry." Words tumbled out of my mouth that I couldn't quite identify. They were lost in the haze of panic blurring my vision. I couldn't get my breath, but I was aware of her scrambling up and off me, her face a pale mask of fear.

Guilt locked chains around my throat. I was scaring her. Here, when I'd been so determined to make her understand she could count on me, that she could trust me, that I'd wait her out and not pressure her.

Now I was losing it in front of her, helpless to do anything more than scoot across the rug and lean against the side of one of the tables while I hauled in deep breaths.

Not enough. Not enough. My heart was a locomotive, vibrating through my body. On the verge of pounding through my flesh and bones and through my skin.

"What is it? Bishop, what do you need? Are you okay?"

Cool hands flattened themselves to my cheeks, making me open my eyes. I focused on hers, shocked to see the same level of concern in her watery hazel depths that I'd seen in Preston's the other day.

Was it possible?

"Water? A cold cloth? Should I call 9-1-1—"

"No. No. Just—come here." I pressed my damp face into her neck, inhaling her vanilla scent as if it was as vital as the oxygen stuttering in my lungs. And I held on to her with everything I had. "Say my name. Just keep saying it. Don't stop."

She did as I asked, over and over. And in her fright and determination and urgency, I heard so much more in her tone than she could ever say.

She'd walked away from me once, but she wouldn't leave me again.

I understood that down to the marrow.

Hearing my name in her husky voice, pitching higher the longer I went without saying anything as she rocked me, stroking my hair, brought me back to myself. I don't know how long it took. It seemed like a lifetime. But when I eased back to gaze up at her, her ruddy cheeks were soaked with tears.

"I'm okay." I cupped the back of her head and drew her down to my shoulder, cradling her in my lap. She was all arms and legs, but we made it work.

I couldn't have let her go right then if they'd used the jaws of life to separate us.

"Are you sure? You were shaking so hard—"

I closed my eyes and forced out the words as my racing heart returned. Not as badly. I could say this. I had to. She deserved the truth. "I get panic attacks. That's what you just saw—just felt." I swallowed hard. "It's so fucking humiliating. I can't control them.

They control me. And I don't know when they'll strike. Can be during times of high stress, but it's usually just…afterward." I made myself slow down and breathe. Last thing I wanted to do was to roll right into another one. "Sometimes it happens during pleasure too. Excitement. My nervous system doesn't always know the fucking difference."

She lifted her head, her eyes filling silently.

"So, you know, I get if this is too much for you, or too awkward or too—"

"Do you get if I want to punch you in the head?" Instead of that particular violent act, she thumped me in the stomach. "You big silly oaf."

Relief flowed through my tensed muscles for the umpteenth time that day. My back and shoulders ached with the effort it had taken just to breathe. "It's a lot. I don't want you to think I'm saddling you with it. No dick is worth…this."

"You're underestimating your own penis."

"Not really. Right this second, I can't see why else you're still here." I lifted my head and managed to smile. "Well, never mind. Forgot this is your house."

"I'm right where I want to be. And you're right where I want you to be." She brushed her fingers through my hair and tenderly kissed my forehead. "Do you think I'd ever doubt for one second how strong you are after watching you fight through that to come back to me?"

The sting in my eyes shamed me more than all the rest. But I didn't duck my head or hide away even though I wanted nothing other than to make a quip or lure her into the shower so I didn't have to reveal these jagged, broken parts of myself.

I was starting to figure out how to take care of someone. God knows I was no expert and had bungled it a million times. Would bungle it a million more. But I was still trying.

I just had no earthly clue how to let someone be there for me. Especially someone who could shatter my heart so easily and didn't even know it.

At least I hoped she didn't know it. And that probably proved how far I had to go.

"Do you like grilled cheese?" she asked hesitantly, running her fingers over my chest. Tangling them in the hair there. Helping me to stay connected to her voice, her touch, her smells.

"Love it. With tomato soup?"

"Is there any other way?"

"Not in my house growing up. My mom used to make the best—" I stopped and rolled my shoulders as they tightened up. "Sorry, sore subject."

"I can handle your mom making better soup than me. Although Campbell's is a tried and true formula."

I brushed my thumb over her cheek. "If you make it, it's my instant favorite." I kissed her softly, holding her in place while our gazes met. "Thank you. You made it so much better."

"I'm glad." She cupped her hand over mine. "Maybe over my award winning soup, you can tell me a little more about it? I want to understand." When I sucked in a breath, she batted her lashes. "Or you can just repay me for my grand culinary skills with some of your own particular talents afterward. If you're up to it."

A quick glance down at my lap made me smirk. "Pretty sure I could get up for you any damn time you please." I kissed the divot in her lower lip. "April."

She released a long, slow breath. "Can you say my name again? Just another thousand more times or so should suffice."

"April." I kissed the corner of her lips before repeating it on the other side. "April mine."

CHAPTER NINETEEN

April

Having a big, broad, ridiculously sexy lawyer sitting cross-legged on the floor in my craft room hot gluing a wooden sign onto an enormous holiday pitcher should've been odd.

Forget that part. That we'd had intense shower sex not an hour before and he was wearing my grandfather's plaid robe because he'd made a mess of his suit—ahem—was even stranger. He'd sent it out to be dry cleaned yesterday and he had no clothes to wear so he could leave.

Not that he seemed to have any inclination to leave. Nor did I want him to. When the dry cleaner had asked if he needed rush service, he'd said no.

The extremely in demand hotshot lawyer had said no so he could stay with me to eat the contents of my refrigerator and binge Netflix and help me make crafts.

Oh, and fuck like we were still in Fiji.

Without condoms. Because we'd officially decided we weren't going to make sense anymore.

We'd even discussed our bad choices. Even when we were being entirely impractical, we still had to talk about it.

I'm not on birth control.

Okay.

So we won't? Though it's not the right time in my cycle.

Are you clean? Late to ask now, but...

Yes. Are you?

Yes.

And that led to more sex sans condoms. He didn't even seem particularly concerned at the implications. But God, the sex was good. Somehow it was even better than in Fiji. My lady airstrip had rolled out a welcome mat for him, and he'd done his best to keep me filled at all times.

That wasn't even much of an exaggeration.

It was now Tuesday evening, and we'd spent the last two days together. My brain had put up a vacancy sign right about when Bishop—God, it was strange to think of him as other than my mystery man—had plucked me out of that gutter. Inviting him into my little place had pushed the fantasy into the reality. I hadn't known if he would take one look at the pillows and tarot bags I was making on my sewing machine and decide I was some homespun hippie wannabe witch and flee into the hills.

Or for him, flee into the concrete jungle he prowled around in so naturally.

But he hadn't. He seemed fascinated by everything I did. By who I *was*. I'd asked him if he was missing something vital at work and he'd mentioned clearing his schedule with Vienna, his admin.

My schedule definitely wasn't that wide open.

I'd intended to go back to work Monday afternoon, albeit a bit later than I'd planned. But after what had happened with Bishop, my job had taken a backseat.

Everything had.

For the first time in my life, I'd called in sick for the next two days, without even knowing if Bishop would hang around with me or split as soon as his dry cleaning was delivered. But Preston had shocked the hell out of me by closing the office for the rest of the week.

The entire *week*.

Bishop had barely seemed surprised when I told him, just

remarking about love being in the air. And then he'd gazed at me as if he wasn't only talking about Preston and Ryan.

The nuttiest thing was that I hadn't even questioned what he meant. I had other concerns right now.

I hadn't felt fear like I had in those terrifying moments on my craft room floor in…well, ever. I'd heard stories of men dropping dead during or after sex, but they typically weren't insanely fit and in the prime of their lives. Still, I didn't know his medical history, and he'd mentioned being under a doctor's care in Fiji. For a couple minutes, I'd been scared out of my mind that I'd lose him just after finding him again.

Amazing how jaw-dropping panic had helped me get real clear about my feelings for him.

Crazy or not, improbable or not, I'd fallen in love with him in Fiji. And the job that had meant the world to me before I'd met him couldn't compete with making sure he was safe.

He'd told me he was okay. That he was handling it. I understood anxiety all too well, even if I couldn't fathom someone like him who was normally so calm and in control being stricken with it so unpredictably.

That didn't mean I intended to let him out of my sight anytime soon. Especially since he seemed just fine with that idea.

To be safe, we probably should have killed the sex stuff. I'd even tried to dissuade him at first. Weakly.

Very weakly.

Even now when my body was still limber and loose from him and warm water, add in a very thorough pat-down from him with my plushest bath towel, I couldn't keep from sneaking glances his way. He was a stupidly attractive man, somehow made even more so by wielding a small hot glue gun in his bear paw. His inventive curses as he tried to lay down a stream of glue around the edge of the sign, without dripping it onto the mat I'd wisely placed beneath, was just this side of adorable.

Until he started slamming his thumb repeatedly on the glue stick release.

"It's stuck, for fuck's sake."

I walked over to him and pried the gun out of his hand. A few flicks of my fingers and the glue squirted out just fine. "You have to maintain even pressure while you're aiming the stream. If you push too hard, you'll just make a big ol' mess."

"Hmm, seems like I know about messes."

His devilish grin made me kiss him, which had probably been his intention. Then I sat back on my haunches and motioned for him to try again.

"Taskmaster," he muttered, doing as I'd suggested. "What are you doing with all of these?"

"Some are for me. I don't have a big house or the whole family thing, but I love to decorate. Kit-Kat enjoys my creations too."

"I just bet. You let her chew on the plastic plants to keep her out of the real ones?"

"Something like that."

"What about the rest?"

I was too fixated on his large capable hands smoothing over the wood. Who'd known this could be a kind of porn? Not me. But I'd subscribe to this channel immediately. "Huh?"

"Now you know how I feel."

I blinked at him.

"When I can't focus on anything but you."

"Did you hate me?" I whispered. "When I left."

Immediately, the softness in his expression vanished, replaced by the worry lines in his forehead I didn't love seeing now that I'd witnessed even a fraction of the turmoil inside of him. "I couldn't."

"I shouldn't have done it. I know you don't want to talk about it, that you'd rather just pretend it never happened, but it did. I did the exact same thing my parents did to me," I realized hollowly, falling back on my ass on the rug.

He started to speak, but I shook my head, shushing him with my fingers against his lips. Saying nothing, he kissed them, bolstering me anyway.

He always did that with me. Always.

"You're going to defend me. To say it's obviously not the same. We barely knew each other. But we did. Didn't we?"

His nod made me close my eyes.

"I was nine," I whispered. "They kept taking me to my grandmother's for play dates. At first, it was just a few hours here and there. Then they started buying me toys that were special, ones I could only play with at my grandmother's. There was this doll. Holly Sparkles. She had this red dress covered with crystals." I laughed self-deprecatingly, hoping like hell he didn't look too closely. So he didn't see the tears.

After all this time, there were still tears.

"I loved that doll. I'd begged for it for months and months, every time we went to the store. And my mom got it for me just before the last time we went to Grams. I cried the whole way home, because why couldn't I play with it now? 'It's for at Grams. You have to wait, April.' So I waited and I got my doll. And they never fucking came back for me."

He reached for me and I started to push him back. It was what I did. The only thing I knew how to do so I didn't lean too hard or need too much or chase someone away because they mattered too much.

But he wouldn't let me, no matter how I shoved at him. Using all my strength to make some space around me. But he just wouldn't let go.

"I'm here," he said over and over until the words lulled me, soothing me into stopping the fight.

I sagged into his arms and spoke into his throat, needing him to understand. I wouldn't take the easy way out again. "I didn't want you to find out I wasn't like you. Not rich and important and valuable. I was damaged goods. When even your own parents won't stick around for you, how can anyone else? Why would anyone else?"

His laughter was soft and ragged as he drew me back to cradle my face in his hands. "I haven't spoken to my father in almost four years. My mother, I talk to at Christmas and her birthday. That's it. That's all."

"Why?"

A muscle ticked in his jaw, barely visible through the two days' of dark golden scruff shadowing his skin. "They chose my brother over me."

"You don't have to tell me—"

"Yes, I do. I have so much to tell you. But I didn't because I didn't want you to run again." He released a laugh that broke at the end. "You're afraid you're not good enough for me, and I'm—"

I couldn't let him say it. My being vulnerable was one thing, but I knew, understood on a bone deep level, what he'd risked by letting me into his world yesterday. He hadn't walked away or tried to pretend it was something else. He'd just told me what he was going through without a shield. Even if I didn't get exactly why he was suffering, I didn't have to. Not right now.

If he could be brave, so could I. And I could trust him.

At least, I could try.

"You're everything." I pressed my mouth to his, drawing on his air, feeding him mine. For that moment, letting it be enough.

But instead of sinking into the kiss, he jerked back and cast a glance at the ceiling. "If this turns out to be the wrong thing to do, so be it. I've tried to plot and plan and orchestrate everything for the last few years, and all it made me was a miserable millionaire."

"You're a—" I fumbled for my locket. Dammit, I should have asked for courage with the confidence. Georgia Rose, can I have a two-for-one? "Okay. Moving on."

"It's not all it's cracked up to be."

"I can guarantee neither is not having money."

"I've had my lean times too."

"Define lean. Because mine included making a single carton of ramen last for two days."

He winced. "Not that lean. My parents were comfortable, so we were too. Not millionaire comfortable," he added quickly. "That's just me."

"So you're self-made."

"Damn straight."

Pride surged through my chest on his behalf. "I'm a self-made thousandaire. My grandmother had money from my grandfather, but once I moved out, I took care of my expenses myself."

He glanced around, smiling faintly. "You did just fine for yourself. Um, does that box have eyes?" He nodded to an upper shelf on the bookcase next to the window.

I didn't even have to look. "Yeah, she likes to peer over that rattan one as if she's an alligator."

"Boxes and baskets are for her."

"Standard cat fare," I agreed, waiting him out. I knew he wasn't done yet and that he'd get there in his own time.

"She watched me pee this morning."

"Also typical."

"She was hanging over the bathroom door at the time. I nearly screamed like a little girl."

I giggled and tipped my head on his shoulder. "If it makes you feel better, her tendency to fall from that height is zero."

"How about jumping?"

"Hey, she already took a nap on your um, dick." *Dick!* I said in my head, channeling my office conversation with Ryan. "Anything's possible now."

He released a long breath. "I was a royal asshole to make that money. I enjoyed it. And now I'm enjoying telling everyone to go fuck themselves when I have meetings and depositions and client reviews out the wazoo. But I told them I couldn't work this week on doctor's orders. Sorry if that doesn't work for you, find another attorney to help you screw over your ex and the pet llama in Peru."

"That's oddly specific. And intriguing." I set the hot glue gun in its stand since he'd dropped it around when I started to tell him my life story and it had burned a glue-filled hole at the edge of my sign. I'd fix it with a glittery brad and call it a day.

I was discovering that "good enough" was good enough indeed.

"I never intended to take this week off."

I set my hand on his knee. "But you told them you needed to."

"Yeah."

"Your doctor didn't really want you to, did he? Just to be clear. I know you took a vacation on his advice."

"My doctor thinks it's a miracle I took a week off. He didn't try for more." Bishop reached down to tighten the belt of the threadbare robe until I wondered how it didn't cut off his circulation. It had already been a snug fit to begin with, since my grandfather definitely had not been built to his scale.

I shivered. Definitely not.

"Cold? Oh, and is it time for more Advil?" He glanced down at his heavy gold watch. "Nope, you have another forty-five—what?" he demanded.

I so love you.

It was a miracle I didn't say it out loud. Knowing it didn't make any sense didn't stop my feelings.

"I probably have daddy issues."

"Okay," he said slowly.

"And mommy issues and a hell of a lot of other ones. But I'm going to admit something extremely dark and personal to you right now."

His brow wiggle was nothing short of lascivious. "Lay it on me."

I placed my hands on his chest and kissed his strong chin. "I think I'm developing a fetish for being taken care of. Usually, I'm the one to take care of others."

He stroked his hand down my hair. "That so?"

"So much."

"Is there a place I can sign up for that job?" His green gaze stayed steady on mine. "On a permanent basis. I don't do temporary."

My heart did a slow roll in my chest. "No?"

"No. Not anymore. I used to be the king of temporary. Now I want to build something real. Something meant to last with someone I can trust."

I'd told him about my taking care fetish. But I'd just learned I had a fidelity kink to go with it.

Probably too much to admit right away. What was the timetable for personal disclosures?

Uh, went out the window when you slept with the dude without knowing a damn thing about him.

"You can trust me. I'm boringly traditional." I bit my lip. "I know being a flight risk doesn't exactly inspire faith in that claim, but—"

"Tell me you won't run again no matter what, and I'll believe you."

"It can't be that easy."

"It can be when I want to be with you more than anything else, including worrying about things that won't happen."

"I won't run again." I pressed my face into his neck, absorbing how he smelled. My vanilla soap on his skin smelled incredibly erotic, although I couldn't wait to breathe in more of his ocean-inspired cologne. "What was in the frame?" I asked suddenly.

"I'll show you."

"You will?"

"Yes. It's in my place and cost a fuckton to ship back. I don't know what I was thinking."

"Is it pornographic?"

His laugh was like a balm to my soul. I'd never tire of hearing it. "No, but now I kind of wish it was. I'd like a giant picture of you naked on my wall."

"Keep dreaming, pal."

"Hey, since we're sharing kinks..." He pointed toward the bookcase. "Page 191."

"You looked?" I smacked his arm.

"I did more than look. I ordered some stuff." His eyes smoldered into mine. "It's not here yet."

My pulse stampeded in my throat. And in other...excitable places. "Stuff like what?"

"You'll see. Preston asked me to take his job."

CHAPTER TWENTY

April

SAY WHAT? The topic change was so abrupt that I might've tripped if I hadn't already been sitting down.

When I would've moved back—to breathe, to *think*—Bishop's hand clamped down on my non-bruised hip. He never forgot, not for a second. "He's my best friend. Basically, my brother. After yesterday, I thought I could say no. That I had to, if it was going to make this hard for you. Or awkward. Or just put one more thing between us. But—"

"You can't."

"No. I can't. And the man you want in your life wouldn't be able to either."

Kit-Kat must've sensed the change in the air because she leaped down from her lofty perch and streaked out of the room. She'd been far more interested in hanging around when we were having sex.

My cat was a pervert.

I got to my feet and paced around the room, picking up and setting down parts and pieces from my various crafts. I was always in the middle of something. A lot of times I moved on before finishing. Always looking for a spark sustainable enough to get me to the finish line, whether it was for a present or a decoration for myself or something I put up in my Etsy shop online.

A lot of pieces, I created on a whim or from something I saw in a magazine, but I grew tired of them before they were completed. But the ones where the glow was strong and true from the first, I always loved, no matter what.

"You asked me what all of this stuff was for." I gestured around the space. "We got diverted, as we usually do. But I didn't really have an answer. Now I do. They're for me, even if I don't keep them all. They make me happy in the moment, and for some of them, that's enough. I don't need to keep them to have loved them or to remember how much they mattered. Some I sell online. I give a lot of them as gifts. That project on the sewing machine right now is a pattern for tarot bags for my girls for Christmas. Assuming I can stop dicking around and focus."

Hey, look at you using dick as a verb. Progress!

"The one thing I don't pick up and put down are jobs. I find one, and if it's a fit, I stay. Like a barnacle on a ship in turbulent seas. I cling."

He studied me for a long moment. Even not looking in his direction, I could feel the weight of his stare. Warm. Assessing. Above all, empathetic. Not pity. I couldn't have stood for that. His sympathy and understanding were so much different.

"You need something you can count on." He cleared his throat. "A place you belong."

"Yes." I couldn't elaborate. Not when I knew he was already so conflicted.

But he'd told me. True, not right away, but he hadn't waited that long, all things considered.

It had taken him a little while, but he'd trusted me with this too.

"My first inclination the other day was to tell him hell no. Then I decided to try it out." He sent me a heavy-lidded glance. "When I figured out you were his assistant, that his new girlfriend Ryan was your best friend...let's just say I had some thoughts."

"I bet you did."

"Yeah. The kind where we test out my boss and secretary kink."

I bit my lower lip and tried to control my sudden desire to climb on him like a carousel horse at the fair. "You have one of those?"

"Turns out if you're the secretary, I sure as hell do."

"Hmm."

"I was at your building yesterday to do a trial run. To get the lay of the land, so to speak. And there you were, walking right behind my SUV. Which, by the way, I asked Preston to move for me with my spare key last night while you were sleeping through *Law & Order*."

I flushed. "Just closed my eyes for a few minutes."

Or like three hours. Whatever. I'd barely slept since I'd come home from the island, other than my first day back.

"Is this your delicate way of saying my current boss knows I'm banging my new boss?"

"No, it's my delicate way of saying I talked to Preston last night and told him I couldn't risk hurting you, even if it killed me to let him down. He helped me at a really tough time."

"Dagger time?"

He glanced at me over his shoulder as I kept pacing and picking up and setting down craft supplies. The fuzzy pipe cleaners I was currently clutching gave him pause before he nodded. "Yeah. The tattoo."

"I was hoping it was related to apex predator activities."

"Well, that too. But the worst of those began after…"

"Just say it, Bishop. I can take it."

I was pretty sure, anyway.

His smile was slow and arresting. "I love how you say my name. Usually with exasperation."

"You like that? I can be exasperated with you more often if it twinks your winkie."

"I don't know what twinks means."

"Me either." I shaped a pipe cleaner into bunny ears to give myself something to do with my hands.

Waiting him out once again.

"I nearly married my law school sweetheart."

The blow didn't land quite as hard in my chest as I would've expected, mainly because he didn't marry her. "Nearly?"

"She ran off with my older brother. Announced she loved him during the vows."

However, that one had me sitting down hard on the loveseat. "God, that's brutal."

"Yeah." His smile twisted like a rope around my ribcage because I could only imagine the hell he'd gone through. "They got married."

"And?"

"And I haven't spoken to my brother in the almost four years since."

"Or your parents. That's why?"

He nodded. "I don't give a shit about Rina anymore. Far as I'm concerned, they deserve each other. But my dad should've stayed loyal to me. It was obvious who was wrong. And my mom pretending she didn't have to choose because she loved us both—"

"No matter what your brother did, he's her son."

Bishop's eyes narrowed. "Really?"

"Yes, really. What would you expect her to do?"

"Acknowledge who fucked up. It wasn't me. God knows I've done plenty of shit wrong in my life, but I did everything I could to make Rina happy. Key just strolled in there and messed with her head and told her crap like I wasn't really ready to settle down, that I'd back out within a year. That I'd never be anything but a workaholic."

I rose and came over to him, sitting at his side even though my hip hurt more sitting on the floor. But I wanted to be at his side. "People do crazy stuff for love."

"You're saying he loved her? That she loved him? Well, hi, remember me? He had a responsibility to treat me honorably as his brother."

"And she as well, as your almost wife." I tried to keep my tone even. "But God, Bishop, people screw up every day. Sometimes they want to take those mistakes back, and sometimes those mistakes lead them to something amazing."

"What the hell about me?"

The desolate question made me slide my hands under his robe, gripping his thighs so he would look into my eyes as I summoned every ounce of my bravery. "Maybe she wasn't meant for you."

I figured he'd argue. He was so very good at it, after all. And clearly, I still wasn't confident in my appeal. I'd probably never be awesome at trusting people. But he didn't fight me.

"I know she wasn't."

Swallowing deeply, I tipped my forehead to his. "But he's your brother. He will always be your brother."

"Preston's my brother."

His stubborn response would've caused me to smile if there wasn't so much on the line. "Is this where you slide in that you're going to be my boss, after all?"

"I have to do this for him. He asked me because he knows Dex doesn't have the dedication to manage a Foot Locker, never mind a multi-million dollar—hey." His eyes narrowed. "Did you know he made Preston think he was sleeping with you?"

I rolled my eyes. "Yes. Before you ask, no, I didn't sleep with him. We've never even flirted. He's like an annoying cousin. Objectively, he's attractive, but we have no sparks."

"I have lots of sparks with him, because I wanted to pop his tires for even *thinking* about you and sex."

It felt so good to laugh after all the epic revelations over the past hour. But I supposed we were way overdue. "To be fair, I think anyone would've been thinking of sex when confronted with the *Debbie Does Dallas*-level kiss between our best friends. It was hot, and I'm not typically aroused by Ryan *or* my boss."

"What do you know about *Debbie Does Dallas?*"

"That I'd rather watch *Boss Me, Daddy.*"

He shifted toward me and tugged me into his lap. Despite the various aches and pains from my butt's collision with that gutter, I wound my legs around his waist as if wrapping myself around him was the most natural thing in the world. "Is that a real movie?"

"Sure, once we make it."

I'd never seen someone's jaw drop before. In that moment, I couldn't have been more delighted with myself—or with him.

Whether he was my boss-to-be or whether he'd almost married a seriously dumb cunt. I'd never used that word before, even in my vilest thoughts. But it applied here. And his brother was an even dumber one. If they didn't grasp the kind of man Bishop was, they didn't deserve to even breathe his air.

"April mine, you're going to corrupt me."

"I'd say you're ahead on that score. But I do wish I could do one particular thing."

Desire flickered to life in his gorgeous eyes. "What's that?"

"I wish I could kiss your ex. With tongue." He stiffened, but I kept going. "Know why?"

"No, I really don't."

"She gave you up." I brushed my fingers through his hair, watching the wavy brown strands shot through with gold tumble over my skin. "And I won't."

His arms tightened around me. "That so?"

"Oh, yeah." I pressed a kiss to each of his temples in turn. "Even if it's hard. Or I'm scared. I'm sticking, Bishop." My breath trembled out. "Bishop mine."

CHAPTER TWENTY-ONE

Bishop

April fell asleep during *Law & Order* again.

That night, and the next, and the one after that. I knew this because other than stopping by my place to spend a few hours each day with my brassed-off parrot—who was not suffering in the least since I was paying his pet sitter handsomely to stop by a couple times a day, as well—I had not left her apartment except when she was by my side.

Even now that I had a couple bags of clothes in my possession, I wasn't going anywhere.

"Were you or were you not the individual who just one week ago chastised me for wanting to live with my girlfriend?"

I grinned at Preston's annoyed voice through the phone. "Chastised is a strong word."

"Right. So you don't recall indicating such behavior wasn't rational so soon in a relationship?"

"Did I? Interesting. Also, I'm not living with her."

"Did you get evicted? Maybe forget your address?"

"She has nice pillows."

"If that's a euphemism…"

"Sometimes a pillow is just a pillow. Although now that you

mention it—" I laughed as Preston made a noise that sounded disturbingly like blowing a raspberry.

We were regressing at a rapid speed. It was a beautiful thing to see. And hear.

"I appreciate you giving me some time to think."

I twitched back the curtain that looked down on the neighbor's lawn. A tricycle was parked next to a sandbox that someone I assumed was the father was dutifully filling with sand. A little boy at his side—likely the tricycle rider—was talking loud enough that I could just hear the pitch of his excited voice over the sound of the shower down the hall.

Must be dad had the day off and the kid was too young for school? Maybe he was a single father and had to juggle childcare with work.

A very pregnant woman toddled down the back steps with a young girl in pigtails riding on her hip. That was a lot of very young children at once. But the dad rushed to his feet and took the girl from her mother, pausing long enough for a quick kiss.

Sweet. They looked happy. Even the woman who looked as if she'd swallowed a large watermelon sideways. Ouch. That had to hurt.

"And he's not listening to me. Again."

I turned away from the scene playing beyond the window and focused on my best friend. "Sorry. Repeat that?"

"I said I didn't give you time to think. I gave you time to live."

"Huh?"

Preston's voice went in and out as if he were changing ears. "You told me you rearranged your schedule this week."

"Yeah, to come in and see what your clients are like, the typical workload, if Dexter really is as much of an ass-munch as I grew to believe after our dinner at Lonegan's. By the way, he did not sleep with April. If he told you he did, he's a lying scumbag."

"Shocker. He didn't exactly say that though, just let me believe the worst and didn't correct me. She didn't, either. But I couldn't quite wrap my head around it. No way does she fit with Dex, even for a little afternoon delight."

"Next you'll say I don't fit with her, either."

His pause was lengthy and I could hear the rasp of his scruff against his fingers as he thought it through. "Actually, I can see it. I couldn't at first. But the picture is becoming clearer."

"Thank you, Madam Vega. Does your witch come with a crystal ball?" Before he could answer, I pinched the tensed area between my eyes. "Ignore me. I've been happy for multiple days in a row, so naturally, I'm preparing to watch it combust in a haze of funnel cakes and ferris wheels."

"You never say what I expect."

I laughed. "We're heading out to lunch and going to hit the fall carnival at the high school. Apparently, Luna and April usually go every year but Luna isn't feeling well and said caramel apples make her want to hurl."

"That's quite the advertisement for other carnival-goers."

"No kidding. So she begged off, and April asked if I was into it."

"Are you?"

"A carnival?" I lowered my voice. "Are you kidding me?"

"Ryan mentioned going too. She usually goes with the girls but missed out last year because Rainbow swung into town and they went yard saling before the cold set in."

"Rainbow? Yard saling? I need to meet this woman of yours."

"Her crystal ball is in the shop."

"Pity."

"Rainbow is her mom, by the way. She has an RV and she makes—you know what? Never mind. So, would it disturb you if we went too?"

"Define disturb."

"April sees me as merely Mr. Shaw most of the time. If I wear jeans in her presence, will she, I don't know, have some kind of fit?"

I snorted. "I don't know if she will, but I definitely might. Do you even own jeans?"

"A couple pairs, thank you very much."

"New, I bet. Since your lady doesn't like you parading around in Brooks Brothers on the weekends. Though I heard you two were reenacting *Boss Me, Daddy*, a very intriguing—"

"Shut up and never mind. I don't want to go on a double date with you. In fact, I actually hate you now."

"You were thinking a double date? That's...wow."

"Humans who are friends do that."

"I'm well aware of that. I'm just stunned that you're the emotionally healthy dating dude now and I'm the one growling about having to eat funnel cakes."

"No one should growl about funnel cakes. They're heaven dusted with sugar. And yes, we already went last night. So what?"

I grinned and nearly jumped a foot as a gray blur streaked under the dust ruffle on the bed. Would I ever get used to Kit-Kat skulking around? Every time, I tested my levitation skills. "My sister mentioned she might go too."

"Accidentally on purpose so she can meet your woman?"

I folded my arms across my chest. "Her idea, not mine. I'm okay with staying in our little bubble right now."

"Intimidating to start moving beyond that. How about if we casually bump into you guys there? We won't set a time, and if it happens, it happens."

"Should we look for the couple a crowd is forming around? You know how people enjoy displays of public lewdness."

"You are not the least bit funny."

"I'm definitely hilarious. But I'm happy for you. She has to be pretty damn great if you're all in."

I could hear Preston's smile through the line. "She is. And I am. Same goes."

"Yeah. I haven't felt like this—" I stopped. Frowned. "Ever. Actually, ever."

I'd suspected it before, but Fiji felt more like a fantasy than reality. Now we'd spent a solid block of days wrapped up in and around each other, and every morning was better than the one before. I used to be the exact opposite of a morning person, but I'd caught myself humming while making our morning coffee. And pouring cereal in bowls. And even while trying to coax the gray ghost to come out and eat her breakfast.

We'd started out so well, but ever since Kit-Kat had been driven out of the craft room by my urgent need to get inside her mom, things had been strained. Now I was just the interloper she had to keep a close eye on from any number of precarious perches.

Last night, I'd fallen asleep on the sofa and awakened to find April snoozing against my chest and Kit-Kat watching me from the top of the television armoire. Green eyes glowing in the dark and judgment twitching in her whiskers.

Preston chuckled. "I could tell at Lonegan's. You were like a feral, wounded bear. A state I understand now too well."

"Um, thanks?"

He laughed again. "It's not a bad thing. Just means you're sunk, buddy. I don't know anyone who deserves it more. Well, other than April, which just makes it better."

"Early days yet, but it's good." I smiled as the water turned off down the hall. "So good."

"Helps you had time together without other people interfering. Or without you throwing your weight around as her boss."

My smile disappeared. "About that—"

"It'll wait a couple more days. Tell you the truth, I'm enjoying letting Dex sweat on his own. Dad left to go to some charity golf tournament in Maryland and has made it pretty clear he wants to be all the way out by the holidays. So, regardless of what happens with you, changes are afoot for my dear brother."

"For all of us, it seems."

I pried the object I'd found on the floor this morning out of my jeans pocket. April's slim Cinderella heel glittered in my palm. Kit-Kat had probably dug it out of the pocket of my bag. I'd taken to carrying it around as a reminder. Not in a negative way. That night had been the beginning of everything.

Time to get those shoes fixed as well as the pair she'd fallen in on Monday. I didn't need diamonds to remind me of her when I had the real thing by my side.

Though I wouldn't mind getting her a new diamond...

I inhaled a deep breath as darkness crept in at the sides of my vision. A whole different kind of panic attack now. Rushing into something that huge didn't make sense.

Right, because having sex without condoms or birth control makes tons of it. Hello?

"Have you ever made a choice that feels really right but is actually really risky, and you don't know why you're doing it except this person makes you just do stuff that isn't like you?"

"No." Preston's tone was dry. "Absolutely not. Do you recall what I said about bench sex? Outside. Under the full moon. There was… witchiness involved."

"Like what?" My eyes widened as I sifted through my limited knowledge of the mystical, mostly gained through movies and TV. "Like a pentagram in blood?"

"Dude, you need to get out more. Stop watching Netflix. Try reading an actual book from a knowledgeable source for a change. Let me email you my reading list." I heard a series of clicks on the other end that sounded as if he was wrestling bodily with his computer mouse.

Corded, because my best friend was born in the dark ages.

"Look who's talking. Here I was just talking about not using protection, while you're casting circles and—I don't know—using crystals in ways not intended. Although maybe they are intended? Enlighten me. I'm game."

"What?"

I had to plug my ear at his shout. "Jesus, warn a guy. I didn't know I hit a sore spot. It was the crystals, wasn't it? Now you gotta tell me."

"No, it had nothing to do with crystals, though points for you for knowing the technical term. I thought they were shiny rocks."

"That's technical?"

"What the hell are you doing, Bishop?" His voice had suddenly gone quiet.

I gripped the heel that much tighter. "We talked about it."

"Oh, really."

"Yeah. The first time was an accident…and then we just didn't. She told me she wasn't on anything and we're both clean and—"

"And you're both ready to be parents?"

That question should've had me running for the drugstore. But it didn't. "You know statistically that it usually takes a while, and that's even if we're both fully operational in that arena. No idea if we are."

"Are these the kind of odds you use to practice law?"

I jerked a shoulder. "It's not like I go around doing this. I've never done it. It's just—"

"This isn't the way to lock her down, man."

The words were like a slap in the face. No, more like a short-armed punch. My head almost reeled. "That's what you think I'd do?"

"No. Not consciously. But you were fucked over in the worst way, and maybe if you didn't want to risk her running again…"

"I wouldn't." Bitterness laced my tone. "I would never want to bind her to me that way."

"Sure, when you're thinking straight. But sometimes smart people make not smart choices."

"Who says it's not smart? Just because we haven't known each other for a hundred years? I dated Rina for years before I proposed. We had it all planned out. We'd marry after we graduated from law school, buy a fancy ass house befitting two esteemed attorneys. And of course, after a requisite three years to make sure our finances were stable, have our prescribed 2.5 kids. We had a plan. And the plan got all shot to hell." I was breathing hard and hadn't said that many words in a row outside of court in years, but I needed to get it all out.

And I needed to say it to someone other than my best friend. This was just my trial run. A good litigator always had his strategy, but here I was, flying by the seat of my freaking pants.

God help me.

I didn't know if Preston was still breathing or if I'd actually talked him to death, but I wasn't done.

"I don't want to live that life anymore. I want to do what feels good and right and just be fucking happy. Even if that means I skip out on my job and toss out the fucking rubbers and fall in love with a woman who might not love me forever or at all. But I don't want to not take the chance because it's *safe*."

He didn't respond right away. "I get it. I get it more now than I would've a year ago. Hell, last month. But Christ, man, I just don't want to see you get hurt. Or for April to get hurt. Or for a kid to get hurt. I may have seen an entirely new world lately thanks to Ryan, but I know all too well the other side of things." He was quiet for a beat. "As do you."

"Yeah. That wouldn't be us. I'm tired of thinking the worst all the fucking time."

"I hear that. And if this is where your energy is, well, then go with it."

"My energy?" I grinned. "I'm enjoying this new woo woo side of you."

"Good, because I just sent you that reading list. Check it off while you're eating some fudge later. I recommend the raspberry chocolate swirl."

"You and your sweet tooth. I'll see you around. We'll probably be there for an early dinner. Mickey has a late class then she said she'd try to meet us."

"Sounds good. And hey, if it turns out you want to live off the grid and have babies with names like Butterfly and Elm Tree, have at it. I won't dissuade you. I even know someone who's all about the RV life. They're surprisingly spacious."

I couldn't hold back a laugh. "Pretty sure we won't be going that far, but thanks for the support."

"You have it, brother. Always." He quieted. "I mean that."

"I know. And same goes. Now go break some public decency laws and scram."

He chuckled. "Later."

I turned around to find Kit-Kat observing me from the pillows on the bed while she washed her face.

"I'm going to talk to your mom about very mature themes. I'd appreciate if you'd give us some privacy."

She turned around and showed me her butt before she wiggled between the pillows and stretched out for her daily siesta. If she could've said *whatever*, I had no doubt she would have.

I wandered down the hall to the bathroom, tucking in my button-down shirt before I decided that looked too lawyerly for an afternoon lunching and hanging out a carnival so I yanked it back out again. And walked right into April wearing a red sundress with tiny flowers and a big hat with a wide brim.

"It's too much, isn't it?" She yanked off the hat and let out an oof as I dragged her into my arms and gave her a hard, deep kiss.

When we finally parted, she rubbed her hand over her mouth. Her lipstick was officially toast. "I know it's been like a half hour since you've seen me, but that was one hell of a hello."

"You look gorgeous. Hat, dress, this hair." I lifted a handful of the sunny waves she'd teased around her shoulders then looked over the rest of her. "Those shoes. Peekaboo heels?"

"They better not break."

"I think we're past that streak."

"From your mouth to God's ears."

"Or goddess's." She gave me a wry smile. "Lu and Ry prefer the female interpretation of spirit."

"Male, female, crowd of many. Whichever. You look incredible. So, how do you feel about having babies with me?"

She blinked. Blinked again. "How soon are we talking? There's a growing period."

I laughed and sagged against the wall, drawing her in so I could rub my lips over her jaw where her delicious scent was strongest. Right now, there was a hint of citrus mixed in with the vanilla. "New shampoo? I smell lemons."

"You can't ask someone to have a baby and then be like, 'hey, new face cream?' Which it is, by the way. A moisturizer Lu suggested from this apothecary shop they brought me to." She touched the locket around her throat. "And they enhanced this."

"Enhanced?"

"Story for later. Now back to a baby."

"Actually, I asked for several, and yes, I can ask about face cream right afterward, because I have many tracks when it comes to you." I touched her locket, holding it for a moment while my gaze roamed her face. It seemed unnaturally warm. Enhanced indeed. "Preston and Ryan wanted to meet us at the carnival."

Her eyes widened. "Again with the new topic."

"Well, I wanted to make sure I mentioned that. I know the whole boss thing makes it awkward."

"If the man I'm sleeping with being my future boss isn't awkward—and yes, it is, but I'm trying this new thing called not overreacting—then eating a funnel cake with my current boss shouldn't be too strange."

"What is with you people and funnel cakes?"

"You've never had one? Oh, you don't know what you're missing."

"Apparently. I told him we weren't using any condoms and it went from there."

The pretty flush in her cheeks drained away until she would've blended in quite nicely with the snow on the ground in December. "You did what?"

"Maybe we should sit down." I started drawing her back down the hall to the bedroom.

She pulled on my hand, bringing me to a stop. "I'm just fine here. You did what?"

"I didn't mean to. He's my best friend. Just…I spewed."

"Do you understand what this means for me?"

"No?"

"This means that if we are now doing couples' things, they will be discussing us."

"As if they didn't before?"

"Yeah, but now it will be open season. Which means Preston probably got off the phone and asked Ry if she knew her best friend was an empty-headed crackpot, but in more sophisticated Shaw-esque terms."

"Why are you the crackpot? I was the one who was espousing free, condom-less love."

Her brow arched delicately. "Men are apt to do or say anything when sex is involved. Women are the protectors of the box."

"Box being pussy?"

She nodded soberly. "And you know what's even worse than Ryan and Preston discussing our sex life on a personal level?"

I closed my eyes. Oh, I knew. "Yeah. Sorry."

"Sorry? You're sorry? What if I went to your job and told the guy who signs your paychecks that I'm hoping you knock me up?"

I opened my eyes. "If that's true, I'd probably immediately dedicate myself to the task."

"Pfft." She wrapped her arms around her midsection and leaned against the wall. "I've tried really hard not to think about it. Now you're making me think about it."

"I wasn't thinking about it either. Then I was. It was the damn kids next door."

"Mister and Mrs. Honeycutt?"

"They have a red-headed little boy and a blond little girl and a very large child in utero?"

She shook her head, openly laughing at me. "In utero. God."

"Goddess," I corrected, and she poked me in the stomach.

I grabbed her finger and lifted it to my mouth. "We aren't on anyone's timetable. Not even our own. We're just rolling with whatever happens. I'm good with that. I guess I'm asking if you're good with it too."

She pursed her lips. "I always used condoms every time."

"Same."

"No, but *you* can't get pregnant."

"No, but trust me, I'm in this. I'm not just fucking around here. This is deadly serious to me." I slid my hand around the back of her neck and tugged her in close. "You have to know that."

"The fact that you basically moved in this week without being invited was my first clue."

My heart started that ridiculous speeding up thing that could even out on its own or take me someplace I profoundly did not want to go. "Do you want me to leave?"

She fisted a handful of my shirt as she arched up on her tiptoes to plant tiny teasing kisses all over my mouth. "No. I want you to show me your place so we can figure out how to blend two households with a smut-talking bird and a man-hating cat. And possibly several babies."

The chaotic rhythm in my chest settled. "I don't think your cat hates me so much as she isn't sure what I want with you."

"Oh, she knows. She's got a dirty mind."

"She and Santiago should get on famously then. So, you're good with this whole double date thing? It's all very casual. No definite plans."

"Seems like that's our state of being these days. And what about your sister?"

"She might casually swing by to meet us too. Possibly with her man." I did air quotes around the word *man*, making April poke me again.

"Promise you won't try to intimidate him. The guy is probably an insecure college student."

"But it's one of my best skills. I haven't even needed to pin you with my best opposing counsel glower yet." I turned her around and started walking her down the hall toward the front of the house. "Here I was hoping you'd say no to the double date so I would be forced to convince you with my tongue."

"I didn't know you wanted to see Preston that badly. But if so, be my guest." She playfully swatted my hand when I made a grab for the bottom of her gauzy sundress.

"Actually, who I want to see is Ryan. I need to meet this witch who stole my buddy's heart."

"She's a whole lot of woman."

I hauled April back into my arms and kissed the side of her neck as her laughter filled the hall. "So's mine."

CHAPTER TWENTY-TWO

April

By later that evening, a certain fact had become readily apparent.

Even hot, delicious funnel cake and three rides in a row on the nausea-inspiring Thrillride couldn't kill the buzz of nerves circling that we were officially on meet the family day.

Except in this case, the family was our best friends who were basically family and his sister.

His sister who he adored and talked of glowingly and who supposedly had a radar for phonies. Michaela had never liked Rina, and he'd been a fool for ever denying her wisdom.

So, of course I'd wondered if she would like me. Awkward, fumbling me who'd run off and left her wonderful brother alone on a tropical island without even an explanation.

Yeah, that should go well. Yuppers.

Bishop and I spent a relaxed afternoon strolling by Crescent Lake in nearby Crescent Cove, kicking through the scant leaves starting to accumulate, feeding the ducks, and people watching. It was a sunny, early fall day, balmy and warm, and just wandering through the little shops and taking pictures of the sailboats skimming over the flawless blue glaze of the lake had seemed like perfection.

"You know, you could sell your wares here." He'd stopped beside

Every Line A Story, a craft store that specialized in knitting, crochet, and also had a section dedicated to painting and other creative pursuits. He tapped on the window full of pieces from local artisans. "That purse thing you're making would be great here. You could do a whole line of them. Do themes."

"Themes?"

"Sure. Like holidays. Or for special occasions. Maybe like specific ones for makeup or girly shit."

I nodded, trying to keep my face straight. "Girly shit is a very popular theme."

"Jerk." He hauled me into his side. "You get what I mean. What are they for, anyway? Women don't usually carry bags that small."

"No, of course not. We all tote around suitcases." I held up my own tiny crossbody flip bag.

"I'm going to ignore you."

"They're not actually purses. They're tarot pouches. They started as gifts for Lu and Ry for Christmas, and then I started working on a pattern."

"I like the moon and stars one."

"Thanks. That's Luna's. A little too on the nose, but it fits with her apartment decor too."

"What is Ryan's? I heard she has a crystal fetish. Or I surmised. I didn't actually hear."

"See, it's already started."

"What?"

"Friendly gossip." I drew up my chin and made a show of studying the items displayed in the window. "I won't speculate about my besties."

"She and Preston had some kind of freaky sex on a bench outside under the full moon. I'm working on him to find out if it's something we should investigate. He's being very close-lipped, so I have to figure it was memorable."

"Hate to break it to you, but I'm not witchily-inclined."

"Me either, but that doesn't mean we can't simulate." He bumped his hip into mine and made me giggle.

We started walking again, hand in hand. I was so euphoric, I wondered how my feet didn't lift right off the ground.

"I have something else in mind," I said as we strolled, dodging dog walkers and couples and young moms pushing smiling—or wailing—babies in strollers.

"Oh?"

"I've been thinking about becoming a paralegal. Would you as my new boss have a problem with that?" If there was a small catch in my voice, it couldn't be alleviated. I was still so uneasy with the whole boss-secretary aspect of our relationship, but I was trying to follow the wisdom I'd gained in Georgia's shop.

With a bit of help from my locket.

"No. Absolutely not. I think that's a great idea." He squeezed my fingers then drew me into a hug right there in the middle of the sidewalk. "Your new boss would even make sure the firm picked up the tab for your schooling."

I forced out a breezy laugh. "But no pressure."

"No." His tone was serious. "After what I've been dealing with lately, I've become allergic to pressure, and just as allergic at the idea of pushing it on someone else. So, just think of it as some extra incentive, but if you decide you'd rather sit home and make tarot bags and flower arrangements, well, that's just fine by me too. Although those bats in the jar were kinda creepy."

I framed his face with my hands and kissed him hard. Sometimes he just took away all my words and replaced them with a warm glow.

"You want a jar of them for your desk then." I laughed as he swatted my ass. "Got it."

The whole day was easy, natural. We talked and kissed and held hands as if we'd known each other for a lifetime instead of a couple of weeks. And even less than that if you counted the actual days.

Which I was not. I was trying to enjoy each one as it came, not mark them off on some imaginary calendar to prove it wasn't too soon to feel how I was feeling.

Obviously, I wasn't alone in that, if he already was thinking about the state of my uterus. It was probably unusual in the annals of dating that he'd skipped right to procreation without considering love or marriage, but maybe not in this day and age. And we *were* kind of living together.

Fine, this whole thing was weird and fast and scary as hell. But I was so happy, and when my Grams called the next time, I was going to tell her exactly what was going on.

She would be thrilled for me. How could she not? And she'd already met him, which felt like its own stamp of approval.

Now if the sister liked me, maybe we'd be getting somewhere.

After that, we drove over to the fall carnival at Kensington Square's high school. I could tell Bishop wasn't at all certain about it, but he gamely walked around with me to the different stands and booths. We'd had lunch not all that long ago, not that it seemed to matter to either of our stomachs. We started eating at one end of the strip with corn dogs and ended with cotton candy, with curly fries and everything else in between. Bishop was more into the rides, so that was how I ended up taking the Thrillride three times until finally my cotton candy threatened to come up all over his shoes.

Good thing I'd left the hat in his SUV because that would've gone flying when we were spinning through the air.

"Just once more," he promised as I dropped onto a bench in the shade.

I waved him off. "Ryan and Preston will be here soon enough. I'll just see how close the weight guessing guy gets until they arrive." I didn't have much choice. The overly sweaty guy in a long coat was yelling his guesses a few feet away.

"Awesome." He dropped a kiss on my head and was in line a moment later. Judging by the length of it, he'd be waiting awhile.

Turned out Ryan and Preston didn't appear, but the infamous Michaela Stone did. And she was very much man-less and ridiculously beautiful.

"He dumped me," she announced after she introduced herself and launched herself at me, almost knocking me off the bench in her exuberance. Evidently, Bishop had shared a picture of me with her, so she knew who she was looking for. She was like a small, energetic puppy with her brother's hair and wide smile.

Not that she was smiling now.

"Oh, no. What happened?"

"He's a pig. All men are pigs." She chewed her gum aggressively enough to make me worry for her former man's safety if she saw him strolling about. "You know that song, 'When He Cheats'?"

"Uh oh. Yeah."

"I could totally do that. Carve the shit out of my name in the seats of his vintage Trans-Am and he couldn't do a thing to me because I have the best lawyer in the known universe and he'd smoke his ass."

If Bishop found out his baby sister had been cheated on, he'd probably do the carving himself, and I doubted he'd stop at leather.

"I'm sorry. That's a really awful thing to do. Did you love him?"

"God, no. But the sex was decent." She sighed heavily and examined her manicure. "Maybe the potential was there for love someday. He killed it dead. Like roadkill over the asphalt annihilated."

I glanced over my shoulder just to make sure her brother wasn't hiding behind a tree listening to this conversation. You could never be sure. "That's really dead."

"Yeah. Sure is. So, he hasn't fucked things up yet?"

"No. Was he supposed to?"

"Well, he is male, and on top of that he was wounded by that she-bitch who wrecked my whole family and I hope burns in hell." Michaela sighed. "You probably are wondering if I need a counselor, but I started my period today too."

"Ahh. I get it."

"Do you?" She shifted to study me thoroughly. "You look...delicate."

"I'm not. I'm actually very—" *What?*

As the sun burned a hole in my scalp through an unforeseen gap in the branches above, I wished fervently for my hat.

Dammit, I really was delicate.

"I'm trying to be less so," I finished.

"Why?"

That was a good question. "I feel tossed around by the winds of fate sometimes. If I was stronger, nothing could touch me."

She snorted in an utterly Bishop-like way. "Sure thing, buttercup. Tell me another bedtime story."

"I'm working on swearing more."

"You don't work on that. You just do it." She put her fingers in her mouth and whistled at a shaggy, dark-haired man walking no less than three mixed breed dogs on a split leash. "Hey, nice ass."

The man stopped. He did not turn around. Again, I wished for my hat, but this time so I could bury my face in it.

After a very long moment where I debated saying I had diarrhea so I could escape this trainwreck, the guy turned around and probably slayed half the women within hearing distance. "Talking to me, love?"

Michaela seemed momentarily taken aback by the Irish lilt in his voice. His killer bone structure and piercing eyes weren't bad, either. "And if I was?"

"I'd say you should respect your elders." He murmured to one of the dogs at his side and they all trotted off as if it was any other ass-catcalling day.

"Wow, burn."

I made sympathetic noises in agreement.

"He wasn't even that much older than me. What would you say?"

I'd really rather not get involved. "Maybe ten years on the outside?"

"Even so, hardly makes him an elder. Now I want to take it back. I've seen better asses. I've definitely heard better Irish accents." She crossed her arms over her chest, straining the seams of her cropped jean jacket. "It's probably fake."

"Your brother has a very nice ass."

At her aghast expression, I wondered how much I could blame on heatstroke versus being extremely conflict-averse. "I mean, objectively."

"Do you have a brother?"

"I'm an only child."

"Makes sense now. Do not ever talk about his body parts, or I'll retch right here. The sibling contract involves not knowing any sexual activities. Better yet if we think a monastery is the next natural step, but not so much that we think we have to rent them a prostitute."

"My God, Mickey, I better not be hearing you talk about renting me a prostitute. Also, you don't *rent* prostitutes, you hire them."

"I rest my case." She leaned up to smack Bishop's cheek. "But you're late to the party. A minute ago, I was talking about guys with hot asses and fake accents."

He shot a wistful glance in the direction of the rides. "Is five times too many?"

"Depends what we're referring to, slugger. And hello, don't you say hello to your sister anymore?"

"I'm trying to string together enough consonants. You're burning," he said to me, frowning. "Where's your hat?"

"I left it in the truck."

"Don't worry about her. She's trying not to be so delicate."

"Why?"

"Beats me. I'm going to get an ice cream." She jogged off, disappearing into the growing crowd.

He sat down heavily beside me. "Did she say anything I have to apologize for? I only drew devil horns on her forehead one time when she was sleeping. In my defense, the day before she'd sprayed whipped cream under my nose while I was in bed so I woke up spraying it all over."

I laughed and leaned against him, snuggling into his chest when he wrapped his arm around my shoulders. "Having a sister must be so awesome."

"What part of a whipped cream mustache is awesome?"

"All of it. I never had anyone to draw things on or squabble with or share the dinner dishes with. It was just always quiet. So you could hear your own breathing kind of quiet."

He stroked my back. "Sorry. I'm the king of insensitivity sometimes."

"Nah, you didn't know." I lifted my head to kiss him. "You taste like cherry slurpee. I thought you didn't like them."

"Who, me? By the way, I missed you." He threaded his fingers through my hair and tilted my mouth up to his once more.

"And the guy says *we're* publicly lewd. Ha."

Recognizing my boss's voice behind us made my tongue retreat like a salamander into a sand hole. Bishop, however, simply lifted his middle finger and drew me back with the other hand.

Laughing and shaking my head, I pushed back from him and tried to stay natural as I locked gazes with Ryan and Preston. If I'd thought about it, I would have assumed facing Preston would have been most awkward. Instead, my bestie had her FBI face on, the one she pulled out when she was in hardcore surveillance mode and had no intention of taking any shit.

And her gaze was zeroed in on Bishop.

"Hi there, we haven't met. Ryan Moon. And you are?" She stuck out her hand, and I waited for flames to shoot out of the tips and turn Bishop into a human baked Alaska.

Preston and I exchanged a glance. He was a surprising source of commiseration, since, you know, he and I had never had much of a personal conversation the entire time I worked there except when he announced he was leaving, and it had been awkward as hell since.

The fact I had a sneaking suspicion he'd closed the office for a week so I could be freely naked with his best friend was just another facet to the weirdness. He probably knew Bishop was seeing a doctor. Maybe that was even part of why he'd asked Bishop to take over for him at Shaw, LLC. Even as busy as Preston was, he didn't work 24/7, as it sounded like Bishop did. Plus, as a considerate best friend, he probably wanted Bishop to relax more, and what was more relaxing than having sex?

Assuming I didn't kill the guy inadvertently, a concern that still had not totally left me. I didn't think it ever would.

But now Ryan was going feral.

Bishop tightened his arm around my shoulders and leaned forward to shake Ryan's hand. "Bishop Stone. I've heard a lot about you." He arched a brow at Preston. "Though not as much as I'd like."

Preston ignored him and smiled at me. "Hi, April. Have you eaten yet?"

"We've eaten everything." I laughed too loud and Bishop slanted me a look, probably due to the imminent popping of his eardrums. Whoops. "But I'm still hungry, so if you'd like to grab some stuff, I'll join you."

Ryan gave me a hard glance I didn't quite understand. "Why don't you and PMS go get some cheese fries and whatever else while I chat with Bishop?"

"Fine by me," he said cheerfully while I narrowed my eyes.

"Chat about what, exactly?"

"Getting to know you things." Her smile was entirely too angelic as she plopped down on the bench on his opposite side. "Go on." She waved me off. "We'll be fine."

I fumbled my sunglasses out of my purse as the late day sun threatened to blind me. "Preston can go for all of us. They have trays."

His eyebrow lifted before he shrugged. "Good luck, man." He saluted Bishop and meandered off in the direction of the many food stalls.

Considering I knew his success rate with remembering his own lunch, I'd be impressed if he managed to return with enough food for even himself. Besides, it wasn't like Bishop and I were starving.

Though I wouldn't have minded some of those onion rings by the slurpee stand…

"Nice day, isn't it?" Bishop's voice was so genial it set my teeth on edge. I didn't like the vibes in the air all of a sudden.

"Gorgeous. Perfect for a light sweater." Ryan adjusted her shrug. "You're burning," she said to me.

"I told her. She forgot her hat."

"Not just her face, though that especially. Her arms too." She tugged her bag into her lap and reached in for a tiny tub of salve, passing it to me. "Try that. It should help protect against further damage and soothe any burn you've already gotten. It's also safe for sensitive conditions." Time for another hard look in Bishop's direction.

I took the tub and started slathering it on. "Thanks."

I knew she was angling at something—and I had a very good idea what—but I didn't want a fight. Even if she was just concerned about me, I wasn't going to go there. Not now. Not when we'd had such a good day and everything was so new and tenuous.

"So, has Preston moved you in yet?"

Ryan wound her flyaway hair into a knot on top of her head. The wind was kicking up as the sun was heading down. "I'm not a refrigerator. He can't 'move me in' without my participation."

I sighed. "Sorry. Bad choice of words. I got too much sun today and—"

"Too much baby juice?"

I'd never known even the soles of my feet could blush. Today was an education in a number of ways. "Bishop, can you please give us a few minutes?"

"No, I'd rather not, if that's okay with you. Obviously Preston told you about our conversation today?"

She pressed her lips together. "He didn't get too specific but I got the gist. He's worried."

"Clearly you are too."

"Hell no. I have ways of bringing pain into your world you can't fathom, Stone."

"Ryan, what the hell?" A quick spurt of panic had me glancing between them. Bishop did not look concerned unlike me. "We really need to talk alone."

"Sorry, Cinderella, no can do. I think your best friend thinks I'm some kind of baby harvester, instead of just a guy who's happy. I'm not trying to get her pregnant."

"Let me explain how this process works. You do things that lead to certain other things, you can anticipate certain outcomes. Or if you just want to know the joys of the latex-free life, you get an IUD or some birth control pills, and you vow to never, ever go to Crescent Cove."

"We didn't go to Crescent Cove." I frowned. "Well, we walked around there today but we both had our underwear on."

"A relief for the townspeople, I'm sure." She pulled her leg up under her on the bench and turned her attention toward Bishop. "How does a player go from being all over the place to oh so committed without actual commitment so fast?"

I started to interject, but Bishop held up his hand. "Preston told you I was all over the place?"

"No. He wouldn't. The guy is more true blue than the flag. I had Luna do a reading. She said you had very intense but inconsistent energy. I surmised that meant that—"

"I'm leading her on for my baby harvesting program."

"Can you not say baby harvesting?" I shuddered and wrapped my arms around my belly. I was losing my appetite fast. "Or else I'm going to go find Mickey and join her in whistling at fine asses with possibly fake Irish accents."

"I didn't realize an ass could have any accent, never mind fake." Ryan tapped her cheek. "Who's Mickey?"

"My baby sister. I wanted her to meet April. She's also my best friend and chief counsel. It was probably neck and neck who wanted her to meet her more, because my sister would hound me forever if she didn't like her."

"Yet she's gone?"

"Yeah, her ultimate seal of approval. Nothing to worry about with her, so she's not going to get in our space—at least not this soon." Bishop toyed with my hair, sliding Ryan a pointed look. "Good philosophy. She's smart for 22."

"You're meeting his family?" Ryan demanded as if Bishop had just said we'd had sex in church.

Actually, she would've been less shocked at that, minus the whole church aspect. Due to her beliefs, she didn't visit them as a rule.

"The most important part of my family. I'm estranged from my brother and my parents."

"Why?"

"Ryan," I hissed. "Did you completely lose your manners?"

"No, it's fine." Bishop's voice was buttercream smooth. "My ex-fiancée ran off with my brother. My parents sided with him."

"Technically, his mother wanted to remain neutral."

"You sure you're not a lawyer too?" he asked mildly, rubbing his thumb over my lower lip. But he didn't seem mad at my correction. Maybe he was thinking about what I'd said the other day.

Not that I knew the players involved or had any right to speculate. I just couldn't stand him thinking his family had all aligned against him except Mickey. I hoped like hell it wasn't true.

Ryan glanced between us as if she couldn't believe what she was seeing. "And you're open and upfront about all this."

"Yeah. Trying. It wasn't exactly easy to share it with anyone." His laughter was wry. "But I want to get this right. Or at least not so wrong."

"And Preston knows about all this," she said slowly. "The thing with your ex and your brother, all of it?"

"Yeah. He was at my side when it went down at the wedding. Think about the most soap-opera-like scene you could imagine and that sums it up. They ran out hand in hand. I walked out supported by Preston." Bishop shook his head and tightened his hold on me as I curled into him to give him support the best way I knew how. "So, if you're wondering why I'm not the most marriage-minded guy, that's why. Though I'm not against it. I just want the family more than the piece of paper." He ran his hand down my hair and then kept going to my arm under my sleeve. "You're still too warm. We should get you inside."

"I'm fine. The sun will be gone in a few minutes." I glanced at my best friend, who no longer appeared ready to take a bite out of him if he said something she didn't like. "We discussed everything. We might be making unusual choices right now, but we're doing it with our eyes open. Remember this?" I reached up for my locket, gripped it in my fist. "Staying open to love in all its forms is what I'm trying to do right now. Trusting if the path is meant to be mine, I'll find my way to it."

She nodded hard, her aquamarine eyes gem-bright in the fading sun. "Yes. That's exactly right." She released a long, slow breath. "Sorry, I forgot myself. I just love you, Apes. You're my sister. I wouldn't hesitate to bind his balls if he did anything the slightest bit funky."

I smiled mistily and started to lean over him to hug Ry when I caught his grimace and laughed. "You're safe. I'll protect your balls. But my besties are both witches, so you know, mind them."

"Your besties or my balls?"

"Both," Ryan and I said simultaneously before looking at each other and dissolving into laughter. I scrambled away from him to go around to the other side of Ryan on the bench so we could have a nice long hug. We rocked and laughed and maybe even cried a little as the night's musical entertainment, a country act, started up on the temporary stage.

When I peeked at Bishop, he was staring at us, mystified.

"About time, my man," he said to someone approaching who must've been Preston. "The girls are having a moment, and I didn't know if I should join in or throw money."

I kicked him and he laughed.

"Ran into a friend working hard as always at the petting zoo. Grant finally decided to take a half hour off and eat."

We broke apart as Preston and the man called Grant started offloading food to Bishop. I smiled and stood up to help until I took a good look at him. When I'd seen him last, he'd been walking three dogs.

"Oh, God," I said under my breath, backing up and frantically looking around for Mickey.

Bishop immediately stood, still juggling the three drinks Preston had all but dumped on him. "What's wrong?" he asked in an undertone.

I just shook my head and accepted a carton of cheese fries from Preston. "Thank you."

"Hello again," Grant said with a smile. "Where's your mouthy friend?"

I did not speak. How did one answer that question?

"She just had a rough breakup," I mumbled. "She didn't mean any harm."

"Ah, so time to inspect the merchandise, I see. Oh, hello, Ryan. Good to see you again."

Ryan stood and launched herself at him, giving him a quick hug. "Same goes, Grant. How's Poppy?"

"Rambunctious as always. And hello to you too, Bishop. Santiago's well?"

"He's definitely well, and as mouthy as April's 'friend'." With an eyebrow wiggle at me, Bishop set down the remaining drinks and extended his hand to Grant. "Nice to see you out and about and not working such long hours for once."

"Oh, the animals treat me well, but people can be a whole other story." He shook Bishop's hand then moved back and sent me a charming grin. "And who's this?"

"This would be my girlfriend." A warm rush of pleasure spread through me as Bishop looped his arm around my shoulders and kissed my temple. "April Finley, meet Grant Thorn, the best vet in the state."

Still flushed—for several reasons now—I smiled at the vet. "Hi. Pleased to meet you."

"Oh, but we met already. In a manner of speaking."

"She's a lovely person," I said quickly. "And I'll be sure to tell her your accent is real."

"Appreciate it." Grant's laughter was rich and long and had Bishop giving me a healthy dose of side-eye as Grant chatted quietly with Preston and Ryan.

"Okay, what did Mickey say to him?"

I shut my eyes and shook my head. "Trust me, you do not want to know."

CHAPTER TWENTY-THREE

Bishop

April hummed to herself on the ride back after the carnival. Her song of choice? "Thriller" on the Halloween satellite station.

She was so freaking enticing, I couldn't think straight. Or keep my hands off her. I kept rubbing her knee underneath the hem of her sundress, occasionally skimming my thumb higher along her inner thigh. At a stoplight, I'd fisted my hand in her hair and dragged her close for a taste, enjoying the doughy, sugary taste of funnel cake.

Preston was right. It was delicious. Especially on her lips.

When "Thriller" rolled into "Werewolves of London", I slid her a sidelong smile. "All things considered, I think our first couples' date was a success, don't you?"

Hearing myself made me groan inwardly. Seriously? Next I'd be asking to help sew tarot bags and little pouches for my balls.

Yet I couldn't really dredge up much concern for my missing swagger. What the hell had it ever gotten me? I'd been miserable most of the past few years. Right now, I was happy. And I was going to master using that hot glue gun, dammit.

It was now a personal quest.

"Yeah. Ry mentioned making Caleb and Lu come next time. She hadn't heard the caramel apple story. She thinks they were just naked."

"It's a valid reason to skip the carnival. Or basically anything." At the stop sign, I leaned over to nuzzle her jaw, inhaling her vanilla scent. "Take off your panties."

Her scandalized look made me hard in a second. "Why, Mr. Stone, surely that can't be proper." She did as I asked, removing them quickly and licked her lips as she dropped them on the center console.

I was never getting this car detailed again.

"I want to fuck you in my apartment. On every surface. In every room. Possibly also out on the fire escape."

Her laughter teased out my grin. "Happy Fri-yay to me."

That wasn't all I wanted to do with her in my place, but it was a start. "Fair warning, we'll probably have to lock out the bird. He's a damn lech."

"He should meet Kit-Kat. She had her face pressed against the shower door this morning."

I grinned. "I can beat you. She curled up in the sink to watch me shower yesterday and when I got out, she tried to lick the water droplets off the floor."

"Why am I not surprised? She's also fond of watching you sleep. I've caught her doing that a couple of times this—uh oh." She grabbed her phone out of her purse and swiped before lifting it to her ear. "Hey, Grams. How are you?"

I slid her a look. Grams wasn't aware of how our relationship had progressed, best as I knew. April had told her we were spending time together, and her grandmother seemed glad to hear it and mentioned us all going to dinner when she and Roger returned home in a couple days.

But spending time together wasn't quite the same as unofficially living together. I just hadn't left since I'd gotten there on Monday, at least not for more than a few hours at a time. When I stopped by home to hang out with Santiago, I made phone calls and handled emails. I was in no mood to sort through the materials Vienna, my admin, compiled for me to keep me abreast of updates with my clients, but I did my job. Yesterday I'd had a Zoom meeting with Eli and Cord, the associate lawyers I worked with the most at my firm, and I'd discussed shifting more work their way. I'd then told them I was considering other opportunities beyond the Pierson law group.

Seriously considering.

They both had been supportive, and privately, Eli had asked if I wanted to bring someone else on where I was going. I'd admitted I didn't know the parameters of the workflow yet or if that would be necessary, but that if I did, he was the lawyer I'd call. He thanked me, wished me luck, and then I'd gone off to clean the cage of my rage-y parrot, who had asked me no less than three times if I was on the rag.

Yes, I'd made the mistake about asking that exact question about one of my least favorite clients when talking to Eli months ago. Santiago had whipped it out at a moment's notice ever since.

I'd learned my lesson not to anger the gods with misogynistic comments.

"Oh, that sounds so nice. Tomorrow? Home? Wow. Yes. Wow. Uh-huh. Wow."

I frowned. That was a lot of exclamations.

"Of course. Sure, he should be available. At least I think so." She peeked at me out of the corner of her eye. "I'll check. He's really busy. Not this week so much, because he took an unplanned vacation—no, Grams, oh my God." She covered her face with her hand. "I still have a couple left."

"I'm available," I mouthed.

She reached over to grab my thigh—or so I thought she was aiming for. Instead, she grasped a part of me far more excited by the prospect and I made a noise that nearly made her drop the phone.

"Shh, shh!" she hissed at me before picking it up again. "Sorry, Grams. No, we're just on the way to his—his size? For what? Oh, Lord, really?"

I was so intrigued by her half of the conversation, I almost forgot my throbbing dick.

Almost.

She hung up a couple of moments later just as I parked down near the end of my block. It was a nice night, and although my building had a garage—with a direct elevator to my apartment—I wanted to stroll with her for a few minutes. I wasn't in any hurry for this day to end.

That had been true of all the days we'd shared so far. Each one had been better than the last.

Dude, you are sunk.

"Dare I ask what your grandmother wanted to know my size for?"

"She bought you something when she was in the islands. She guessed your size as extra-large."

"My size what as extra-large?" I was afraid to verbalize the question.

"Boxers," April said in a low voice, waving me off when I started to speak. "She assured me they're tasteful."

"Um…" I took a breath. "This whole meeting and getting used to the families thing is going to be an experience, isn't it?"

"I think you're correct. Also, she said she knew I'd used all the condoms she'd given me and was startled I had not."

"Wait til she finds out why."

For about the fifth time in the last half hour, she covered her face with her hands. "She's going to think I've lost my cocoa puffs."

"Your grams ran away with someone she met in Fiji for a couple of weeks. I don't think she'll be too judgmental."

"Yeah, but she can't get pregnant."

"Let's hope not. That would be noteworthy for an entirely different reason."

She dropped her hands and grinned, undoing her seatbelt and sliding across the seat. "You inspire me to act like someone else."

I ran my fingertip down her nose. "Same goes. Or maybe we just never knew ourselves at all." I unclicked my seatbelt and lowered my head to kiss her, sucking her lower lip between my teeth while she made that hungry sound that made me so crazy. I pulled her against me and she wrapped her hand around the back my neck, dragging her nails over my skin while I drew on the tip of her tongue and wondered if I could just fuck her right here.

"No," she said between kisses, caught between a laugh and a moan. "Take me inside."

"Did I...say that out loud? God, your mouth."

"Mmm, you sure did. Inside." She drew back and patted my chest, releasing a laugh as I hauled her in for one more kiss.

Or five.

Once we finally made it out onto the sidewalk, I bent forward and lifted my brows. "Climb on."

"What?" Her giggle was perilously loud although she tried to keep it down. "Like a piggyback ride?"

"Sure. I can handle you. Besides, you have a bad track record with heels."

"Low blow." But she clambered up onto my back and gripped her legs around my waist as she slung her arms around my neck and kissed my ear. "Oh, this position has its benefits." She wiggled her foot free of my hold and managed to run her low heel over the base of my cock, eliciting a string of curses that made her laugh in delight. "Let's see you walk with that nine-iron in your trousers, Stone."

"Here I thought you were so sweet and kind. You fooled me, you sexy wench." I came to a halt outside the double doors to my building, quickly typing in my code and standing still to allow the eye recognition scanners to do their thing. Squirmy McSquirmerson barely stopped moving long enough for me to remain motionless, but a series of beeps finally heralded the doors opening.

"Fancy building for a fancy lawyer." She bit the top of my ear as I carted her inside and went straight to the elevators. The night doorman cast a dubious glance my way but said nothing.

It was completely normal to carry a beautiful blond woman on your back across the lobby of a multi-million dollar building, right? Sure thing.

And here, I'd bypassed parking in the garage where I would've had direct access to a private elevator that led to my apartment. More examples of my sensible thinking.

Whatever. Living dangerously was my new motto.

Once we were in the elevator, I still didn't put her down. I wasn't sure why I liked carrying her around so much, but the way she laughed so freely every time made me just want to do it again.

Bringing joy to someone was so much more satisfying than beating them in court or finding a piece of missing evidence that would poke holes in their case.

Who knew?

"I think you were a horse in another life with all your toting me around." She covered my eyes with her hands as the elevator dinged on my floor. "Let's see how well you know your building."

"Oh, now you're raising the bar." I headed out in what I hoped was the right direction and she laughed uproariously as I overcompensated and pivoted into the wall instead of around the corner.

"Left. At least I think that's where you were headed." She giggled. "Guess this wasn't too smart since I haven't been—Bishop."

At the sudden worry in her tone, I reached up to drag her hand away from my eye. And came face to face with someone I'd never wanted to see again.

The fact that it was a man I'd once idolized and had considered my best friend made it so much worse.

"Bishop." Key's voice sounded ragged as he walked up the hall toward me. His jacket had seen better days. His shirt didn't fit him right. He smelled of his preferred whiskey and as if he hadn't showered recently.

I didn't feel concern. Not right away. I'd hardened my heart toward my brother years ago, and the walls were thick. But one emotion cracked through immediately.

"Jump down," I said softly, calmly, to April.

She did as I asked and then I turned to her, trying like hell not to show what was in my head as I withdrew her panties from my pocket and pressed them into her hand. "My apartment is at the other end of the hall. 11B. Code is 89912." The last part I mouthed so we couldn't be overheard. "I'll be right in. Please get dressed."

I couldn't believe I'd had her take off her panties when she was wearing a dress. A long one, but still. Then I'd paraded around with her on my back where anyone could see if she moved wrong.

I was a damn fool.

Her brows knitted together at the final thing I'd said before she peered over my shoulder in Key's direction. Her pupils enlarged as if she understood who he was. We'd always looked a lot alike. He was just the taller, leaner version. We still shared a strong similarity, even if he appeared far rougher than he had the last time I saw him.

At your wedding.

April reached up to wrap her hands around the back of my neck, drawing me into a long, slow kiss without any concern for who was watching. As she eased back, I fumbled for something to say, but she spoke before I could.

"I love you, Bishop." Her expression held so much emotion that I couldn't breathe.

She walked away, confidence in every step. Was this still the same woman who'd seemed so shy at first in Fiji? We both had changed in the very best ways in such a short time.

Having someone who cared about you made everything different. Better.

Made *me* better.

When she passed my brother, she didn't pause, just gave him a scathing glance that could've torched him where he stood.

She went down the hall, tapped in the code I'd given her, and then walked inside to a loud series of parrot screams that barely made her miss a beat before she closed the door.

Despite everything, I grinned. I didn't have to worry about intruders. Santiago could do a good imitation of a murder victim on cue.

And besides that, April Finley loved me. She hadn't even hesitated. So, really, what did I care about Key showing up here like the prodigal brother?

He couldn't hurt me anymore.

Couldn't hurt *us*.

"You look good." Key scraped a hand over his over-long golden brown hair so like my own. His was more on the golden side thanks to lots of hours spent working outside. He had his own successful landscaping business. He loved nothing more than spending hours cultivating a client's outdoor space, even though he'd built a talented team to support him.

Or at least that had been the case a few years ago. After the wedding, he and Rina had moved to a town halfway between here and Buffalo, and I'd assumed he'd transferred the business, as well.

The Key I'd known hadn't worn ripped jeans or baggy shirts and let his hair grow unkempt. The light that had always been in his eyes was gone, and his ready smile had disappeared behind a thick beard.

He was still my brother—but not.

Hell, he could dress and live however he wanted to. His choice. In the end, I hadn't really known him at all. So, maybe this was simply the real Key.

"You don't," I said shortly. "What are you doing here?"

For a moment, his blinding white smile slashed through his beard. "Right to it, huh?"

"I don't want to keep my girlfriend waiting. We have plans."

"She's beautiful."

With effort, I didn't growl. I trusted her and this was a whole new situation. But it was really hard not to let echoes of my past resurface while I was standing a few feet away from the man who had literally helped to change the trajectory of my life.

For the better, I could see now. April had been absolutely right there. Rina had never been meant for me.

"She is, and even better, she's smart and funny and sweet."

And I can believe in her and us and what we're building.

"You're happy."

"I am. Very much so."

"I'd like to talk to her, get to know her—hell, Shoop, get to know you again. A lot of time has passed."

I locked my jaw. Hearing my old nickname from him reopened ancient wounds and dumped in a dollop of salt. "What did you hope to gain from coming here?"

"Didn't I just tell you?"

"You wanted to meet my girlfriend you didn't know I had. Right." I crossed my arms. "How did you even get in here?"

"I said I was your brother, showed ID. The woman in the lobby took pity on me."

"Woman. Right." He wouldn't have been as lucky with the doorman working now. "So, flashed her the old Key charm. You never quit."

"Actually, I do. But I'm desperate. I need to apologize to you. I need to make amends."

"Oh, you need. It's all about you again." I shook my head and started walking up the hall toward my apartment. I wished it didn't hurt to turn my back on him, that I could be as cold as I'd purported to be these past few years. But I'd loved and admired my brother so much. Deep down, some part of me still longed for his approval.

Especially longed for my family to be whole and okay again. We'd been so close and tight knit before all of this. I'd give anything to have not proposed to Rina if it meant I'd get to keep my big brother and my parents in my life.

In fact, I wished I could erase her existence entirely. I'd thought I'd loved her, but my feelings for her paled compared to how I already felt for April.

She was my forever. Rina had been my right then.

"Shoop, I divorced Rina. We're through."

I didn't turn around. "So? Is that supposed to change anything?"

"I guess I hoped…" He puffed out a breath. "I did this all wrong."

A flicker of compassion tried to build inside of me. I didn't want it. I also didn't think it was entirely my own doing. Someone was already making me softer. Turning my apex predator into a teddy bear with quills.

I hoped I still had the damn quills. Somewhere.

I closed my eyes and hoped like hell I wasn't making a mistake. Wanting something didn't mean it was the smart choice. Sometimes the only decision to make was to move on. Which I thought I'd done.

Not so much.

A lot harder to move on when he was standing here in my hallway, and I knew he was struggling. What the hell kind of man was I if I could turn away from my own flesh and blood, even if he'd wronged me? Everyone made mistakes. He hadn't had a pattern of them with me. Just the opposite. We'd always been so tight and losing him for these past few years had been agony.

If I could get him back again...

"Let's go inside." Before he could take a step, I held up my hand. "This isn't any more than a conversation. Don't make it anything else."

"I know. I won't. I'm grateful for even that, man." He exhaled again, the tension in his long, lanky frame leaving him for a moment. "You don't know how much."

"Yeah, yeah. If you look at April sideways, I will make your nuts into ponytail holders. Don't think I won't."

His lips started to twist before he schooled his features. "Noted."

I watched him over my shoulder, making sure he kept his distance while I typed in my code. He kept a proper distance back. I opened the door and ducked and almost rolled into the couch as a low flying, shrieking African Grey sailed over my head and into the hall.

It sounded suspiciously like he was screeching the word, "pussy!"

My brother also ducked, but he wasn't expecting the dive bombing parrot so wasn't able to correct himself before he cannonballed into the wall. April raced into the hall after Santiago, shooting me a panicked look before Key shot to his feet and whipped off his jacket, covering the bird who had momentarily landed on the floor to examine some speck he'd considered might be a snack. Key grabbed him like a football and sprinted down the hall, doing his best to contain the squawking, flailing parrot before tossing him in the direction of my open apartment door and pulling it shut as if he'd locked away some evil spirit.

He wasn't evil, but he did a pretty good imitation when he was irritated. Which was often.

Panting, Key turned around and sagged against the solid steel core door while Santiago shouted his word of the moment on the opposite side.

"Pussy! Pussy! Pussy!"

I glanced at April, who was wide-eyed and staring back at me. "So, that's my bird. What did you think?"

CHAPTER TWENTY-FOUR

April

THIS EVENING HAD TAKEN an unexpected turn. Why was I even surprised?

Looking at Bishop and Key sitting side by side on the couch—well, with two cushions between them—was vaguely disturbing. Not only were they both insanely handsome specimens, they strongly resembled each other, right down to the stubborn set of their chins. The biggest difference was that Bishop was broader and more muscular, where Key had more of a runner's body and was taller. And of course, Bishop's eyes were gorgeous gem green where Key's were more of a muted shade.

Not that I was biased or anything.

But as much as they looked alike, they definitely were very different men. I'd just met Key, and I knew that already. Bishop was so naturally outgoing, although Key might've been more reticent because of the awkward situation.

Oh, boy, was it awkward.

I glanced over to where the formerly pissed-off parrot was now sitting at the top of a miniature sized bird slide complete with small wading pool, daintily eating a whole banana—including the peel. "Santiago is enjoying himself."

The mere sound of my voice had him lifting his head to give me a beady stare. I expected him to yell his favorite word but he just kept eating.

"The way to his heart is through his stomach. Shove a banana at him and he chills right out. It's basically parrot weed."

I coughed. "Maybe I need a banana then."

"You aren't the only one," Key muttered.

"How did you get the name Key? Seems questionable with the last name Stone."

"No kidding. That would be my father's idea, since he apparently impregnated my mother in her dorm room on the campus of Keystone College. They thought it was a sign."

Lifting my brows, I looked at Bishop. "And let me guess, your dad is a chess fan?"

"Nope, Bishops are the mascot of a football team they saw play the day he knocked my mom up." He rolled his eyes. "By the time they got to Michaela, they'd given up that nonsense and Mom just picked a name they both liked. Mickey was eternally grateful because by then our father was taking graduate courses at Syracuse University. She had no desire to be named Orange for their mascot or any variation therein."

"Aww, good thing. I was hoping we could save Orange for ours." I didn't know what made me say it. Probably some deep down desire to demonstrate without a doubt to Key that Bishop was doing just fine after his betrayal.

The emotion that moved through Bishop's gaze made my fingers twitch on the arm of the recliner. We'd spent so much time holding hands today that I didn't know what to do with him being so close and not being able to touch him.

As if he knew, he patted the seat beside him. I went to him without a word, catching Key's mystified look as I curled into his brother's side.

"You two are cute," he said from my other side.

Still mystified? Check.

"Thanks." I spoke when it became clear Bishop had no intention of it. "I'd say you're cute too, but your brother is cuter."

Key laughed. "Hooked this one good, Shoop."

"He sure did. What does Shoop stand for?"

Bishop wrapped his arm around my shoulders and tipped his head to mine. "This is not a chance for you to find out all my embarrassing stories."

"You think not? C'mon, spill it."

"He loved that song by Salt 'n' Pepa. Every time it came on, he tried to rap. It was fairly sad."

"I was six," Bishop informed me before leaning around me to speak to his brother. "Tried to? I rhymed with Pepa like it was my job. Shows what you know."

I swallowed a laugh until Bishop pinched my side and it tumbled out of me, unrestrained. "I'm trying to picture you rapping."

"Oh, he did it all the time, even after he was grown. I can't say he got any better. There was even talk of playing 'Shoop' at the reception, but Rina—" Key cut himself off, but it was too late. The mood was ruined.

I cut a glance toward Bishop, but he didn't look pained. If anything, he seemed…bored. His gaze locked on my legs, pulled up under me with the hem of my sundress just barely covering them. He slid a possessive hand over my knees, and it might've niggled at me if I hadn't understood all too well why he'd feel proprietary.

"You married Rina," I said after a moment, silently imploring Bishop with my eyes. I didn't know what the hell I was doing, but sitting in this uneasy silence wasn't helping anyone. Better to excise the wound and move on if that was all that was left.

I hoped it wasn't, for Bishop's sake. From little comments he'd made here and there and even how he'd looked at his brother, I knew he missed the excised parts of his family. If this could be the beginning of getting them back in some shape or form, then the discomfort would be worth it.

Key stared at me as if I'd just swallowed a flamethrower. Even Santiago dropped his banana peel in open shock before he flapped his wing and hopped down to retrieve it. I could just imagine his thought process.

Human dramas are so tedious.

"Yes," he said slowly.

"And you divorced her?"

He nodded.

"Honestly? Or did she cheat on you too, and you're trying to preserve your questionable masculinity?"

Bishop smothered his laughter in a cough.

"No. At least, I don't know it if she did. We grew apart. Classic story. I've had friends it happened to, and most of them say there's nothing to be done to avoid it."

"Sure there is." I shrugged. "Don't marry a woman you can't trust. But then again, you'd be screwed anyway, since you're not exactly batting a million on the trust score yourself."

Key blinked. "You're a cute little bunny with vampire fangs."

This time, Bishop didn't temper his laughter. I cocked a brow in his direction as it rolled out of him, but I much preferred him laughing than something else.

I crossed my arms. "What exactly did you come here to do?"

"Sharp vampire fangs," Key muttered.

Bishop laid a hand on my thigh and squeezed. "You don't have to do this."

"I can interrogate people too. Take a night off, counselor."

"I only have one brother." Key lowered his voice. "I screwed up, okay?"

"Would it be okay if he'd done it to you?"

He cracked his jaw. "No. I wouldn't even be sitting here right now. But he has you and is happy. He said it himself. So, what does it—"

"What does it matter that you're a faithless whore?" I asked pleasantly. "A hell of a lot, actually. Loyalty is the foundation of a relationship. *Any* relationship, and it seems like you need some remedial work on that subject."

Bishop's hand turned into a steel brace on my leg, but a quick glance at his face told me he wasn't angry. Try the opposite. His steady green gaze roamed my face, settling there with the sort of hungry promise that told me he wasn't thinking of any other women but me right now.

"Damn, Bishop, no wonder you don't care about Rina anymore. You've got ten times the woman sitting right here, defending you." Key didn't give Bishop a chance to reply. "You're right. I hate that you're right, but you are."

"I am?" I cleared my throat. I was new at this whole 'being kickass' thing. "Yes, I am. So there."

Bishop's pressure on my thigh grew even more intense and hotter somehow. As if we were now alone, no matter who else was physically with us.

They didn't exist anymore. Simply didn't matter.

"I have 100 times the woman Rina was at my side." Bishop's mouth brushed along the side of my neck, and I shivered so visibly that Key's eyes widened. "And you did me a favor by making sure I didn't marry the wrong woman, so someday I can marry the right."

Oh, God. Now I was really shivering. Inside and out. I didn't bother trying to hide it, either.

Bishop needed to know exactly how I felt. No more guessing games. No more tucking parts of myself away.

He was getting all of me from now on. Good, bad, and horny.

Leading with horny at the moment.

Key leaped to his feet. "All right then. Guess that's my cue to go."

Bishop let Key walk a few steps toward the door before speaking. The whole time, his gaze remained on mine.

"Key."

Key waited.

"I appreciate you coming by. We'll talk again."

That was it. No long drawn out acceptance of the apology I hadn't heard Key give, but I assumed maybe he had in the hall. No false platitudes. Not even a hug.

But even that much of an olive branch made Key's tight frame sag for a moment before he shored up his defenses and smiled briefly.

"Thanks, Shoop. It's damn good to see you—and to see you like this. It's different now with her, isn't it?"

Bishop nodded but he didn't elaborate. He was too busy trying to make me come with nothing other than the power of his stare.

It was on its way to working too.

"I'm glad. Truly I am. Nice to meet you, April."

"Same." I waved at him over my shoulder without turning toward him. I'd given him enough of my attention for one night.

Now I had an all new focus. My favorite one.

"As for you, bird," Key said, "it's been real."

Santiago threw what was left of his banana peel at him. Then after Key left, he retrieved it and started nibbling at it again.

"Waste not, want not." I laughed.

But Bishop wasn't in the mood to laugh anymore. "Did you find your way to my bedroom?"

"What, for those five minutes I was alone in here?" I shook my head. "No. I texted Lu to see if she was feeling okay enough to check on Kit-Kat tomorrow morning."

"Oh?" He fingered my windblown hair, twirling it between his thick fingers. "Reason why?"

"Yes. I want to suck you off in front of those big, wide windows over there." I nodded toward the big transom windows on the other side of the open space that made up his living area, cut off on one side by the surprisingly spacious galley kitchen.

One I intended to investigate after I made a meal of *him*.

"Jesus, baby, you're going to have me messing up my rug this time instead of yours."

"No, I won't." I swallowed hard and tugged at the bodice of my sundress as I climbed onto his lap to straddle him. "I have a much better target for you to aim for."

"Yet you're climbing on top of me…"

"I don't want to wait. I'm greedy. What can I say?" I leaned forward and yanked down the collar of his T-shirt, feasting my mouth on his skin. Trailing kisses from his neck over his collarbones and then farther down to where his dark hair started. "I love this. Think it does something to my pheromones." I ran my fingers through the crinkly strands while he let out a chuckle. "Do you think you're up to performing similar feats to what you did on Monday?"

"Depends. Be descriptive."

I peeked up at him as I licked his skin. "I've never actually given a blowjob."

"Ever?"

"Never." I yanked his shirt downward as much as possible, well aware I was stretching it all to hell. He didn't seem to have any complaints as I circled his nipple with the tip of my tongue. "Let's just say I tried once and decided it was a dismal failure."

"You don't have to. I don't expect—"

"Yes, I do. I expect. I want to taste you. I want you to know you're the only man I've wanted to be with that way. Only you." I licked my way up his throat to nip his chin, placing my hand on his heart to feel the steady thud that centered me so easily. "I love you, Bishop, and I'm going to keep saying it until you believe me."

He shut his eyes. "What did I do to deserve you?" His voice was broken like glass and made a lump form in my throat.

I'd figured admitting it once would be scary, never mind twice. But it wasn't. And I wasn't going crazy because he hadn't said it back yet.

He would. For the first time in my life, I just *knew*.

"Well, first of all, you went down on me for like twenty minutes that first night." His eyes flew back open as I grinned, desperate to see him smile again. "That kind of sealed the deal."

But his expression remained serious as he wound my hair behind my ear, his gaze searching mine. "I love you too, April. You know that, right? Please tell me you know."

I smiled even through the gathering heat in my eyes. "I know. I think I knew right away. It's why I had to run. No one ever had chosen me first, and I couldn't bear to watch it end. It couldn't last—"

"It will. I won't change my mind. We're just at the beginning. I love all of you I know today and the you I'll learn more about tomorrow."

He kissed me so gently that there was no holding back the tears.

He didn't shy away from them, kissing them too as they slipped down my cheeks.

"I believe you. With everything inside me, I'm believing in you, Bishop Stone."

He drew me down on the sofa, rolling me beneath him so he could frame my head with his muscular arms. Then he just smiled down at me with every ounce of the naked emotion we'd both tried so hard to hide from each other.

No more mysteries.

He reached down to draw off my panties, grunting as he realized how damp they were already. Then he glanced up and narrowed his eyes, pointing with a handful of silk.

"You. Hit the road, pal."

Santiago stood on the coffee table, blinking innocently.

I knew what was coming even before he opened his beak.

"Pussy!"

"Not for you. You know where to go." He pointed down the hall off the living room and the bird danced from foot to foot. I was waiting for him to mutter under his breath. I wasn't sure parrots were capable of that, but I had a feeling Santiago had his own rulebook.

Rather than flying away, he hopped down off the coffee table and, head held high, marched down the hall. Where he went, I couldn't see, but I wasn't altogether sure there wouldn't be destruction in his wake.

Bishop shook his head, a smile playing around his mouth. "Sorry. He's mostly well-behaved, so I try not to cage him more than I have to."

"You're a good daddy."

"I will be." His breath stuttered then he dropped my panties on the floor and bent to kiss me, filling his hands with my hair. "I can't wait."

It was insanity. So much of this was. But I'd never felt saner or more me in my life as I reached for his belt, yanking it free of its loops. He arched up to give me room to scoop him out of his boxers, to caress his hot, hard length while I teasingly drew on his tongue. He groaned and thrust into my fist, his movements chaotic and untamed already.

"I had a plan," I breathed between kisses. "I'd start the traditional way. BJ, then sex."

"Valid plan," he breathed back.

"But I figure we've done stuff differently so let's mix it up."

I shoved his jeans and boxers down over his ass and thighs. He kicked them off along with his socks and sneakers. When I would've just pulled up my sundress, he shook his head and drew me up so he could tug it over my head. With a few flicks of his fingers, my bra went flying.

Instead of immediately pulling me down again, he commanded the lights to dim and shifted me until I faced the floor-to-ceiling windows. Beyond the glass, Downtown Kensington Square's lights glittered along with the backdrop of nearby Syracuse. The glow reflected off the expanse of Crescent Lake just visible in the distance, and I gasped as if he'd just shown me the Eiffel Tower.

I didn't need any of that. He'd given me the world even when it was just us two. The rest was just ambience.

He bit my earlobe, and I rolled my neck to give him more access as he nudged my hair over my other shoulder. His fingers skimmed over my breasts, tugging and twisting my sensitive nipples while moisture pooled between my thighs.

I couldn't be embarrassed. He knew exactly how to touch me. Had from the start. Knew that when he dragged his fingers through my wetness and lifted them to my mouth that I'd need the nip of his teeth on my shoulder to encourage me. I sucked them in and he groaned into my hair, banding his arm around my stomach to pull me backward. He was sitting on his feet, so when he drew me back, his cock parted me. I flowed open around him, sliding down in one fluid move. He groaned again, pushing into me so deeply I had to pant through it for a long, trembling moment.

"Take me in, baby."

I already was. Couldn't do anything else.

Falling forward, I braced my hands on the arm of the sofa as he speared into me and retreated over and over again, the sounds erotic, filthy, and desperate. His dark shadow loomed over me in the glass, somehow just a little bit dangerous and that only turned up my desire. His grip on my ass wasn't tender, but even as his hold bruised me, he was careful to avoid the fading bruises from earlier in the week. These he made on me would only bring pleasure, not pain.

He reached around me, aiming for where I needed pressure most. His thumb was an insistent force, making me drop my head to bite the couch to keep from screaming. He was relentless, his hips slapping mine, his thrusts so determined that he kept driving me up the sofa until I was draped over the arm and bracing my hands on the floor. I wasn't even sure how I'd gotten there. It was just blinding speed and need and drowning bliss.

My body convulsed, twisting in on itself as I lifted my head. The lights blurred as sweat dripped into my eyes and I fought to memorize the shape of him hammering into me from behind. But I couldn't focus, couldn't see.

I was just his receptacle now in the very best way, taking him into me until there was no more space between us.

No more doubts.

I slickened his strokes with orgasm after orgasm, stretching on and on. He fisted his hand in my hair and one around my middle to pull me up so we were body to body, frantic shadows in the glass. He fastened his mouth on my neck, imprinting my skin with his shout of release. And still, he fucked me, his strong thighs forcing mine apart for his brutal thrusts.

The sharp ache of raw need finally ebbed into exhaustion. But I wasn't done.

Not even close.

He rolled me into his arms, going into his usual spooning pose. I'd discovered this week he was all about the spoon, even if it didn't last long. His cuddle game was strong until he got too hot, turning away and kicking off the covers. I was amazed he hadn't kicked me one of these mornings yet.

But I didn't let it get that far tonight. Not that there were covers on the sofa. Even the throw pillows were on the floor. Handy for what I had in mind.

I extricated myself from his hold, barely resisting rubbing my hands together. This would be fun.

His arm flailed out, eyes still closed. "Master bathroom's at the end of the—whoa."

I kneeled on the nearest pillow and carefully pried his shaft off his thigh. Even spent, he was half hard. Seemed like he always was. We'd made a mess, as usual, not that he cared much about cleaning up if he'd gone hard enough. Such a male.

Such a delicious *tasty* male, if my first testing lick was any indication.

"Babe, what're you doing?"

"Tidying you up." *Before you make a mess of me...*

"April." His sleepy voice had an edge to it now. "You're not—you don't think—"

"I warned you." I licked around the head, slowing down near the rim at his inward hiss of breath. "You're going to have to help me get it right."

"You're off to a rip-roaring start. I don't want to deter you but recovery time—I'm young but not that young."

A giggle bubbled out of me. "You managed it the other day."

"Right, but you can't expect every time—Christ, how did you learn to do that?"

"Porn." I squeezed my eyes shut and slid him into my mouth, our combined flavors and scents making me take too much too fast. I started to choke and then realized his eyes were on the verge of rolling back into his head.

Messy. Tears. Choking. Possible death by cock. Keep going.

I moved my hand up and down fast and hard like I'd seen, gauging the speed and pressure by his uneven breaths. Curiosity had me reaching beneath to feather my fingertips over his sac, judging he liked it by his unintelligible curses. His cock pulsed in my grip, one quick throb, and the vein along the side seemed even more pronounced as I sucked him up to my tolerance level. He threaded his fingers into my hair, his gaze riveted on my lips as they spread around him and I tasted a quick hit of salt in my throat. It wasn't an ice cream sundae, but his canting hips and bunched thighs might as well have been the hot fudge.

From 'I'm not sure I can get it up again' to full body shudders in under five.

Good job, Finley.

At least I thought it was under five. Hard to tell from my current discomfort level. My jaw ached fiercely. My lover was *built*.

My love.

"Dammit, April, how? How do you do this to me?"

I might've tried to answer if my mouth hadn't been full of him.

"God, baby, you're so beautiful." His gasps between words made me press my drenched thighs together. "Look at you…taking me like a fucking champ. Get up here so I can fuck you…again."

I ignored him and kept pumping and sucking and squeezing and licking.

All I wanted was for him to blow.

When I sensed he was close, I clamped my fingers in a vise around the base of him to stave it off. The sound he made was pure agony.

"Do that again and I'll drag that pussy over my mouth and make you scream."

I yanked my head up to breathe, razoring my teeth over his lower belly before I dove down again. Fighting against a laugh and a moan as he reached down to spank my ass.

"I'll pay you back," he promised darkly as I deliberately bounced my ass in time with my ministrations on his cock.

He fisted my hair. "I can't hold on. Fuck, I won't. If you want this —" He broke off as our gazes locked electrically in the darkness.

God, I wanted it. So much that I couldn't stop rocking my hips, crazed all over again to be filled.

Fingers, tongue, or cock, I wasn't choosy.

Somehow I managed to pull him free just as he erupted, dousing my lips and chin and breasts before I swallowed him down to get every last drop. But he yanked me off before I was finished and pulled me right up to where he wanted me, just as he'd said he would.

I balanced on one leg while he tongued my pussy and I gripped the arm of the sofa so I didn't fall over. The pose was awkward and I was shaking too hard to keep upright, but it didn't matter. A few flicks of his fingers against my clit as he buried his face against me, and I threw back my head, digging my nails into his scalp as I soaked his lips and chin.

I screamed. I begged for Jesus. I said things I'd regret if I even knew if they were English.

Then I lifted my leg off the couch and half slid, half collapsed on the probably priceless carpet. At least he probably had a maid.

And hopefully soundproofing…

When I opened my eyes the next time, I expected a tiny pair of yellow eyes to be peering back. I'd landed right beside the coffee table, the perfect height for Santiago.

Instead, I was looking at my own arm. I'd blinked out with it over my face.

Before I could move it, the honors were done for me. Bishop was grinning down at me, looking positively overjoyed at himself and the state of the world.

"Do I know you?"

"Pretty sure I'm the dude who made you come so hard you blacked out."

"That's not a thing." I sat up and rubbed my damp cheek. Yeah, I needed a shower immediately. "Is that a thing?"

"Think so, since it just happened."

"Do you have a bathtub?"

"I sure do. A nice big one with jets."

I lifted up my arms like a sex-drunk concubine. "Can you carry me? Possibly forever?"

He lifted me with that baffling strength of his and pressed his face into my hair as I looped my arms around his neck. "If only you'd let me, April mine."

CHAPTER TWENTY-FIVE

Bishop

AFTER A WEEKEND OF DEBAUCHERY, fun with pets, not fun with pets, and an eye-opening dinner with April's Grams and her much younger boyfriend Roger—how a twenty-nine-year-old man was named Roger, I didn't know—I was hardly well-rested for Monday's meeting with my best friend about his job.

Or my job.

Actually, neither of our jobs if it played out the way I hoped.

First, I had to drag my attention away from watching April dress and do her makeup.

Yes, in this short amount of time, I had devolved to become a man who was so twisted up, he even found exfoliation creams fascinating when applied by his woman.

There was also the matter of her curvaceous ass sticking way out as she examined her face in the mirror. A curvaceous ass that starred in many of my fantasies lately.

And there I was, off again. Hard-on number 50 in the past week. Who needed Viagra when you had April Finley around?

Still, I didn't want her to assume we'd be performing vertical sex acts throughout our relationship. At least beyond the first half dozen years or so.

"We have to have a chat about expectations."

April switched beauty implements to outline her already perfect eyes in smoky gray stuff. "Hmm?"

"Just because a man performs stupendous anatomical feats once, you can't expect him to do it all the time. A man needs regenerating time. Especially a man in his mid-thirties—don't poke out an eye," I muttered, grabbing her eyeliner before she stabbed herself from laughing.

"Yeah, well, I think I dislocated my jaw. There's a technique to blowjobs, and I ain't got it. But I appreciate you reacting as if I do."

"I came twice in like 20 minutes on Friday. That isn't supposed to be possible." I only preened slightly.

"Beginner's luck." She shrugged and stepped back, tilting her head to examine herself in her bathroom mirror. "What do you think? Do I look appropriate to be the boss's saucy girlfriend?"

How about the boss's saucy wife?

I did not ask that question. Even as a man who was embracing a new, possibly bonkers side of life, I wasn't ready to go whole hog and propose after such a short amount of time. Even if I was sure she held the key to my sexual satiety from now until the end of eternity, amen, we didn't have to rush.

Other than the baby we may have made or could still make at any moment, but who was keeping score?

Oh, and other than the living together thing.

And the one other aspect that would be revealed in due time today.

I didn't know what the hell I was doing. For a guy who'd plotted and planned every step of my career and everything else, I had shot completely out of my comfort zone. I was riding a Thrillcaster of my own making, but the best part was that April was strapped in at my side.

Of course she could slam on the brakes at any time. And she might after what I had in mind for today.

Hey, I was thinking outside the box. That was a good thing, right?

Sure, baby harvester.

"You look incredible. I want to take you back to bed." I grabbed her waist and lowered my mouth to hers.

Before I could kiss her, she grinned and placed her fingers against my lips. "We're already running late."

"For the very best of reasons."

"Even if I had to take a second shower since you thought the first was a chance to get me dirty again." Playfully, she shook her head. "Gotta say, I don't think there's any birth control that could withstand you."

"From your lips to…" I pointed upward.

A series of parrot-style bellows emerged from the bedroom and I rolled my eyes. "I'm going to call my pet sitter to stop by today. I thought he could handle a few hours on his own getting used to the place, but he isn't happy to be sequestered away from his new love."

April snorted. "Isn't it odd for a bird to like a cat that much? They usually threaten to eat birds."

"Not in this case."

Kit-Kat had taken one look at Santiago and galloped for the nearest closet. He'd immediately let out a piercing cry and stationed himself outside said closet for hours.

"She just doesn't know what to make of a horny bird pursuing her. Or any bird pursuing her."

"The more she runs from him, the more he wants her." I tapped my chin. "Hmm, my bird isn't unlike me. That's disturbing."

April shifted back to the mirror and started dusting some powder on her cheeks. I coughed as some flew in my direction, but she didn't seem to notice. "What are we going to do about our living situation?"

I leaned against the counter beside her and resisted kissing her neck so I didn't get powdered again. "It's a consideration."

"You're not freaking and rethinking since I put it right out there in a forceful manner?"

"I like you forceful."

"You are a pervert."

"Already noted. Maybe we should build a place. Find some land just out of town so we can have some room. How do you feel about that?"

The brush in her hand clattered into the sink. "It's really that easy for you?"

"Babe, I have a lot of money. It's fairly easy, yeah. Minus the required permits and building schedules and such. Those are pains in the ass, and pretty much why I rented an apartment in the first place. Also, it's been just me and my loud nuisance. Now it won't be."

"I didn't mean the financial part. I mean, it's a big step. Far bigger than just endless sleepovers. Which would be fine with me, too, except we have pets and—"

"It's not fine with me. We're building a family. Families need to be together. You, me, the kooky pets." I took her hand and kissed her knuckles. "I can't ask for anything more."

"So, when Grams comes over for dinner again, I get to tell her now we're moving in somewhere together. On top of the 'hey, who needs condoms' conversation I did not want to have, but apparently, you did, because I'm still blushing."

"I'm willing to bet a woman with a boyfriend nearly forty years younger than she is can understand living however you want."

"Non-traditional for the win."

"What's more traditional than falling in love and making a family? I'm gonna say that's as true blue as it gets."

She smiled up at me and linked her fingers behind my neck. "I see why you're such a good lawyer. You can persuade anyone."

"Yeah? So, how do you feel about one more shower?"

Grinning, she kissed me, soft and sweet. Although I would've definitely pressed my advantage if my phone hadn't buzzed with a ringtone I'd nearly deleted a hundred times.

Damn sentiment.

She eased back. "Do you need to get that?"

"No. Now where were we?"

Her eyes narrowed. "Is that Key?"

"No. Worse. My father." I grabbed the phone and meant to swipe away the call. Instead, I accepted it.

"Bishop? Is that you, son?"

My hand clenched at my father's deep baritone. I hadn't talked to him for so long. This man that had once been as much a friend to me as a father was now practically a stranger.

"I can talk to him." Her voice was barely a whisper. "Tell him never to call again."

Her expression was so fierce. She was so ready to defend me, to take up sword and shield in my honor, even if she didn't agree with my shutting him out. Not that she'd detailed her feelings exactly, but I was willing to bet. She was so kind-hearted. So longing for family in her desire to build a cozy home with her crafts and decorations.

And I was a shark now wearing a onesie, because I was going to do this for her—and maybe for myself too. Besides, if he went too far, I'd just hit the trusty X and make him go away again.

"Hi."

"Bishop? Oh, God, it's really you. Son, you don't know how good it is to hear your voice."

"It's—it's good to hear yours too."

April smiled at me and turned toward the bathroom door, but I caught her hand in mine and tugged her against my side. I didn't have secrets from her. That was one of the mistakes I'd made the first time. Sectioning off pieces of my life so Rina never questioned my decisions. Spending more time on cases rather than dealing with potential problems. Focusing on the future so I didn't have to handle the present.

Not again. April might get sick of being privy to every damn thing, but she was getting the option to be as involved as she wanted to be.

"How have you been?"

"Good." Hearing myself, I let out a laugh. "Let me correct that. Now? I'm fucking awesome. I'm in love with the most amazing woman on the planet, and we're making a life together."

April curled her arms around my waist and laid her head on my chest. She made me feel like freaking Superman. What had happened with my father in the past couldn't touch me—touch us—if I didn't let it.

"But before her, I was in hell. A lot of it I did to myself. But not all of it."

"No, not all of it. I'm sorry. I made mistakes. A lot of them." He released a long breath. "You'll find someday if you're lucky enough to have a child that no one hands you a rulebook. There's no standard for how to face a situation as a family. That goes for a marriage too."

"I get that. More so now than I did then."

"But that doesn't mean I didn't screw the hell up. I tried to do what I felt was best. Your brother always struggled so much more than you did."

There was no stopping my laughter. "Key? He aced everything on the first try. Had a million friends, a thriving business, even swimming trophies. The only athletic medal I ever got was in ninth grade track."

Then he'd taken the woman I'd proposed to. I didn't think of her as my wife or even my fiancée anymore. As far as I was concerned, only one woman deserved those monikers, and it wasn't Rina Kent.

"And he's divorced at thirty-six and without his business and his home and rebuilding from the bottom all over again."

I frowned down at April, who mirrored my expression.

"I didn't know all that, but even so, what does that mean? That because he lost everything doesn't mean he—"

"Made mistakes," my father said quietly.

"Still making excuses for him, I see. Nice to know some things will never change. How about mom? Is she making them too?"

"No. Your mother hasn't spoken to him for the same amount of time you haven't. She feels like she lost both her sons on the same day, if you must know."

April braced against me, but if anything, her grip on me tightened. She understood me and my reactions so well already. And above all, she wouldn't let me face this alone.

"And what? Now I'm supposed to feel guilty?" Before he could reply, I kept going. "Worst of it is, I do. I feel guilty for cutting him out of my life when he hurt me more than anyone ever has. Or ever could. At least I thought so then. Now I get that Rina was just a waystation for me. Just a rest stop. She wasn't the whole journey by a long shot."

April massaged my hip, over and over. Reminding me silently she was there.

She would always be there.

"No. You aren't supposed to feel anything except how you do. I won't judge you for that. I'm just asking for you to do the same. Especially when it comes to your mother. Her heart is broken over you two boys. And she won't reach out to him if you don't make peace with her. She just won't."

My throat tightened until I wasn't sure I'd be able to get the words out. "I need time."

"You'll have it. This was more than I ever expected. Bishop, I love you. We both love you so much."

"I'll be in touch." I managed to end the call and then faced myself in the mirror, my breaths already coming quick and fast.

"Motherfucker," I muttered as the now familiar spots lingered at the edges of my vision. "It's happening again."

"What—oh. Oh, okay." I could hear her breathing quicken almost to match mine as she rubbed my back. "We'll get through it. I read something online—here, wait." She yanked open a counter drawer, jabbing me in the leg. She grabbed a roll-on bottle, flicked off the cap, and jammed it under my nose. Actually, *in* my nose. "Try this."

Lemons. Strong lemons. My head swam and not just from the panic attack. "What—"

I gave up and sniffed that perfume roller like it was my job. I didn't know why she wanted me to, but I needed to do *something* so I didn't focus on the throbbing of my heart throughout my body.

"Scent can reroute panic. Interrupts the neural pathways or something like that. It's supposed to be peppermint, I think, but I only have that kind. I'll get it. Don't worry. Ry and Lu can get me some from the—oh, baby, sit down." She shoved me toward the toilet, just getting the lid down before I sank onto it heavily. She pushed my head between my legs and something about the moment was just so pathetically hilarious that I wheezed out a laugh.

But then it made it even harder to breathe, so I started counting in my head in time with the particular breath patterns my doctor had suggested.

Throughout, April stayed close, stepping back to give me room to pace. Saying nothing when I stalked out of the bathroom and down the hall to the craft room to draw up the window and stick out my head. The fresh air on the brisk fall day slapped me in the face, exactly what I needed. I closed my eyes and hauled in great big breaths, the sounds of April arguing with either feline or parrot soothing me even when I didn't have the oxygen in my lungs to tell her so.

She was already my heart, literally beating outside of my body.

After it started to ease, I sank to the floor and just sat for a minute. Then two. Then I reached over to pick up a frilly band thing that had obviously fallen off the sewing machine. "Are you sewing your own bridal garter?" I wondered aloud.

If so, I'd probably better propose soon. I didn't want her to have a garter with no place to go.

"What? No." She let out a baffled laugh as she came over to grab a bottle of wine off her sewing table. "It's for this. Housewarming present for Ry, since I know she's going to shack up with Preston soon enough. Though, hmm, if it's big enough for my thigh, I may have to go back to the drawing board."

I laughed too and then stilled her with my hand at her hip so I could just lean against her legs. She sifted her fingers through my hair, yet again easing me without words.

"You make it better. You make everything better, including me. I don't think I deserve you, but God, I'm going to try. I swear to you, April Finley." Swallowing hard, I gazed up at her. "On my life."

"I believe you. You do the same for me." She knelt down next to me, still brushing her hand over my hair. "We can call Preston, say we're playing hooky."

"Nah, I'm okay. I'll get there. I can't stay home and make these go away. They don't work that way."

"Is there anything that can help?"

"Reframing my brain." I smiled weakly. "In lieu of that, being patient with myself. Learning not to go so goddamn hard."

"What about writing legal briefs in bed at four a.m.?" she asked innocently as I slid her a look. "Just wondering."

"Even sharks in onesies relapse."

"Not even going to ask about that one."

I sighed. "My doctor also referred me to a therapist, said there was medication that could help. I haven't gone that route yet. But I'm considering it."

"It's a lot to think about." She pursed her lips. "You could just quit your job."

"Yeah, that was on the docket."

"Not to take Preston's. He'll find someone. You know he will. And you could even assist as an adjunct attorney or whatever it's called. But you don't have to take the job. You don't need any job if you don't want one."

I stared at her. "What the hell would I do all day? Make wreaths?"

"Sure, if you wanted to. Or you could oversee that house you want to build. Or you could, I don't know, write a legal thriller. Or just retire, Mr. Moneybags." She poked my belly. "There's no shame in choosing to walk away. You're just making another choice."

"But I don't want to leave Preston in the lurch."

"You won't be. He's leaving too. Besides, he's your best friend, and you know he'd care most about you being happy and healthy. Taking care of yourself isn't selfish."

I frowned. "I can't believe I'm really thinking about this. I used to be an—"

"Apex predator, yeah, yeah. Now you'll just bite into other things, subject to change." She wiggled her brows.

I cocked my head as I tucked her hair behind her ear. "Sure this isn't you not wanting me to be your boss?"

"Absolutely sure. I'd actually grown to kind of love the idea. Assuming you respect the boundaries and don't act like an overbearing dick." She beamed. "I can so say that word now."

I was still stuck on not being an overbearing dick. "You definitely can."

"But I figure if it doesn't happen right now, we can always make it happen at home." The look she gave me tried and failed to be lascivious, but it made some of the heaviness in my chest lift just the same.

"I still need to talk to the managing partners at my current firm. They could sweeten the deal. Up my percentages. Make it harder to walk away."

"So? You don't need any more money. What you need is your health and happiness." She circled her arms around my shoulders. "You can just say no. No more."

"It feels too easy."

"Sometimes easy is the best answer."

Which was exactly what I intended to tell Preston an hour later once we were sitting opposite each other in the conference room at Shaw, Shaw, and Shaw, LLC.

I didn't plan to start with that, of course. I wanted to give him time to run through his spiel first.

"Yeah, so I appreciate you considering this gig, but we're going a different direction."

I blinked at him like a teen fresh out of high school trying to get into Kohl's. "Gig? Direction?"

"Oh, for fuck's sake." He braced his forehead on the heel of his hand. "She's contaminated me with her lingo."

"Come again?"

"Ryan referred to April's position as a gig when she was about to start here." His fond smile would've made me smirk if I wasn't pissed he'd fired me before I'd even accepted the damn position.

Not that I was going to, but still. What bullshit.

"Let me get this straight. You invited me to take a position and now you're taking it back before I even spent a few hours here?"

"Well, we're a week behind schedule."

"You're the one who closed the damn office on a whim. Though you forgot to inform Dex, since apparently, he was working last week."

"His choice," Preston said lightly. "And I only decided to close it because you were having...a situation in your personal life and Ryan told me I should."

I rested my chin on my fist. "Interesting. You sound entirely—"

He pointed at me. "Do not say it, my friend. Do not even think it. I saw how you and my assistant looked this morning when you walked in here together. You were cuddled so close, I wasn't sure how you were both still walking."

"I was going to say 'in love' but I can't imagine what you thought I would say. As if I would ever refer to you being...whipped in a certain way."

"You would say it because you're a jackass, and April's out of earshot."

A quick rap sounded on the connecting wall. "Wrong. I'm in the records room."

If Preston had laughed any harder, he would've needed to lie down with a cold compress.

"Also, if we're talking about being pussy-whipped, that means it's very, very good."

"No arguments there," I called back.

Preston stared at me and pulled out a sheet of paper, writing quickly in his slashing handwriting.

What did you do to my assistant?

I grinned and shrugged. "Now back to firing me."

April thunked a box loudly next door, which I assumed was in disapproval, but sometimes a thunk was just a thunk.

"I'm not firing you. You never accepted the job. In fact, you never tried out the job and looked at so much as one legal brief for this firm. You don't need this job."

I narrowed my eyes at the wall between the rooms. "Did you talk to a gorgeous blond recently, per chance?"

Another thunk. Apparently, that was a new communication technique, similar to Morse code except with cardboard.

"Not about that particular aspect, though I did talk to my assistant about things that pertain to her."

"Hmm."

"I also talked to a man of average attractiveness with brown hair, depending on his hours on the beach or usage of hair dye." Preston withdrew his phone from his inner jacket pocket, swiped a few times, typed, and slipped it back in his pocket as the door opened.

Dex strolled in, hands in his pockets, pecs bulging in his Ant-Man T-shirt under his designer suit jacket. "Hey, man. I didn't sleep with April, just so you know."

In the adjoining room, there was a high-pitched sneeze.

"Thank you for the bulletin. I already knew that."

Dex rattled something in his pocket. "Good, good. So, yeah, I'm going to be taking over this candy stand."

I exchanged a glance with my best friend. His shrug was almost imperceptible.

"Issac's okay with this?

Dex leaned a hip against the conference table. "Issac is golfing, his main preoccupation now, other than schtupping his caddy."

"His caddy?" Preston coughed.

"Yeah, her name is Felicia. Coincidental? I don't think so. His admin Courtney just quit, so I doubt we'll see him around here again other than to collect his degrees off the wall."

I locked my hands behind my neck. "Yeah, this place is a hotbed of something."

Dex dropped into the chair at the end of the table with an exaggerated sigh. "That won't be the case anymore. We're condensing the staff considerably, between natural attrition and disgust at being dumped."

I frowned. "Who's disgusted at being dumped?"

"That would be Courtney, our father's admin." Preston held up a hand. "Don't get me started. I made sure she had a generous severance package." He lifted his voice. "And speaking of generous severances, April, would you join us, please?"

More thunks next door and then the door closed in the next room.

I leaned toward Preston. "I hope you know what you're doing."

His expression was implacable as always. "Me too."

"The all-knowing Preston always has all the answers." Dex tapped his fingers on the edge of the table. "Question is, is he asking the right questions?"

April opened the conference room door and stuck her head in. "Yes?"

"Please come in and sit." Preston indicated a seat at the table.

She shut the door behind her and walked to the table, giving me a long look as she sat at my side. I reached for her hand and she slipped hers into mine, causing Dex to positively cackle.

"So sweet. I can't bear it. All this young love around here. Hope the pheromones aren't catching." He tilted his head toward April. "Hey, since your one bestie is occupied with PMS, what about your other one? Lunestra, is it?"

"Luna and she'd kick your ass."

Dex rubbed his hands together. "Ooh, even better. Let me get the digits."

"She's very taken."

"She's also a witch," I put in, "and would freeze your balls off if you pulled your usual shit."

Dex clutched his chest in mock disapproval. "Bishop, my man, I can't believe I'm hearing this from you. A guy falls in love, and suddenly, he becomes a changed man."

"Try it. You might even grow up a little."

Preston shook his head and shuffled papers in his folder. "Doubtful. Now, if we can move this along, I have a meeting with a client in half an hour."

"Why don't you sum up the finer points then?" I suggested. "Repeat how you're firing me before you even hired me for the record."

April cut me a glance. "What?"

"No one is being fired. Just as I explained to April, we're making a lot of changes around here. Since the personnel is shifting, we understand some of our support staff may not be onboard with the changes, so I wanted her to know if she chooses to leave, she'll be granted a hefty severance package as well as placement assistance into a future position."

"You can always work for me." Dex smiled widely. "My admin is staying part-time, but I'll likely need more help depending how things go. I'm also hoping to bring on another lawyer on a part-time basis. Bishop isn't looking to work part-time."

"You know that, how?" But he was right.

Part-time would make sense as I figured out what to do next. I wasn't much for the fate stuff under normal circumstances, but maybe there was something to it. I was more the sort to either go too hard or not go at all and take a step back. Half measures weren't my style.

"Tell me I'm wrong."

"You're not wrong. I'm happy to help out here and there on a case if I'm needed, but I know of someone who's looking for a new opportunity who'd probably be a better fit than I am." I shot Preston a dark look. "And who hasn't been fired here already."

"I didn't fire you, you ass. I want you to choose your work, not feel like it's your responsibility to help me out or because you're picking the lesser of two evils."

April's fingers tightened on mine.

I nodded. "Yeah. Guess you're getting wiser in your old age."

"Funny. We're basically the same age."

"I'm younger than both of you, however." Dex jerked a shoulder as we glared at him. "Just pointing it out."

"If you ever want to start over working shoulder to shoulder on something we'll build ourselves, you let me know." Preston stood and motioned for me to rise as well, then gave me a quick one-armed hug. "Until then, thanks, brother. I know you'd upend your whole life if you thought I needed you to, but I don't. This is Dex's firm now." Preston looked skyward. "Heaven help the clients of Shaw, LLC."

"I'm ready to tackle a new adventure." Dex grinned. "Look-out, divorcing townsfolk of Kensington Square and beyond. You're in for a wild ride."

I shifted my hold on April's hand to her thigh. "So, I guess I'm not your boss anymore."

"It was nice while it lasted," she said seriously, her lips twitching at the corners.

"I'm not sure I was ever technically your boss."

"But we thought you were—or on the way to becoming my boss—so that's all that matters." She leaned in close to whisper in my ear. "Earlier offer still holds."

Again, she tried the lascivious look that only made me laugh before I framed her face in my hands and kissed her.

"I'm out of here," Dex announced. "Good to see you, Stone. Glad I was never tempted to sleep with you, April, although you're a damn fine assistant."

Her brows drew together as she pulled back from me. "Thank you. I think."

I held out my fist for a bump as Dex passed us. A moment later, the door shut behind him.

My best friend cleared his throat. "I'll follow his example as soon as I know what direction you'd like to go in, April."

April tangled her fingers with mine. "I'm staying here for now. Dex could use some help with the transition, and of course you too. You've got a couple more months here, right?"

I wondered if he could hear the slight tinge of nerves in her voice like I could. Already I knew her so well. She'd become so brave in going after more, in keeping her mind open to possibilities, but the April she'd been such a short time ago was probably clinging to the shore.

Whatever she wanted to do, however fast or slow she wanted to go, I would be right by her side. Loving her through it, just as she was loving me.

Thank God.

"I do, yes. Closing out my cases is a process, not to mention shifting the ongoing ones to Dex and whomever he chooses to bring in."

"I know someone he might want to talk to. Eli's a fine attorney. I'll have him call Dex, set up a meeting."

"Your referral will go a long way, I'm sure. Thank you. I appreciate it. In the meantime, I'll be more here than I'm not, April. And even after I've left, I'll still be available if something comes up. Dex is my brother. This firm was a big part of my life for many years. I don't foresee I'll ever truly cut the cord."

She nodded, smiling tentatively. "So, I'll be here for a while then. In a couple months, I'll reevaluate as necessary."

Preston nodded. "Your loyalty is something we treasure. We always have. Well, I always have. Dex will learn the importance of a good admin in keeping a business running the way it should."

I turned my hand over to grip April's. "What about you? Won't you need an admin?"

The tips of my best friend's ears went red. "I have a candidate in mind. We'll see how it goes."

April and I exchanged a look as Preston scooped up his file and headed to the door. "Ryan," she mouthed while I nodded.

"Dinner later this week?" he asked from the doorway. "The four of us."

"Are you going to cook?"

"Hell no. We'll get takeout. Denny's has a good sandwich." The door shut behind him.

April dissolved into giggles. "Denny's? Really?"

"The guy's in love. Or he's lost his mind. Seems like basically the same thing." I grabbed the arm of her wheeled chair and rolled it over closer to mine. "Come here often?"

She glanced around. "I've actually *never* come here. But Ry and Preston defiled the records room."

"Hmm. I do have a fondness for conference tables. But I don't even work here."

"So? I do." She rose and shrugged out of her sweater before strolling over to the door and flipping the lock.

And when I swiveled my chair to face her, already loosening my tie, her suggestive expression was exactly on point.

EPILOGUE

April

I CLIMBED out of my car down the block a short distance from my destination, my attention on my shoes. I wasn't trying not to fall, although with my history and the current light snowfall, it wouldn't have been a bad idea to be mindful.

But no, my focus was more on my footwear than my footing. I was as riveted now as I had been the very first time I'd laid my eyes on these heels almost three months ago.

So much had changed since then. Most of all, me.

They weren't the least bit appropriate for where I was going or the weather. I didn't give a flying fig. For today's mission, I wanted everything to be perfect.

We would remember this day for the rest of our lives.

The office building looked so quaint in the snow. Thick storm clouds gathered overhead, spitting fat flakes that already coated the ground. I took small steps since I'd already snapped the heel of one of these once. Walking in snow like this was pushing my luck. But they seemed…ceremonial somehow.

I'd found them waiting for me in my closet a few weeks ago, sitting neatly beside the other pair I'd damaged the day Bishop and I had reunited in the gutter.

There was a title for a tabloid love story.

He'd saved both shoes and had them fixed. Or repaired. Or employed some high priestess to wave her hands and make them whole again. Whatever he'd done, both pairs of shoes were as good as new.

Not that I'd be wearing many heels for a while after today. I was going to get nice and acquainted with my slippers—bunny, because what else?—as often as possible. I might even sport them around the office.

I was almost positive my new bosses wouldn't mind.

Drawing my shawl in tighter around my shoulders, I hurried up the steps, smiling at the little sign in the door. A warmth enveloped me. A sense of rightness that somehow through all the twists and turns my life had taken, they'd all combined to lead me here to this time and place.

I was so lucky. So happy and excited and maybe just the smallest bit afraid that with so much good in my life, maybe I was tempting fate. Surely some rock would fly through the window and shatter everything.

Grams kept telling me that was anxiety talking. Bishop and I were a pair in that way, even if he never seemed the slightest bit uneasy. On the outside, he was a solid, strong man who never faltered. I was the only one he allowed to see the other side, other than his doctor and new therapist. He'd just started going once a week a few weeks ago, and so far, so good. We were taking it one day at a time. There were no quick fixes, unfortunately.

We'd just had dinner with his parents for the first time. For his sake, I'd hoped for it to be easy and natural after a bumpy start. Instead, we'd sat quietly over roasted chicken and green beans and fancy potatoes until the silence had made me mental. I'd started chatting with his mom about sewing techniques just to fill the room with something other than tension.

When she called me the next day, I'd almost told her what I'd literally just found out, but I decided to wait. That was Bishop's call where and when to tell them, not mine.

No matter how much I yearned for a textbook happy family, life wasn't always like that. And wishing wouldn't make it so. But Bishop and his parents were trying, so there was hope.

Key was still trying too. He called Bishop every week or two. Half the time, Bishop even answered the call. Key hadn't been at the family dinner. Neither had Michaela. She was almost as stubborn about avoiding Key and their parents as Bishop was.

But Mickey spent lots of time at our places—both of them. We hadn't found land yet. Or even settled on a general location other than near Kensington Square.

So much was in flux, and that was hard for a planner like me. I was learning to ride the waves. And when I got too stressed, I took time to enjoy the very naughty self-pleasuring panties Mickey had picked up for me.

Bishop didn't know where they'd come from. He never would.

Just like he'd never find out his sister had catcalled the neighborhood vet.

The vet in question had asked me about Mickey in a sidelong fashion when I'd brought Kit-Kat to see him to get microchipped. I expected her lusty parrot paramour to send her fleeing out the front door any day now.

I did not tell Grant anything about Mickey. I also asked his age in a super casual way.

So, how old are you, exactly?

36.

And Mickey was turning 23 in a few weeks.

Certainty of Bishop flipping his wig if they spent *any* time together, even just to have a conversation such as, '*do you have a kitty?*' 150%.

No, Grant, I haven't seen Mickey again and have no idea of her location. She's probably in Iceland. Thanks for the cat chipping. Bye now.

But that was a concern for another day. Thank heavenly biscuits.

Oh, biscuits. I could eat. I wondered if they'd had lunch yet. Or maybe they could get delivery. Or maybe takeout from that pizza shop on the corner. I could go for a double cheese with a side of more cheese.

Easy does it, Finley. Breakfast was just three hours ago.

With a sigh, I pushed open the front door, wincing at the creak of the hinges. Inside, I could hear my best friend's voice.

"Do you people hear that door? I need WD-40 to fix it. One of you needs to get off your ass and—April," Ryan said delightedly. "No one told me you were coming by, dammit. We just ordered lunch."

A tear of joy came to my eye. "Blessed be."

She pulled me into a hug and then hauled me back before tugging me close again. "Lu told me something about you," she whispered in my ear.

Uh-oh.

"What?" My trepidation had little trepidation babies. I didn't want to share with them before I told Bishop. It had to be a law somewhere. I could right afterward, though.

"You know what. Oh my God, your shoes are fabulous." She bent down to haul my leg up by the ankle, sending me teetering backward.

I had one thought as I scrambled to right myself. *Not freaking again.*

And then as if I'd suddenly found a grace I'd never possessed before, I didn't land on my keister like in the past. This time, I stumbled and stayed upright.

"Oh, whoops, I didn't mean to—" Ryan paused and tilted her head, studying me far too intently. "You look different."

Misdirection. Deflection. Those were the tools to use.

"My shoe didn't snap! Wonder if he used some kind of super wonder glue to fix the heel last time."

She snorted. "Right. Wonder glue. Girl, you are something else." She turned to walk across the still chaotic office—remodeling was a bitch—and I released an inward sigh of relief. Somehow I'd gotten by without responding to her comment.

Then she turned back and pointed at me. "You didn't distract me, by the way. But a woman's allowed to have some secrets from her best friends. For *very* short periods of time."

I grinned. "Lucky me, having intuitive witches as my besties."

"You are very lucky." She smiled, and if it hadn't been Ryan, I might've thought that twinkle in her eye was a hint of wetness.

Not badass Ryan, though.

"I ordered a giant sub, so we can share. If that's enough for you." She lifted her brows pointedly as she gazed at my midsection, then glided over to the desk with Preston's fancy nameplate in front of the big window.

A window that was basically begging to be decorated for the winter. I had a can of spray adhesive snow I could use to make snowflakes in the corners and add some curlicues that would look like blowing wind gusts. Oh, and I could add a couple of skinny trees with the glass-safe paint I'd gotten on sale last week. Maybe add a few cute elves. Nothing too holiday specific, but with a little bit of extra whimsy.

"Oh, sure, that'll be fine. Thanks." My attention was still focused on the window. I had some glitter paint too. I'd have to see if that was safe for glass. Some of the trees would be so pretty with a hint of sparkle on the boughs. "What kind of sub?"

"Turkey and cheddar with tomatoes and lettuce—"

"Oh, no." I clutched my stomach. Turkey sounded vile right now, and I didn't think I was supposed to eat that stuff, anyway. "I'll just take the cheese and veggie parts. Thanks though."

"I ordered a pudding cup too," she offered. "Chocolate."

"Bless you." I rushed around the desk to give her a hug. My appreciation was probably over the top, but I'd acquired an excessive love for sweets just recently.

"You're welcome. You know, the guys aren't back yet, maybe I can catch them and we can add on to the order. Celebration lunch and—" She held me at arm's length. "You knew it was celebration lunch day. Duh."

"Yeah. I just didn't know if I'd be able to get here in time." I bit my lip. "I registered for school today. Begins in January. I'm starting my paralegal courses."

"Oh, Apes, that's so awesome." She bounced with me in our version of a dance, complete with leg kicks and high-pitched squeals.

Which of course was when the guys returned, their laughter cutting off abruptly as they rushed through the door with their arms laden with bags. "What is it? What happened?" Preston shouted at the same time as Bishop chimed in.

"Who's hurt? What's wrong?"

Ryan and I turned toward them, arms linked, and she was laughing as she responded. "Aww, look at the big brave boys, thinking the helpless wimmins need to be protected."

Naturally, she could still speak, because she was used to withstanding the sight of Preston in full work garb, also known as a three-piece suit.

Me? Not so much. I'd seen Bishop get dressed this morning, but somehow the office environment added extra personal value. My tongue was stuck to the roof of my mouth. Other parts of me were fluttery, and tingly. Hmm…was there such a thing as double-paneled panties?

Before I could fully ponder that question, Bishop smiled at me, and I forgot I was supposed to be cool like my untouchably chill bestie and rushed toward him like I hadn't seen him since last Christmas.

In reality, it had been like four hours. Not even. He'd dallied as long as he could before heading off with Preston for some big meeting.

Since they were now officially partners and all.

I still couldn't quite believe Bishop had asked him about joining Preston's new firm. They'd be practicing family law, among other kinds, but nothing involving divorces. My guy's apex predator days were over.

However, a shark in a onesie could still be arranged. Or maybe a shark onesie...

More than anything, he'd wanted to come with me to registration, but I'd told him it was good for me to take this step on my own. I was getting better at doing that. It helped that I had so much support. Amazing how that worked.

Grams had wanted to drive me too, but she was starting a new part-time job in Crescent Cove and today was orientation. Roger was gone, and she didn't seem to mind.

For a reason or a season, she always said, and that applied to men too.

Well, not for me. Mine was for a lifetime. I was trying really hard to have faith in that—in myself, and in Bishop. And in everything we'd build between us.

He tossed his bags of food on the table near the door, almost toppling the large vase of fall flowers, and caught me in his arms, hugging and kissing me while Ryan and Preston groaned in unison.

"Is this *Casablanca?* It's damn lunchtime," Ryan whined.

"Right. Besides, I'd rather greet you with my hand up your skirt."

She laughed. "You sweet talker, you."

Distantly, I heard their snickers, but my focus was on Bishop's hard body and his soft lips on mine. And the silky vest I couldn't help touching under his opened suit coat. That I had probably opened. His pants may or may not have been next.

At least after I got some food in me.

"Do you two need a room? Sheesh."

Bishop finally pulled back with a laugh and pressed his cheek to mine as he spoke to Ryan. "Actually, we have one. My office upstairs, right, Pres? It's not quite up to my standards yet, but at least the space is split into two quadrants."

My head was still reeling from the kiss—kisses, plural—and I was in a starvation fugue state, but I wasn't quite understanding yet.

"I have an incredible interior designer, Shelby, coming in to help get the place up to what it should be for two such esteemed," he cleared his throat, "attorneys and their very capable admins. Or co-pilots. Or whatever term we want to use, since secretary is a word I only like in porn. Just saying."

"Are we getting jets as company perks?" Ryan rubbed her hands together. "I'd be onboard with that."

A buzzing started in my ears. "Are you getting an admin?"

I hated the insecurity I heard in my voice. I was doing just fine working for Dex as the office transitioned to whatever it would eventually end up being, but working with my love and my bestie and my old boss would be so incredible. I'd feel like I had a personal stake in every part of my work.

As if I was part of a real, genuine family. I did already, but this would be just the cherry on top. And maybe that made me nuts, because I didn't want to stay at home all the time. I'd be working reduced hours, at least for a while, but I loved the idea of being involved and productive and doing work that I enjoyed.

This was what I wanted.

Bishop started to reply, but I shook my head. "Let me speak. Please." I took a deep breath. "I realize you might have had other plans, and you have every right to make the best decision for your office, but I think I would be the best admin for you. Or co-pilot. Or co-fluffer." I flushed as everyone laughed.

"Should I wonder how you know such things? Or just be grateful?" Bishop gave me a raised brow.

"A woman has to have some secrets, even from her besties. Though for only a very short time."

"Wait, now I've been demoted to bestie?" Bishop jangled his keys in his pocket. "Rough crowd."

"Hate to tell you, Stone, but we best bishes were rolling as a crew long before you and PMS swung up to the plate. And now PMS and I are going to eat and talk about how smushy mushy you two are and how above it all we are. Before we screw like minks."

PMS—I mean, Preston—frowned, verging on a pout. "You can't leave before he gives his answer. You're like those people who leave a concert before the encore. Who does that? Monsters, I tell you."

"Wow, you've actually *been* to a concert?" Ryan grinned. "Let me guess. James Taylor's greatest hits. Oh, I know, double billing with Barry Manilow."

"You're a harsh woman and I only love you because you're the most staggeringly smart, beautiful woman I've ever met."

"See, this is why I keep him. C'mon, PMS." Ryan linked hands with him and tugged him to the opposite end of the room where the stairs led to the second floor. "Make good choices," she said in a singsong voice before she shut the door.

A half minute later, she opened it again and ran over to the table where Bishop had tossed the food. "Forgot my food. You can share *his* sub. I'm starving. Besides, you two live on love. Peace." She hurried out and closed the door while Bishop and I grinned at each other.

"She's a sweetheart."

"She is. She just doesn't like people to know it. She's also going to listen at the door."

"You bish, I am not," Ryan called, making us laugh even harder. Especially since I was almost sure her mouth was full.

"Pres has no chance of dragging her away."

"Nope, he doesn't, so just get the romance over so I can have my lunch in peace and not leaning against a door. Thanks in advance."

"Do you want to go outside? We don't have to be subject to this abuse." Bishop was grinning, so I knew he didn't care if we were overheard.

I didn't either. I probably would've been okay with skywriting our news. *All* the news. And Ryan was basically my sister and Preston was…well, I had fond feelings for him. I still hadn't quite slotted him into the friend zone, but I'd get there someday.

We had time.

"Okay, so for your last point, you are absolutely my fluffer. I'd consider no one else for the job. So, you know, try hand exercises."

On the other side of the door, Preston mumbled something that sounded like, "Good tip for you too, Miss Moon."

"If my hands get any stronger, you'll need a prosthetic, pal."

"Too much information." I covered my face.

Bishop tugged down my hands. "Ignore them. Now they'll just try to outdo us."

They started to talk on the other side of the door, so Bishop just raised his voice. "As for co-pilot, didn't you say you hate to fly? I mean, practice makes perfect. Especially since Ryan needs a jet as a company perk. I thought she had a broom at her disposal."

I shook my head. Ry and Bishop had an oddly adversarial relationship that they both seemed to enjoy. She always tossed the zingers right back.

"You are not the least bit funny, Stone. And watch yourself. You might need to use hair regrowth on your eyebrows if you keep it up."

"She's a fearsome woman. Anyway, back on topic, as for the admin job, of course I meant you." Bishop's face softened as he cupped my cheeks. "Who else? How else could I ever want anyone else with me as I do this new crazy thing? Not to mention Preston says you're the best he's ever had."

Ryan started coughing so fitfully that Bishop cleared his throat. "In a manner of speaking, of course."

I smiled. "Aww, did he really say that? He told me that too, but telling you is different. Thank you, PMS—I mean, Mr. Shaw, sir."

"I certainly did, not counting present company. All true, April. And we can dispense with the formalities. I beg you. Your best bish makes fun of me for days afterward."

"It's not making fun, it's enjoying a laugh at your expense. And too late now, pal. Get ready for the couch," Ryan muttered.

Bishop cocked a brow. "Should I be worried you're more touched by Preston's praise than by my lovely speech?"

"No, because duh, I know you love me. Just as I love you more than the sun, moon, and stars, plus about 500 known galaxies."

"Only 500?"

"Today at least 1000. And I'm thrilled to accept your job offer." With a grin, I stood on my tiptoes to cover Bishop's face with his kisses while he laughed and brushed me off. "We can work on the benefits package later."

I expected some *eww, ick* noises from beyond the door, but the dynamic duo was strangely silent. Either Ry had stuffed the end of her sub in his mouth or they were making out, most likely. I wasn't focused on them right now, anyway.

"But there's just one problem."

Bishop frowned. "I won't be a taskmaster. Hello, new kinder, gentler Bishop Stone is playing in theaters now. Haven't you noticed?"

"I have. Though you were never anything but amazing to me, a little—okay, a lot—of highhandedness aside. I never got to see the shark. But I heard the horror stories." I gave a mock shudder, smiling as his forehead furrowed. "But I'm going to need to take some leave in six months or so. Non-negotiable."

"Okay, that's fine. Is there some craft thing?"

"No. Not a craft thing. But you're the sweetest man on the planet for thinking there might be." I sucked in a long breath and cupped my belly. "More like a baby thing."

He just stared at me. Not blinking. Not breathing.

Oh, shit. What did I do? I should've picked a better time and place. Maybe eased him in somehow.

You know that whole theory of how babies are made? Turns out it's real.

No, this wasn't the time for jokes, dammit.

"God, did I—are you having an attack? Just breathe through it, baby. I've got the peppermint—" I patted my arm for my purse and realized I'd dropped it at some point. Bad habit of mine.

I glanced around the wax figure Bishop had become toward the front door. My purse sat on the table. One of them had picked it up for me when I wasn't paying attention.

Not one of them. Bishop had. He always noticed the details and always took care of me. He'd given me so much. Most of all, himself. That was the biggest gift of all.

I rushed toward it, but he stopped me in mid-stride. He didn't pick me up, didn't kiss me. Just hauled me into the hardest, tightest hug I'd ever had.

The absolute best.

We stood there, rocking for the longest time. Sometimes there weren't words. I swallowed over and over, finally slipping away from him to go to my purse. There was something he needed to see.

I pried out the two little overalls I'd been working on here and there when he was busy closing out the rest of his old cases or during the rare times he went to sleep before I did. He slept easier now, but there were no quick fixes.

Even miracles took time.

He watched every step I took toward him, his gaze riveted on what I held. I held the green one out first. Daddy's little girl was embroidered on it.

His shattered eyes met mine and he grabbed it in one hand and me with the other. "Is it?"

"I don't know. Figured we should find out together. So, I did one of each." I pressed the other into his hand. This one was yellow with Daddy's little boy.

He pressed them both to his face and I clutched my locket, hoping I'd done the right thing. I didn't want to upset the balance—

Then he lowered them and grinned at me, his emerald eyes sparkling. "Or maybe twins?"

I was literally shocked for thirty seconds. "I just gave you your firstborn, and you want to cram in more? Typical overachiever. Also, rent a uterus, dude."

He threw back his head and laughed. Then he drew me into his arms and kissed me soundly enough to make me forget he was on thin ice. "I could not love you more, April Finley Stone."

I went still. "Huh?"

"Sorry, getting ahead of myself."

"No, I'd say you're behind. Catch me up." I was the one breathing fast now, not him.

We'd talked about marriage in abstract terms. I understood it would never be easy for him, considering his past. And we were so new. And I was blissfully happy.

But I wanted it. Getting married had been one of my most secret dreams since I was a little girl. Marriage, kids, a life built together. He was giving me all of that except one thing. A ring that didn't really mean much at all.

Except it did.

He went to the pile of takeout parcels and withdrew a tiny box from a bag labeled utensils. I let out a laugh that veered toward a sob.

"I've had this since after the carnival."

"What?" I lifted my stunned gaze to his. "Dally much?"

He grinned. "I wasn't sure you wanted—"

"Are you kidding? I want." I threw myself at him and he spun me around, laughing as I kissed him.

The door opened and our friends rushed in, laughing. Well, Ry laughed, Preston smiled and bumped fists and did the one-handed hug thing with Bishop. With me, he started to shake my hand, until Ryan knocked his shoulder and basically shoved him into me. We hugged to avoid being human pinballs.

Then Ryan swooped in and wrapped me in a hug that of course led to side-to-side dancing. "I totally knew, you bish. And Lu picked up the baby's aura. She's known for weeks. It's been killing us to play cool."

I reared back and stared at her for a second before encompassing Bishop in my gaze. "Really? Did she see a color?"

He wasn't making fun now. He was completely serious and focused on Ry's answer. Luna sometimes saw colors that corresponded with a person's energy. I didn't understand it all, but she had a gift with it.

"She sure did. Her own skills in that arena are extremely highlighted right now."

I frowned. "Oh, yeah? Good for her."

"Especially when you find out why." Ry looked skyward. "Help me, goddess."

I didn't get any of this, but as much as I loved Lu, it would have to wait. "What was the color?"

"Purple."

"Like Barney? That kids' character?" Preston mimed zipping his lips. "Sorry. I'll shut up now and enjoy this blissful moment."

"What does that mean?"

Ryan shot PMS a dark look. "It's a very peaceful, relaxed, happy sign, so the baby is very glad to be coming soon."

"Aww." I sniffed and locked hands with Bishop. "Imagine that, *we* got an optimist."

He laughed and squeezed my fingers. "The surprises keep coming."

"As for a sex, I'm sorry. Could go either way."

"That's okay. Either one is exactly right." Bishop slid me a glance and held up the two sets of overalls he still held. I wasn't sure where the ring had gone. "Or both."

"Don't push it, buddy. I still haven't eaten, and now I'm eating for two."

Preston held up a hand. "That's our cue to leave. Well, go upstairs until you need us. Or whatever. Yeah, uh, so happy for both of you. Congratulations. Going now. Let's go, Miss Moon."

Clearly fearing imminent violence from the hangry pregnant lady, Ry actually followed him for once. "He's got a point. So glad for both of you. This is the very best news! We have so much to plan. Or you can plan with Lu, and I'll drink heavily. Congratulations! Bye!"

Bishop's eyes crinkled around the corners in the very best way. "Just one second, guys. I need witnesses for this."

"Huh?"

Then he dropped down on one knee.

"Oh, I kinda forgot this part."

"Obviously." Amused, he dug out the ring box from his pocket and popped the top.

Inside was the smallest, most glittery red stone I'd ever seen surrounded by what seemed like a million diamonds set in gold. I gasped. "It's so gorgeous."

"Dude, really? That's like a chip." Ry crossed her arms. "Apes, you can do better. Consider this the opening argument. He can try again."

Bishop ignored her as he started to speak. "This is a red diamond. One of the rarest, most expensive gems that exists. It's the most prized diamond. The red reminded me of the dress you wore that first night. And even as rare it is, you're still more rare than a million of these. Nothing competes with your beauty, but hopefully, this comes close." He exhaled. "Will you marry me, April Anne Finley?" The corner of his lips lifted as he mouthed for my ears only, "Cinderella."

By then, I was crying. Openly. Like the romantic fool I'd always been and hadn't ever felt comfortable sharing with anyone.

But he'd known. And he'd given me my fairy tale every day since we'd met.

I went down to my knees and held out my shaking hand. He slipped on the ring—jamming it a little since sausage fingers, *thanks, baby*—and dipped his forehead to mine as Ryan and Preston laughed and cheered.

Easing back, I rubbed his scruffy jaw. "As beautiful as this was, you forgot something."

"Now what?" His slightly cross tone made me laugh.

"Remember Fiji?"

"Slightly, considering the ring."

"You never showed me my gift. You've put me off for months now."

"Waiting builds character, April mine. But I suppose now is as good a time as any. Though I wanted to wait to put it in my finished office after Shelby gets done with it."

"Yeah, yeah, you're always waiting. Get to it."

He grinned and rose to go to the closet. I didn't know how he'd fit it in there, but the man was skilled at such tasks. He withdrew the wrapped package while Ryan and Preston glanced at each other, and then yanked off the paper.

The stained glass piece made my jaw drop. The blond woman in red faced the ocean with her hands up with the waves rolling in the distance. As if she was commanding the water. Harnessing it. A million colors came through the faceted panes of glass, and she was made up of every one of them. No boundaries.

Ry gasped and moved closer, sinking down to get a better look. "Stone, this is *witchy.*"

"Is it?" Bishop sounded proud of himself. "When I saw it, I immediately knew it was April. The red dress, but also the hidden power. Untapped. I knew she'd only begun to find hers inside her."

"Bishop, this is stunning." I came closer to crouch beside Ryan, riveted by the piece's beauty. I'd never imagined it could be something this epic.

That *I* could be this epic.

"You really see me in this?" I whispered.

"Absolutely, baby. This is you." He stroked his hand down my hair and I reached up to grip his fingers. "And when the baby comes, I'm going to commission another with him or her in your arms."

I was too busy sniffling to speak.

"Oh, you are so getting laid." Ry punched Bishop in the shoulder. "Almost a miss on the ring, but this saved it. Priceless, but little. *Pfft.* But this is a masterpiece." She grabbed his cheeks and planted a kiss on him. "Good job, dude."

He laughed. "Thanks. I think."

"We're going now. Congratulations again." Preston waved and dragged Ry with him upstairs.

"So, how do you feel about roleplaying that boss and secretary thing now?" Bishop teased, encircling my waist with his arms.

But only for a minute. Almost immediately, his hand came to rest on my belly.

I laughed and tipped back my head to look up at him. Somehow I could still see him through my happy tears. "Try feeding me first, and we'll talk."

Dexter is up next in our series! Did you miss Luna and Ryan's stories? Read on for more details!

**We appreciate our readers so much!
If you loved the book please let your friends know. If you're extra awesome, we'd love a review on your favorite book site.**

Want to keep up to date with us?

Please visit our website, tarynquinn.com, for details!

Next up is Dexter & Shelby's story!

For the first time, I'm chasing a woman who has no interest in my good looks, my endless charm, or my money. In fact, Shelby is a single mom who wants nothing to do with me at all. So, with the help of my brother and his best friend, mission make Dexter Shaw into forever material is underway. Send beer.

Did you miss Preston "PMS" & Ryan's story? You know you want to know all about that romance too!

Oh, and wait! What about Luna? We got you covered there too.

Turn the page for a special sneak peek of HIS TEMPORARY ASSISTANT & WRONG BED BABY now!

HIS TEMPORARY ASSISTANT

PRESTON

Just when I thought my day—week, month, life—couldn't get any worse, my assistant said she was taking a vacation.

In a week.

Not a year.

Not a month.

A week.

"Look, sir, I'm really sorry. I never expected to get this opportunity. My grandmother was supposed to go to Fiji on her honeymoon, but they broke up, and Biff is taking the Tahoe so she's taking the vacation."

I pressed a fingertip to my aching temple. "Biff? Your grandmother? Fiji?"

"He's taking the Tahoe," my assistant April repeated slowly, leaning forward. Her blond hair fell down around her shoulders, escaping whatever pinned-up thing she'd done in the back. Unless that was the style.

Must be. April Finley was never anything but perfectly put together.

Before today, she'd also never been late. Or taken a vacation beyond a standard and reasonable long weekend. She'd called in sick precisely twice and worked from home.

"We had an agreement." My voice remained even. "I hired you on the spot approximately eighteen months ago on the condition you realized this was not a position that afforded you—"

"What, I can't take some time for myself?" Unlike my own, her voice rose in pitch to match the lifting asymmetrical hem of her dress. Not to indecent levels, mind you, because April was always proper.

Yet somehow my lack of sleep and brewing tension headache was bringing to mind ocean waters creeping higher on the Titanic.

The dress was sea blue too. Or hmm, was that more of a blue-green? I never did get why women had so many colors for things.

Look at my closet. I had black and navy suits. More navy than black because it was less severe for court. My tie collection was more colorful, but I certainly didn't know the names for the damn shades. Who had time for all that nonsense?

Not me. I didn't even have time to complete the work on my plate. I also didn't have time to further engage in this conversation.

April was still blathering on about mud masks and self-care and did I realize how long it had been since she'd even slept in?

No, I could honestly say I didn't.

"What exactly does that mean? I rise every day at precisely four."

She stopped mid-tirade and stared. "You what—why?" She tapped a glossy pale nail against her mouth. "Actually, that's better than I assumed. Rising means you sleep."

"Not necessarily," I said under my breath.

That certainly wasn't the case this month. My father was on the verge of retirement, which meant we would be looking to hire a new partner soon, and my brother and I were overloaded with work. Well, I was overloaded. Dex was strictly a nine-to-fiver—sometimes a ten-to-twoer if the water looked good. In the winter, he was all about the slopes.

I wasn't just talking about skiing. He made just as good use of the lodge as he did the hills. The guy dated more women in a year than I had in my entire life.

I was too busy working. And that was when I'd had an assistant.

Dear God, how was I going to get through a week without April? She kept my life running smoothly. Or at least it was less bumpy than it could've been without her.

"You remind me to eat," I said accusingly.

She frowned. "No, I don't. You just saw me with a donut or a sandwich a few times."

"Right, but seeing you with food reminds me I haven't eaten."

"Sir, your growling stomach should do that without my help."

As if I paid attention to such physical cues.

I would soon find out exactly how good I'd had it before.

Before vacations.

Before retirements.

Before I'd succumbed to a life of no meals and no sleep.

I grunted. "This is not enough notice. How am I supposed to hire a temp in," I consulted my Apple watch, "six days, eighteen hours, and eleven minutes?"

"I know it's short notice."

"Short? Try miniscule."

"But I have the perfect solution."

My shoulders unknotted for the first time since she'd walked into my office. "You've decided to cancel?"

April scowled. Until today, I'd never seen anything but a serene, unruffled expression on my assistant's face. That was one reason I appreciated her so much. She wasn't prone to mood swings.

Mood swings were a good part of why I was single. My mother had enough of them to change the weather from across town.

I didn't need any additional stress in my life. The calmer a woman was, the better. That went for men too, although that was a different dynamic because I didn't get naked with them.

For that matter, I didn't get naked with women much recently either.

Moving on.

"I can't cancel. My grandmother needs me. She and Biff were together for two years."

It took everything I possessed not to give a mock shudder. "I'm grievously sorry for her loss, but why does her misfortune have to become mine?"

April huffed out a breath. "Biff isn't dead. Have you been listening at all?"

"Of course I have." I adjusted my cuff links. "You're cruising to Alaska?"

"Seriously?"

"Look, I have back-to-back meetings this afternoon." Normally, at this point in a conversation I did not want to have, I would text my assistant to call me with a made-up appointment. That was hard to do when she was the one seated across from me.

One more reason I hated unplanned, unnecessary vacations.

"Not according to your Daytimer."

"There were a few last minute additions."

"Mmm-hmm. You know, I'm beginning to rethink my backup plan."

Hope bloomed inside me like a daisy in spring. "You are?"

"I always thought you were a fair, equitable boss who didn't play power games."

"I do not. Ever."

"You never so much as pinched my ass—rump," she corrected, thereby putting the image of an ass-rump in my head—luckily, not hers.

I had never so much as glimpsed her backside. I wasn't that sort of employer.

"Of course not."

"You don't take advantage of your position, and you see everyone as equals."

I couldn't help preening. Slightly. "I am careful to do exactly that."

"So, naturally, I figured Ryan would be the perfect choice to assist you while I'm away. I would never introduce you to a friend if I didn't believe you were fair-minded. Some look at having an assistant as an opportunity to lord their elevated status over them."

Why did it sound as if she was lecturing me? "I have never done such and I never will."

She rose. "Good. It's settled. Ryan will start for you next Monday at nine. Possibly nine-fifteen. No more than nine-thirty. Mornings are iffy." She crossed the office to the door. "Oh, and thanks! I'll bring you back a souvenir."

The door clicked shut on my curses.

I stalked over to the coffeemaker and discovered I was down to five pods—inhumane considering my current level of tension.

I popped one in the brewer and returned to my desk to stab the intercom button on the phone.

"Yes?"

"I'm almost out of coffee. Can you kindly place an order before your vacation?" The question held the same level of wrath as a death threat.

Preston Michael Shaw was not someone to tangle with without his caffeine.

"Already taken care of two days ago. Tracking says it should arrive by Monday afternoon. Your preferred flavor of Columbian coconut-caramel was backordered."

"Of course." I had no reason to feel ashamed I enjoyed coconut and caramel. Those were extremely manly flavors.

And Monday afternoon meant I would have to deal with April's friend who was "iffy about mornings" without the benefit of my early morning pick-me-up unless I grabbed one on the way in. My own kitchen at home was stocked with an assortment of possibilities that I rarely took time to actually make there, other than my restorative Friday night meal. For the most part, I only used my place to shower and sleep.

"I actually paid for rushed shipping."

"Why, does Ryan enjoy coffee too?" There was no keeping the edge of sarcasm out of my voice.

"Hardly. Tea is much more Ryan's speed. Coffee is a dangerous stimulant and can lead to hallucinations."

"Such as fantasizing about murdering someone when you don't have any?"

"You have five pods left," April said crisply. "Ration."

She hung up before I could reply.

In the old days before vacation, April never hung up without making sure I had everything I needed. Now she seemed dismissive. Perhaps this was her way of weaning me off the teat of capable assistantship before she took her leave.

It was hard to imagine Ryan, with his inconsistent start times and love of tea, could measure up.

Maybe I was being unfairly judgmental. Usually, water seeking its own level was a factor in friendships, but I had no idea if this was a former ex of April's or someone she merely had an acquaintance with. Many people today called everyone their friend, from the mailman to the barista who made their latte. I was far more selective.

My old school buddy, Bishop, counted as a close friend. I also had numerous acquaintances. I wasn't looking to add to the roster.

I grabbed my coffee from the brewer and disposed of the pod before sitting at my desk. I slipped on my glasses then typed a missive to April.

Memo: Ryan Moon

Ms. Finley,

Upon further reflection, while your effort to provide someone in your stead while you are vacationing is commendable, I need more information before I blindly accept someone into my employ, even temporarily. Does this individual have a CV? A work history? Applicable skills? References? I will need to see these materials before I hire anyone.

Yours,

Preston Michael Shaw, Esquire

Addressing her as Ms. Finley was a bit much, as was signing my full name and using Esquire. I was annoyed on multiple levels and needed an outlet.

I didn't believe in gyms—communal sweating had never been my kink—so I'd be going for a nice long run tonight to get out my frustrations. God knows I didn't have any other healthy outlets, other than playing Mario Kart on my ancient Super Nintendo system.

Vintage. Not ancient. I needed to learn the lingo so I didn't sound like someone caught in the past.

I drank a mouthful of hot coffee and flicked through screens until I came to my notes about one of my biggest cases, Terrance vs. Yorn, a multi-million dollar divorce with drama worthy of *Judge Judy*. I did not do drama. I also didn't relish reviewing notes that amounted to little more than a record of personal attacks rather than anything based on legal precedent.

I had pulled up my email program to dash off another email, this time to Donald Terrance, when said program dinged.

I frowned. I had turned off all notifications. How had one gotten through?

The frown grew as the most recent email in my box seemed to loom larger than all of the others. The sender? Ryan Moon.

Mental note: tell Ms. Finley not to share my email address with outsiders before asking.

Narrowing my eyes, I clicked it open.

To whom it may concern:
   I have attached my resume. References are at the bottom. **The first one is the person who got me this gig.**
   Sincerely,
   Ryan G. Moon

I cocked a brow. *Gig?* That was a new one.

Rather than reply to Ryan G. Moon, I opened my email to send another memo to April.

> **Ms. Finley,**
> I just received correspondence from one Ryan G. Moon. Kindly do not share my email with strangers in the future. Also, did you make clear what sort of position this is? Your friend referred to it as a "gig."
> **Yours,**
> **Preston Michael Shaw, Esquire**

I'd barely hit send and sat back to drink smugly from my rapidly disappearing coffee when my email dinged.

Yet again it had bypassed my no notifications setting. How was this happening? I did not want unanticipated noises interrupting my blessed silence.

> **To whom it may concern:**
> I am well aware what kind of position this is, as April (Ms. Finley to you) has told me all about her job many, many times. I am also well-versed in the likes of you.
> **Sincerely,**
> **Ryan G. Moon**

I set my coffee mug down with a snap. My gaze narrowed on the jaunty saying on the side of the cup, a gift from my last secretary right before I'd fired her.

Lawyers do it in their briefs.

She'd laughed uproariously upon handing me this item at the

company Christmas party. Then she'd pinched my ass. I'd been quite certain she'd dipped into the punch, but I couldn't have the other employees thinking I'd crossed a line.

As if I'd willingly have sex with a woman with nails as long as tongue depressors.

I begun to type again. Forget Ms. Finley. Evidently, Ryan G. Moon and I were meant to communicate solely with each other.

Ryan G. Moon,

What do you mean by 'the likes of me'? If you have formed a bias against me due to Ms. Finley's description of her workplace, perhaps you would like to seek employment elsewhere. Ms. Finley should also discuss any concerns she may have with me herself rather than through a questionable intermediary.

With all due respect,

Preston Michael Shaw, Esquire

I wasn't even surprised when the reply came through before I'd managed to finish even half my email to Donald. At this point, the resulting ding was also non-climactic.

Clearly, my notifications setting had gone as rogue as my obviously displeased assistant.

To whom it may concern:

April actually loves her job. I find it hard to believe, since my interactions with lawyers over the years haven't led to a feeling warmer than luke at best, but she is more generous than I. She has no concerns. I just read between the lines.

So, have you checked out my resume or what?

Sincerely,

Ryan G. Moon

What kind of feeling was *luke*? The word lukewarm was not meant to be split as if the first half counted as an adjective on its own.

I rubbed the knot in my forehead. If this was an example of Ryan's grammatical skills, I was nearly giddy with anticipation.

Also, I had forgotten to download Ryan's résumé. But I had one other salient point to attend to first.

Ryan G. Moon,

    The word is resumé with the accent mark over the e. Without it, the word is simply resume. Which the dictionary defines as: to take up or go on with again after interruption; continue. Example: to resume a journey.

    Sincerely,

    Preston Michael Shaw, Esquire

Her response took all of three-point-five minutes.

To whom it may concern:

    You forgot the accent mark on the first e. It should be résumé.

    Insincerely,

    Ryan G. Moon

This time, I did not answer the missive. Instead, I summoned Ms. Finley via the phone's intercom. "My office, please."

That *please* constricted my throat.

She knocked and appeared in my doorway, without seeming the slightest bit contrite. "Yes?"

"Sit."

She sat. Waited. Blinked innocently.

"Do you have some rapid-fire system that allows you to forward my emails to your friend in an instant? I've never seen anyone reply so quickly."

April's lips twitched. "She's very conscientious."

Now there was no doubting my throat was tight. "She?"

"Why, yes. Didn't you realize? Ryan is a woman." Now she did smile, widely. "She can't wait to meet you."

Would you like to read more?

NOW AVAILABLE!

One-click HIS TEMPORARY ASSISTANT now!

WRONG BED BABY

MOVING SUCKED.

Moving because your bachelor pad for half a decade was being torn down by Gavin Forrester, the hotshot big time developer in town who wanted to build more condos, *really* sucked.

But getting a hefty payment to help compensate for the inconvenience of moving helped ease the pain. Slightly.

"You gonna get a move on or just keep staring into the back of this SUV like it holds the answers to good sex?"

I didn't even glance at my best friend Lucky. I knew he'd be looming over the back of my vehicle to show off his biceps to maximum advantage, just in case any ladies happened to wander by.

"I know the answer to that," I muttered. "And it involves me and a glass of merlot."

"That's how you warm yourself up? You sound like a chick, but hey, do what works for you, man."

I had to laugh. "Shut the hell up, Roberts, and grab the other end of this hutch."

He elbowed me out of the way. "You might prefer group activities, but I can handle this one on my own, son." He hefted up the handcrafted oak piece built by my older brother August with a grunt.

The sound made me grin as I stepped back and waved him toward the propped open door to my apartment building. "By all means. I'll just stand here and cool off with a refreshing beverage." I popped open the cooler and grabbed a can of lemonade before flipping open the top. "Ahh. Tastes good," I said as I took an exaggerated swallow.

In a truly spectacular feat, Lucky managed to flip me off before hauling the hutch toward the open door.

Music suddenly spilled out, loud and unrepentant. It wasn't something you'd hear on the local station either. This was a sinuous, exotic beat, the kind that brought to mind warm breezes, a gorgeous sunset, and an even more gorgeous woman belly-dancing with a colorful snake wrapped around her upper torso.

I took another drink. Or maybe that was just me.

Lucky didn't seem to pay it any mind as he barreled through the doorway and headed up the stairs with his latest bulky item of furniture.

I turned toward the back of the SUV to take stock of what was left. In short, it was a lot.

This wasn't the first trip I'd made over here, but we were in early innings. My new apartment was still mostly a barren wasteland. I'd skipped hiring a moving company, considering I hadn't had far to go and could call on a number of fit dudes like myself to help out.

Oddly enough, most of them had become suddenly unreachable despite knowing for weeks the days I'd planned to move. August would be over later after work, but I couldn't count on any of the rest of the slugs I knew. As if wives and children and gainful employment could keep them *that* busy.

Whatever.

Lucky, however, used any attempt to show off and looked at carrying heavy furniture as the best opportunity going. So far, his plan had not borne much fruit, although a couple of the gooey-eyed young baristas at Macy's coffee shop had come out a few times to offer us refreshments. Lucky hadn't been too keen on any of them, since most of those girls were barely legal.

He had some standards. Not a lot, mind you, but some.

He jogged up beside me as I was dragging out the small bookcase that doubled as a nightstand in my bedroom. "Dude, there's some kind of chick party in there, and I think they're stripping."

I snorted and set my bookcase on the pavement. "I think heat stroke has finally warped your brain." I swiped my forearm over my sweaty forehead and grabbed for my already sweating can of lemonade. "It has to be ninety out here."

"Ninety-five," he informed me, flashing me his smart watch. "Not that you've been doing much to get sweaty, you lazy fuck."

I shrugged. "Conserving energy for when the help is gone is a valid strategy. We both know you'll only stick around as long as there's a chance you'll get laid."

He waggled his brows at me. "I didn't know that was on the table."

"Not in your fondest dreams, pal. I don't care if you unload every piece of furniture by yourself and decorate too."

"I don't fucking decorate. That's what sisters and girlfriends are for. You've got one."

"A sister? Definitely. Not that she has enough time for that shit. She's not even around right now, remember?"

My baby sister Ivy was in LA with her husband and their baby daughter Rhiannon for a week, which had been a tactical error on Ivy's part since we were smack dab in the middle of a heat wave. Her ice cream truck Rolling Cones would've made a killing if she'd been open for longer than the banker's hours she kept the truck operating on while she was away. She had a good crew to help her, but she preferred shorter shifts when she wasn't around to manage things. If she'd been able to stay open until 10 pm on these sweltering nights as she usually did, she probably could've funded Rhi's college education.

Not that her fancy rich husband needed any help with that.

I wasn't bitter, toiling away on a teacher's salary. Mostly because I loved my kids. I enjoyed their curiosity and enthusiasm and sometimes even their mischief-making. Aug claimed my affinity for children came from the fact that I hadn't matured past twelve myself, but I would've said at least thirteen. Maybe fourteen on a good week.

In any case, I was happy with my lot. I wouldn't have minded a bit more green to grease the wheels, but then again, who would?

Lucky tied back his long hair, swatting away the sweaty pieces sticking to his neck. "Yeah, Ivy's getting used to that high-rolling life. Next thing you know, she'll move out there. Probably get a pad on the beach. That'd be something to have a place to crash at on the west coast, huh?"

I didn't say anything. My family was close. Sure, we had our occasional spats like any other. Now and then, we didn't speak for days at a time. Life got busy.

But I didn't want to lose my sister across the damn country. I definitely didn't want to only see my niece on FaceTime and for occasional vacations. I was her favorite uncle. The fun one who'd hired a clown for her last birthday—Lucky, of course—and helped her whip up and down the sidewalk on her tricycle. She'd had a small accident and busted open her lip on account of the raised lip on the sidewalk, but she'd healed fine, right? And she had a hell of a story for the kids at playgroup. You know, for when she could talk coherently.

She was a sentient toddler now, so I was enjoying my little RhiRhi more with each passing month. But infants were another story. My other niece, Vivian, was a bit younger, so we were still working on communication beyond *goo-goo gaa-gaa*.

I wasn't one for babies. Nope, never. Not my bag. I preferred kids once they got past the drooling and excessive pooping stages.

Lucky straightened and grabbed a soda for himself, popping the top. "Well, if Ivy can't help, then you gotta get your mom involved. They live for that stuff."

"Are you kidding me? She's on like fourteen town committees. She barely has time to sleep, when you factor in her work at the gallery. Besides, who says I need a damn decorator? I didn't at my old place."

He laughed and took a long drink. "Yeah, and it looked great. *Not.* Most of the rooms didn't even look lived in. You can't do that in a swank place like this, man. Forrester's taken all these apartments up a notch." He let out a belch. "When you invite over that sexy chick who strips for tuition, you don't want to make her sit on the floor. Then again, if you do, I have a better chance." He nudged my shoulder. "I still owe you one for the Sanders' sisters."

He'd imparted so much in that barrage of information, I didn't even know what to unpack first. "Uh, the Sanders' sisters were almost a year ago."

"Hell no. They were this spring." He frowned and drank more. "Weren't they?"

"Try last fall. And I didn't hook up with both, just Judy. You just didn't like that they both weren't immediately bowled over by your baby greens."

"Says you. What happened with you guys?"

I shrugged. "We went out a few times. We're still friends. Just no spark."

"But she's smokin'. Doesn't that count for something?"

I shrugged again and finished off my lemonade, feeling like a class A chump. How could I tell him I was developing an aversion to casual dating? Not because I wanted something serious. Hell no.

Lucky and I were Crescent Cove's original bachelors. When all the single men around us tumbled like timber for the whole marriage and babies scene, we stood strong. We didn't want any of that. Pleasures of the flesh were enough for us, thank you.

No commitment. No stress.

No way, not in baby central anymore. How could you possibly enjoy a no-strings hookup in a place like the Cove? We'd become known across the northeast for ease in procreation. The damn town bird might as well have been the stork.

I gestured to the remaining items left in the back of my SUV. We'd packed that sucker like a Tetris game, taking advantage of every millimeter of space. "You going to help me with this stuff or what?"

"*Help?* I've been carrying most of it while you stand around out here sipping lemonade like a southern belle." To show off—as usual—he picked up my bookcase under one arm and grabbed another small shelving unit with his other hand. Then he winked at me before heading inside.

Since I knew quite well his posturing probably had to do with the woman he'd mentioned probably innocently dancing in her own apartment, I grabbed a couple of small end tables and followed him toward the sexy music.

After we went upstairs, I stepped around him to open the door to the hallway before we continued on toward my apartment. The music only grew louder as we walked.

Apartments branched off in two directions. There were only a few on each floor, and for now, there were three levels. There was still room for more on the very top floor, but Forrester was taking his time there, gauging interest, before he decided to make it one big place or split it up like the other ones. On the roof, there was a communal gathering space for all the tenants' use.

This property right across from the lake was in a prime location, what with Macy's Brewed Awakening on the bottom floor and the Cove's real estate market booming. I'm sure Forrester liked being the hottest ticket in town.

"Holy shit," I mumbled as I walked into the back of Lucky, who had stopped dead outside my door.

And who could blame him, because the door across the hall was cracked open, just enough to reveal a scantily clad blond winding around a pole that had been drilled into her floor. Or attached there somehow, well enough to support the gyrations she was doing around it.

To it.

"Told you," Lucky said smugly, panting slightly from what he held. He appeared to be glued in place and had not set it down yet.

"Does she realize the door is open?"

I was fervently glad that it was, even if I felt a bit like a pervert watching her. Her eyes were closed as she moved to the music, so she didn't know we were out here, but she *was* dressed—albeit in a minuscule way.

When Lucky didn't reply, I tried again. "Since the door is open, maybe she wants us to see?" It was a mostly hopeful question.

My conscience was screaming now. I had a sister and a niece and of course a mom. I taught kids. Spying on her wasn't kosher.

Unless she had some exhibitionistic tendencies and didn't mind if we peeped on her. At least she wasn't naked.

I would just keep telling myself that.

"I cracked the door open a little, wanting to see where the music was coming from," Lucky admitted, voice low. "She hadn't latched it though. I'm not *that* bad."

"Asshole." I jabbed the pointed corner of one of my end tables into his back.

He grunted and dropped the bookcase on his toe. His unholy bellow of pain made the gorgeous blond stop dancing, just as I set down my furniture and moved toward her door to firmly pull it shut.

Well, that had been my intention anyway. I didn't make it all the way to closing the door, because her face fucking slayed me.

I could admit I hadn't noticed it before, as occupied as I'd been with her fluid movements. She was seriously coordinated. Flexible. Hot as fuck. But then she just had to have a stunning face to match, with fiery eyes—color undetermined from this distance—and full lips and enough cleavage to kill a man who'd been abstinent for, oh, close to eight months now.

The last woman I'd asked out had ended up engaged to the sheriff within weeks. So, that kind of gave a reading on the state of my love life.

"What in the goddess are you doing?" she demanded, lowering the music and marching to the door at a rate of speed sufficient to make all the dangling threads from her top flutter over her abs.

She had a twinkling jewel in her navel. I was reasonably sure the beam of light from it had rendered me cross-eyed. Possibly altered some of my bodily functions as well.

That was as good an excuse as any for my current…pants predicament.

"Eyes up here, pal." She tapped her forehead. "Were you breaking in?"

"Hardly. The door was open. I was shutting it for you. Never know who's around."

"Wind did it," Lucky muttered from behind me.

I glanced back to see him leaning against the wall, gripping his foot. His boot was lying sideways on the floor.

I probably should've felt guilty, but he knew better than to pull stunts like that. Nudging a door open wasn't cool. She didn't know us. The last thing we wanted to do was scare her or make her feel uncomfortable. And I was her new neighbor, for fuck's sake. If he made things weird between us, *I'd* be the one dealing with the fallout.

"Look, we apologize." I cleared my throat. "The music lured Lucky to your apartment, and the door wasn't latched, so he made an ill-advised decision to open it. *We* apologize," I repeated, glancing back at my best friend, who nodded with a sigh.

"Sorry, ma'am."

"Ma'am?" She frowned and crossed her arms. "Just how old do you think I am?"

"Barely legal?"

She arched a brow at my quip. "Since I suspect that's your attempt at flattery, I will say you're both wrong. I'm not old enough to be called ma'am, though who is? And I'm also not young enough to remember having a fake ID to get drinks. Although I rarely imbibe to excess." She flushed. "Well, unless bestie service calls."

"How do I call you through that bestie service?" Lucky pulled on his boot and flashed her a winsome smile. "Truly, you won't meet a friendlier guy in all of the Cove."

"She's new in town. Don't scare her off already. At least I assume." I gave her a smile of my own. One far less toothy than Lucky's.

"I'm fairly new to actually living in town, but I've worked here since last year." She squinted at me. "Are you sure we haven't met before?"

"Unless I was drugged unconscious, there is literally no way I could forget meeting you." It was probably the most sincere thing I'd ever said, but Lucky snorted out a laugh just the same.

She just kept squinting. "I've seen you before. Are you—" She snapped her fingers. "August."

I scowled. "I'm definitely not August. If you think I am, I'm leaving." Not that I could go far.

Across the hallway. Yeah, that would soothe my wounded ego.

"His reputation as the hotter brother is on the line," Lucky informed her. "Mind you, the only one who ever said he was hotter was Caleb himself, when he was preening in the mirror."

"Caleb." She rolled the name around in her mouth as if she was tasting a fine wine. "I definitely can tell the difference between you."

Was that a subtle dig? Or maybe not so subtle? I threw back my shoulders and puffed out my chest. I didn't think I was the equivalent of a body-building male model like my best friend, but I cleaned up quite well.

I'd definitely never gotten any complaints.

"August has a picture of you guys on his desk," she continued. "You two and your sister."

"How do you know August?" I wasn't over being compared to him, even if it had happened my entire life.

I wouldn't have said I suffered from middle sibling syndrome, but I had to admit I got testy sometimes. August was one of those guys who did everything well. He was a supremely talented craftsman, a good friend to practically the whole town, and now he had a perfect little happy family with Kinleigh and their baby.

But that was neither here nor there.

"I work for him. Well, technically, I worked for Kinleigh, before their stores and everything else merged." She spun a damp curl around her finger. "They're so happy. It's lovely to see."

I grunted. As did Lucky when he picked up the furniture he'd dropped, along with my end tables, and somehow managed to heft them all into my apartment in one trip. Then he banged the door shut.

"What's his problem?" she asked.

I turned back to her and sent up a silent apology to Lucky. Technically, he'd spotted her first, even if that spotting had been through shady means. Bro code and all that.

But I was the one who was moving into this building. She was my new neighbor. I was honor bound to chat with her and get to know her while she looked so attractively sweaty.

Okay, so side benefit.

I lifted a shoulder. "His paper plane has been unexpectedly grounded."

"Don't think its made of paper. Unless he's one of those who stuffs toilet paper rolls in his jeans. Do guys really do that?"

I had to grin as I leaned against the jamb. "Guys really do a lot of things, though I think socks are more common." I shrugged. "Sorry, can't say definitively."

"Oh, right, because of course you've never needed to do anything like that."

I didn't bother to hide my smirk. Hey, she'd continued this particular line of conversation, not me.

"If I was the ogling sort, I'd just look to see myself. But I prefer a little mystery."

"What's your name, Mystery?"

"Luna."

"Nice to meet you." I held out a hand and she clasped it after a moment. I waited for sparks. Expected them, for some weird reason. When there was nothing, I frowned. "Do you have a last name?"

"Nah." She released my hand with a satisfied smile. "I'm like Madonna. Who needs more than the first?"

"Us ordinary people who teach school, for one. I don't want my students calling me Cal."

"But that's what the hip teachers do, isn't it?" She smiled again, this time in a much less practiced way. "What do you teach?"

"Second grade at the Catholic school."

Her expression warmed exponentially. "It's Hastings."

"What?" Why was she so damn beautiful? It shouldn't be legal.

"My last name is Hastings."

"Mine is Beck." I rubbed the back of my neck as Lucky turned on the music in my apartment and started singing along loudly.

Since when did he like Sinatra? Or like butchering Sinatra, because wow.

Her lips twitched. "I know that. You know, August and all. But thank you for the confirmation."

When I lingered in the doorway, not wanting to leave just yet, she arched a pale brow. "Since you're just moving in, you can't need a cup of sugar."

"Oh, you'd be surprised what I might need. You don't happen to have any children you'll be enrolling at school?"

"No."

"Any husband to help you make those nonexistent children?"

She glanced over her shoulder at her fully furnished apartment. I couldn't see much with her blocking my view, but the place felt relaxed and serene. Much like the woman herself. "Appears not."

"How about a boyfriend?"

"Are you auditioning?"

"I'd like to know what the audition consists of before I sign up. If it involves that shiny pole over there…" I gestured into her spacious apartment, which seemingly had the same layout as mine. "Regrettably, I'll have to pass."

"Let me think about it and get back to you."

I knew a brush-off when I heard one. I needed to seal the deal. "Why don't we discuss it over lunch tomorrow? I'll cook," I offered, before remembering that my apartment was half empty and the rest was a disaster zone.

"A second grade teacher who cooks," she mused, tapping her irresistibly glossy lips. "In the package of an outrageous flirt. Very interesting."

"I wouldn't say I'm outrageous. Exactly. More like persistent." I flashed her a grin. "So, what do you say?"

Now Available
For more information go to www.tarynquinn.com

KENSINGTON
Square

His Temporary Assistant

My Boss's Secret

Her Billionaire Bargain

For more information about our books visit

www.tarynquinn.com

KENSINGTON SQUARE CHARACTER CHART

BEWARE...SPOILERS APLENTY IN THIS CHARACTER CHART. READ AT YOUR OWN RISK!

Kensington Square's office park is a hot bed of sizzling legal briefs, occasional dick-tation, and lots of hot sleepless nights! Never know what will happen in this small town romantic comedy series, but beware of the steam fogging up your glasses...

April Finley: Executive assistant to Preston Shaw
Involved with Bishop Stone, friends with Ryan Moon and Luna Hastings

Adrienne "Dre" Jenkins: Owns The Honey Pot Bakery

Bishop Stone: Divorce Lawyer at Pierson Law Group
Involved with April Finley, brother of Key and Michaela, friends with Preston Shaw and Dexter Shaw

Dexter Shaw: Partner in Shaw, Shaw and Shaw, LLC
Brother of Preston Shaw

Eli Turner: Associate Lawyer at Pierson Law Group

KENSINGTON SQUARE CHARACTER CHART

Elizabeth Finley:
Grandmother of April, friends with Bess Wainwright

Grant Thorn: Veterinarian, Owns Thorny Paws Clinic, volunteer vet at Kitten Around Clinic
Father of Poppy Thorn

Issac Shaw: Started Shaw, Shaw and Shaw, LLC
Father of Preston Shaw and Dexter Shaw

Key Stone:
Brother of Bishop and Michaela

Luna Hastings: Works at Kinleigh's Attic, later known as Kinleigh and August's Attic, tarot card reader
Involved with Caleb Beck, sister of Xavier, friends with Kinleigh Scott, Gina Ramos, April Finley, and Ryan Moon

Michaela Stone: Student
Sister of Key and Bishop

Preston Michael Shaw: Partner in Shaw, Shaw, and Shaw, LLC
Involved with Ryan Moon, brother of Dexter Shaw

Rainbow Moon: Artist
Mother of Ryan Moon

Ryan Moon: Artist and tarot card reader
Involved with Preston Michael Shaw, friends with Kinleigh Scott, Luna Hastings and April Finley

as of November 2021

Crescent Cove

Have My Baby

Claim My Baby

Who's The Daddy

Pit Stop: Baby

Baby Daddy Wanted

Rockstar Baby

Daddy in Disguise

My Ex's Baby

Daddy Undercover

Wrong Bed Baby

Lucky Baby

Daddy on Duty

Crescent Cove Standalones & Shorts

CEO Daddy

Fireman Daddy

Mistletoe Baby

For more information about our books visit
www.tarynquinn.com

MORE BY TARYN QUINN

Kensington Square
His Temporary Assistant
My Boss's Secret
Her Billionaire Bargain

Afternoon Delight
Dirty Distractions
Drawn Deep

Deuces Wild
Protecting His Rockstar
Guarding His Best Friend's Sister
Shielding His Baby

Wilder Rock
Rockstar Daddy
Rockstar Lost

Holiday Books
Unwrapped
Holiday Sparks
Filthy Scrooge
Bad Kitty
Saving Kylie

For more information about our books visit
www.tarynquinn.com

QUINN AND ELLIOTT

We also write more serious, longer, and sexier books as *Cari Quinn & Taryn Elliott*. Our topics include mostly rockstars, but mobsters, MMA, and a little suspense gets tossed in there too.

Rockers' Series Reading Order

Lost in Oblivion

Winchester Falls

Found in Oblivion

Hammered

Rock Revenge

Brooklyn Dawn

OTHER SERIES

Smoke & Glass

Tapped Out

Love Required

Boys of Fall

If you'd like more information about us please visit
www.quinnandelliott.com

ABOUT TARYN QUINN

USA Today bestselling author, *Taryn Quinn*, is the sexy and funny alter ego of bestselling authors Taryn Elliott & Cari Quinn. We've been writing together for years, but we have found a love of small town romance that doesn't quite fit with our crazy rockers and romantic suspense.

And so…Taryn Quinn was born!

Do you like…

* Ultra sexy—check.
* Quirky characters—check.
* Sweet mixed in with the sexy—check.
* RomCom shenanigans—check.
* Office romance—check.
* A crazy baby town that has exploded into a few side series—check.

So, c'mon in. Pour a glass of wine—or grab a coffee if you're like us—put your feet up, and lose yourself in one of our books.

For more information about us...
tarynquinn.com
tq@tarynquinn.com

Made in the USA
Coppell, TX
31 October 2022